I0824354

CONTAINER ZERO NINE ELEVEN

From the author of:

Finally Africa

Houseman Press
August, 2007

CONTAINER ZERO NINE ELEVEN

A Novel by Jim McDonald

Printed in the United States of America by Houseman Press.

Cover art by M Susan Broussard
www.susanbroussard.com

Patricia Fry, Editor

Book Jacket Design by Marcos Hernandez

Art Direction: Norma Kass

Cover photo by Robert French

Contributing Editors:
Stan Mays, Alan Weinkrantz, Bruce Jenkins,
Rhonda Graves and Pam McDonald

ISBN 978-0-9837868-0-1

Sydney and Sam
And Pam
The Loves of My Life

CHAPTER 1

Unhappy Camper

Heavily marinate one fifty-one-year-old, third-generation Irish American in pure melancholy. Add a long night of staring blankly at the campfire's errant sparks and star-filled sky. Mix with liberal portions of rum, red wine and beer. Fold in about four hours of tossing and turning sleep with Hunter S. Thompson-type borderline hallucinatory dreams, and stir for effect.

The recipe that made up one Murphy Morrison, a.k.a. Murf, rumbled to life at 10:15 that May morning with a groan and a blast of acrid sphincter smoke. His bladder and head now throbbed powerfully in unison. "Jesus, I need to piss like a fuckin' racehorse," he mumbled.

Standing up now in the spacious olive green sleeps-six-waterproof-fabric-floored Coleman tent his wife and daughter gave him for Father's Day, this former Madison Avenue wonder was a sight. He had a four-day growth of beard, baseball hat hair, and he was ripe with need of a shower. "GA-A-A-W-D DAMN IT!" Murf bellowed when his head slammed against the horizontal support pole as he struggled to plant his bare right leg inside the jeans he held open before his teetering body. With a quick and decisive thrust, the leg was successfully encased in his jeans. And then a silly idea popped into Murf's foggy head.

With no bed to sit on, he'd just balance temporarily on the one be-jeaned leg and in a single, swift Karate Kid-wild-monkey-fu-like move, he'd lift the other leg up toward his chest and slam it down into the pants. Then he would pull the pants up, and zip on the fly as he headed for the tent's zippered door. An increasingly urgent need to pee pressed him into immediate action.

In seconds, the tent erupted with gut-busting screams and molten streams of profanity—a sound not unlike an all-out attack by a mutant pirate band. A toe on Murf's bare and flamingo-lifted foot snagged as he attempted to plunge it into the pant leg. His six three, 210 pound mass swayed wildly to and fro like a woeful entrant in the balance beam competition at the Foster Brooks Memorial Drunkards' Olympics. His fingers were now savagely pulling at the belt loops as he executed desperate full-body pogo-sticking up and down, while trying to free the snagged leg and still maintain balance. But it was no use. The panicked beast was hopelessly ensnarled at the ankles and teetering toward the inevitable calamity.

He went down hard, his face sliding the length of the tent's zipper, and landing in a small pile of gravel, grass and dirt that had collected at the bottom of the door. He lay dazed for what seemed like several minutes, aware that he was bleeding from his friction-burned cheek. "Damnit," he muttered as he shook his shaggy and battered head from side to side in search of coherence. He could feel his face flush bright red as his simmering anger boiled over.

"COCK-SUCKIN', SON-OF-A-FOOKIN'-BITCH jeans!!!! I'll kill you, you lousy fookin' B-A-A-A-S-S-T-A-R-D!!!!!" he screamed from the deepest recesses of his lungs. Spitting gravel from his saliva and dirt covered mouth, Murf awkwardly stood up inside the tent. When he saw the jeans on the floor in front of him, he began kicking them across the ground and against the tent walls. He attacked them with vengeance well suited for insidiously evil inanimate objects that cross quick-tempered, hung over Irishmen.

Finally, having beaten the lifeless denims into submission, he succeeded in pulling them on, all the while cursing nonsensically ("Shit bitin' cock fooker") like a Tourette's syndrome poster child. Suddenly he became keenly aware of his even more agitated bladder as if it was saying to him, "I'm starting without you!" The obvious sense of urgency caused him to wince and bend at the knees and waist in an attempt to stop the rebellious piss monster. He had to get out of the tent and NOW.

Carefully, Murf stretched up and out from his crouch and reached for the tent door zipper. After three off-balance blurry-vision grabs, he secured the zipper flap between his thumb and forefinger. Fittingly, as he began to tug the zipper upwards, it rose only about ten inches worth, and then snagged firmly on some loose threads—now refusing to move either up or down. Desperate for relief, Murf thought for a moment about trying to crawl out of the too-small-to-do-so opening. Then the anger washed over him like a large wave smashing ashore.

"Mutha-fookin' stuck!!!! I'll kill you too you shit eatin' ass-breath," Murf bellowed, kicking the thoroughly tangled tent door flap in vain. And then the dumber idea compounding effect kicked in. On top of the immediate past stupid jeans idea, he now contemplated upping the ante by sticking just his penis out of the partially opened tent door to pee. This way he could relieve his throbbing bladder while remaining in the shadowy privacy of his roomy tent. As a bonus for his brilliance, he would also altogether avoid the sunlight's probable nasty affect on his pounding, hung-over head.

Without hesitation or further consideration, he successfully mastered his jean's zipper, unleashed the beast and let forth a foamy torrent of peanut-smelling, dark yellow urine which, unbeknownst to him, set the campground awash like an early morning flash flood inundating a peaceful meadow. Twigs, leaves, beer cans and cigarette butts were suddenly sent surfing on the yellow tidal wave. In the three to four full minutes it took to empty his bladder—including over a minute and a half of the I'm-still-not-done-yet jerk and spurts—a Grand Canyon-esque ravine was grooved into the campground soil by Murf's piss fest. A few feet downstream, a wooden pole and canvas camp chair now teetered precariously on only three legs, the dirt beneath the fourth having been washed away into oblivion.

Task completed, Murf tucked his business in and zipped up his jeans. Then he untangled the tent's zipper, and unfettered the door flaps for his exit. His right hand cupped over his bloodshot eyes, he strode out into the morning light and immediately went into a massive arms aloft, fist clenched full-body stretch and a yawn as loud as a Deliverance hillbilly on steroids. "E-E-E-E-Y-A-A-W-W-F-O-O-K!" he thundered, eyes still squinted shut against the painful sunlight. As he opened and focused them, he was more than a little surprised to look up and see that the entirety of the thirteen scout strong Woodchucks Webelos Pack Nine stood spread out before him a mere fifteen feet away, stunned and petrified, jaws agape at the spectacle that had interrupted their morning hike. The look of shock and awe on the kids' faces was outdone only by their bespectacled scoutmaster's expression of horror and disgust.

"Show's over buckos; ship on out!" growled Murf. The now scrambling Webelos fell in behind their Don Knotts look-alike leader and fled away from the grumpy, Sasquatch-smelling camper.

Ad Man Extraordinaire Murphy Morrison took "The Package" known as early retirement from corporate America and was done at fifty-one. Ten years ago, he was a dashing advertising agency wizard at the top of his game. The clients loved him; so did his colleagues. His efforts had helped build one "hot shop" after another as he moved from New York, the one time capital of the advertising world, to San Francisco, where the most exciting creative work in the land was now routinely done.

Murf pretty much had it made. Then a very slick, senior executive type from the Selectronics Superstores mega chain persuaded him to take a walk on the wild side by leaving the agency and joining their SS ranks. Looking back, he realized that he had sold his soul to the devil in pursuit of what Murf called "building a super brand," but it was really about his own vanity and building a super bankroll. Take the money and run, as they say. And he did, leaving behind the ad agency world he had long since conquered. And now look at him.

"Should NEVER have jumped on the 'client' side and left the agency world," he'd said to himself several times a day for the next ten years.

But after those ten years of mindless meetings and corporate horse-shit, he had just over $2 million stashed in stocks and mutual funds. With his marriage now on the rocks as well as his career, he had decided that all of it should pretty much go into a trust fund to provide for his family. "And besides," he thought, "Old Murphy Morrison still has plenty of fire in the belly and I'll come up with some kind of new money-making ideas now that I'm no longer stifled by the boring, bureaucratic and bullshit world of corporate America." So he told the wife and kid back in San Francisco that he needed to get away from it all by going up the north coast by himself for a few days of "alone-time," camping in the great outdoors to help him sort it all out. There he planned to dream up a new gig that would be a lot more impressive than having to tell everyone he knew that he was suddenly "retired."

When you drink hard for a few days, they call it a "binge." But what Murf was on, a drinking-alone, sleeping-hardly-at-all, mind-numbing-more-than-a-week-of-trying-to-figure-it-all-out stretch, was better defined as a "bender."

And now here he sat on a picnic bench at Salt Point State Park some three hours north of San Francisco, unwittingly terrorizing Webelos. With his foggy brain settling back into melancholy overload, he now stared blankly at the Pacific Ocean waves crashing into the craggy black rocks and shiny black sand of the shoreline. "It must be happy hour somewhere," Murf said as he opened a breakfast beer and killed two-thirds of it in one prolonged pull. This was followed by a carbonated-explosion as a massive belch ensued, rounded out by three staccato farts. "Kisses for George W. Bush," Murf said to himself and the now deserted campground.

He took another chug of beer as he continued to stare out over the sea. Suddenly, something caught his eye. He slipped into an almost trance-like state as he fixed his gaze on the distant horizon. After about two to three minutes spent holding hand over brow, eyes trying to penetrate the grey coastal haze, Murf was finally able to discern the object slowly coming into view. It was a cargo-laden container ship like the thousands he had seen in San Francisco and Hong Kong. As the ship drew near, Murf could read the word Hanjin painted on most of the containers. Inexplicably, he broke into a broad smile as he muttered, "Of course!"

CHAPTER 2

Fifty-One Sure Was Fun

Murphy Morrison definitely looked the part of the decidedly dashing Ad Man, in his impeccably tailored, double-breasted dark blue with faint gray pinstripes, gabardine wool suit. Though festooned with bright white cuffs and collar, his crisply starched dress shirt was mostly sky blue. His M.M. initials had been monogrammed on the pocket. A dazzling light purple paisley print silk tie rounded out his ensemble.

Tall and ruggedly handsome with flashing green eyes and salt and pepper colored, slightly curly, Kennedy-esque hair, Murf personally preferred the comfort and unpretentiousness of more casual clothes. His off duty garb was typically a snug-fitting, well-worn pair of Levis with a long-sleeved baseball undershirt—white body with navy blue sleeves. His preference in shoes was the always comfortable and fashionable black low-top Converse sneakers.

Nonetheless, Murf had long since adapted to precisely dressing for the part of Ad Man and especially on a day when he'd lead an all-out pitch for a prime target advertising account—the Selectronics Superstores chain—worth more than $160 million a year in billings. Murf had perfected his brilliant advertising executive power wardrobe, with mainstays like the eight handmade suits he procured on a business trip to Hong Kong. There he had invested a lunch-break half hour of his time to be fitted for a molecularly precise-fitting wardrobe at a tailor shop. And amazingly, each suit cost the same as an off-the-rack suit would in the U.S.

So Murf now possessed a killer repertoire of Madison Avenue snap—major presentation suits worthy of an international tycoon. The suits featured hand-stitching work done around the clock just across the border from Hong Kong in mainland China, in the close-by, rapacious growth, hub city of Shenzhen. Once measurements were received by fax, the suits took a mere two days to spring to life from wide, rolled bolts of the most fabulous fabrics. Each suit also came with a different colored, monogrammed dress shirt thrown in. Murf already owned dozens and dozens of sensational silk ties and several pairs of hand tooled Italian shoes (which he amassed in a memorable two-week vacation to Florence some ten years back).

The personal touch to his outfit came from his eclectic collection of infallible conversation-starting cufflinks. The treasury included one set made from shipwreck-salvaged pirate doubloon coins; a pair of sailing cufflinks that housed miniature compasses under glass domes; dazzling opal cufflinks he purchased near the mine they came from in the desert outback of Australia; two converted civil war confederate uniform CSA buttons; and finally, one pair that supported his favorite, lovable yet perpetually cursed Chicago Cubs baseball team. They were actually made from the remnants of wooden seats removed from "The Friendly Confines," otherwise known as Wrigley Field.

Getting ready for the big presentation today, Murf laid out his wardrobe like a highly paid mercenary warrior preparing armaments and armor for battle. After all, this would take place at the Hal Lively &

Partners impress-the-shit-out-of-clients, downtown San Francisco advertising agency offices. After completing a vigorous five-mile run along the San Francisco waterfront at 6:00 a.m., he was now sipping a cup of freshly brewed French roast coffee and mentally rehearsing the insightful and witty presentation he would make later in the day. The master of multi-tasking, Murf was also simultaneously helping his wife get their eight-year-old daughter, Molly, ready to drop off at daycare, so mom could swiftly move on to her job as head of the private banking group at Wells Fargo's downtown bank.

"If the pitch today goes well, I guess you'll go out celebrating with your barstool buddies," said Murf's wife, Terri, in a very matter of fact way.

"It would be rude to say no," replied Murf grinning broadly at the prospect. Terri was an exceptionally attractive lady. She was a tall and slender, blue-eyed brunette with an eye-catching figure and a sensational pair of legs. She and Murf met twenty-some-odd years ago when they both worked summers off from college on Nantucket. Terri had only become more attractive since then and turned many a head, no matter her demur intentions. As was appropriate for her uppercrust clientele, she generally wore a pulled-back and clip-held hairstyle and light, yet luminescent makeup. She sported tortoise-shell designer glasses and today, a highly professional looking and well-tailored black silk suit. In spite of it all, she remained a disruptively enchanting vision in any boring boardroom she graced.

"Leave your car at work and take taxis with those deviates," warned Terri pleasantly. "You won't look nearly as handsome in a DUI booking photo as you do now."

The barstool buddies Terri referred to were better known to each other as "The Pirates." The six of them were advertising professionals by day and roughhousing rummies by night. The crew melded together slowly over a year and a half. They tended to be the ones consistently congregating at the watering hole at the endless stream of agency celebrations.

They were the ones who stayed too late, drank too much, told and laughed raucously at outrageous jokes and in general—after a few pops—became the antithesis of the dressed-in-nice-suits, gentlemanly advertising professionals they portrayed by day. And then there was softball.

While the Pirates were still bound by decorum to quasi-control themselves at work functions, when the agency entered a team in the San Francisco ad agency league, they really came together as mates. Softball was the one work-related activity where they got to let their Mr. Hyde sides show. And once softball season was over, it was only natural that they continued to come together outside the office once a week or more to attend hockey and football games together—for betting, drinking, swearing like sailors and drinking some more.

All of the six bore generally deserved nicknames never uttered by anyone at their workplace. There was Mike the Medic, Danny Boy, PD, Cat Man, Fig Newton, and The Captain. The particular night the drinking buddies formally bonded as The Pirates, and whence Murf earned the nickname "The Captain," was at a large hotel ballroom speech. While the other five mingled with their Pizza Hut clients, Agency Account Director Murf Morrison and the senior management team of Pizza Hut all gave speeches in front of the crowd that night. But Murf's had the assistance of a Hollywood stuntman friend; so he literally set his hair on fire.

He did so ostensibly, to underline his and the agency's absolute commitment to the new product rollout program the agency was helping a client company launch. After his drinking buddies saw Murf's way-over-the-top bit of theater that day and its thunderous reception, he was quickly anointed as "The Captain." The moniker came about both for what was called "the supreme act of an insane attacking pirate" and given his preference for drinking fine, barrel-aged rums.

The meticulously planned ruse was staged before 2,000 pizza restaurant operators and franchise owners gathered to hear their company's operations launch plan for its new deep dish pizza and to preview the agency's ad campaign for the new product. To make the stunt convincing, Murf had been fitted with a toupee constructed and styled to look as much as possible like his own real hair. Beneath this realistic looking rug that had been soaked at length in highly flammable liquid, Murf wore an asbestos skullcap over his real hair, which had been flattened and saturated with a non-flammable, protective gel. The same clear, fireproof gel veneer had likewise been applied to his eyebrows and lashes by his stunt man friend Connor, whom he met at a TV advertising commercial shoot in Hollywood a few years before.

That night, as Murf stood in the spotlight mid-speech, with hands boldly on his hips and legs opened dramatically, he was surrounded by a small group of very attractive female and male dancers, theatrically costumed in sparkling formal wear outfits and wearing firemen's helmets. Murf told the crowd, "When I spoke with the Hut's head of marketing, John Reynolds, for input on this presentation, he told me to do something really memorable to kick off the new deep-dish pizza launch." He smiled broadly with confidence and supreme projection. "Specifically, I think John said, 'It needs to be something really special, so you'd better really set your hair on fire.' Is that what you folks want to guarantee our success?" Murf asked. "If I set my hair on fire right now will you make sure Deep Dish Supreme Pizza is a huge success????!!!!" he shouted resoundingly, doing his spot-on carnival barker imitation.

After multiple mass-responses of, "Yes, yes!!!" punctuated with a few cries of, "Hell Yes," Murf waved over a dancer, who promptly lit up a blowtorch he had been carrying. As the faux-haired Murf further exhorted the crowd with shouts of, "Are we committed??? Are we gonna do this???!!!" and thunderous responses of "YES, YES," resounded, crazy Ad Man Murf Morrison's hair was set ablaze by a dancer-stuntman named Connor. The flames leapt and danced unbelievably high—about two feet above Murf's head. Once the NASCAR-type crash-and-burn, disaster-loving crowd had massively and sufficiently cheered his thirty-five second long flame-on insanity, Murf removed his hands from his hips, which was the prearranged signal to Connor, who was standing right beside him. Connor quickly covered Murf's head with a wet towel, at the same time using the towel to pull off the now charred wig in one swift motion. Murf then straightened and fluffed up his slicked-back real hair. To the crowd, he appeared to be a mad man checking to see how much of his hair had been burned away. So the illusion they created of Murf having really set his hair on fire was maintained for the now delirious mob of pizza purveyors.

"Y-A-A-A-A-H-H-H-H!!!" the crowd screamed in adulation and bewilderment.

Having witnessed Murf's grand spectacle that evening, whenever one of them flicked a lighter or lit a match around him thereafter, Murf always feigned panic at the sight of the flame.

The Pirate that was birth-named John Hannon, a.k.a. Fig Newton, was pony-tailed and gangly. A very talented yet twisted copywriter, he was legendary for his outlandish pranks. The Fig Newton nickname was born when a highly annoying, low-level client marketing representative named Mark Steinman came to visit the agency. He was there to make an unimportant, yet time-consuming, all-hands-on-deck presentation, which he had broadly boasted of working on for weeks. Everyone knew that, in actuality, the agency's interns had been abused by this prick to complete the presentation and on a completely unreasonable turnaround basis.

Steinman's second mistake was leaving his briefcase on the agency's coffee and snack bar counter while he went to the washroom to preen just prior to his presentation in the agency's large conference room. Shortly thereafter, as he opened his briefcase in front of a crowd of about forty, he pulled out a file filled with printed decks to hand out. To his chagrin, each copy of the presentation was infused on almost every other page with smashed, smeared and gooey Fig Newton remnants.

After stammering for a few minutes about "some wise guy," Steinman attempted to give the presentation without the prepared material. This, of course, only underlined his poor command of the topic and over dependence on others to do his work. After twenty minutes of floundering and with considerable giggling from a very pleased-with-himself John Hannon in the audience, a red-faced Steinman grabbed his briefcase and fled the room.

Murf subsequently had to put in some overtime smoothing things over with some higher-up client muckety-mucks that Steinman had complained to. Murf bought them countless cocktails that evening and, as it turned out, he learned that many throughout both the client and agency ranks had developed considerable dislike of the unctuous bastard John had pranked. In the end, "The Fig" was permanently endeared to both the agency's and client's staffs—save one—for his quick thinking and Robin Hoodesque deed.

Mike the Medic, a.k.a. Michael Mills was a beefy and mustachioed African-American and an up and coming account supervisor who worked on Murf's accounts. He was also the agency softball team's third baseman and much valued and beloved team medic. The affection stemmed from Mike's pharmacological prowess in treating muscle pulls, hangovers or just the popular "I had a shitty day" blues from his magic, jangling backpack filled with different types of pills, and a dazzling assortment of airline serving-size booze bottles. Needless to say, with every slide into any base or acrobatic tumble while catching a fly ball—or even just the act of falling off a barstool—cries of "Medic! Medic!!!" always ensued.

William Johnston, a.k.a. Danny Boy, was in his mid-thirties and handsome with sparkling blue eyes and a baby-face. He was the consumer trends analyst in the agency's research department. He came by his nickname one St. Paddy's Day when, in a fit of drunken brilliance, he suddenly broke into an astoundingly rich, tenor rendition of that timeless and melancholy dirge, "Danny Boy." The entire bar immediately grew silent and several patrons were brought to tears. It was touching. William looked askance and sang pensively as though singing only to himself while sitting in some far away Irish glen plucking clover. His heretofore-secret talent likewise blew his Pirate mates away. They were also amazed and quite pleased by the four adoring "Ruby Breasted Swallows" his siren song attracted to their table afterwards.

Apparently, delivering commanding a cappella ballads was a skill he began developing as a teenager, forced by his mom to sing in their church choir. He refined his repertoire during two semesters as a foreign exchange student in Dublin, in his junior year at Stanford. After returning to Stanford, there was supposedly some kind of "incident" that led to his expulsion. Johnston would never speak of it. He left Palo Alto and finished up his psychology degree in the city at San Francisco State University. An internship at Lively & Partners the summer after graduation congealed into a full-time gig in the research department, where he made friends quickly with his droll wit and rapier tongue. And boy did he like to drink.

Paul "PD" Reading was a forty-two year old, thrice married and divorced manager in the agency's print production department. He supervised the specialized area of purchasing and printing for Lively. His highly undesirable nom de plume was bestowed upon him by an angry wench whose rear end—with a little helpful shove of Paul's arm by Mike the Medic—he had "accidentally" groped in a crowded bar.

"Watch it, Pencil Dick!" she snapped at him with eyes blazing like searing hot coals. Nearly everyone in the entire bar had seen this go down and the derision for Paul thereafter was non-stop.

"Another beer, Pencil Dick?" inquired the waitress. "Perhaps a SMALL one?"

"Telegram for Needledick. Telegram for Needledick," chimed in the three girls at the table next to The Pirates.

Cat Man or Big Cat was by day known as Stan Harold, and the bespectacled, six-foot five, 190-pound lovable dufus was the agency's controller. He was an Ichabod Crane-looking, gangly man with rosy red ball cheeks and an Adam's apple the size and shape of a casaba melon. "Sweet but off-the-charts klutzy," was how Terri described the affable but ever-bumbling and stumbling Big Cat. And the strangest stuff always seemed to happen to the lovable lunkhead.

In sarcastic deference to his nickname, The Cat was, in fact, the antithesis of feline agility. His pratfalls were the stuff of legend. Were there fines for calamitous clumsiness, he would live in a state of perpetual bankruptcy. Two very classic Big Cat incident examples—which occurred on separate occasions in different restaurants—illustrate his potency.

In the first one, Cat Man was telling a funny story and gesticulating wildly while doing so. At the same time, a self-absorbed waiter, trying not to spill his load, approached our table with six large mugs of beer and two overflowing baskets of popcorn on his serving tray. Just as The Cat thrust both arms up in the air to emphasize his point, the overloaded waiter moved in with the tray directly behind him. When The Cat's right arm struck the underside of the tray, the beers sailed high up in the air and then seemed to hit and spill their entire contents in succession, one at a time as though orchestrated by the devious creator of those Tom and Jerry cartoons. As bad as all who witnessed this spectacle felt for the waiter, there was no such evidence of this at first as the Pirates unanimously exploded in howling and shrieking laughter. It continued unchecked on a stop and immediately start-up again basis, until the lads were practically weeping.

The second and even more inspired act of Big Cat calamity happened at a trendy, white tablecloth restaurant with multi-level seating throughout. After a sublime luncheon that Cat and Murf hosted for the VP of finance and one of his accountants from a key account at Lively, the group continued to make small talk. Stan—as The Cat was known—began to stretch and tilt on the back two legs of his chair. As he added a yawn and a full-arm stretch to his precarious chair tilt, he was blissfully oblivious until his eyes filled with panic at the split second realization that he had irreversibly lost his balance and was tumbling out-of-control backwards and down. Unfortunately, he sat on a raised platform, so when he fell, he came crashing down on the fully set table below. The sound of dishes breaking, glasses shattering, and people screaming was only slightly more out of place than Stan's very embarrassed apologies after he had rolled off the table and staggered back onto his feet. Adding insult to injury, the Big Cat as he was apologizing, used a napkin to wipe the tomato bisque off of a horrified bald man's soup-covered dome. Nervous tittering built to a howling crescendo from the dining room crowd and, as the two horrified clients, still sitting at the table with Murf, looked down from above. That's when Murf, in his best Howard Cosell imitative accent muttered, "Down Goes Frazier! Down Goes Frazier!"

CHAPTER 3

The Code of the Buccaneer

Beyond enjoying the physiological buzz and the escape from high-pressure careers that came from consuming adult beverages, the Pirates also consistently focused on the pursuit of loud and raucous repartee. They loved creating the kind of lighthearted mischief that provoked frequent explosions of unbridled, teary-eyed laughter. And boy did they amuse easily. Their favorite running gag was rooted in the old "Liquor????!!! Hell, I hardly knew her!" punch line. Their collective sense of humor could best be described as Murfassian. And their ability to never tire from the same joke no matter how many times they heard it or any of its derivations repeated, was infinite. For them, this single, simplistic "Liquor??!!!" quip was as constant and reassuring as breathing. The response, "Hell, I hardly knew her!" became a non sequitur group retort to any word uttered by anyone anytime that happened to innocently end with the letters "er" or "or."

While such a juvenile response was expected and even necessitated by a word like "poker" ("Poker???!!! Hell, I hardly knew her!"), the joke was often carried beyond the predictable. For example, when an unsuspecting guest lecturer took to the podium and asked for a "clicker" to advance his slides, a Pirate voice in the crowd shouted out to the speaker's and many others' consternation, "Clicker???!!!! Hell, I hardly knew her." And the smattering of Pirates present and a few wannabes in the crowd would laugh in supportive appreciation.

And, of course, the more inappropriate and formal the setting—say during a speech by an agency holding company senior executive visiting from New York—the more points scored by the Pirate quick enough to jump on a phrase like, "The campaign was a world beater..."

"Beat Her???!!! Hell, I hardly knew her!"

Or one like "…it's a wonderful revenue generator..."

"Gener-Ate Her????!!! Hell, I hardly knew her!"

Or perhaps "…the effective use of a simple customer statement stuffer…"

"Stuff her???!!!! Hell, I just met her!!!"

In the next half hour of this presentation, the pitiful and much harassed New York executive, to his great chagrin, unthinkingly incorporated the words "tester," "pester" and "sequester" into his oratory. Those in the audience listening intently because they were playing ER-Bingo, silently mourned his thoughtless exclusion of the words "zester" and "molester." They recovered their mirth as the very red-faced man from corporate cited a closing example of a highly promotional flyer intrusively placed under an automobile's window wiper. "WIPE HER???!!!! Hell, I hardly knew her!!!!"And so on and so on. Ad infinitum and ad nauseum.

Babe spotting, or "moisture detection" as the boys called it, was another primary Pirate fixation. Whether the crew was in a bar or at a hockey, football or baseball game, crowd scanning was a constant, and alerts of "Sweater Meat dead ahead" (a.k.a. Ta-tas, Dairy Treats, ICBMs, etc.), were continuous. To Murf's dismay, he did come to learn of other unfamiliar breast descriptors while on a business trip to Sydney to address a gathering of top Australian advertising executives. In his speech at the conference, Murf repeatedly referred to happy-meal type "Fun Bags" as a proven promotional tool developed by his agency for use by the pizza restaurant chain they represented. Unfortunately for Murf, he did not know that Australian Pirates refer to women's breasts as Fun Bags. The result of his ignorance of Australian slang was intermittent outbursts of uproarious laughter every time the unknowing and increasingly frustrated Murf repeatedly referred to the Fun Bag tactic "that American kids just go bug-eyed over!"

When the Pirates attended hockey games, babe spotting was at its best. "Outstanding rackage at four o'clock!" one of the Pirates practicing the art of the scout would mutter, after locating a single or pod of hockey game hotties.

"The real deal is at twelve o'clock high," said The Captain after instantly and thoroughly assessing the stands with his primo-female body heat seeking vision. "And gentlemen, she is MOIST."

"Hear-hear, hear-hear. Moist, very moist Captain," echoed the Pirate throng in enthusiastic acquiescence to his superior spotting skills.

"More beers, guys?" inquired a roving vendor.

"It would be rude to say no," the thoroughly rehearsed crew said in near unison.

"Goal scored by number fifteen, Jamie Langenbrunner," boomed the PA announcer. "Langenbrunner????!!!! Hell, I hardly knew her!" replied the Pirates uniformly.

A key statute in the Code of Babe Spotting was the Don't Lock-on Rule. As the name implies this corollary decreed that the spotter or another Pirate enjoying a mate's good spotting, should never "lock-on" or stare in an obvious manner. To do so was to risk being seen by the spottee, thus spooking the quarry and spoiling the viewing for others. Not to mention the bad form of being detected and then receiving the "You're an Asshole" look or sometimes getting the finger from a lady not appreciative of a lustful Pirate's gaze. And, of course, if the crowd at a ball game should notice the goings on, they might just deservedly boo the sexist pig offender(s).

For most of the reasonably pleasant looking wenches the Pirates encountered, mustering a casual glance without locking-on was not a problem. But the occasional Super Babe or ten point rack could easily result in gang accusations of, "You locked on dude," followed by claims that a round of beers must be bought by the offending party. Of course, the Captain was thought by all to be too smooth to ever lock-on—that is until a certain bad-boy boondoggle, advertising awards ceremony trip to Saint Tropez.

The trip put Cap and Fig Newton in harm's way via a topless beach with a bounty of bodacious ta-tas therein. After too many lock-ons to count—in a setting where this is about the most un-European, obviously an American swine move to make—the Captain and Fig retreated to the hotel gift shop wherein they hastily procured two pairs of Cool Hand Luke mirrored sunglasses.

Another favorite Pirate practice at hockey games was the giving and receiving of head butts, rendered with considerable pop whenever the home team scored a goal. Murf had often found himself the day after a hockey night, with perceptible lumps and bruises on his forehead from having attended a high scoring head banger with the Pirates the night before. The primary Pirate game activity was, of course, over-ordering rounds of beer. Each Pirate would take turns ordering a foaming round whenever a vendor passed—and a different vendor passed by the group through the aisle every few minutes. Therefore, the group was forced to constantly chug the goods to keep up with the new arrivals and impending next orders.

At one particularly festive hockey outing, the boys were ensconced upstairs in a luxury suite instead of their usual lower box seats, compliments of a local TV station seeking favor with the agency. Late in the third period, Big Cat ordered two cases of beer with five minutes to play in the game—just in case of overtime. His move was seen as prudent at the time because the Pirates' team was only up four to one. Shortly after the beer arrived, the buzzer sounded signaling the game's end. Within ten minutes the stewards were knocking at the door to clean the suite and encountered a locked door when they attempted to enter.

Security was the next group knocking at the door and they were, likewise, ignored as the Pirates kept chugging beer. Finally the security detail entered the suite next door. From there, they were able to climb over the railing from the arena-side seating and enter the back door of the suite the Pirates occupied. Thus the detail was able to re-take a suite that had been commandeered by scurvy Pirates. To stall the stern-faced security guards for the additional time needed to empty all of the recently purchased beers, PD feigned chest pains as a rear guard tactic. Security had no choice but to take him seriously. Therefore, they immediately called for the all-white clad EMS guys who showed up with a square orange medical chest, stethoscope and a white sheet-covered gurney. The lead guy's first question to PD naturally was, "Have you ever had a heart attack before?"

"Heart attack???!!! No never," stammered PD with a completely straight face. "Well, not in the last six months!" he quickly added. PD's blood pressure and pulse were closely monitored for ten more minutes, and a ton more cans became dead soldiers before the paramedics wised up and all of the conspicuously giggling and snickering suite occupants were unceremoniously ushered out. But anti-lawsuit medical malpractice protocol still required PD to be wheeled out of the Ice Center's doors on the gurney, which made for an epically memorable exit to cap a stellar Pirate adventure. The story of this escapade was much re-told and celebrated thereafter around the campfire or whenever and wherever adult beverages flowed between Pirates.

Another favorite pastime of the group was the art of telling off-color jokes so loudly that most of the nearby tables were forced to listen in on the joke, whether they wanted to or not. Murf's personal favorite, which was always a crowd pleaser, took a good five or so drawn out, over-done Irish-accented minutes to tell. It's the classic one about the parish priest who announces to his parishioners during his sermon at Sunday mass that he's heard tales in confession of GHOOSTS in the parish!

"'Now tell me children, consider this a mass confessional. Has anyone of you, man, woman or child, (volume building) actually SEEN a GHOOST?!!!' asks the priest. And low and behold, about thirty hands go up among the seated parishioners. 'JESUS, MARY AND JOSEPH!!!!,' says the priest. 'Well let me ask dear children, has any one of you, man, woman or child actually TOOCHED a ghost?' he says. And lo and behold about fifteen hands go up among the parishioners. (Even louder) 'JESUS, MARY AND JOSEPH!' says the priest. 'So many of ya have tooched a ghost and I've heard nary a word of it from you at confession,' he says. 'Well now, let me ask all of you one last question,' says the priest. 'Has anyone of you, man, woman or child, (almost screaming) had SEXUAL INTERCOURSE with a ghost?!!!' says the priest. And lo and behold, from wa-a-a-a-ay back in the crowd one very shaky hand is raised up. 'JESUS, MARY AND JOSEPH!!!!' says the priest. 'I cannot believe it man, you've had (extremely loudly) SEXUAL INTERCOURSE with a ghost and you've not spoken a word of it at confession,' he says. 'Well stand up man and confess it now!!' says the priest. And way in the back, O'Malley who is three sheets to the wind staggers to his feet and says loudly, 'Ghoost???!!! I thought ya said a GOAT!!???'"

The telling of jokes too loudly was actually a deliberate Pirate attempt to create social interaction. It was commonly a safe way of intercepting hearty wenches who might listen in on a round of jokes, reciprocate with one of their own and possibly even join in on a round of drinks or six. Of course, the best-laid plans sometimes went awry, as was the case when one eavesdropping blonde heard Fig Newton tell a fairly predictable and off-putting dumb-blonde-gives-a-blow-job joke. Immediately afterwards she asked aloud if the Fig liked sex. And the Newt took the bait readily. "Of course I LOVE sex!" he proclaimed with supportive whoops from his crew.

"And do you like to travel?" she then purred.

"I LOVE to travel, honey!" he responded.

"Then fuck off," she said quite demurely as the group roared with approving laughter at the disemboweling of the Fig Man.

Many of the guys, including Fig, were already on their second wives or were at least, given their lack of tact with the opposite sex, diversity training dropouts. The sharp-witted blonde quickly followed up with another question for the shrinking-into-his-seat Fig. "Do you know why men whistle when they're on the toilet?" she queried. As the Fig shrugged an unspoken no, she closed him out. "Because it helps them remember which end to wipe," she quipped. And the thunder of uncontrollable gut laughter exploded again.

Tonight's somewhat sloppy, loud joke-telling session began with Danny Boy. "This bar's for jerk-offs," he bellowed loudly and to the visible disgust of the macho young jocks at the table next to theirs. "I got so shit-faced here last night I was falling all over the place and then I threw up all over my shirt," he continued, making obnoxious vomiting sounds to recreate the moment and thoroughly disgust as many people as possible. "I knew my wife would kill me when I got home and she saw my condition, so I made up a lie about the guy next to me in the bar being so drunk he threw up on my shirt," said Danny Boy, again making the driving-the-white-truck, hurling noises, only longer and louder. "I told her that he felt so bad, he gave me this five dollars that's right here in my pocket," Danny said holding up a 10-dollar bill. "And then she says," he continued, "'Hey, that's a ten dollar bill!' And then I said, 'Oh that's right, he shit in my pants as well.'"

As Danny, along with the Pirates, chortled heartily at his own joke, he heard a cry of, "What an ASSHOLE," ring out from the table behind him. Five late-twenties and very full-of-themselves stockbrokers who were celebrating a city league basketball victory occupied said table.

"Yea, well Fuck YOU Tweety Pie," responded Danny Boy as he

angrily rose from his seat turning around toward his none too amused adversary. Accompanied by the sound of many chairs being pushed back all at once, Danny Boy was immediately flanked by the other, now equally incensed Pirates, who moved into face-to-face, feel-each-others'-hot breath proximity to the slummin' Wall Streeters. All too quickly, each of the sea dogs was paired up with one of the landlubbers. With much threatening and posturing, each pair mutually grabbed hold of the corresponding adversary's shirt at the chest or collar opening.

And then, as the offended B-Baller began to tell Danny Boy what a loudmouth asshole he was, Murf hollered the signal word, "A-R-R-R-R-H." Almost simultaneously, five full-force Pirate head butts were delivered to the shocked recipients, followed by fists flying, lips splitting, bodies crashing and tables smashing before the entire group was separated and tossed out by a phalanx of massive bouncers.

As the Pirates looked back from the street and through the bar's window, they spotted the fight's instigator Danny Boy, now seated at an adjacent table with two pretty ladies, acting as though nothing significant had transpired. After the head butts, the fisticuffs' catalyst had instantly ducked down and slipped away from the fracas which he had caused.

"All in all, this has been an exceptionally memorable Pirate evening," said PD. Murf noticed that Mike the Medic and the Big Cat both had steady streams of blood flowing from their foreheads. The Cat was also quite wobbly and a bit concussed, but nothing that a few rounds of adult beverages at the bar just down the street wouldn't fix. The other Pirates just had unsightly knots and red, puffy spots where clenched fists had landed. As they tumbled into the next bar to celebrate their battle royal, the two skull-bleeders held napkins, secured from a hot dog street vendor by Murf, on their foreheads to stanch the flow. Rather than ruin the remainder of the evening with stitches at a neighborhood doc-in-a-box clinic and a lengthy wait that was sure to spoil their rum-induced buzz, Murf made a bee-line to a couple of nice looking ladies at the bar counter and could be overheard smoothly asking to borrow something from them to help out his needy friends.

"The boys got a bit nicked up defending a lady's honor," he lied with a completely sincere expression. He returned and showed the wounded duo their salvation—a tube of the super glue females often carry to repair a broken fingernail.

"Here's a little trick I learned working in restaurant kitchens at night while I was in college," he said. "We cut ourselves with sharp knives all the time and needed a quick fix," said Murphy glibly. "My word as a Pirate on this, lads. Surgeons use the exact same chemical compound that is sold over-the-counter as super glue, to close up after certain kinds of delicate surgery. Secretaries at work also swear by it to immediately seal up and stop the ache of paper cuts because the glue instantly stops the air from irritating exposed nerve endings," said the Pirate king expertly to reassure his new patients. First on Mike and next on Cat, Murf grabbed the forehead skin at the newly opened seam and held it closed together before applying a thin layer of super glue atop the split. He held it closed for maybe thirty seconds before releasing, and voila! The bleeding had stopped with very little visible evidence of the injury. A huge group chant of "A-A-A-A-R-R-R-H!!!!" went up and Murphy's drinks were covered for the rest of the evening's revelry.

Come the next morn, Murf got up early and went to the gym to sweat the poisons out and immediately pay the piper. He had a religiously kept rule. In order to maintain a reasonable home life and a functioning liver, he did not drink and carouse two weeknights in a row. But what was it about Murf Morrison that made an otherwise dependable soldier/citizen, with a highly successful career, a sparkling wife and an adorable daughter, so wickedly impulsive and secretly edgy and conflicted within? And though he deeply loved his family, why did he spend the time he did in the comfort and camaraderie of his dubious band of buccaneer brothers instead of with them?

Maybe it was the influence of his kooky grandmother whose idea of babysitting him as a six-year-old was to take him to play the nickel slots at the booze and smoke-filled casino bar. Afterwards, she'd take him to the local theater and then pass out in her seat as he enjoyed one of the hilariously slapstick early Woody Allen movies. Elsewhere in his gene pool, his own retired army sergeant father was quite the practical joker. On the night the MIR Russian Space Station was supposed to free fall out of orbit into an uncontrolled smash landing that scientists projected could be anywhere on earth, Murf's dad was fast at work in his garage plotting a prank to avenge some ridiculous slight his next door neighbor had committed. He spent almost three hours stenciling with black paint, the letters MIR and carefully painting a red hammer and sickle on an old kitchen sink garbage disposal he had forgotten to throw out. For effect, he uglied it up by first randomly hammering it in spots and then by bending at odd angles the metal edges of the strange looking lump of steel. He also burned it in several spots with a blowtorch.

A little after dark, he spirited the bizarre looking object over to his neighbor's front yard along with a shovel to partially embed it into the dirt. Then he doused the fake space debris with gasoline. He also artfully trailed an eight-foot long straight tracer-line of gas in the grass leading up to the supposed strike point. Finally, he set the twisted metal beast on fire, and lit one of his teenage son Murf's purloined M-80 firecrackers, which he tossed at the neighbor's window as he ran back toward his own home. After the local 10 o'clock news team began filming their MIR feature story next door, Murf's dad kept running back and forth to the window, laughing hysterically and clapping his hands with extreme glee while his fried fish TV-dinner-eating family alternately stared at him and at the news on TV in utter disbelief. The next day, when accused of the hoax by his angry neighbor and an accompanying newspaper reporter at his front door, Murf's dad rolled his eyes toward Murf who was sitting in the living room inside and said "Teenagers!!! Ha!" before slamming the door in the faces of both of them.

Murf's upbringing was, indeed, atypical. But at the same time, it was a richly diverse, globetrotting adventure.

CHAPTER 4

The Formative Years

As with Murphy Morrison's upbringing, on the other side of the world, Abdur Nidal's life growing up was comfortable and middle class in the small 8,000+ population, four-mosque northern West Bank town of Azzun. The country, known as Palestine—which many still refused to recognize—was originally comprised of the land between the Jordan River and the Mediterranean, bordered by Lebanon to the north, Syria to the northeast, Egypt to the south and Jordan across the river to the east. But, of course, since 1947, the burgeoning state of Israel had become heavily intertwined with the now more loosely defined area called Palestine that the British inherited after WWI and the fall of the Ottoman Empire.

The indigenous Arab population had fled into refugee camps in Lebanon and Syria or had largely been relegated to the two landmasses still referred to as Palestine. The smaller was the intensely populated southern coastal Gaza Strip, which shared a southern border with Egypt, faced the Mediterranean to the east and was surrounded by Israel on the other two sides. The larger portion, the West Bank, derived its name from its location on the west bank of the Jordan River. It shares borders with Israel and with Jordan—which occupied and annexed the West Bank after the first Arab-Israeli war in 1948, only to lose it to the Israelis in the Six Days War fought in 1967. Since then, most of the West Bank has been under Israeli military occupation with numerous Jewish settlements constructed.

As the eldest son of Doctor Nidal, the lead physician at an Azzun private clinic, and his middle-school teacher wife Sari, Abdur's friends viewed the seventeen-year-old, his older sister, Amal, nineteen, and little brother, Khalil, seven, as well-to-do and extremely fortunate. Though Abdur's parents together earned only a modest annual income of $24,000, a single employed parent was a rarity in this place, let alone two. The Nidals lived in a nice upper middle-class, six-room home built of concrete blocks, with a smoothed beige plaster fascia. Unlike most neighboring houses, the Nidals had indoor plumbing, electricity, a refrigerator and overhead ceiling fans in most of the rooms to keep the heat of this arid land somewhat at bay.

Weekends were sometimes spent at his aunt and uncle's four-acre farm, a half hour's ride north into the heights. When the extended Nidal family gathered there, it included Dr. Nidal's brother Nikki and wife Marta, and their four teenage and young adult sons, Omar, the twins Fathali and Waheed, and Shafik. A weekend with eleven Nidals meant the chicken population on their hilltop hideaway would be reduced by five or six for every family feast undertaken.

Though soccer game outbreaks were a constant for Abdur and his older cousins, the boys also pruned and tended the olive trees, herded goats and fed chickens. Afterward, they would relax and nap a great deal in the modest ancestral Nidal sanctuary set amidst the rolling green and brown hills and finely terraced groves. The high points of the weekend, however, were the timeless and leisurely family picnics, awash with the golden light of sunset and constant buzz of conversation punctuated by unchecked roars of laughter.

As a rule, the family tried to avoid talking about politics and they were likewise fairly secular about religion. In fact, Dr. Nidal was born a Shiite Muslim in North Yemen and sent by his poor mason father to live with a well-to-do uncle in Lebanon. He later met his wife at a university in Beirut. She had been born and raised a Sunni Muslim. But love found a way. Though doubly Muslim, the family only said prayers together at the morning and the evening meals and did not kneel and pray to Mecca five times per day unless they were in a public place where it would be customary. Their more pragmatic Islamic beliefs were rooted in humanitarian actions and in service of their fellow man—a constituency largely comprised of agrarian workers, tradesmen, mechanics, marketplace peddlers, and itinerant laborers.

Since unemployment seemed to be the most common "employment," life for most in Azzun was very challenging. And rather than just giving alms to the poor on religious holidays, the Nidals' entire lives were dedicated to their fellow man, channeled through medicine and education. And everyone in the family pitched in with both. Amal and Abdur, and even young Khalil helped out at the school and the clinic when they were not studying.

Dr. Nidal had little time to spend maintaining his facility, so the family tended to functions there ranging from janitorial to administrative. His work kept him at the storm center of a constant stream of riot-injured Palestinians who poured into the clinic almost daily. There were also frequent late night flowing blood emergencies that were brought to the Nidal doorstep by neighbors with nowhere else to turn. And they were never turned away.

At seventeen, Abdur was a handsome young man, an excellent student and a gifted soccer player. He idolized the retired Brazilian superstar Pele and dreamed a not-at-all-unrealistic dream of earning a spot on a national team someday. Beyond his five-foot, ten-inch lean and muscular body, his slashing speed, dazzling moves, and booming kicks, he had a great head for the game like no other local athlete. Perhaps that came from his grasp of strategy and battlefield tactics garnered from his history studies of ancient and modern warfare. His offensive and defensive brilliance and prescient leadership quickly landed him the team captain's role on every team on which he played.

As his friends dropped out of school to work or were redirected away from academics to trade schools or for many, into radical insurgent activities, Abdur held steady. He was driven by the soon-to-be realized dream of a college education just like his parents had. Perhaps, he fantasized, with a bit of luck, he may someday live the whirlwind life of a professional soccer star. Another huge advantage Abdur enjoyed over his Palestinian-born friends was that he had actually been born in Lebanon while his father was in medical school there. So, whereas poverty and Israel's ban on Palestinians leaving the country for study abroad killed the dreams and future for most Palestinian youth, Abdur's Lebanese birth certificate left him with a way out—that is, assuming he could muster a scholarship or grants in aid to fund an overseas education, which his family could otherwise not afford. Of course, he would still have to maintain a spotless record in the eyes of the Israelis in order to secure his exit.

At his parents' insistence, Abdur steadfastly avoided the rock-throwing confrontations with Israeli soldiers that most of his friends regularly participated in. This occasionally deadly-fire precipitating "sport," seemed to have become the neighborhood teenagers' everyday alternative to America's national pastime of baseball. And that was evidenced by the far worse than a stint on the disabled list stream of amputated limbs and scar tissue-covered exit wounds that some of his friends sported as the result of these unrelenting and horrific street skirmishes. And they were supposedly the lucky ones who had lived to boast of bravely battling with "the cruel oppressors."

Abdur and his father had spoken many times of the need to break the endless cycle of violence and destroyed lives. “Do we not have the right to resist occupation of our village by the Israelis?” implored Abdur.

“Yes, but our resistance shall take other forms than hurling rocks and setting cars on fire,” responded Dr. Nidal with quiet confidence in his delicately balanced, tightrope-walking approach to a nearly impossible situation for the village. The plan he had fashioned called for Abdur not to be drawn into the hopeless abyss where he would take part in any kind of lawless protest, let alone a major uprising. Abdur was taught to stand up for Palestinian human rights, but to do so through non-violent actions and intelligent advocacy. In fact, with Dr. Nidal’s persistence and help from a generous and large Arab-American community in the Dearborn, Michigan area, Abdur was leaving soon to attend Michigan State University in East Lansing on a combination of academic and hardship scholarships.

The paradoxes of life for the Nidals in Azzun were many. In some circles, in spite of their stubborn and noble dedication to civil service, the parents were reviled for possessing the intellect and affluence to play leadership roles among the intifada or uprising, and yet choosing not to. Their commitment to Islam was sometimes questioned, as well. This was because, though they were all raised in the Muslim faith and considered themselves to be a family of faith and service, they were not at all dogmatic. Abdur’s dad even enjoyed the occasional glass of wine with dinner—a practice he picked up in med school. The Nidals, in fact, practiced exactly the kind of life the Quran emphasizes—one of kindness, love of one’s neighbors, a strong sense of family and generous and selfless hospitality. And yet the proponents of suicide bombings—who always invoked God and jihad in the name of killing not just soldiers and policemen, but innocent women, children and civilians—were absolute in their intolerance for any deviation or moderation from their fundamentalist dogma of radical Islam.

While the family had the means to escape their precarious neighborhood, leading by example, they chose to remain and serve. Ironies abounded in Palestine. While contempt and hatred blossomed among all Palestinian youth like Abdur and his best friends Ahmed and Badr for what they viewed as the imperialistic and blood-thirsty West, they granted high esteem to wearing counterfeits of American brands of sneakers, tee-shirts and jeans and taking in badly overdubbed Hollywood-produced movies.

At eighteen, Abdur became even more atypical from his peers as he traveled to the United States to begin his freshman year at MSU. While in-flight from Damascus to London en route to and contemplating the many wonderful new experiences he might enjoy in America, he also thought about the many good times he had back home with his family. He smiled contentedly as he sipped his juice and remembered one particularly festive Nidal family gathering in the Palestinian countryside.

His recalled a picturesque holiday celebration with the centerpiece goat slowly roasting on an open fire pit in the courtyard in front of Uncle Nikki and Aunt Marta's place. The rugged hills were an explosion of wildflowers. Hundreds of butterflies flitted from one plant to the next on that sun-drenched afternoon. The citrus orchards were swelling with plump oranges and limes. A promising crop of purple and green olives hung from several olive trees. That evening's spread of fresh breads, olives, roasted tubers, date cakes, and other sweet treats were on the counter and ready to be spread out on the massive wooden table inside the seventy-five-year-old stone and mason country house. The wonderful smell of a wood fire and roasting meat filled the air, as the family members drank honey-sweetened tea and made ready to feast. The occasion was the holy day of The Eid Milad un Nabi, or the birthday of the Prophet Muhammad. This Muslim holiday is usually celebrated in late March—with calendar variances factored in—very close to the also renewal-centric holidays of Passover and Good Friday, in the Jewish and Christian religions respectively.

Amal, Abdur, Khalil and their aunt, uncle and mother were seated outside near the fire in the late afternoon. They chatted as they shelled lentils for dinner into a large wooden bowl. None of them noticed when a perturbed billy goat took aim at a weary Doctor Nidal.

The good doctor, was swaying blissfully in a brand new woven hemp hammock that he had purchased and brought to the farm to set up for serious naps like the one he was enjoying. The hypnotic sway back and forth of the hammock clearly did not sit well with the large and ill-tempered male goat. He seemed to grow more irritated with each movement of this new and foreign addition to his domain on the farm. By the time the family noticed the angry animal, it was in full attack mode—head down, horns heading directly toward the prominent target that bulged though the backside of the amply filled hammock's mesh.

"Babba, look out!!!" Amal screamed. But it was too late. Abdur couldn't help but chuckle as he recalled the spectacle. It wasn't the blow struck against the target that led to the explosion of rollicking laughter that followed. It was that the goat's head butt spun the good doctor completely around in a full 360-degree spin and, in doing so, pinned his arms to his sides inside the hammock that now entombed him.

Abdur squelched a giggle as he envisioned his father shouting loudly for help and the goat quickly striking his now even more irritatingly wagging bottom and spinning him completely around once more. And even as the accustomed-to-farm-animals cousins came running to the good doctor's rescue, the goat struck a third and final blow, with the same spectacular Olympic-gold-medal-caliber, full-circle-spin results. The party at the table, who were genuinely concerned for Dr. Nidal as the attack unfolded, were now laughing so hysterically that several had fallen to the ground and were clutching their sides in near convulsions. And with each subsequent re-telling over time of the infamous and now beloved goat attack story, the animal would become larger and angrier and the full body spins even more numerous.

Abdur adjusted his passenger seat back and attempted to nap, with occasional, goat-story-induced chuckles still slipping out from time to time.

CHAPTER 5

Mother Nature's Son

Growing up as the son of an army sergeant was for the most part a real hoot for Murf. One of seven brothers and sisters and a middle child to boot, Murf was ever the clever antagonist who precipitated fights among siblings and then disappeared into the woodwork when Dad's Irish wrath and retribution exploded on the scene. But it was good to be part of a big family, given all the instability of regularly moving to a different place every few years.

In addition to all the various military bases the family lived on in the U.S.—in Maryland, California, Florida, Texas, and Kansas—there were exotic foreign locales as well, such as when they were stationed in Germany and then Panama. Murf especially loved the many swimming pools and Pacific Ocean beaches their Fort Amador home in the Canal Zone had to offer because he was the definitive water child. He repeatedly and voluntarily went underwater in his baths as an infant, and he quite precociously begin to swim in the pool when he was just two.

Accustomed to watching all of the older kids in the water, Murf just jumped in one day and instinctively began to swim—mostly beneath the surface—as though he'd been doing it for years.

While he possessed no underwater photos of himself as a young fish, those sumptuous scenes we've all seen of open-eyed, smiling California babies hovering underwater, was very much how Murf envisioned his early childhood. And back then he did, in fact, routinely swim underwater for as much as ninety seconds at a clip, as though he had built-in Aquaman gills.

At age ten, his daily routine, when school was not in session, was to rise in the dark of early morning, make the deliveries on his newspaper route, and then grab a few still hot, fresh donuts when they were just delivered to the base canteen. Then he'd go fishing off the pier for grouper by dawn's early light. And when he'd caught his fill, or by the time the sun rose high enough in the sky to push the temperature into the 80s, he'd toss his tee-shirt off and take a cooling dip in the surf. Then he'd ride his bike to the pool to meet his friends and spend the rest of the day swimming. In fact, Murf spent so much time in the water that his curly hair sported bright blonde and subtle green highlights because of the effects of constant sun, water and swimming pool chlorine.

Murf also played baseball with his friends, went to matinees at the movie theater and generally goofed around with complete abandon. When he showed up just in time for the mandatory family dinner of meatloaf and potatoes on a Sunday evening, his dad would ask sternly why he hadn't been with the rest of the family earlier that day at mass?

"I went to the early service at the hospital while doing my paper delivery rounds at 6:00 a.m." was Murf's foolproof ruse. "Seeing all those poor folks sick and hurt, I just had to stop in right then and say a prayer for all of them," he'd say straight-faced and earnest a la Eddie Haskell.

His dad would shoot back a look that said, "You'd better not be bullshitting me!" And then he let it lie, knowing that his kid had not been any closer to Sunday mass than he had been to giving up Scotch.

Though there was never a lot of money or fancy possessions, the family always had an ample supply of cereal, hamburgers, hot dogs, pork and beans, to feed such an army of hungry Catholic whelps. And, of course, there were always fish sticks on meatless Fridays.

"Cat-lick" schools are what Murf called them when he started putting on a school uniform and reporting to Catholic school in the first grade. The nuns and priests of that era seemed to be driven by a philosophy of beating and threatening religion into kids. Fear was a card played daily by them and usually via shouting, "Only Catholics free of mortal sins can go to heaven. All of your little Protestant friends are going to burn in hell forever unless they get baptized by the Catholic Church!" went the typical catechism lesson. "If you lie to me, you'll burn in hell! If you steal candy, you'll burn in hell! If you have impure thoughts or touch yourself down below, you'll burn in hell for all eternity!!!!" That's what the big burly priests would yell at the boys, as their neck veins bulged and spittle flew.

The avoidance of burning in hell provided little motivation for Murf because his days at Catholic school felt a lot like being in hell already. Plus, he didn't buy into the punishment-obsessed, mean and vindictive version of Jesus he was threatened with daily. He preferred the smiling, beatific face of Jesus he saw in the stained glass at church while those peaceful and reassuring hymns were playing. Given all the wonderful things the bible said the Lord did and how crazy so many of the priests and nuns acted, Murf, at a very early stage, decided he liked God, but just didn't care a bit for God's wacky, screaming friends dressed in black robes with white accents.

Years later, Murf moved to San Francisco—a liberal and fiercely independent city where the Fashionista police seemed to have declared that the citizenry must always dress with a penchant for all things black. San Francisco Gap-dominated fashion sometimes reminded him of the priests and nuns. When it did, his brain screamed, "Fookin' nuts, they are."

His dad's favorite profanity was always rooted in the Irish accented descriptor "fookin'" and it had likewise become the son's. Fookin' as in fookin'-nuts, fookin'-crazy, fookin'-bastard, fookin'-lame brain, fookin'-liar, fookin'-looney, "I'm fookin' serious now" (when you are about to get smacked) and the twinkling-eyed observation, "she's fookin'-garjus" (gorgeous).

Murf continued to love water thoroughout his life. Being in or on the water made him happy. One of his favorite ocean voyages was on a camouflage-splotched, olive green-colored landing craft. This particular trip involved taking Murf's troop of army-brat boy scouts some fifteen miles off the northern Panama shore to a tiny, unnamed and uninhabited, pineapple-growing island in the Caribbean Sea. Murf's scout troop was being rewarded for their many civic good deeds, with an exotic day trip. But what Murf loved most was the ride in the made-for-troop-transport, open-air belly of a naval landing craft. Way cool! That's right, the kind our men stormed out of on Omaha Beach and into withering German machine gun volleys.

While all of the other scouts stayed down in the troop and equipment carrying center of this strange looking shell of a ship, Murf was perched up on the bridge of the wheelhouse at the captain's invitation, with the wind ripping through his highly tangled hair as the craft's powerful engines pushed it forcefully through the waves and swells. Many of the scouts aboard that day got majorly seasick and repeatedly hurled their egg breakfasts down into the ship's seawater-splashed wooden floorboards. Murf never got seasick, even when tossed unmercifully by an angry ocean. He actually enjoyed surging up and down through the rollicking troughs of water that severely tilted the craft from one side and then savagely twisted it back to the other. And he loved every minute of staring out across the sea with its endlessly mesmerizing, glittering-blue expanse. Though he had tried to warn his fellow scouts to pass on the greasy scrambled eggs and mystery-meat sausage at the dockside café, he felt bad for those who were loudly and repeatedly blowing chowder down below.

When the landing craft reached their destination—the pineapple plantation—the scouts spent the afternoon with the grower. As they stood among the seemingly endless rows of plants, he told them far more than they wanted to know about pineapple farming. Finally, he showed them something they all thought was really cool; how to cut the golden pineapple fruit away from the sword blade-like green leaves with a machete. Then he lopped its body in two and a feast of deliciously ripe and sweet slices ensued. Little wonder that, in later years, Murf would rekindle fond memories of that day every time he bit into the chunk of pineapple that adorned the top of his rum drink glass. It was Panama that instilled in Murf, at a fairly young age, a life-long love affair with the water.

CHAPTER 6

"Blown up, SIR!"

Growing up, Murf was impetuous, resilient and more than a little lucky. He was smarter, quicker and more athletic than most of his friends, which meant that succeeding at sports and assorted adventures came easy to him. Murf also had an inordinate number of silly, impulsive ideas that popped into his head, and were usually put almost immediately into action, with little consideration for the consequences.

To wit, Murf particularly loved mayhem and football. Overall, he was a pretty nice kid, but with a wicked sense of humor. Even as he readily partook of good-natured teasing, his style of humor was more self-deprecating. He liked acting silly and making people smile. He thought nothing of pouring an entire bowl of chili over his head at lunchtime if he had the impulse and believed it might make for some good fun. Murf was not a bully. He did not put up with bullying from others, either, and so he often fought in defense of those being picked on. And, regardless of the just cause, Murf's occasional fistfight at school resulted in detention for both combatants. But a far worse consequence for Murf, was the subsequent punishment with the belt he'd receive from his dad. He was a tough kid, and his dad was firm but fair with him.

Football was the last great bastion of sanctioned violence and chaos and that's why Murf loved it so. Later in life you usually go to jail if you publicly assault someone. But in football, it is not only legal, but encouraged, to smash someone with complete abandon, and with no repercussions, save the later retaliation that might come. Sweet. While Murf was a skilled starting running back and linebacker on all the various level teams he played on, his favorite football experience was when he joined in with the special teams players for kick-offs. Running full-tilt down field and steamrolling blockers and blowing up the return man was such a gas. His favorite takedown was the sideline tackle, which Murf always initiated at the edge of the boundary line. However, the force of his tackle was typically such that the momentum sent him and his victim flying into steel and chain first-down markers, water coolers, wooden benches evacuated by scattering reserves, or good old-fashioned mud or gravel. The more spectacular the collision and the closer he brought the hit and its aftermath to the gasping folks in the stands, the more Murf relished it.

Murf's best friend Nicky Banachek was the team's quarterback and Murf's equal in terms of impulsiveness and unchecked spontaneity. Often they would abandon the scripted play during the game, and pitch the ball back and forth to each other rugby-style. That way they both eluded tacklers in the process; but they were also daring each other to handle the surprise last-second pitch without fumbling. They usually accomplished enough, results-wise, on the field to mollify their coach's objections, but it was this kind of "freelancing, gol' darned undisciplined behavior," as one coach described it, that kept them from sticking long at the more serious college football level. The very same modus operandi predominated with these two merry troublemakers outside the world of sports, too.

For instance, in junior high school, Murf and Nicky both lived in base housing at Ft. Detrick, Maryland where Nicky's dad was a major. That summer, they went to a boyscout summer camp along the Maryland coast for two weeks. The "what-in-the-world-were-we-thinking" adventure du jour involved aluminum canoes on the Chesapeake Bay. Paddling furiously and alternately racing each other on the rippling waters along the shoreline were the soon-to-be-no-longer-laughing boy scouts of Murf's troop. They were packed three to a boat in a dozen or so canoes. Unfortunately, it was shortly after Murf first screamed, "Canoe wars" and then, "Ramming speed!" that the participants realized what a bad idea Murf had come up with. As one canoe after another was struck and overturned, all who went into the water that day soon discovered the stinging horror of a jellyfish saturated bay. The scouts swam to shore and then howled and cried in pain as they had to slowly use their fingers to remove tentacle after tentacle from all over their bodies. For all of them, that still remains a very hard-to-forget day.

The next year, the duo went on a camping trip with the scouts in the Cumberland Mountains of northern Kentucky. The twin terrors soon tired of torturing the younger "tenderfoot" level scouts with the old standards like: secret Ben-Gay underwear coatings; midnight, use-paint-instead-of-water balloon attacks; undulating garter snakes hidden in the victim's bedding; or assorted bugs embedded at the bottom of red or green Jell-O desserts. Little did they know that this year, a fairly innocent instance of ignorance and curiosity would get them permanently booted from boy scouts and enshrined in the Hall of Fame for Colossally Dumb Ideas.

Every morning after breakfast, Murf and Nicky left their campground in the deep green, shadow and nettle-coated piney woods. As they hiked on the rocky trail that ran from camp through the babbling brook dissected grassy meadow, to the clearing where the camp's central parade ground and mess hall were, they passed it. "It" was the round open-mouth of a massive rusty pipe embedded deeply straight down into the ground. It should have had an accompanying sign that said, "Herein Lies the Entrance into Hell."

The diameter of this three-inch thick, steel pipe's hole was greater than fifteen inches across and, when a passing scout tossed a pebble into the black abyss, it would make a succession of ever-farther-off plinking sounds as it descended potentially thousands of feet down. Now, never did these two enterprising lads stop to think about the meaning behind the heavily rusted abandoned drilling and mining equipment they passed while hiking in the nearby mountains. Nor did they contemplate the origin or the implications of the Sinclair signs attached to some of this long-ago abandoned gear. They just loved the sound a pebble made as it fell into the seemingly bottomless pit they had discovered. So logically, they reasoned, bigger stones would make even cooler sounds as they ricocheted downwards. And, indeed, they did.

So cool a sound did they make that Murf and Nicky were compelled to demonstrate their amazing discovery to two other buddies later that afternoon. And then Murf had an even better idea, "Let's try to see how far down the pipe actually goes. We'll light some dried grass on fire, drop it into the pipe and then we can see the bottom when the flame reaches it."

As the four curious teens pushed the burning grass down the hole, they knelt and stared down its throat; watching as the orange and yellow flames traveled further and further down.

"It must be a mile deep or more," said Nicky as the light dimmed in the distance.

And then to their surprise, the pale yellow flame turned into a bright neon-blue color.

"Holy shit, something blue is coming back up," observed Murf with the word "up" barely making it out of his mouth before the massive burst of lightning-fast blue flame and an enormous whooshing sound exploded from the hole. The foursome didn't move even slightly—they were seemingly frozen in fascination as the very flames of hell roared upward toward them.

Scouts elsewhere in the camp reported that the flames soared some thirty feet high into the air. The combination of the sudden gush of fire from out of nowhere and the other-worldly roaring sound it made, had scared the bejesus out of the entire troop of campers and counselors, with many falling or ducking to the ground with their brains instinctively screaming, "INNNNCOMIIING!!!!"

In terms of injuries caused by the Pearl Harbor-like surprise attack: there was an inconsequential assortment of minor scrapes and bruises among the surprised campers; several sets of pants were allegedly involuntarily crapped in—including, unfortunately, the head scoutmaster in charge of this now legendary outing; and one bug-eyed kid didn't speak for several days afterward.

As for the four perpetrators, the Las Vegas-style magic fountain of flame tossed these criminally idiotic teenagers like ragdolls about six to ten feet from where they had been crouched. Not having been previously blown up, the boys could not comprehend the brevity of the big blue flame burn-off. It seemed to them to last an eternity. Exacerbating their inflamed perceptions of the fireball from the deep-earth pocket of natural gas they had just ignited, were their own bizarre conditions. Though not seriously injured, they had no sense of that being the case. They had been thrown into soft grass some ten or more feet away from the flame-spouting pipe. But they could still hear the roar of the burn-off and feel the heat. Plus, their eyesight was really fuzzy—literally. Not only was every hair on their heads massively singed together into a curly, crumbling fusion of dead, fuzzy strands, but also the tiny hairs on their eyebrows and eye lashes, as well. The combination of the tingling feeling on their arms and faces from mild skin damage and having their vision impaired by the melting together of their eyelashes convinced them of the worst case scenario.

"A-A-A-G-G-H-H!!! I'M ON F-I-I-R-R-E!!" they all screamed in near unison as they picked themselves up and staggered ten feet or so toward the nearby stream where they hurled themselves into the shallow water. Even as they splashed savagely to put out what were only imaginary flames, they continued the high-pitched chant, "I'M ON F-I-I-R-R-R-E!!!" Though when all was said and done, miraculously, none would have worse than a whole day at the beach-type sunburn on their hands and faces—plus some amazingly weird, Afro-style frizzy singed hairdos. Murf, in particular, was wondering if he had just received the burn-in-the-flames-of-hell promise that those fear-spewing, men in black robes had so often threatened him with at Cat-lick school.

When the assistant scoutmaster (now temporarily in charge since he had not crapped his pants), ran up to them huffing, and quickly ascertained that they were alive and mostly just badly shaken, he calmly inquired, "WHAT IN THE HELL HAPPENED????!!!!!!"

Years later, when Murf watched the movie Stripes—one of Bill Murray's finest—he would hear, way too late, the perfect response to the scoutmaster's inquiry. Murray's character—the new recruit in Army boot camp—was asked by his superior after a mortar mishap, "Soldier, where's your sergeant?" And Bill came right back at him with the perfect screaming, stentorian response, "Blown up, SIR!"

Right now the bewildered, burnt-haired scouts could only shake their hung low heads and mutter, "I dunnow."

In Murf and Nicky's final summer of scouting, they had missed out on becoming Eagle Scouts by a subterranean mile, and by taking the time honored practice of scouts lighting natural gas—usually from their sphincters—to a new, historic level. All who camped there afterwards, would oft speak of this day with hushed reverence, as they gathered around their campfires at night.

CHAPTER 7

The Great Atlantic City Newspaper Boys Caper

In spite of young Murf's mischievous nature, he was extremely hard working. He consistently mowed about a half-dozen neighborhood yards each weekend for around ten bucks apiece. While the money he earned from his jobs was not needed to provide income for his family, without it there was insufficient means to buy the comic books, baseball cards, records, movie tickets and piping hot French fries from the base canteen that he loved so much. Plus Murf actually dug the physical toil of manual labor.

As far as Murf was concerned the bigger the yard, the better in terms of hours of satisfying struggle. All the while he was cutting and bagging the grass, his imagination was running amok. A favorite lawn-mowing fantasy was Murf versus the WWII Japanese Army. He imagined himself to be a grizzled, helmet wearing, and Tommy gun-toting, American soldier. As he mowed row after row, he envisioned each bit of recaptured land to be another machinegun nest captured from the stubborn, resist-at-all-costs Kamikaze foes. A particularly large and difficult to assail clump of weeds that threatened to choke the mower to a complete stop, called for the flamethrower—or pushing down on the handles and lifting the mover up on its two back wheels. Murf would then lower the whirling maelstrom of flashing blades of death directly on top of the tall weeds as he yelled "A-A-A-A-A-R-R-R-G-G! Die, You Dirty Jap Bastards!!!!"

The multiple yards he cut were, of course, seen by Murf as the re-taking of multiple islands as the Americans hopscotched across the vast Pacific, drawing ever nearer to the Japanese mainland. He even envisioned that his rinsing off of the mower after the day's work was actually the swabbing of the wooden decks of the mighty U.S.S. Missouri, upon which the Japanese finally surrendered to end the war.

Murf's other early morning income stream came from delivering the morning newspaper. This activity also led to some of Murf's and Nicky's adolescent misadventures. At age seventeen, the lads hatched a clever scheme to earn themselves a trip to the fabled summertime beaches of Atlantic City, New Jersey. The opportunity was presented to them through a sales contest organized by *The Baltimore Sun* newspaper that each of them delivered in their respective neighborhoods. Six enterprising newspaper boys in the area would win vacation trips to Atlantic City based on who sold the greatest number of new subscriptions in a two-month sales drive period. Nicky, as the more devious of the two, came up with the scheme to net each of them the prize.

Since the military was notorious for the transience of its members, in addition to knocking on doors and cold-call selling like all their competitors, the two of them would also take turns entering the names and addresses of every individual posted to the Temporary Officers' Quarters. Each of them became a new *Baltimore Sun* subscriber in name only. Said individuals were rarely housed there for longer than a few days to a week and, with each of these special new subscriptions they turned in, Nicky or Murf always included a thirty day payment to eliminate any suspicion of bad paper being submitted.

As the number of newspapers for them to deliver each morning increased, the boys simply took the leftovers and regained their false subscription front money by selling them to passing soldiers—often, ironically, in front of the Temporary Officers' Quarters. "It's legit because, in the end we are getting more paying readers for *The Baltimore Sun*," rationalized Nicky. "Besides we shouldn't be penalized because our routes are on a military base where people put off subscribing because they might be shipped out at a moment's notice."

"That totally makes sense," chimed in an initially reluctant Murf. "Why, to disallow our approach is an affront to our soldiers in the military and would be simply un-American," he added. Sixty days later when the subscription contest was over, their names were atop the list of prize-winners who would be staying at the fabulous Traymore Hotel overlooking the white sands and bikini-infested beaches of Atlantic City.

The hotel looked quite like one of those grand designs featured in the Metropolis skyline of Superman's crime-fighting big city home. With its massive multiple towers, smoothed tan-colored concrete fascia and art deco accents, the 1915 constructed Traymore Hotel was a boardwalk landmark. Plus it was at the epicenter of fun in the tourist Mecca of Atlantic City. With six twelve-to-seventeen-year-olds versus only one elderly chaperone who went to bed around nine each night, the stage was set for the unique Nick and Murf brand of mishap and mayhem. The only complication that might impede their after-hours escape was the hotel security guard in the front lobby who had been tipped, by the not-yet-too-senile chaperone, to be on the lookout for the boys.

Murf told Nicky that he had seen a metal stairway fire escape protruding from the backside of the hotel's third floor. "Cool, we'll slip out the back way, get some winos to buy us beer and then pick up some hot college girls," strategized the ever confident Nicky. About fifteen minutes past nine that night, the two freedom seekers slipped out of a third floor hall window and clambered out onto the massive steel stairway suspended some fifteen feet off the ground and locked in its "for emergency use only" recessed position. While an experienced-with-fire-escape-lowering-procedures individual might have thought to release the emergency lever and lower the stairwell BEFORE getting on top of a steel ladder that was suspended above the street and parallel to the ground, the fearless duo were far too anxious to launch themselves into freedom. And so, without hesitation, they climbed aboard the four thousand pound fire escape, yelled out a "Three, Two, One" countdown and then hit the unleash-hell lever. Instantly, they plummeted to the street below riding the wild steel stallion, which slammed the bottom of its ladder down onto the street at a sharp perpendicular angle.

Murf wasn't sure which injury was more memorable. First there were the shock waves that reverberated through his wrists and arms and then right into his body. Said waves emanated from the force of steel striking hardened concrete and it felt like the penultimate arm-stinging gigantic foul ball struck by a mega-sized metal bat. Second, there were the countless scrapes and bruises he got from head to toe, when he was thrown clear of the steel demon and into the now badly chipped cement and gravel street they had just bludgeoned with their Paul Bunyan-sized Excalibur sword. With the combination of the thunderous, clanging ladder striking ground noise and the earthquake-like vibration it created, the entire hotel population simultaneously turned on their lights and rushed to the windows to see precisely where the airplane that must have just struck the hotel had crashed.

Nicky was as dazed, scraped and bloodied as Murf, but the "Hey you!" shouts from the hotel occupants that were raining down on them from above, prompted the boys to quickly struggle to their feet and run like hell. As they did so, they started whooping loudly in immense glee, like two "Great Escape" prisoners of war who had jumped the barbed wire fence on a motorcycle Steve McQueen-style.

The guys deduced that in all likelihood, there would be no second night spent at the historic Traymore Hotel. Surely, upon capture, they would be prematurely and rudely shipped home the next day. The on-the-lam duo became determined to make this one evening count big time.

It was easy enough for the young men to score two six packs of beer with the aid of a wino, who would get to keep the third one. Satisfied with their haul, they began slamming down tallboy Schlitzes beneath the boardwalk. A couple of massive foamy fusillades and several whole-body belches later, and the guys were stoked and ready to "PAR-R-R-TAY!"

Next, they slipped on over to a nearby pizzeria and hurriedly gobbled two slices of cheese pizza each, washing them down with two more beer blasts. Then they headed for the bright lights of Steel Pier where they persuaded two comely blonde girlfriends to join them on the Tilt-a-Whirl.

In spite of their handsome, athletic, and dangerously attractive scraped and bloodied features, the lads soon learned that there is no possible means of kiss-inducing persuasion that can overcome the act of blowing chowder all over your dates on a sweet summer's night. As the open-air seats of the thrill ride made the first of their characteristically sudden and violent outward thrusts, both Murf and Nicky were immediately hit with unstoppable waves of motion sickness that could result in only one outcome. As fate would have it, the guys both lost their lunches on the ride's second outward thrust as the girls' faces flooded with panic at the realization of their impending doom. As it happened, when the ride's arm was extended outward, it also positioned the two Olympics-caliber hurlers out over the carnival goers meandering down below. The combination of the Tilt-a-Whirl's forceful thrust and the quickly consumed beers and slices, made for twin high velocity streams of pungent spew that broadly sprayed both the girls and the horrified crowd below. And, we all know the response that the sudden appearance and smell of vomit on slippery-when-wet wooden boardwalk slats can cause. Oh, the slipping and sliding and chain-reaction retching HORROR of it all!

Needless to say, after fleeing the angry crowd, the guys knew that the probability of them now meeting some other girls and successfully procuring sex—given the puke breath they now sported—was infinitesimally small. With their epic adventure nearing its end, they retired to the beach about 4:00 a.m. to sleep it off before turning themselves in at the hotel.

A few years later, Murf was just getting started in college at Brown when he heard that his best buddy Nick Banachek had dropped out of the local community college after one week, and enlisted in the Marines. Nine months later, Nick was killed in Kuwait in the first few days of The Gulf War. Thereafter, Murf decided not to play football anymore. It reminded him too much of his lost friend and no longer seemed to hold much fun for him. He settled into a fairly austere life of going to class, studying whenever he could and working at nights in campus restaurants to pay the bills. Murf would not bond closely in true friendship with any other males until more than ten years had passed.

CHAPTER 8

The Turning of a Wheel

Abdur's newfound affection for all things modern and American was second only to his immediate love for all variety of Spartan sports. Sports helped keep his mind off of fear for his family's safety back home and his deep-seated desire to do something about the regularly occurring tragedies there. For all of his delight in his new campus activities, Abdur was secretly and constantly torn between two worlds he now loved. He was rarely seen without wearing some manner of green and white MSU athletic gear and his dorm room walls were covered with MSU/Big Ten Conference/Beat Michigan posters and pennants. The grand scale mayhem of fall football and winter basketball games enthralled him the most. But he did far more than just quickly master his engineering school studies and go to watch MSU games. As one of dozens of uninvited walk-ons for the soccer team, his dormitory roommates were astounded when he easily made the Spartan team. Abdur was not surprised, however, for it was always a part of his life's plan.

Though rare for a freshman, he received considerable playing time as one of the reserves and he even scored a few very impressive goals in several games.

On one of the few weekends when he wasn't playing or taking in a college game, Abdur and a Jordanian MSU student he'd met named Ali, traveled together by bus from their East Lansing campus to nearby Dearborn, which, with its large Arab immigrant population and prevalence of Middle Eastern culture, offered the food, music, religion and languages of home. While there, Abdur stopped in at the Arab American center to pay his respects to the sponsors that facilitated his scholarships. He also met a very pretty young American-born Arab girl named Aya at a nearby shaved-meat and pita bread shawarma stand where he and Ali stopped for lunch. Though she had plans to attend the hated rival school Michigan when she finished high school in a few months, they were mutually smitten and subsequently occasionally dated in the months to come between school classes and soccer competitions.

All things considered, his new life in America seemed profoundly blessed. Abdur even thought his future might include living in the U.S. long term. That is, until a week before his second semester's end, when he received the frantic phone call that would dash his halcyon days of college life at MSU. It was from his mother who told him, sobbing, about his father's arrest by Israeli security forces. He was handcuffed and taken away, all the while screaming of his innocence, by heavily armed Israeli commandos who came to their home one night. She had spent an unsuccessful week pleading with authorities at the Shin Bet, the Israeli security service, in vain to free him. "We need you back home, my dear son," sobbed his mom.

For the next two years back in Azzun, Abdur served as the head of the family in place of his unjustly imprisoned father. The charges brought against Dr. Nidal of engaging in terrorist activities, were vague and could not have been more ill-founded. Nonetheless, Abdur drove a taxi both day and night to help make ends meet for a Nidal family that now—like most of its neighbors—was struggling to survive with hopes fading fast. Even after the release and return of Dr. Nidal, the downward spiral for the Nidals continued. It would accelerate significantly due to the increasingly aggressive actions of the small, but very virulent Hamas militia, now staging missions in both Gaza and in some parts of the West Bank.

First, Israeli undercover forces killed five militants in nearby Ramallah. The killing was a long and carefully planned revenge strike on a group who, in the preceding years, had organized numerous missions that killed many innocent Israeli civilians and several soldiers, as well. For many decades, the longstanding policy of Israel has been that any terrorist with Jewish blood on their hands will be pursued and brought to justice no matter how long it takes.

Two days later, the Hamas Brigade Martyrs responded with five straight days of long-range missile and mortar attacks on Israel's southern border communities, killing four. During that five-day span, the daily street battles—orchestrated by Hamas in Gaza, and by Fatah in the West Bank—grew in scale and intensity in defiance of Israel's extended curfews. Rock-throwing quickly escalated to Molotov cocktail tossing, and cars were turned over and set afire. When a column of Israeli Humvees and Jeeps sporting big bore machine guns took its first causality from a single gunshot, the Israeli response escalated from stun grenades and tear gas against the mob of 400, to a very deadly thirty-second volley of heavy machine gun and light weapons fire. Seventeen bodies were stacked outside Dr. Nidal's clinic that night and almost sixty wounded were treated, as well. No such horrific scale or depth of tragedy had befallen Dr. Nidal in his fifty-five years of living in Azzun.

Earlier that day, Abdur finished up at school and met up with his sister to walk home together. They were joined en route on their long, but usually pleasant, jaunt home by his good friends, Ahmed and Badr. Badr had long been infatuated with the very handsome woman that Amal was rapidly blossoming into. Badr had even quizzed Abdur about the likelihood of Dr. Nidal allowing them to marry once Badr found respectable and regular employment. As Badr pulled a piece of Amal's favorite candy from his pocket much to her delight, Abdur wondered about the seemingly skulking countenance of Ahmed and how overly dressed he seemed for a such a hot day in his heavy, bulky jacket.

Ahmed spoke sparingly and seemed nervous and agitated as the foursome walked and chatted about the small-scale uprising of recent days. In response to brief mortar attacks on its military posts from the general direction of Azzun, the Israelis, earlier in the week, had demolished the house of a known Hamas leader. This was followed by two other mortar attacks, and then, this morning, by the Israeli demolition of the Azzun Community Center with its school, playground and women's center. Across the board, the people of Azzun were livid and had taken to the streets in a show of defiance.

As the friends passed the typically noisy marketplace and neared within a block of the main square, the sounds of a large, chanting crowd were apparent. Seeking to reroute his sister and his friends to safety, Abdur turned around to look for an easy exit from the suddenly teeming area. But as he did so, Ahmed sped quickly forward directly toward the noise. Unbeknown to Abdur, he did so with the very curious Badr and Amal in tow. When the three of them turned the corner, they immediately joined in with the tightly packed, chanting and bouncing mob. Most carried aloft the Palestinian flag with its flush left, angular red pennant jutting over the black, white and green descending stripes, as well as painted signs denouncing Israeli repression and occupation. Soon they saw the column of Israeli soldiers ahead of them ducking and dodging the many rocks being thrown or hurled by slingshots their way. Both Badr and Amal screamed "NO!!!" at Ahmed as they saw him flash open his jacket, pull out and point the pistol hidden beneath it. And then he fired his gun at the soldiers.

When Abdur heard the first gunshot, he began to turn back toward his sister and the others. The shot was almost instantly followed by a massive Israeli response. As he ducked and recoiled at the thunderous sound of a thirty-gun volley, he realized too late that his friends and sister were nowhere in sight. In an instant, a mass of screaming, terrified people were heading straight at him as they fled the square. Fighting his way through them, the smoke and dust, and the bodies strewn all about, he finally found Badr on the ground sobbing, "No, no!!!" as he clung to the now motionless body of Amal.

Abdur shrieked in horror. Determined to save his sister, he scooped her up in one athletic move and turned around to take her back to his father. As he began to run with Amal in his arms, the bullet that would drop him tore through and shattered his right kneecap. The pain was intense, but his horror at this sister's plight somehow helped him transcend it. Screaming in anger and through the searing pain in his knee, he willed himself to his feet and struggled successfully to lift Amal into his arms once again. Blood flowed steadily from his leg and then from his lip when he chewed deeply into it as he began an excruciatingly painful hobble some three-quarters of a mile back to the clinic. He arrived covered in her blood and his own, eyes streaming from tear gas and sorrow and screaming loudly for his father, "Babba, help her!"

With such a mass of horribly injured casualties overrunning the clinic, the scope of the emergency quickly overwhelmed the outnumbered and ill-equipped medical staff. Dr Nidal went into classic triage mode and rapid-fire-directed the actions of his team, even as arterial bleeding sprays erupted seemingly every few minutes from another of the wounded. His almost super-human calm and ultra professional response was powerfully shattered the instant he saw his weeping, screaming son Abdur in the doorway with the slackened body of Amal in his arms. Dr. Nidal's deep and bellowing screams of anguish rose above all the pain-filled and panicked cries of the wounded and stunned them all into temporary silence.

His screaming of, "Amal, my beautiful girl," continued unchecked for a seeming eternity. He was of no use for nearly two hours as he collapsed sobbing atop his daughter's body. He was beyond consolation.

And then later, as if a switch had been flipped, he arose without any emotion and continued to treat the survivors for a shift that lasted a full forty-eight hours before he collapsed from sheer mental and physical exhaustion.

In the six months that followed before Dr. Nidal took his own life, he struggled to hold on to his mind and to function with any semblance of normality. The philosophy of humane service and a selfless dedication to medicine that had defined his adult life, quickly dissipated. Long before his son, Abdur, would leave Azzun to train to fight infidels in holy jihad, the good doctor would slip into a despondent state from which Abdur repeatedly tried, but always failed, to arouse him. He stopped properly feeding himself and shaving. He kept very irregular hours and worked erratically at the clinic. Largely, he just wandered the streets of Azzun rambling to himself and railing against both God and the inhumanity of his fellow human beings.

When Abdur could no longer stand to see his father like this, he packed his meager belongings. The soon-to-be-wayward son gave a teary-eyed hug goodbye to his incoherent father. Before walking away, he tenderly stroked his father's face looking for, but not finding, any signs of recognition in his father's expressionless eyes. And then Abdur gave him over to his very distraught mother. He kissed her and then hugged his completely confounded and wailing little brother, Khalil. The always supportive Uncle Nikki and Aunt Marta were also there for the sad parting.

"Go now, Abdur with the blessings of Allah, on the difficult path you have chosen." said Uncle Nikki. Abdur was keenly aware of the finality of the farewell, as his family all seemed to act as though none expected to ever see him again.

CHAPTER 9

"Order Up!"

In lieu of financial aid to the Ivy League liberal arts bastion, Brown, Murf had to pay his own way. So he would work after classes at near-campus restaurants in a variety of jobs that ranged from dishwasher, to kitchen prep, to eventually learning to become a very good cook. And as usual, he had tons of crazy ideas and bizarre scenarios running though his head as he did so.

Murf also loved the grit and colorful language of folks who worked the long and late night hours with him. One cook in particular named Smitty mentored Murf, not only in the foundations of culinary excellence, but also in the time-honored tradition of teasing and torturing waitresses. Smitty's favorite ploy was to heat the underside of a dinner serving dish under the broiler, before filling it with the food that had been ordered, and then setting it on the serving counter. "Order up," he would shout to lure his unsuspecting victim. Of course, caution in grabbing the underside of a dish would not normally be warranted, since the heat lamp above the shelf that held orders awaiting delivery only glared down on the top of the plate to keep the food warm. But with Smitty's help, when the waitresses' fingertips hit the plate's normally cool underbelly, a red-hot reception and loud and profane reaction awaited. Invariably, the dish was reflex-reaction flung or at least dropped and broken, scattering the contents across the kitchen floor.

"Way to go butterfingers, now I'll have to rush-cook another entree to replace the one you just wasted!" Smitty would yell at the shocked waitress, who was now sucking on her seared fingers. The words, "You, you, you rotten son-of-a-bitch," usually followed when Smitty failed to keep a straight face and began laughing hysterically—revealing his complicity.

"You sound like a dog that's been eatin' peanut butter, baby. Get your slab-ass out of my god-damned kitchen," he would shout in response as the angry, teary-eyed victim retreated through the swinging kitchen door to the safety of the dining room. Later on, he would usually corner the still-bitter lass in the back of his stainless steel lair and try to make up with her by plying her with a glass of chilled champagne or a fresh-made chocolate-covered profiterole, while he told her about how much he actually admired her work (not to mention her lovely tush).

Smitty was some piece of work. He spoke an arcane language of crusty similes, absurd alliterations and twisted metaphors. He constantly spouted favorite catch phrases like, "She's hotter than a fresh fucked fox in a forest fire, ain't she?" But odd in manner as he was, Smitty was a great cook and he had taken to young Murf Morrison and was determined to teach his apprentice all of the tricks of the trade.

"You keep workin' in those flat-soled sailing shoes," Smitty advised Murf, "and one day your feet will be flatter than road kill …and they will hurt worse than grinding your dick in a broken glass and razor blade-filled garbage disposal. Stop sweatin' it like a whore in church and get yer-self down to the Kinney Shoe Store. You get some extra thick, rubber-soled black leather Hush Puppies like mine. They'll last you forever and your feet will thank God like a nun who's riding over potholes on a bicycle she just removed the seat from," said Smitty as he shared his infinite wisdom.

And Murf, in turn, did as he was advised and bought a pair of comfortable black Hush Puppy work shoes just like Smitty's.

There was also the initiation task that Smitty put his new assistant up to. It involved the careful placement of a harmless, but very real, live snake in the bread-warming drawer. Unfortunately, the resultant screams that emanated from the poor waitress who opened the drawer to fill up her white-linen-lined breadbasket, were of such ear-splitting volume and abject terror, that it made it difficult for the restaurant's manager to explain away the incident to the alarmed patrons seated outside. That little stunt cost the restaurant quite a number of comped drinks and nearly cost Murf and Smitty their jobs.

The life of a restaurant worker was not exactly a normal one. They endured tough hours and long shifts. Everyone, seemingly, smoked and drank together with co-workers, and then fooled around after work with them—cheating on the spouses and significant others who were nestled in their beds at home awaiting them. After torrid, but brief (and not very secret), dalliances with several married waitresses a few years his senior, Murf after being egged on by his buddies in the kitchen, schemed for two months without success, trying to get two of the prettier twenty-something waitresses drunk and naked in a friend's hot tub. He tried his damnedest to put together the much idealized-by-males ménage a trois dream team in the face of ten-to-one odds against him succeeding in the betting pool his male cohorts were running. Instead of a simul-tryst with both ladies, in the end he spooked the prey and bedded neither. Even Smitty had to give up some begrudging respect for Murf's pluck and persistence during the failed quest.

"Careful now, Murf," Smitty advised. "Those two girls are hotter than two rats screwin' in a wool sock. And they'll steal your seed faster than an albino Irishman gets a sunburn."

Over the next three summers, Murf typically left the campus once school let out and moved up to The Cape to spend as much time as possible near the water he so loved. There, without Smitty around, he'd skip most of the practical jokes while working in one of the endless array of Cape Cod seafood restaurants to stockpile tuition money for the upcoming school year. It was on the island of Nantucket at a charming whitewashed and wood-shingle-covered seaside restaurant where he met and fell hard for a cute pastry chef and also off-for-the-summer college student named Terri Brewster.

Terri was quite the stunner to be found working in a kitchen. At five-foot ten, she was taller than most young women, which suited six foot three Murphy to a T. She also had million dollar legs that further accented her height. Her blue eyes contrasted greatly with her long dark brown hair. At work, she always kept it pulled back, tied up and very subdued. Terri's subtle use of makeup and self-confident and thoroughly professional air made her come off as smart, yet beautifully feminine. And she immediately upon arrival captivated the attention of all the males working with her at The 'Sconset Bistro.

The Bistro was off the beaten track for Nantucket. It was a ten-minute drive away from the cobblestone streets and whaling captains' houses found in the Nantucket-proper harbor area (twenty if transported by the more ubiquitous rental mopeds). To get there, one simply took Milestone Road out of Nantucket, which led to the tiny village of Siasconset—or 'Sconset—on the southwest side of the island. There standing alone, a quarter-mile down the road from the central cluster of tiny, picturesque wood-shingled summer cottages, was the stand-alone wooden structure that housed the restaurant. The modest building and parking lot were surrounded by windswept sandy bluffs and blessed with stunning 180-degree Atlantic Ocean crashing surf views. The Bistro's neutral interiors were quite understated, but in stark contrast, the walls were filled with dazzling impressionistic paintings of the maritime world, featuring streaks of vibrant aqua, sky blue, sea-glass green, angelfish yellow and bright lipstick red.

The edgy and eclectic cuisine at the 'Sconset Bistro, was centered around the local and organic produce and caught-that-day seafood that the far-from-the-mainland island was famous for. The menu, which was refreshed weekly, was broadly popular with both the bronze-skinned, hair always tousled-from-sailing, year-round islander types, and the preppy, blazer-clad "summer people" from Boston and Manhattan.

Behind the dining room's highly appealing nouveau bistro facade, lay the kitchen. From open 'til close, it was a beehive of activity, heavenly aromas and visual and gustatory creations—a swirling blur of constantly-on-the-move, crisp-white-linen-uniformed workers, set against a backdrop of brushed stainless steel and non-stop chatter. Yet when Murf had the chance to talk with Terri, all that dissonance fell away and he could see little else beyond her lightly freckled, pert nose, perfect smile and sumptuous, dancing eyes. He loved the way she spoke with the eloquence of an ambassador and the wry sense of humor of a brilliant satirist. Truth, be know, she was actually rather shy around large groups of people but on an interpersonal basis she was composed, confident and sparkled with wit and confidence.

As their courtship began, the bombast that was so much of Murf's M.O. quickly proved ineffectual and was abandoned. His buddies were quick to see the difference whenever she was around him. Even Murf felt like he was under a seeming spell in that he became a much more attentive listener and opened himself up more in her presence. He spoke with more sincerity and candor to Terri than he had with anyone for many, many years. And Terri broadened Murf's repertoire in every way. Her interests were diverse and unexpected. She could enthrall with acute and extremely knowledgeable insights about Brazilian samba music, diving ancient Mediterranean ship wrecks, everything Degas, obscure spices and fragrances, Russian playwrights, Woody Allen movies, ancient Scandinavian wooden ship-making techniques, and even the perennial plight of the hapless, yet tirelessly supported by New Englanders baseball club, the Bosox or Boston Red Sox.

Terri had, from her early youth 'til late high school years, traveled the world extensively with her parents and her nice-looking, but-not-nearly-as-pretty-as-Terri older sister. They all lived a rich and exciting life. But not without tribulation in that her well to do father—an international businessman—had died in his forties and left his large family largely insolvent. And yet Terri persevered and was working her way through college and still sending some money home for her siblings with nary a whine of self-pity. Eventually, she really opened up and even taught Murf to master her specialty—made from scratch killer muffins and sublime desserts. And that was in between their bouts of spontaneous and frequent, hot-monkeys-and-goats storage room sex, moonlit skinny-dipping on the beach, sailing Nantucket Harbor in a tiny, wooden sailboat, or the very best of times—lying together on the hammock outside Murf's small, summer bungalow for endless breezy hours spent gently caressing each other and napping blissfully.

Many relationships experience one poignant moment when there is a mutual realization that two people have fallen in love. For Murf and Terri it happened one Saturday night after the kitchen closed up around one a.m. After borrowing a friend's VW beetle convertible, Murf invited Terri for a drive down to a remote beach for some serious smooching and grubbing to the sound of crashing surf. He could not be held responsible, however, for the musical tastes of the car's owner. When Terri turned on the radio/tape player as they drove toward the beach, a Frank Sinatra cassette tape boomed to life.

While taken aback at first because it was not Rock 'N Roll, the couple quickly started to groove on The Chairman of the Board's shtick and masterful phrasing. In fact, the song selection was just perfect. First there was "I've Got You Under My Skin" and then "You Make Me Feel So Young." As they set up their blanket in the sand, they left the tape in the nearby car playing and heard Frank's quintessentially tender "In the Wee Small Hours of the Morning" as they made passionate and then especially tender love in the moonlight.

Murf and Terri knew that night they were meant to be together forever. They fell madly and profoundly in love that summer and would marry one year later upon graduation. In Terri, Murf knew he had found a magical and miraculous soul mate for the ages. In the months soon thereafter, Murf also realized he needed to get serious about finding a job in a field he was well suited for and where he could earn a decent living without surrendering to a quiet life of desperation. So he became an advertising copywriter.

George Orwell is credited with saying about the business of advertising, "Advertising is the rattling of a stick inside a swill bucket."

CHAPTER 10

Young Mujahedeen

One year later and after the bomb-making blast deaths of two of his likewise radicalized cousins, the still regularly aching, zipper-like, scar tissue-covered knee was evidence of both the shattered bone and dreams of Abdur Nidal. Although he walked with only a slight limp, the bullet and his bone on bone, tendon shredding run to the hospital had completely ended his dreams of soccer stardom and a life less ordinary.

After the U.S. attacked and deposed the dictator Saddam Hussein in Iraq, the entire Middle East became even more highly unstable. With U.S. military personnel now on Muslim soil as occupiers, the majority view among Palestinians, Syrians, Iranians, Egyptians, Saudis, Lebanese, and even Moroccans was that the Americans were oil-obsessed imperialists. If left unchecked, many believed they would follow the Iraq invasion with attempts to overthrow the governments in Iran and Syria. In doing so, they would place millions of Muslim homes, families, and the heart and soul of holy Islam under an all-out Western assault.

Meanwhile, Arab aristocracies like Saudi Arabia, which many viewed as oppressive and corrupt, were allied with the West and viewed with extreme contempt for blatantly crushing the human and civil rights of their own people and also attacking, with impunity, any reform-advocating or dissident movements. Given that outlook, the radicalization and progression of even an educated, sober and decent young man like Abdur, toward becoming an extremist, hardened terrorist, had a very high likelihood; and it was now well underway.

Whereas most hate-filled jihadists are lonely youths in their late teens and early twenties from large, lower income families, Abdur, with his comparatively privileged and highly-unusual-for-a-Palestinian background, would defy most of those norms. For one, he had no intention of becoming a soon-to-die suicide bomber. Instead, he wanted to live to kill as many Israeli soldiers as possible. But the prospect of partaking in Katyusha rocket attacks and occasional raids against Israeli settlers struck him as a frustratingly slow and a minimal-impact way of exacting the broad-scale revenge he dreamed of inflicting.

Abdur sought counsel from the local imam at his neighborhood Azzun mosque. The wise one said that the route to achieving such a glorious fate would be to go through training at an overseas al-Qaida camp that produced warriors who are given the opportunity to fight as part of insurgencies in places like Afghanistan, Iraq and Yemen. This was serious food for thought for Abdur. Though he saw Americans as invaders, he harbored a distant soft spot for Western culture and did not look forward to someday encountering American troops in battle. He initially sought his revenge through means closer to home.

After spending six-months in Gaza as a guest of the Islamic Resistance Movement better known by the acronym Hamas, Abdur was still frustrated with his lack of action as a jihadist. His assignment was to train to kill enemy soldiers and train in the arts of guerilla warfare. Yet his Hamas benefactors were overtly preparing him to return to the West Bank after training, to fight fellow Palestinians by battling with the

Fatah faction of the PLO, which still controlled the West Bank. Though Hamas had routed them militarily and politically in elections that left them in complete control over Gaza, Fatah still ruled the roost in the larger West Bank territory. Abdur, and many radicalized Palestinians, were suspect of Fatah for its willingness to negotiate with Israel in pursuit of a two-state solution (Israel and Palestine) and a unified national Palestinian state. Whereas Fatah received considerable Western aid and support after renouncing its prior vow to destroy the Jewish state, Hamas remained foresworn to Israel's destruction and continued its resistance even during times of truce. Launching rockets twenty to thirty miles away at southern Israel towns like Ashdod and Ashkelon was the primary Hamas tactic. Said rockets came from fundamentalist allies in Syria and Iran, smuggled into Gaza through a vast system of border tunnels used to arm Hamas and also to supply the people of often blockaded Gaza with daily sustenance.

For the record, Abdur was now a student at the Islamic University of Gaza, a well-known hotbed for Islamic militants. But the majority of Abdur's time was actually spent in secret training camps studying the Quran, and at intensely political Hamas meetings. As a mujahedeen in training, Abdur played only a distant observational role in the ongoing cat and mouse game of sporadic and often ineffective (in terms of casualities, as opposed to creating terror and instability) surprise Hamas rocket launches. Invariably, these were followed by devastating Israeli reciprocal economic blockades and pinpoint air attacks on Hamas leaders and buildings.

The Gaza Strip, where Abdur now lived, was a small seaside enclave teeming with a 1.5 million population. The combination of the ever-smothering presence of Israeli security forces and Abdur's desire to ultimately do something bigger than just to participate in intersectional Palestinian militia power plays, inevitably led Abdur to conclude that he needed to leave Palestine and his shattered, shard-of-its-former-self family behind in pursuit of serious jihad.

Returning to the West Bank, ostensibly to visit his family, Abdur again sought the aid of the imam at his family's mosque. With unspoken-of funding and connections, the imam arranged for Abdur to leave Palestine in order to dedicate his life in support of the global jihad declared by al-Qaida. His valid passport with entry stamps and a visa that had previously permitted him to get into the United States, made his entry into Pakistan a breeze. What followed after an extensive precautionary screening was one year of terrorist training at an al-Qaida camp in Pakistan's Northwest frontier. Beyond the physical training, which a slowed but still-athletic Abdur found underwhelming, bomb-making was a core curriculum. The IED or improvised explosive device—the most successful insurgent tactic for attacking Western troops without taking casualties—was a specialty of the camp he was assigned to.

Abdur quickly became adept at creating IEDs with a variety of readily available materials including plastic explosives, TNT, and fertilizer. Cell phones were the preferred means of triggering the detonator from a safe distance. The trainees were taught to make IEDs by cannibalizing the explosive charges within government supplied artillery shells, which were easily purchased on the black market. Abdur also quickly mastered the use of conventional firearms and became adept at launching surface-to-air missiles. Where he really excelled and distinguished himself was in the area of battlefield tactics. His soccer leadership experiences had honed him in terms of developing methodical game plans, splitting defenses and utilizing feints and misdirection.

Upon completing his training, he was one of a group of a dozen jihadist volunteers transported to Iraq to fight with the al-Qaida in Mesopotamia faction. Passage was obtained with the assistance of other militant groups who moved the men through Syria and then Iran, and finally across the porous border of eastern Iraq. Once settled with his unit in the southern province of Diyala, he was quickly integrated into small raiding parties comprised of mostly former Iraqi military mixed in with a small number of foreign Arabs. Their mission was to regularly attack coalition forces in and around the hundreds of villages that fanned out from the city of Baquba, east of Baghdad. They were also to prevent the Coalition forces and their local allies from bringing any semblance of order to the villages and towns their forces had occupied and were attempting to stabilize.

The typical attack his team employed was hardly sophisticated, yet consistently effective. It combined a roadside bomb to stop a mobile patrol with opposing-sides ambushes by two heavily armed groups of four to five of their men. Occasionally, they would attempt to drive the defenders into a second and bigger IED planted a quarter-mile behind the first. But the key was to mount the attack and inflict as many casualties as possible within a ten-minute span. After that time frame, they would always break off just before the expected Coalition air response arrived on the scene. The first step after an ambush was to hide their weapons—usually at a home where the residents' cooperation would be mercilessly assured by the threatened slaughter of the entire family—beginning with the children. Then Abdur and his men would separate and disperse into more populated areas, reuniting later back at their camp.

In his very first action, Abdur's unit leader was killed, but so were two British soldiers in a well-executed ambush with an IED and small arms fire. Abdur had planned the attack and built the IED and then he assumed command of the directionless men when the Coalition counterattack killed three mujahedeen. Abdur reflected later on this momentous first action for which he was being highly praised. He had seen the faces of the British troops and one of them was a ringer for a teammate of his on the MSU soccer team named Scott Allister. He, like Abdur, was a foreign student. But Scott was from Birmingham in the U.K. from what Abdur remembered. As pangs of doubt seeped in, Abdur wondered if his original ambition to avenge his sister Amal's death by killing Israelis had gone very much awry with his redirection toward global jihad. "They are still infidels and invaders," he sneered to himself to reassert his dedication to jihad. "And that young Arab soccer player at MSU lives no more," he reminded himself. "He died along with my sister on the streets of Azzun!"

Abdur was silently opposed to some of the tactics employed and taught by the Sunni Salafist extremist group he had joined. Using civilians to shield their forces from counterattacks struck him as unconscionable, but often, regrettably, necessary. He viewed the frequently used al-Qaida tactic of setting a secondary explosive to kill emergency personnel responding to the first blast, as cowardly and related it to his father being punished for helping injured neighbors. A variation on this use-the-first-bomb-as-bait theme was taught to him at the training camp (but only in theory). It was the use of a secondary killing device of a very different kind—a cyanide-gas bomb that the instructor said was intended for use in large cities should a jihadist be dedicated and lucky enough to someday earn a mission abroad in Europe or America. Such was the depth of al-Qaida's resolve and willingness to sacrifice innocents.

Propaganda was another key focus, and not just to properly imbue each revolutionary with the appropriate motivation and justification. Given that mainstream Islam did not sanction murder or suicide, martyrdom was a central and oft-repeated instruction regarding what, in Arabic, was referred to as Amaliyat Istishhad. The first ancient act of supposedly noble suicide cited therein was committed by Hussain ibn Ali (the Prophet's grandson) and his family in the ancient battle of Karbala. The more modern debut of the martyrdom tactic—which supposedly comes without pain and insures an immediate trip by the suicidal attacker straight to heaven—was during the 1980-88 Iran-Iraq war. As part of an effort to clear the battlefield of mines, poor and hungry Iranian children were trained to walk out into minefields and blow themselves up in the process—all for the glory and far better-than-their-life-on-earth rewards that awaited them. Each was given a plastic key to heaven as they were led out for their final walks.

With the aim of inciting the withdrawal of American troops, the suicide truck bombing was introduced with massive casualties at the

Marine barracks in Lebanon in 1983. And in more recent pre-Iraq War times, Hamas used explosives-strapped suicide bombers to persistently attack civilians within the Israeli inhabited towns of Afula and Khidarra in 1994.

In Iraq, Coalition and American soldiers were the highest priority targets, with Iraqi government forces and police personnel considered secondary. Abdur, with his stealth and leadership skills had gotten close enough to American troops on several occasions to hear their enemy-bashing chatter. “Fuckin’ Hajjis,” they would say disparagingly about all native Iraqis. Seemed to Abdur to be an odd sort of slander in that it literally meant “fuckin’ religious pilgrims.” And it was never said John Wayne-style (“Pil-grim”). Nevertheless, Abdur came to respect American troops and he exercised great caution in dealing with them because they were highly disciplined, brave in the face of fire and extremely tenacious. In contrast to the targeting priorities in Iraq, back in Abdur’s home in Palestine, the top priority was naturally killing Israeli soldiers. But it was closely followed by the proudly sanctioned objective of also attacking Israeli women and children, too. Attacking innocents—women and children—was something Abdur could not reconcile and had never undertaken, and he was determined to continue to avoid.

Ironically, following the Coalition forces’ invasion of Iraq, the quick defeat of the Iraqi Army and the onset of sectarian violence during the subsequent insurgency, it became open season for his al-Qaida in Mesopotamia team to begin killing fellow Muslim men, women and children. Rival Shiite and Sunni Muslims deliberately targeted each other’s civilians—even committing atrocious attacks on the real pilgrims engaged in hajj and visiting the holy sites of Islam. These regular acts of horrifying terrorism against fellow Muslims tormented Abdur. He knew that many a bomb he was making and the young suicide-vest-wearing martyrs he was told to train, would inflict decimating results on civilian populations in predominantly noncombatant marketplaces that often intermingled both Shiite and Sunni Muslims. In Saddam Hussein-ruled

Iraq, the Sunni Muslims, though a minority numerically, had come to be the ruling sect through their powerful Baathist Party. After Saddam's fall, the Sunnis now saw the majority Shiites, whom the Baathists had actively repressed, as puppets of Shiite-dominated Iran, whose influence in the Middle East was surging in Syria, Lebanon and Iraq.

Soon Abdur found that he was no longer attacking American forces. Instead, he was engaged full-time in sectarian violence—attacking Shiite Muslims in a power struggle and a religious war between Muslims. When he saw the grisly, shredded and strewn body-parts aftermath of an attack by one of his suicide bombers in Karbala—the holy city south of Baghdad—Abdur was disgusted and ashamed beyond imagination. In this consummate act of barbarism, fourteen pilgrims were killed and sixty wounded—mostly women and children. Many of the pilgrims were Persian-speaking Shiites from Iran. The blast left a crater with a twelve-foot radius. The fifteen-year-old suicide bomber named Faisal wore a vest charge that Abdur had packed with nails to kill and injure as many as possible. The wannabe martyr set off his bomb at a crowded rest stop amidst the tens of thousands of worshippers near the Imam Hussain shrine, where the grandson of the Prophet Muhammad was buried in the seventh century. It was immediately known by all to be the work of al-Qaida in Mesopotamia, with intent of re-igniting ancient enmities and open sectarian warfare between Shiites and Sunnis. Which would, of course, in turn, lead to even more collective Muslim deaths.

"But how can we countenance the killing of innocent civilians?" Abdur recalled asked the imam in Azzun in a conversation that seemed to have taken place a lifetime ago.

"The innocents become Allah's martyrs. They feel no pain from the act and go straight to heaven, having helped to further the Prophet's greater glory," said the unquestioning and rote-sounding imam.

This kind of horrific terrorism-driven warfare underlined that propaganda was also a primary weapon of the extremists. Such acts were intended to maximize fear and generate publicity—which might tout the success of an insurgent raid or the detailed horror of innocents killed in the retaliatory strike by the occupiers. Customarily, the local coverage would also include the airing of a pre-taped "confession" of faith by the now dead suicide bomber. The tools of the terrorist communications trade included not only using cellular and satellite phones, but also fax machines, digital video cameras, and computers for web postings of the video documentation of their acts. Sometimes the terror squads would even commandeer a radio station to broadcast their news. Wire tapping of phone conversations was a useful practice too, with a favorite application being to play re-edited versions of secretly recorded phone conversations that featured a trusted source. The altered messages could then be used to lure more impending victims into their clutches.

Another aspect of his service, that Abdur found terribly disillusioning, was the organized crime they spent the majority of their time engaged in. Since these crimes were staged to raise funds for waging their war of terror, it was deemed to be righteous. Trafficking in illegal drugs, robbery, kidnapping, car and fuel-truck theft and money laundering were everyday activities, with identity theft, counterfeiting documents and fundraising fraud thrown in for good measure. Abdur so hated the incessant stealing and criminal behavior. His self-image was one of a virtuous and honorable warrior who would eventually die in battle defending his faith and his people against the infidels.

Abdur spent the next two years alternately arguing with his superiors over strikes against rival factions that deliberately targeted civilians and occasionally attacked Coalition forces. Distrust and paranoia were rampant throughout the militants' ranks. Al-Qaida's leadership cherished Abdur for his significant battle skills. And yet he was reviled by the local leadership and by the rank and file for his "arrogant Arab" obstinacy and his outright resistance to "political" missions. Abdur was now nearing a phase where, in spite of his personal accomplishments, fed-up men who were on his own team might, any day now, kill him.

As he opened a message that had been transported to him by a foot soldier from district command, Abdur winced. He expected to read orders to once again attack civilians and Sunni Muslims versus American soldiers. Instead, he read, to his great surprise and relief, that the high command was going to the considerable trouble of retaining his skills by reassigning him and sending him out of Iraq entirely. One month of furtive travel later, Abdur slipped across the Pakistan border with a new team bound for his new mission in Afghanistan. There, he could do what he did best and focus on thwarting Coalition troops' efforts to occupy and control key territories in order to defeat al-Qaida's top leadership and the Taliban allies that had so long sheltered them.

Once settled in, Abdur staged attacks on enemy forces as he moved from safe house to safe house with a band of fifteen Taliban warriors—a few Arab militants like Abdur from assorted Middle Eastern countries, but mostly Uzbeks, Afghans and Pakistani nationals who fought as part of the insurgency in far flung rural and frontier areas of southern and eastern Afghanistan. Though the Taliban were removed from power and smashed in Afghanistan by U.S. forces in 2001, soon after 9/11, the subsequent refocusing of American might on Iraq had allowed them to rebuild their potency and retake considerable Afghanistan territories. To their opponents' great chagrin, the insurgent high command was usually safely ensconced in Pakistani tribal areas that were off limits to Coalition ground forces nearby in just-across-the-border Afghanistan.

To coordinate with their leadership, Abdur's team sent daily text messages back to their al-Qaida commanders in Pakistan. Abdur's specialty became sneaking his men and munitions like phantoms past the enemy's sandbagged checkpoints and then staging well-coordinated and highly visible raids—often in broad daylight—on well-fortified Coalition positions. His peers preferred to, instead, attack the far softer targets of Afghan policemen or government troops versus the well-trained and better-armed Coalition troops. Though losses were often quite high for Abdur's always-on-the-move band, the considerable psychological advantage that striking at the heart of Coalition entrenched and heavily fortified positions rendered, was invaluable to "The Cause." The propaganda machine back in Pakistan loved Abdur's attacks. They would proclaim broadly that, "another bold, frontal Taliban attack had succeeded in inflicting heavy Coalition losses." And naturally, they always stressed repeatedly that no part of the country—even Kabul—could escape the reach of Allah's heroic Islamic warriors. Abdur's leadership and fearlessness quickly became well known in the area.

He was shot and wounded peripherally, by both gunfire and shrapnel, several times over the course of dozens of raids that he led and fought in during the next three months. Soon Abdur had won over many new high-level Pakistan Taliban and al-Qaida allies, and even a few friends among the many formerly formal allies within Pakistan's Inter-Services Intelligence Agency. It was well known to all that Pakistan maintained little control over its borders in these tribal lands and that many high-ranking officials in its government still secretly supported the Taliban, in spite of public proclamations to the contrary. The leadership's true intent was that this transparent alliance would taunt Pakistan's reviled neighboring enemy India, with the prospect of an extremist and Pakistani-dominated Afghanistan at its other border.

Almost four years after leaving Palestine and many mind-numbing attacks and atrocities behind him, Abdur bore little resemblance to the handsome young soccer star he once was. Now he had a long scraggily beard and was dressed in traditional Afghan tribal garb—a shalwar kameez or long, loose-fitting long-sleeved grey tunic with a black vest over it; in combination with baggy pajama-like grey pants. For extra warmth, he wore a black burka coat and a black cotton headscarf interlaced with a white checked pattern that swept over the top of his head and around his neck and chin, revealing only his piercing brown eyes and angular nose. He was covered with numerous ammo belts slung over his shoulders.

Abdur had become a highly respected warrior and mid-level Taliban field commander. He now rested his AK47 against a large rock within one of several Pakistani/Afghan Taliban sanctuaries outside of Miran Shah, the main town in North Waziristan. Squatting closer to the fire, he used a stick to push red-hot glowing embers beneath the blackened teapot he hoped to heat.

"Rafik, come and warm yourself by the fire. You will be of no use to Allah in tomorrow's travel to our next ambush if you get sick from this bitter cold," he directed his fifteen-year-old charge who had just finished training three weeks before. Abdur needed to introduce replacements into his warrior team at a rate of about a half dozen every two weeks and he did so with a mixture of young Arabs funneled to him from the training camps, and with more seasoned Pashtun tribal warriors that had long supported the Taliban.

Rafik was an orphan—an only child whose parents were both killed in a marketplace bombing a year earlier. As opposed to some of the recruits his own age that looked old and hardened by tragedy well beyond their tender years, the five foot two, slight of frame Rafik looked closer to twelve years old. And he had far more innocence about him. In fact, he still regularly broke into a huge and unrestrained smile.

It was as though Rafik was straining to wrench some joy out of life before it sped by him all too quickly. Abdur had taken a liking to Rafik in spite of the close call he had caused last week when he had been directed to scout ahead for police or Afghan troops in the village they were slipping into. Distracted for an instant by a vendor's blanket covered with music CDs, Rafik failed to spot the two soldiers coming around the corner in time to warn the others. Abdur was forced to shove Rafik out of the way as he sprayed the troops with bullets from the gun that had been hidden beneath his heavy wrap. With both of the men now down and bleeding badly, Abdur spun and grabbed Rafik by the collar and darted away down the alley with him.

Rafik had been doing extra chores for punishment ever since. And right now, as he listened through ear buds to an up-tempo Michael Jackson tune on his hidden-in-his-tunic music player, he was not only smiling but jangling and bouncing. Though he was actually making a conscious effort not to, Rafik was still dancing just a little bit as he gathered firewood. Unbeknown to Rafik, a slight smile grew on Abdur's lips as he watched the young man's humorous movements. He thought about himself at that age. Abdur quickly snapped out of it and threw a stone that struck Rafik in the rear end and which drew both a yelp and his rapt attention to his mentor.

"You know that among the Taliban, music is deemed highly improper and dancing is punishable with a lashing," said Abdur with a stern tone that masked his mild amusement.

"Sorry, sorry. I cannot help myself, because I do so love these sounds," said the now cowering, head-bowed youth. Both his genuine regret and his dedication to jihad in remembrance of his parents were heartfelt. This was Rafik's family now.

"Take this cloth and wrap it around the pot of tea," said Abdur. "Without spilling it, take it to the commanders in that house over by the big olive tree."

"Yes, yes right away," said the now beaming Rafik, ever so pleased that he had been given an opportunity by Abdur to be in the presence of such esteemed leaders. As the boy scurried with the tea toward the house, Abdur's neck craned back and his eyes scanned the clear blue sky in search of the almost imperceptible humming sound he detected from far on high. "N-O-O-O!!!" he screamed an instant later as his mind snapped to the conclusion that a jet powered drone missile was quickly descending upon its target. In a split second, it struck with an initial "W-H-U-U-M-P-P!-like" sound immediately followed by a horrendous, earsplitting explosion that leveled the house and threw Abdur's suddenly limp body through the now brown dust-and-smoke-filled air.

CHAPTER 11

When the Career Comes A-Calling

Before starting his first day as a copywriter for the New York City based agency, Benton & Bowles a.k.a. B&B, Murf Morrison took a two-day class on using a computer. Murf thought that knowing his way around a CPU and monitor would be advantageous since big agencies were rapidly converting to personal computers instead of typewriters. As he stared at the black and white screen and the pulsing cursor that awaited his DOS operating system instructions, Murf wondered why these seemingly math whiz-constructed instruments of torture were quickly displacing the good old Underwood typewriter. He had only to see the clattering printer spit out the first page of practice copy to appreciate why. It felt smooth and pristine to the touch and looked picture perfect, versus the bumpy and uneven, almost chewed up pulp of a sheet of paper that had been rolled into and hammered by the jagged keys of a typewriter.

Cordovan penny loafers, grey slacks, a white buttoned-down shirt, red club tie and navy blue v-neck sweater made up his opening day ensemble. He dressed carefully in order to make the statement that, though he was a serious minded creative, he was definitely not one of those Ivy-league MBA management-trainee types known as "The Suits." Of course, as he familiarized himself with the overcrowded and tiny bullpen space he shared with two other writers, he learned at a glance that junior copywriters used typewriters and didn't yet have the new computers that were being bestowed first upon the senior executives and top-paid creatives. Undaunted, he smiled a very satisfied-with-himself smile as he settled into his new, yet very well worn, chair.

Murf licked his lips and instantly tasted the remnants of Terri's lipstick. He smiled once again. Just a few hours earlier at home, after showering and dressing for his first day on the job, he had spied his gorgeous wife deliberately wearing only an apron as she made him breakfast in the kitchen. Terri was not to start her new job as an assistant manager at banking behemoth Citicorp for another week, so she had time for a little mischief. The ensuing on-the-breakfast-table quickie required him to shower anew and suffice to say, it was so HOT and Terri so damned sexy and seductive, that it nearly dissuaded him from ever going in to begin his new career.

George and Marco were his copywriting suite mates and both very affable guys. Marco was big-shouldered and a bit chunky. He possessed an over-the-top and outlandish wit. He had a huge, bellowing laugh that would crash down the hallways for the entire floor to hear every few minutes. George was shorter than Marco, bespectacled and with prematurely thinning hair. His sense of humor was much more acerbic and wry.

Together, the daring duo had become dedicated to mounting elaborate practical jokes—a great way to avoid doing real work, after all. The writer that Murf was replacing was named Quincy and he had resigned very suddenly without notice and actually fled the agency offices, as it turned out. Curiously, the very next day, he joined the army, of all things.

His coworkers said he was far from patriotic, nor was he a particularly physical guy. It seems that Quincy's strong suit was being both quite paranoid and irritating—always going on and on about how sure he was that he and many others were about to be let go due to budget cutbacks. He was pretty much certain that every day, when he left the office, he would, summarily and without notice or cause, be fired over the phone the moment he got home. He was totally convinced, and told everyone who would listen, that he knew he would not even be let back into the building the next morning to collect his personal effects. As the final act of his humiliating corporate beheading, his belongings would just be boxed up and sent to him. Though completely atypical for a B&B employee termination, ultimately, that one scenario did kind of turn out to be true in Quincy's case.

After listening to him drone on and on about his fears of getting fired for weeks on end, George and Marco took it upon themselves to—very much unlike themselves—stay late one evening after Quincy, the incessant whiner, had left. With this opportunity, they boxed for next day shipment to his home, all of Quincy's possessions. In their place they set up an alternative reality on his desk: a new name plate that said "Ned," two potted plants, a framed photo of someone else's smiling wife, a green and white New York Jets mug with pens and pencils inside (Quincy hated sports), and even a Tupperware-packed lunch for "Ned" with a lipstick-imprinted note atop it that said, "I love you, Snuggums," as the coup de grace.

Well, when Quincy arrived at the office that next morning, promptly at 8:30 a.m. (George and Marco never showed before 9:00 a.m.) he saw the complete and total displacement of his workstation and possessions and he just went berserk. Quincy freaked out and began ranting up and down the hallways loudly extolling his demise and the soon-to-be-repeated outcome for everyone else. Security was finally called, he was escorted from the building and, before he could be discharged for being nuts, he beat the company to the punch that afternoon by submitting his resignation.

Murf was not to be left unscathed in terms of being pranked. Called upstairs to meet with the head of HR the afternoon of his first day at B&B, Murf took with him the new attaché case Terri had given him—along with the quickie. As he simultaneously clicked the dual shiny brass latches on the case to open it and remove his note-taking tablet, the case practically exploded open with the pressure from within from about twenty unfurled rolls of toilet paper that George and Marco had jammed under great force into the shiny and now even more impressive black leather box. Welcome aboard, Murf.

In the first few months at the agency, with George and Marco's "wise" counsel, Murf labored along with them on a variety of tedious assignments. All three of them were charged with revitalizing the agency's ads on the Gaines-Burger Dog Food account that had been a client for more than a decade and that few at the agency were highly motivated to work on. The clients didn't really want anything edgy in their advertising and seemed content just to hold endless meetings to "strategize" as they called it. Nonetheless, the three creative idiots in the bullpen became convinced that they had the big idea Gaines-Burger needed.

It came to them after watching endless video of the small dogs the product targeted, eating the hamburger patty-shaped, clear plastic-wrapped dog food packets and then subsequently doing their "business." The main product benefit, the trio proudly declared, that should be boldly proclaimed on every Gaines-Burger package, was that it would make your dog's stools dry, less smelly, uniformly firm and easy to clean up afterwards—otherwise stated, "Nice Turds." Needless to say, they were sent back to the drawing board by the much-displeased account executive for Gaines-Burger .

"Texans, Swallow Yer Pride," was the slogan Murf singularly penned for the agency's Texas Pride Beer account in the first month of his employ. He'd never even been to Texas, but his play on words resonated greatly with the Houston-based Pride client, prompting the agency's copy chief to blurt out that he had coached the rookie Murf—which, of course, was completely untrue and grounds for subsequent prank-targeting by George and Marco. Murf learned quickly that with success came an increase in the pressure to continue to perform well. And that was within ever-decreasing time frames and while enduring an ever-increasing workload. Over the next two years, his work continued to get him noticed by both superiors and clients. In the biggest pitch of the year for the Evergreen Power Company, Murf came up with a big campaign winner.

The utility wanted a campaign to encourage energy conservation and Murf coined a simple and poignant theme line, "Save Your Energy." The tagline was always spoken in the announcer voice-over after another notorious "spokesperson" had been cited in the ads. For example, "Convicted and Imprisoned Hotel Magnate Leona Helmsley is Appealing Her Sentence Again. Leona, Save your Energy." Or "Dave Duke, Former KKK Leader is Running for President of the United States Again. David, Save Your Energy." Or "Imprisoned Unabomber Requests Parts Be Shipped To Him by RadioShack. Ted Kaczynski, Save Your Energy." And so on. The ads were so smart and topical that they got free bonus coverage and became the talk of the town.

Murf became what is called a "fast-tracker" as in someone who is on the fast track to success. And with that unofficial designation, came agency perks like regular raises and the use of the company's executive retreat condos on Long island, in London or on the Caribbean Island, St. Thomas. Murphy Morrison was very quickly seduced by success. With a head full of brilliant ideas, limitless charm-the-client skills, a beautiful and witty wife, and a predisposition for travel, Murf and Terri began to enjoy a Nick & Nora-like existence (referring to the old black & white Thin Man movies) of fast-paced urbane living, high-rise luxury and exotic travel for the next several years.

And during this time of heady success is when Murf made a very savvy move. He completed B&B's management training and switched sides—from a "Creative" to a "Suit." You see, Murf had astutely noticed that the agency's account executives held great sway with the clients. Plus they had almost limitless time with them, whereas "Creatives" usually abhorred the clients and spent as little time as possible with them. And as a result, their big ideas were often mis-targeted, mis-understood or just mis-placed in the hubbub of account executives and their clients doing real business.

But Murf liked clients and the power that came with persuading them. Sure that he could master the strategic and business counseling skills that Suits possessed and still come up with his own smart creative constructs as well, Murf set about to become a serious tour de force in the agency world. And ultimately, that led him to switching agencies to get ahead, getting more money, being assigned to bigger and better accounts, and going "Bi" as they say. By that they meant being bi-coastal, as in working out of both New York and one of the leading West Coast cities like Los Angeles or San Francisco—having offices and clients in both places and jetting on red-eye flights back and forth between the two. "Bring it" was Murf's confident reply. And thereafter, amidst the back and forth "Bi" chaos, Murf's successes and acclaim grew with each passing month.

CHAPTER 12

The Big-Time West Coast Ad Man

The gruesome travel involved in being "Bi" soon took its toll on Murf and Terri as his work and their relationship hit a pronounced plateau. It was Terri who first suggested the move out west, knowing they both needed a change and that her financial services expertise would be even more marketable there. "Go west young man," proclaimed newspaper editor Horace Greeley back in the era that spawned the transcontinental railroad, which truly united America. And Murf and Terri did so because the new epicenter of great creative work within the advertising industry had become San Francisco. His fellow "Creatives" now called New York, "the place where the dinosaurs roam."

Murf was actually recruited to leave New York by an industry legend named Hal Lively. Lively headed up Hal Lively & Partners, a 400+ person shop based in San Francisco that had become well known for its droll advertising, like the campaign done for Bartles & James featuring two very low-key wine country farmer-types. They were homespun and quirky, and made hilarious spokesmen for the B&J Wine Coolers brand. Lively had personally targeted Murf. He took the time to wine, dine and charm him as if he was some very large and important prospective client. Lively was a tall and handsome man with sparkling eyes and a shaving brush-thick grey mustache. Murf enjoyed the attention Lively heaped upon him and he liked the man. Even though Lively was older—in his early sixties—Murf could relate to him because of his always fresh and original perspectives.

The "close" tactic he employed to snare Murf was unveiled after they had finished a fabulous dinner at a 100-plus-year-old Italian downtown restaurant called the Tadich Grill. The killer meal they shared was an Italian cioppino—a medley of sumptuous fresh local seafood in a rich white wine and tomato-based soup served in a pottery bowl about the size of a Buick. Fresh grilled, garlic-laced sourdough toast was served as an accompaniment and the two men washed it all down with two sublime bottles of Adelsheim Pinot Noir from the Willamette River Valley in Oregon. After sipping hot, frothy cappuccinos, Lively invited Murf on a short walk over to see the agency that bore his name. Once there, he unlocked the door and lit up one of the coolest and most modern, art-laden, loft-style office spaces Murf had ever imagined.

After whisking him through the fabulous open-ceiling digs with total nonchalance, Lively took him directly to a corner office on the fourteenth floor with a stunning view. There, with bright spotlights accenting every architectural detail, was the waterfront Ferry Building clock tower with the awe-inspiring grey steel Bay Bridge looming just above it, and the blue waters of the San Francisco Bay behind it.

"This is where you would work and your title would be Senior Vice President/Management Supervisor," said Lively offhandedly. The office sported a jet-black leather couch and antique cherry wood desk. Atop it sat a brand new curved, black monitor and sleek companion computer. This mind-numbing office was Murf's if he decided to make the switch. It also came with a numbered executive parking space in the building's multi-level parking garage.

"Oh by the way, I've got more cars than I'm able to drive; so if you take the job, you can use my Porsche rag top," said Lively in a way understated and unconcerned voice, "until you pick out the new model car the company will lease for you."

Murf was mentally signed, sealed and delivered on the spot. Yet he tried, in vain, not to appear overeager or rash in affirming the deal. He was taking a fabulous, top-paying job in a world-class city that he would've killed for—even if it came without the perks and the praise Lively had lavished on him that evening. "H—m-m-m, very compelling. Cool, let's do it," a smiling Murf said with his voice breaking revealingly as he shook the big man's hand.

With Terri's unsurpassed organizing skills, the couple made the move to San Francisco the weekend after Murf's and Terri's two-week notice times were fulfilled. In the first week there, they moved in and set up their things in a four-room water-view condo on the other side of the bay from downtown. They also managed to christen each and every room in the abode that week with another round of way-hot sex for a married-going-on-ten-years-now couple. The quick transition allowed Murf to throw himself into his new assignments with abandon and unbridled passion. With one hefty paycheck established, Terri was able to take a few weeks to find a fabulous private banking job with Wells Fargo that gave her opportunity equal to or greater than Murf's.

Every morning after he worked out and showered, Murf took a delightful, coffee-swilling, San Francisco Chronicle-scanning, fifteen-minute ferry boat ride to work. The BMW convertible he chose for the company to lease for him mostly sat unused in the condo garage. The dock was a two-minute walk from their place in Belvedere. The ferry plowed across the bay and right past the island anchored by the notorious Alcatraz Prison-turned-tourist-attraction, to the Ferry Building dock on the downtown Embarcadero Street waterfront. Sweet.

Murf's new client roster included the B&J Wine Coolers brand, plus steady work from a diverse variety of Levi's jeans brands and a huge petro-chemical company called Boron. The latter's vast exploration, refining and gasoline retailing business was the biggest challenge for Murf in that it involved a multitude of endless, mindless corporate boardroom meetings at the client's downtown headquarters offices. Boron had over 10,000 gas stations throughout the U.S., yet its culture was decidedly oil patch and advertising was a topic about which most of its executives were only politely interested in. The Hal Lively & Partners campaign for Boron featured colorful animation of a variety of gasoline station fixtures that magically sprang to life to energetic music and sizzling sound effects. The zany characters like Perry the Gas Pump, Wally the Car Wash, and Dip Stick Dave, helped fuel, check-up or clean appreciative visiting cars. All the ads for Boron featured the "Clearly Better," tagline. In fact the agency actually had succeeded in persuading Boron to add white dye to its gasoline in the refining process and to combine this ploy with clear plastic hoses instead of black ones. This allowed the customer to see what actually appeared to be clear gasoline going into their tanks—versus the yellow or gold-colored product their competitors sold.

Research showed that the gas performed no better than regular gasoline. However, consumers, who heard the "Clearly Better" slogan and saw the cleaner-appearing gas, believed the Boron product made their cars' engines cleaner, higher performing and ultimately happier. Fucking brilliant—and good for a dominant share of the market and millions in profits for Boron.

The agency creatives didn't win impressive chrome statuette awards for the Boron work, but the over $100 million in Boron advertising billings that Lively enjoyed paid for a ton of talent that could also be used to do edgier, more critically acclaimed advertising for other smaller accounts. Thus this "anchor" account indirectly maintained the Lively's illustrious reputation as a "hot creative shop." Though Murf always gave Boron his best effort and perversely liked the challenge of making a fungible commodity like gasoline into a preferred brand, working on this account also reinforced to him that there was a great deal of truth to the old adage that clients get the kind of advertising they deserve.

And Lord knows that the resident agency whackos and Boron's cadre of oddball executives they interacted with included some very amusing characters, indeed. The guilty pleasure of ridiculing an idiotic client behind their backs was something nearly everyone in advertising did with regularity and relish. Some did little else. But Murf just joined in on rare occasion because he genuinely didn't view all clients as idiots equipped with bigger budgets than brains.

Even though Murf liked his primary Lively client contacts, there were always a few snakes in every woodpile. And there were also a few egomaniacs and just plain fools within both the clients' and agency's organizations. And with the incessant pressure to succeed bearing constantly down on one and all, the advertising people regularly got crazy and ultimately did some stuff that was funny as hell. After all, having a bit of sport now and then helped preserve one's sanity in a pressure-packed world.

Usually it was just silly personal stuff like mocking the manic and perpetually twitching and sputtering client executive who was in the habit of MS or muffin spraying. MS was the act of rapid-fire eating the heads off of multiple breakfast muffins while speaking at a too rapid a clip simultaneously. The resultant spray of muffin particulate had earned him the nickname of "Machine Gun Kelly" and also moved several of the agency's creatives to show up for a Monday morning briefing by this client with all four of them nonchalantly wearing clear, thick plastic industrial safety goggles to deflect his muffin missiles. One of them had even ingeniously attached battery-powered and squeaky mini-windshield wiper blades to his goggles. The accompanying Lively account executives wore none, but all who gathered, save the client, could hardly contain their giggling. At midday, all six had drinks and lunch at a nearby pub to regale the brilliant act and the client's blissful obliviousness.

He, seemingly, was so caught up in his own mindless blathering and self-importance, that he was none the wiser that he was the brunt of this goofy goggles gag.

On another occasion, when traveling with this very same client, an enterprising art director secretly recorded at a "watering hole," the client's very drunken and ironic—given his Machine Gun Kelly gangster-sounding nickname—karaoke version of the Bobby Darrin-made-famous song, "Mac the Knife." On numerous occasions thereafter, when Machine Gun Kelly began his ceaseless and loud pontifications in the agency's large conference room, barely audible, yet completely recognizable, snippets of his sloshed and slobbering "Mac the Knife" karaoke rendition would suddenly air on the intercom for just a second or two. It was just long enough so that the practical jokers would begin their almost unchecked eye-watering, nose-running giggling, followed by uncontrollable roaring laughter and the client saying, "What? What? What's so funny??!!" On these occasions, at meeting's end, the creatives would file out of the room all humming that melody with one of them under his breath singing, "Oh that shark, babe, has such teeth, dear. And it shows them pearly white."

Then there was Dan, the all-night porn watcher and daytime meeting sleeper. This young and naive, rural Iowa born-and-raised copywriter wannabe made less than a sterling impression during his first week of employment while attending his first-ever TV shoot. The TV ad was being filmed at a studio in Los Angeles and he was neither a well-traveled nor sophisticated individual. It seems that, upon checking into his hotel room, he discovered a free adult entertainment channel, whereupon he proceeded to stay up all night watching non-stop porn.

"You won't believe what was showing on my TV set last night!!!" he excitedly crowed to his colleagues over breakfast the next morning. You'd have thought he, and not Christopher Columbus had been the first to discover the New World. By ten o'clock, just an hour and a half later, Dan was filmed in thirty-five millimeter by the eager-to-get-going director of photography, who stealthily captured Dan sitting in a director's chair at the shoot's final big pre-production meeting, not only soundly sleeping and snoring, but with a huge stream of drool emanating from his slightly parted lips. When this primo video was later shared with the rest of the agency a few weeks later at a town hall after-hours-agency-beer-bash, the scenes of blissfully sleeping Dan in the chair had been inter-cut with nanosecond quick takes of bared breasts, heaving buttocks and the superimposed title of "Porn King" in big block letters. As the camera slowly drifted in closer and closer onto Dan's contentedly dreaming, and now smiling face, the crowd's laughter grew to a crescendo. Thereafter everyone called Dan, "Porn King" or his new nom de plume, "Gregory Pecker"—or just "Pecker" for short.

Three months later, the Pecker became a target once again in an elaborate ruse wherein his three direct superiors called him into an end-of-day meeting. He was astounded to see that they were all wearing elaborate, billowing silk red, green and yellow costumes meant to represent Italian opera characters. All three also wore medieval painted animal facemasks. Dan was thereupon informed that they were all going to the client's big Italian opera costume soiree held at the Palace of Fine Arts rotunda and catered by the top chef from Napa Valley. Told that he had been selected to take the place of a sick colleague, he was given a silky white and black Harlequin outfit to wear to the all-important client gig. He would be dressed as Canio, the sad clown from Pagliacci, who murders his wife. The elaborate costume came complete with a cone-shaped pointed hat and whiteface with red ball cheeks makeup to boot, "which Miriam, the secretary outside would be glad to apply."

Given that the three of them were already wearing elaborate costumes, Dan suspected nothing. He thanked them profusely for the opportunity to rub elbows with the senior-level clients. One of them then gave Dan the address and told him to take a cab and meet them there forty-five minutes later. He was then told that the evening would be extra fun because the San Francisco Advertising Federation's Gala Clio

Awards Ceremony was also being held that night—coincidentally at the Palace in an adjoining auditorium. All four of them would therefore get to jump back and forth between the two parties with their opera costumes still on, adding to the zaniness of the already gonzo Addy Awards gathering. Dan was to check on both venues and to find them once he got there.

When Dan (or Pecker) did show up later at the supposed combination Opera soiree and Clio Awards, he found no opera party at all. But he did locate his three colleagues drinking pre-show cocktails in the crowded main foyer of the Clio Awards. And to his surprise, the three of them were all now wearing elegant black tuxedos instead of costumes. Their wives or dates were in long evening gowns, and all six were in complete hysterics. Dan was the only one among the hundreds of industry luminaries gathered there, who was dressed in an elaborate costume—let alone as Canio. He was immediately asked to pose for pictures, not just with his effusively laughing "buddies" but with many other complete strangers in attendance that had quickly gathered around to partake of the impromptu fun.

On one occasion, after Murf had been there for two years and had become a favorite of the Boron management team, he actually had the temerity to take on, at risk of losing the account, a mid level client and big-time asshole. Unbeknownst to his superiors at Boron, this jerk was abusively yelling at some of the agency's junior staff members and making ridiculous demands for personal favors like picking up and delivering his dry cleaning. And then this prick really crossed the line by ass-grabbing one of the young female part-time interns at Lively, which left the sweet and well-liked girl in tears. When Murf found out about this, he asked for and got an immediate meeting with Boron's supervisor of marketing. Therein, Murf spent five minutes recounting how much he and the entire Lively team loved working on Boron and the many contributions they had made to building the business. Then he informed the client of the actions of the offending executive and that the agency had decided that the individual was no longer welcome at their offices. The marketing headman thanked Murf for his candor and conviction and apologized on behalf of the company. The dickhead, and not Lively, was fired by Boron some twenty minutes later.

Why was Murf so good at what he did in a fairly jaded world of advertising wherein people all too quickly became casualties? Unquestionably, because he was determined, deliberate and very discerning. He generated tons of highly original and off-the-wall ideas and he coupled this gift with the discipline of methodically assessing and pursuing only the best of them. Though many agency-types hated it, Murf often used research as a tool to sort through message issues and strategic alternatives. Murf used research diagnostically instead of destructively. Using it to choose between creative ideas was dangerous in that most focus groups are quickly polarized and rarely reach consensus. In other words, half of the room loves the idea and the other half hates it. Unfortunately, if a client was behind the two-way mirror, even a single consumer's emotional reaction might just kill an idea in their mind versus identifying communications issues to further work on. Murf had learned that great ideas, almost always upon first testing, got at best mixed reviews—but they usually elicited visceral reactions from highly stimulated consumers. So he used research to spot what he called "scratchy" ideas that sparked reactions from consumers, and to yield insights, as to how to make those rough ideas even better.

But Murf's success was also rooted in his philosophy about the work. The craft of advertising has been described by its industry academics as both an art and a science. On the science side, there was the practice of steering the creative development process with a process of narrowing down options toward what advertising legends, Ted Bates and Rosser Reeves, called the USP or Unique Selling Proposition. The key for agencies that focused on developing a strategy first before brainstorming creative ideas, was to consistently pinpoint for its clients, the precise product difference or benefit that would make it sell.

In some agencies, creatives would actually come up with zany ideas to call attention to a given product and afterwards try to devise a basis in strategy that would support the idea whether it really fit the product or not. Within most agencies, good and bad, there was also an ongoing power struggle between the account executives who interfaced directly with the clients and were supposed to be in charge of strategy, and the creative masterminds who usually saw the client only at presentations and during TV shoots (and condescendingly preferred to keep it that way). The infighting between account executives and creatives was rooted in the argument over whether advertising should move the business forward and ingratiate the clients; or aspire to be highly artistic, win lots of awards for creativity (and flesh out the creatives' portfolios and fame), even if it came at the expense of the client's sales and ultimately keeping the account.

Murf never accepted this either/or proposition and would have none of such polarized debates and petty and unproductive inter-agency squabbling. His advertising philosophy was more centrist and business savvy. He described his craft as one of "commercial persuasion" that required advertising that was creative and attention getting, but purposely so. It was not to be considered art for art's sake, but instead had to be artistic in creating differentiation and also effective at moving consumers into action. What Murf believed was that it starts with an idea that would get noticed or break through the clutter of over 5,000 advertising exposures per person per day that academics estimate are inflicted upon the average consumer. And the odds are decidedly against success with only one in fifteen ideas succeeding at being noticed. In Murphy's experience, ideas that touched both people's hearts and minds were the best ones. He also particularly liked to use the juxtaposition or deliberate contrasting of dissimilar factors that captured attention and involvement in that they demanded resolution. Throw in a mnemonic device in the form of a benefit-based slogan that is scratchy and easy to remember—and bingo!

Ironically, according to Murf, most consumers staunchly deny that advertising has any effect on them at all. Yet most can readily tell you in detail about their four or five favorite TV ads (usually the funniest ones). Though rarely can they tell you what brand was actually being advertised. And nowhere is this phenomenon more pronounced than when large or aggressive brands use the Super Bowl to premiere major new advertising. This tactic has elevated the thirty-second TV spot to the big time in terms of idle conversation favorites.

"No doubt," Murf once opined as he attempted to impress a lady who inquired about his profession, "there has always been a mystique about the business called advertising. It has show biz elements to it, a pinch of celebrity and sports. It includes exotic travel and a fair amount of 'entertaining' clients or prospects in nice restaurants or at incredible events that are all but impossible to get tickets to. But it also has all of the pressures of any big business, and then some given its volatility. You can be fired both by your employer, and by the client—as in, 'He was asked off the business by the client.' You can also be whacked with a totally impersonal and unwarranted major account loss," said Murf now fully in stride as he waxed philosophic about advertising. In truth, he thought it a respectable profession that also had more than a touch of creepiness when it came to kissing the client's asses or playing agency power politics to vanquish one's competitors.

Like most other jobs worth having, Murf believed that to excel in advertising involved a huge amount of hard work, constant stress, exceptional resourcefulness, innovative thinking, ridiculous hours, and endless selling of ideas and budgets to the clients, who control your ability to do great work and, in turn, your destiny. He also believed that it took quite a bit of luck to gain or sustain success. And Murf was acutely aware that eventually disenchantment, cynicism or just wear and tear felled most industry practitioners. Murf, on the other hand, had a seemingly bottomless well of resilience and he rarely flinched when taking a good punch. But then again, the real insidious threat to a practitioner was not a sudden debacle but the slow-creep death of simmering drudgery and discontent. As Murf would tell it, there was death by endless, unproductive meetings, and death by brainless and controversy-avoiding committee-made decisions. There was even death by clients that gave this feedback at the end of an enormously invested agency presentation. "I can't quite put my finger on what it is, but I just don't feel comfortable with it."

"A-R-R-R-G-G-H!!!! Die you Rat Bastard!!" Murf would groan afterwards over a beverage at the bar. But the ugliest one of all was death by hiring and firing. In terms of hiring, it was great in the boom times when you loaded up your team with the best ringers money could buy—and for good measure, threw in a few bright, young "dark horse" candidates who could eventually be melded into champions.

But with the inevitable account losses would come the Black Fridays. On a Monday you might get word that your client's company was to merge with another larger company and the business would be moving to the larger company's agency. That Wednesday, you would then be directed to draw up a list of the ten most expendable employees who had worked on that business' agency team. "Need it by end of the day," the boss might say. And the ten so noted would be out by the end of the week. Ergo Black Friday, when the identity of the ten lepers became public and the procession of these damned souls walking out carrying their personal effects in a box unfolded.

The recessions in American business in 1987 and 2001 were astounding to Murf in that during these periods, the scale of this kind of tumult was enormous with hundreds, and sometimes thousands, of otherwise talented people suddenly losing their jobs. One fellow's outcome in particular just took Murf's breath away. The guy's name was Harold Morgan, and he was a mid-level executive and an older fellow in his late fifties. Smart, talented, hard working, well liked and dependable he was, but maybe not quite as hip or fashionable as some of his largely more youthful contemporaries. Murf was really sad to see him let go in one highly broad-scale bloodletting and even more disturbed to learn that, after trying for six months and failing to get any other job, Harold deliberately stepped in front of a speeding bus one day on the streets of Manhattan.

But Murf, after all, was incredibly buoyant, and always stayed one step ahead of his contemporaries. He was a chameleon with irrepressible enthusiasm and charm. And he was a superb salesman because he genuinely believed in the efficacy of the products he chose to represent. He was laser-like at touting the most compelling reasons to prefer and proffer them. Clients who were desperate to know their money was being spent well, trusted his advice because he didn't BS them and he personally saw to it that they got perceptible results and never got screwed. He was extremely adept at recognizing the BIG ideas and revising and burnishing them until the maximum potential return on investment was yielded for the millions of dollars the client had invested.

As for his employers, Murf was also keen about generating momentum from complete torpor. His specialty was helping languishing agencies effect a turnaround toward becoming perceived as a creative "hot shop." He was also willing to leave relative safety of a big shop and clients who loved him, for a smaller yet growing one and a new set of challenges. Since this was also the fastest way to move from a salaried staffer to a principal with a piece of the action, this served Murf's advancement particularly well. Lively understood Murf's talent and marketability when he recruited him and he tried to stay ahead of the game over the years by steadily moving Murf up the ranks with new titles, pay increases, generous year-end bonuses and perks. After just two years at Lively, Murf was one of only a half dozen individuals who had a stylist visit inside their own offices for a bi-monthly grooming and manicure, compliments of the agency.

Another thing that is oft said of advertising and life is that the only constant is change. In the years to come, Murf would continue to enjoy great successes and pull down major-league money to boot. Yet he would also see the advertising industry go through a watershed period of enormous change. During this span, it quickly evolved from a world of three martini lunches and comfy locked-in fifteen percent commissions on gi-normous broadcast media spending, to one where too-numerous-to-survive agencies lived on single digit commissions and scrapped for straight fees or received only temporary projects. At the same time, radical change also came in terms of Americans' media consumption with the advent of the Internet. These days, only half of Americans still read a daily newspaper. Within a short span, the change in media habits would lead not only to completely redefining the basis for advertising agency compensation, but to major media mix upheavals with more and more movement toward online advertising. There would also be a downsizing in the basic role of advertising agencies with innumerable specialist companies causing reallocations that ate into their budgets. And due to mergers and acquisitions, the advertising industry changed from a largely privately owned one, to the predominance of publicly traded agencies. And that meant that agencies were now driven by short-term financial objectives that often undercut the strategy of investing in great work and keeping the most talented people.

Meanwhile, Murf's personal drive and motivation for work, as well as life on the home front, was also in flux. One evening, as the ferryboat cruised from the city over toward his home in Belvedere, Murf's mind wandered as he stared into the splashing wake off the stern of the ship. He thought about the real meaning of life in general, but specifically about all the time he wasted on entertaining clients or hanging with his fellow Pirate drinking buddies. He also contemplated the validity of the values he had spent so much time and effort pursuing in his career. Most of all, he thought about the melancholy that had silently crept into his now twenty-plus year relationship with Terri.

CHAPTER 13

Terri and Little Miss Molly

Living the good life in San Francisco had far exceeded Murf and Terri's wildest expectations. Their Belvedere condo with its sleek black and white marble floor and trendy slate grey walls, had a killer view. The couple could look across the bay at the silhouetted downtown San Francisco skyline. The tip-of-a-fireman's-hose-reminiscent Coit Tower and the elongated pyramid-shaped Transamerica Building were highlights of this vista, with Alcatraz Island and the creamy-blue bay waters in the foreground. There was a round-the-clock doorman in the lobby of their building, plus a dry cleaning center, a fitness area and a rooftop swimming pool with an even more expansive view. And the delightful smells that poured in the power couple's wide-open bay windows included not only wafting hints of the expected salt water and ocean breeze, but also blowing in were alternating rushes of fresh wood-grilled seafood with garlic-laced pasta, or the sizzling Szechwan food scents from some of the best restaurants in the Bay Area. Many were within walking distance of the condo. Their neighborhood streets were alive with charming "Mom and Pop" groceries, exploding-with-vibrant-colors-and-fragrances flower stands, aromatic Cappuccino shops, and sidewalks that broadly intermingled a fascinating people-watching mix of locals and snapshot-crazed tourists.

When they first arrived in San Francisco and started to take in the local scene in earnest, it seemed to be an endless and exhilarating blur of dazzling and daring restaurants, epic city-view sailing, and weekend ocean forays to view migrating California grays on whale-watching expeditions. Another weekend favorite was going to quaint wine country bed and breakfast inns that facilitated wine-tasting trips to the nearby vineyards. And there were skiing weekends at Lake Tahoe, jaunts down to Carmel or Big Sur for coastal retreats with couples spa massages and wonderful and barrier-breaking sex.

Between work and pleasure travel, Murf and Terri were always on the go and into something new and exciting. Terri's career was flourishing just like Murf's and hers was a whirlwind of constantly entertaining and hand-holding rich and powerful clients of the bank. One year, with Murf boondoggling on a client-sponsored multi-stop trip to visit Far East manufacturing companies, he met up with Terri in Hong Kong for an exotic stay at the decadently luxurious Peninsula Hotel. They staged trips to shop for hand-tailored clothes, pearls and to enjoy a traditional twelve-course Chinese feast. The next year, they hooked up in the small but sophisticated rural Japanese ski resort town of Shiga Kogen, for sensual steam baths in snow-surrounded natural pools where long-haired macaque "snow" monkeys were often photographed bathing and preening.

During their first five years in San Francisco, West Coast-based travel across the Pacific also took them to Tahiti and New Guinea for mind-blowing experiences. And other than their odd penchant for dressing only in all black all of the time, the San Francisco people they met were lovely, open and warm and embracing to newbies. They made lots of new, casual friends and life was sublime. But deep down, they knew it still lacked something.

Terri was the first to begin to back off a bit off from the not exactly unpleasant grind of client entertainment parties, office functions, and travel for co-mingled work and fun. Knowing that Murf was so very full of life, she didn't protest his increasingly more frequent softball and hockey games and outings to blow off steam from work with his merry band of Pirates. In reality, Terri's quiet strength actually far surpassed Murf's. He just had a far higher tolerance for pressure and intensity related to work and for adult beverages. And Terri was still captivatingly beautiful, smart and conversant. Though graying at the temples, Murphy was still handsome, athletic and virile. And yet their relationship was plateauing. While still affectionate, they seemed a bit on autopilot. Murf for all his bluster and bombast was the first to have the epiphany. One evening when they were alone, he blurted out a most surprising idea, "Hey, sweetheart, let's have a kid!"

Murf adored buying Terri cute little pregnancy outfits and together they bought a crib, baby toys, a fancy Italian-made stroller and a plastic bib for their baby called the Pelican Pouch because it had a pouch that caught the food dropped by the baby and allowed the tot a second chance to devour it. The actual birthing was a visceral experience for both parents and when Terri was informed that it was too late to receive an epidural, Murf asked if he could have it in her stead. On the day that their daughter, Molly, was finally born, Murf was out of his mind with happiness. He joyfully shouted out her name over and over again and cried a lot, too. Later, he uncharacteristically handed out ATM-fresh $20 bills to three homeless people he encountered on the street. Terri was also overjoyed but, by comparison, she was quite pale and exhausted from the ordeal. After Terri and the nurses finally sent him home from the hospital so she and the baby could rest, he hooked up with the Pirates to give them all some "proud Papa" cigars and to hoist a few too many to his "sweet little darlin'."

Molly was the prettiest and sweetest baby ever, with Murf's sparkling green eyes, her mom's brown hair and stoic beauty, and a heart-melting smile that beamed like the sun. Tragically, the dancing-on-a-cloud-with-joy-couple were given the news a few months later that Molly had become deaf as the result of a side effect of a strong antibiotic she'd been given to battle a meningitis bacterial infection she developed. Terri snapped back from the initial shock very quickly and dedicated herself to raising Molly and insuring her a great education and life in spite of the impairment. Terri learned sign language in just a few months and fervently began teaching Molly at nine months. By year two, she and Molly were both chatting away in sign language as if they always had, while Murf had, instead, thrown himself even more into his work and could sign only a feeble hello, good bye and kiss/kiss to Molly.

But Molly never begrudged him that and she always hugged her daddy dearly whenever he left or came home from work. At home, Murf would usually lose himself in preparing yet another Power Point presentation on his laptop—though he regularly stole glances from afar of Molly and Terri signing and playing. And when he traveled, he often watched videos of Molly as a tiny baby on his laptop and cried while he drowned his sorrows in rum. In particular, he liked to watch the one of Molly dancing. Molly had the most uncanny habit of swaying to and fro and dancing rhythmically to the beat of music on the stereo—though she, in fact, could not hear. But she did feel music or more specifically, the vibration of sound emerging from the speakers. At first Molly had placed her hand against the speaker's black fabric covering and felt the hum of the music as it emerged. And then she started swaying and dancing with her eyes closed and in perfect time to the beat.

Terri was handling the massive challenge that was Molly's disability quite heroically, and would deal with the consequences of Molly's lifelong affliction with a mother's unconquerable determination to make it right for her child. Meanwhile, Murf was cracking inside. He spent more time these days gazing quietly at and sadly mesmerized by the swirling wake of the bay ferry's stern propeller. He stared vacantly at the undulating water more than ever before in his decades of infatuation with the sea. Sometimes in either going to or returning from work, he'd just keep riding the ferry back and forth across the bay several times before finally disembarking. Murf was accustomed to having the weight of the advertising world on his shoulders but that was nothing compared to his near-constant contemplation of his sweet little Molly who wasn't quite right. And even with all his drive and resourcefulness, he could do nothing to change that. It ate at him and ate at him.

CHAPTER 14

Dancing With El Diablo

With the torment of Molly's condition ever present, agency work had come to be less motivating for Murphy. But he still loved taking on new assignments and learning new businesses. He had once boasted—over adult beverages with the buccaneers—that he could even find it intellectually stimulating to head up a new brand of rectal thermometers. That naturally led to one bad joke after another about how Murf would, "get it done in the end" or he'd "dive in and take a bottoms up approach to it," or "Paging Phil McKraken. Paging Phil McKraken."

But things were slow right now on the new business front for the agency, so that meant concentrating on serving the existing roster or more of the "same-old, same-old." And though he had a bevy of clients who loved having him on their businesses, the excitement of developing new launch plan strategies and brilliant campaigns for them, eventually gave way to more of a stewardship role, wherein the job was more about trying to keep a thoroughly familiar type of advertising, fresh and hard-working. His task was not just about sustaining a long running, successful campaign—but doing so working with creatives that were bored and didn't want to work on it any more.

So Murf had to prod both creatives and clients not to become too complacent. Both types often presented the attitude and attention span of thirteen-year-old ADD-riddled adolescents who had spent time preparing for Murf's meetings by wolfing down multiple bags of M&Ms while chugging double espressos laced with grain alcohol and Woolite (accounting for the frequent foaming at the mouth). Somehow Murf, nonetheless, miraculously orchestrated good work out of these insane and potentially destructive gatherings by serving as the chief catalyst and interjecting his own good strategic and creative ideas into the mix. That usually got everyone else's juices flowing and captured focus where only chaos had existed before. But as good as he was at it, he was secretly losing his grip and tolerance for such mayhem and dysfunction.

One such meeting and "emergency" that nearly melted down Murf and a good number of others, occurred when the team was hurriedly called together one Friday afternoon when many at the agency were already planning to leave work early for getaways at Lake Tahoe or the wine country. Boron had just called with word that the agency's help was needed to mitigate a disaster wherein the company had inadvertently sold gasoline that did not make cars go, but that made the cars' engine unable to start back up after the tanks had been filled. The resultant disaster of dozens of cars killed at the pumps by bad Boron gas, were centered at the company's eighteen gas stations in Sacramento, California. Turns out that the gasoline in question was mis-processed by a middleman company which negatively affected the finished product that several national brands of gasoline sold in Sacramento that day. But the press had captured the calamity on film at a Boron station and the company was already fiercely under fire.

Murf's counsel to Boron was to, above all else, tell the truth and don't try to duck responsibility the way so many other companies facing a PR disaster do. "Boron Stands Behind Every Single Drop of Gas We Sell," crowed the headline of the press release at the hastily called press conference. The same headline was carried by the full-page advertisement that ran in the Sacramento paper the very next morning. Though they could have blamed the responsible supplier—thus sounding evasive and disingenuous—Boron, instead, took responsibility and pledged to drain and re-supply every car that had been affected for free. They also pledged to replace, if necessary, any carburetors that needed fixing. The Sacramento bad gas disaster was handled almost as a public relations textbook example, and the stories that ran as a result complimented the company for its honest and immediate response.

Several months later, Murf was attending an all-market sales data meeting at Boron when the Sacramento results, in particular, were examined. "My gosh!" said the mid-level executive reading the report out loud to all. "Sales in Sacramento, after the initial hit, actually rebounded in the days that followed and for the whole month, actually increased to an above prior-to-the-mishap sales level! If the whole thing had happened nationwide, we'd have made, uh, wait a minute…" as he rapidly pounded out the individual figures and the projected total on his handy calculator, "$28.5 million dollars of additional profit!"

The looks of amazement and wonder were consistent all around the room and the Boron Marketing SVP thanked Murf and the agency for their quick response and wise counsel on that eventful day. Then the marketing honcho's boss scratched his head, looked at the ceiling and wondered out loud, "If this whole thing could be replicated elsewhere in the country or even nationwide…" A nervous laugh ensued from several at the table and then all joined in for a heartier guffaw when the big boss man confirmed that he was "just kidding, of course." But it was clear to Murf that, at least for a moment, many in the room actually had contemplated deliberately repeating the episode on an all-across-the-country basis.

"A decidedly creepy moment," Murf thought to himself over a

cocktail that evening. “Very creepy, indeed.”

In spite of his ever-growing mental fatigue, one ritual Murphy did still love was the escape of going on TV shoots. It meant travel to Hollywood or a location outside of San Francisco, only to return with an out-of-summer-season tan and everyone back at the fort believing he’d been just goofing off. But what it really represented was an escape from the tedium of work in an office setting, sitting through intolerably dull meetings, and the growing uneasiness of his time at home with the family. When Murf went on a TV shoot, it meant living out of a hotel for weeks on end and spending from dawn ‘til late night working with a small army of production people to execute on the agency’s big idea or to bring their storyboard of a thirty second TV commercial to life.

Murf’s days were spent trying to cast just the right actors (one sometimes had to review dozens and dozens of possibilities), costuming them just so, deciding on the exact locations or sets, rewriting and honing the dialogue, and planning out and preparing for any special effects, stunts, or unique music. The culmination of all of this was several extra-long days of the thirty-to-forty-takes-per-scene filming. And then it was on to the editing process of cutting it this way and then trying it that way—tweaking the sound and the color and such. For thirty seconds of finished product, it might take a week or even two of constant activity to complete. There was always something pressing to resolve; that is, with the notable exception of the days on which they were actually filming. There was a ton of down time on those days because there was so much set-up time required to get all the lights just right; move the camera, dolly and its tracks into place; and hook up the miles and multitudes of anaconda-like electrical lines and the generators that powered everything. Portable dressing rooms and toilets on wheels also had to be motored into place, and the vital craft services kitchen and dining areas had to be set up to constantly feed the high energy group of over fifty technicians, production specialists, creatives and executives that had been gathered together for the task. To do just one scene could easily take an hour and a half of setting up. Then it might take only twenty minutes of repetitive single take-after-take to capture the one-sentence-long best bit of action and dialogue that might constitute four to five actual seconds of the finished commercial. And then all the equipment had to be broken down and moved to the next location and set up anew.

For Murf, nothing beat waiting out the lengthy time it took to set up, in a stretched canvassed seat and seat back directors chair, placed strategically in the sun. When he did so, he'd light up a big fat cigar and, hiding behind sunglasses, take unobserved and intermittent naps. Sure, Murf liked shoots for those precious moments—the travel and escape—but also because, on the road, it became all about the work and not about meetings and the agency's executive committee's grand pronouncements of new busy work, or inane client handling issues. Ironically, in the grass-is-always-greener mode of planning shoots, West Coast or SF/LA agency creatives always said they "had" to shoot in New York, and those at New York agencies only wanted to shoot in California. Both could agree they really wanted to shoot in Hawaii or Tahiti, but the client's budget limitations usually ruled that out. In reality, if not based in Hollywood, shoots more often than not happened in Chicago or Vancouver or Des Moines rather than in a tropical locale with a fabulous beach.

Regardless of the location, Murf always found a nearby river, lake or some body of water to anchor his early morning run around, or to just sit and stare at for hour after hour as he battled his inner demons. Seattle and Vancouver were favorites of Murf's. Seattle's harbor area was abuzz with ferryboats taking folks to the various and sundry nearby San Juan Islands. Vancouver had swarms of floatplanes constantly taking off and landing in its city-side waters. A long run along the waterfront at either locale seemed the only way for Murf to get mentally and deliberately "lost" and find momentary peace. But the self-torture returned as soon as the running stopped. Maybe that's why Murf actually had begun to turn his daily five-mile run into longer solitary jaunts of ten and twelve miles.

While in Chicago for a two-week shoot, on a whim, he signed up for and, one Sunday morning, completed a half marathon that wound in and around Lake Michigan and the varied neighborhoods of the so-called Second City. This led Murf to run more than a half-dozen full marathons over the next two years. That's when he discovered that he could run, but he could not hide.

The pressure at Lively these days was incessant and seemed to be getting incrementally greater year after year, as every single success lead only to the need to precipitate even greater ones. As the agency grew and the pressure to increase profits grew with it, the agency's leadership, though ironic and self-defeating, became more risk averse, or creatively conservative. The leadership then compounded this by being less discriminating about the quality of the work and new staff hires. And beyond the much-respected Lively, also known as the Old Man or The Chairman, Murf's other so-called superiors (the agency's president, chief operating officer and chief creative officer) were all about appearances and not about the work. Their sole contribution seemed to be saying no to great ideas and blowing tons of money leasing new car after car, traveling to unnecessary industry conferences at resort cities, and entertaining clients (and a lot of their friends) at the trendiest and flashiest restaurants. And of course, in a Peter Principle-born fashion, they constantly avoided really difficult problems. They delegated them to Murf to resolve, instead.

As Murf grew more jaded about the business, he began to save up bonuses and lessen his monthly personal expenditures to compile what he called the "Fuck You Money" which would afford him a comfortable transition were he ever to be suddenly pushed by management, or even a client, in a direction he was unwilling to go. There had also recently been the prospect of a merger/takeover with a bigger European-based agency. "Maybe it's the Saatchi brothers?!!!" Slowly that rumor died off, but Murf knew it could raise its head once again. And then there was the supposed inevitability of that "age and advertising thing," otherwise known as age discrimination. Advertising is, after all, a business that worships youthfulness and the latest trends and fashion. Three times before in his career, clients who loved Murf's contributions had tried to lure him away "to the client side" with lucrative offers. "I really think I can do more good for you staying at the agency," Murf would demur diplomatically.

Murphy Morrison, the wonder boy, was now forty-five years old and although still genuinely handsome and dashing, the graying at his temples was noticeable. Terri always told him it made him look very distinguished. "Sounds like the kind of thing you'd say about a sweet old dog..." Murf said to himself skeptically, "just a couple of weeks before you put the old wart down for good."

Post partum, Murf and Terri's sex life had certainly lost some serious sizzle. Murf was constantly off-balance with work, travel and worry. Terri was still a highly attractive package any man would strongly covet, but usually she was just completely wiped out—and rightfully so—from a day of rushing Molly to and from daycare, wrestling with Pacific Rim clients on protracted conference calls, and then supplementing Molly's education with tutorials and overlays befitting a special-needs child.

In their prime, Murf and Terri were like oyster-loving chinchillas in heat. The spontaneity, frequency and intensity of their sexual unions were formi-DABLE, as the French would say. Although usually discreet—whether indoors, outdoors, in the car, on a plane, or on a train—they were good to go in a nanosecond and both were pretty much multi-orgasmic sex machines once they got going.

On the road over the years, Murf was more than occasionally propositioned by a co-worker or someone he'd met and worked with at a shoot or an advertising conference. Though naturally turned on by the theoretical prospect of hot sex with an attractive, new and different woman, he didn't like the prospect of workplace and personal entanglements. Besides, down deep he just loved his wife so much that the thought of her being hurt by a lustful indiscretion he committed was always sufficient to stop him.

However, there was the ONE time he was traveling on a shoot with a couple of the Pirates, PD and Fig Newton, working on the same assignment. The three were not only in a different zip code, but out of the country altogether in Costa Rica, where the TV spot just happened to require a beach-side jungle village locale. "Can't believe the client bought that one," PD rejoiced at the time of the sell-in.

A legendary-level night of Cuba Libre consumption led to a taxi-driver-directed trip to a "very special" casino, which to their surprise turned out to be a front for a local whorehouse. Though Murf spoke only passable restaurant-Spanish, he enjoyed being surrounded by the many lovely caramel and dark skinned beauties that were conversing with the boys in bits of broken-English, and preening and caressing like sex-crazed slink-monsters. As other men on the left and right were clearly and quickly being picked off by the girls, Murf, PD and The Fig, held-out saying they wanted to thoroughly examine all of the wares before choosing. In truth, they were unsure of themselves and whether they were really going to go through with it, given they did not frequent prostitutes, were in another country and unclear on the relevant laws there—not to mention being totally linguistically challenged.

All of a sudden, a busty Latina with dyed red hair and pretty green eyes grabbed Murf. "Hey guys, she's an Irish lass," he chortled. Then a svelte and stunning black woman with sparkling dark eyes and a sumptuous smile joined her at Murf's side. His interest was piqued even more so when the red-head now nuzzling him, gently rubbed and gave a warm squeeze to the other girl's firm breasts. Then she locked lips with her in a seemingly hot and passionate kiss.

When The Newt and PD, who now each had a girl in their own laps, saw this action they cheered and encouraged Murphy to go for broke with repeated, "Threesome. Threesome. Threesome." chants. Finally Murf stood up, with his girls in each arm, and said in his best Willie Mays fashion, "Ladies, let's play two." And off he went to admiring cheers from the boys in the bleachers, as his two lovelies guided him toward the transaction area in back where all the other men had gone with their pairings.

What it the world was Mr. Showboat going to do now? After paying his money in advance to a man at a window and curiously being given a fresh towel, the two ladies led Murf up a stairway to a way too brightly lit room with a bed, a small sink and a table. Murf was puzzled but minimally cooperative as the customary washing and quick inspection of the penis unfolded. All he could think about was that his big mouth had written a check his he had no real desire to cash. As he used the towel to dry off afterwards, he noticed that the mood of the two ladies had completely changed from seemingly bi-curious to as clinical as an asexual, rubber glove-snapping proctologist. Clearly their intent was to impersonally process another customer and get back to the bar as quickly as possible. No more were there any showy spicy Latina kisses. Now the two acted deliberate and unemotional as they prepped their client and the bed like they were factory workers standing at an assembly line and brusquely handling the wares.

Following Murf's genitalia scrub, they both quickly disrobed without looking at him. The slender black woman indeed had an attractive and curvy figure with a flat taut stomach and firm, upturned breasts. But when the busty faux red-head with the pendulous figure removed her low-cut dress and its built-in wire support structure, Murf saw her breasts plunge faster and further than a pensioner's 401-K stock portfolio the day before retirement. After the disrobing, the girls began chatting in Spanish. Murf wanted to bolt for the door but instead started to, likewise, remove his clothing.

Even as he desperately tried to figure out how he could politely beg off and depart, he eavesdropped as they chatted away like he wasn't even there. From what Murf could make out, one asked the other about "la Nina" or her daughter. It became more and more apparent to Murf thereafter, that this woman was a relatively new mother. From what little Murf could discern, she was responding to her co-worker's questions about her new baby when "la leche" came into it, and the discussion turned to baby care and breast-feeding. This was confirmed for Murf when the mom repeatedly began to squeeze the thick and quickly hardened brown nipple of her own left breast. She did so for several moments until her actions produced a drop of milk at the tip. With total nonchalance, the woman wiped the drop of milk onto her fingertip and suddenly reached out and placed it right at Murf's lips.

"Oh great," Murf thought to himself, "Just what I wanted for Christmas. The gift of AIDS courtesy of the LACTATING HOOKER'S Dairy Association!"

And then somehow without a snuggle or any kind of sexual entreaty, the new mother lay back on the bed naked and in readiness to be penetrated by a completely sexually disinterested Murf. The other woman stood near the bed, apparently to receive the tag team hand touch signally her entry into the contest to spell the first woman after she had been suitably intercoursed. Murf, though he had prepaid, slid his trousers and shirt back on, peeled off two Andrew Jacksons—giving one to each lady—and hit the road shaking his head side to side all the while. "That was about as sexy as taking your elderly grandmother and her sick cat to the veterinarians office," mumbled Murf as he made his way back down the stairs, down the hall and out into the street. "And who am I trying to kid, my precious Terri is the only girl for me."

A quick cab got him back to the waterfront near his hotel where he went for a nice walk. Several ladies of the night approached him and he could only think of that great Jack Nicholson movie line, "Go sell crazy somewhere else, we are all fuckin' full up here."

Later he met Fig Newton and PD back at their hotel's bar and they regaled him with details of supposedly the best sex they had ever had in their lives. Murf, who declined to reciprocate, simply said, "I don't kiss and tell lads." He could only wonder if their real experiences in any way resembled his.

A few days later and back in San Francisco for the weekend, Murf caught up on the week's events over Saturday morning coffee and chocolate croissants with Terri. Naturally, she had risen early and made them from scratch—mixing the batter, rolling and cutting the dough, embedding a stick of chocolate inside each one and buttering the tops. The condo was saturated with the wonderful smell of baking pastry. As they made small talk, Murf suddenly blurted out to Terri's great surprise, "Maybe I should try switching to the client side."

CHAPTER 15

Land of Disenchantment

After two months of healing and rehabilitation, Abdur had largely recovered physically from the explosion that vaporized the sweet young martyr Rafik, and the intended target—the seven-man complement of Taliban district commanders. The remotely piloted aircraft was part of a specialized joint CIA and U.S. Air Force taskforce that had successfully attacked al-Qaida's leadership in both Afghanistan and occasionally even in Pakistan, maybe thirty times a year. It was an extremely high technology and covert program that regularly struck terror behind enemy lines. Since insurgent leaders were the targets, it was greatly feared by all who advanced through the ranks of al-Qaida.

The blast from the missile completely flattened the house and most of the surrounding compound. It took more than two days of sifting through rubble to find the remaining pieces of the mostly Afghani, Pakistani and Uzbek militants that had been killed within. Until replacements arrived, there would be little insurgent activity from the remaining and much disheartened mujahedeen that Abdur had been leading. A key aid in Abdur's recovery was to bolster his returning stamina by taking daily and solitary walks of ten to twelve miles into the surrounding hills. Though he still had the slight limp from his life-course-altering tragedy back in Palestine, his gait and endurance, respectively, grew quicker and stronger every day. But these days, as he roamed the hilly countryside, he would contemplate his life and recent-years' jihad activities—repeatedly and without reconciliation—questioning the meaning and purpose of it all.

When replacements did arrive, Abdur was reassigned from front line duty attacking American and Canadian troops in Afghanistan, to a location much deeper inside Pakistan where his assignment, unfortunately, resembled the personally problematic aspects of his Iraq tour of duty. While Abdur's theater of operations had been centered on moving back and forth between Pakistan's arid western tribal areas and mostly into the unforgiving and forsaken terrain of eastern Afghanistan, he was now moved to the Swat Valley in the Northwest frontier province of Pakistan.

The Swat was relatively inland from the fringe tribal areas that bordered Afghanistan and it was far more fertile and photogenic by comparison. This area, famous for fruit orchards and even a few ski resorts back in the day, was within easy reach of the capital city of Islamabad. Though garrisoned by 15,000 Pakistani army regulars, they largely stayed within their fortifications and avoided interfering with the Taliban, who had taken de facto control with about 4,000 warriors. These warriors were primarily charged with enforcing the Taliban's strict interpretation of Islam or enforcing cultural repression on a moderately religious Muslim population that the Taliban considered lax and decadent. They did so with extreme cruelty and maximum visibility. Usually in action at night, the Taliban also occasionally acted in broad daylight to underline their fearlessness and ruthless control—especially when they acted against those who defied their repressive decrees against singing, dancing, shaving beards, watching DVDs, using or selling drugs or worst of all, allowing girls to go to school.

Assassinations of policemen and other opponents were routine, and beheadings were the preferred "statement" killing method. As a man who considered himself a holy warrior, Abdur was reduced to persecuting innocents and terrorizing schoolgirls to keep females uneducated and in their subservient place as Wahhabist doctrine decreed. This loathsome role was difficult for Abdur to reconcile, especially given that his mother was a teacher and all the girls he grew up with, including his sister, Amal, had been schooled. He wanted to "kill Fucking Salibi (Crusaders)" or enemy soldiers, not women, children and civilians," he said to himself in a brief fit of despair before composing himself anew.

Zahadid al-Aboud, his new senior-level and quite infamous al-Qaida commander, was well aware of Abdur's past resistance to political warfare and determined to correct this flaw in an otherwise highly acclaimed and valuable warrior. Zahadid was legendary for his excessive savagery and personally had served as the vanguard or spear tip of multiple campaigns of terror against mostly civilian enemies. Though deliberately just off camera, it was his hand that wielded the blade that beheaded the three kidnapped Belgian tuberculosis disease prevention specialists from Doctors Without Borders. He had used a petroleum-laden tanker truck to immolate alive, 114 men standing in line for jobs as police recruits in order to feed their families. And he had led the mob that stomped to death as a harlot, a nineteen-year old female returning home college student who ventured into her childhood village's marketplace sans headscarf, which she had accidentally dropped en route.

"We are heroes" boasted Zahadid to any who would listen, "and soldier-servants of Allah bound for glory and victory in a great war against the West."

A man of slight stature with a long, pointed nose, exaggerated by beady eyes that seemed jet black, Zahadid was infamous for his sinister appearances which he amplified by always dressing all in black and highly traditionalist clothing.

To insure that Abdur became more consistent at literally and unquestioningly following his commands, Zahadid let it be known to Abdur that his own personal operatives were now tracking the comings and goings of his mother back in Azzun. Her throat was to be slit should Zahadid just slightly raise an evil eyebrow to signal the go ahead. Though Abdur abhorred Zahadid and thought often about killing him, in due time he, in fact, became more compliant. Those who did not know him assumed he was Zahadid's willing, murderous henchman for the unspeakable deeds and prolific number of murders he was regularly forced to commit. Zahadid was, in fact, hoping to drive all semblance of conscience from Abdur—to make him a blindly obedient servant. So he steeled him by ordering him to personally perform acts of incomprehensible, soul-numbing cruelty, while nursing secret future plans for Abdur to later help him perform atrocities on a grander scale than either had witnessed or partaken in thus far.

Besides thoroughly malevolent one-off missions from Zahadid, Abdur's regular assignment was to train, equip and motivate newly recruited suicide bombers to optimize their terrorizing acts against civilians from a rival sect.

"I shall be given seventy-two virgins in heaven," shouted the seventeen year-old pock-faced Jordanian bomber Waheed Shakil, as he was strapped into his heavy-with-TNT, nails and steel ball bearings suicide vest by Abdur.

"Here is the detonating cord and trigger. Remember, we do this for Islam and not for other worldly gain," Abdur said in a quiet but strong voice to him and the other two callow jihadists in his charge. The four of them squatted on wooden boxes in a dingy room with peeling plaster throughout.

"We go to punish the Crusaders who have invaded Islam," said a voice-cracking eighteen-year-old named Umar from Tangiers. He looked all of fifteen.

"We will destroy the keffar (unbelievers) with Allah's mighty sword," said the third young bomber, Abdulla, with growing confidence.

"You are ready now, young martyrs," said Abdur as he finished their preparations for massive death of innocents and debilitating destruction. "May Allah be with you."

After four months of willfulness-breaking dictates by Zahadid, like Abdur having to cut off a twelve-year old thief's hands, and shooting a postal worker in the head with a pistol in front of a mosque gathering crowd "for spreading infidel lies," Zahadid now viewed Abdur as his own completely broken and blindly loyal servant-soldier. Zahadid soon thereafter informed Abdur that the two of them would shortly join a team of specialists for advanced training at a supposedly Iranian-financed secret camp in Hezbollah-dominated Lebanon. Given the sectarian violence he had committed in Iraq against Shiites, it was extremely ironic and strange that Abdur was now supposed to be trained at a Shiite Iranian-sponsored camp. Truth be known, that was only a cover story. Zahadid and other top al-Qaida leaders above him envisioned a glorious fate for Abdur Nidal. It was a fate that was far more profound than that of the typical young, Islamic-martyr-wannabe grist that the terrorist machine was fueled by.

Because the regular use of satellite phones by al-Qaida was limited to prevent triangulation, which could lead to a missile attack, Abdur was only rarely able to call his mother back home. With personal money he had set aside for just such a need, he stole out of camp one evening and he made a Skype phone call to Azzun from an Internet café. "Momma… you… you are alive??!!" he said, weeping upon hearing her long unheard voice.

"They told us you were long ago dead, my sweet son," she replied.

"I am dead, Mother, for I have become a horrible monster," said Abdur with a hushed and completely resigned tone.

CHAPTER 16

Down to the Sea in Container Ships

Murf was unlike his contemporaries who, at mid life, railed against the encroachment of their own mortality by going through Meno-Porsche (as it was called by senior executives in the business), and blowing major loot on a hot and expensive new sports car or mistress. Instead, he drove the same BMW ragtop he had originally leased by the company upon arrival in San Francisco. Since he was not that into new and flashy cars and didn't drive all that much, he bought the Beemer from the leasing agent when it was time to upgrade to a new lease vehicle. The kelly-green convertible was great for occasional wine country trips and rides to the airport-parking garage when he went on his countless business trips. As for a mistress, that sleek and only slightly used thirty-five-foot single-masted sloop he'd seen for sale and moored in Sausalito, had been making seductive and siren-type calls out to him of late.

As his job satisfaction and comfort in his own home waned, his obsession with the solitude of wind and the water and any and all kinds of boats and ships at sea was waxing or rising. Really, Murf's fascination with the sea sprang from his childhood and almost a life-long proximity to different major bodies of deep water. This started when, as a child of about three years old, his military family was transported on cruise ships to Panama in the mid 1960s—or to "The Canal Zone" as U.S. personnel then called it.

In those days, airline travel was sparse, so even though Murf's dad held only the rank of sergeant, the whole family was transported from New Orleans to Panama on a fairly luxurious commercial cruise ship filled with well-to-do vacationing families. Murf just loved the fact that he got to spend over a week on this magnificent ship—the first ocean going vessel he'd ever traveled on. And while on board, Murf and his two brothers and his sister got to act just like what they called the "rich kids," eating whatever they wanted and whenever they wanted, as the ocean liner with a salt-water pool on deck, meandered the Caribbean Sea with brief stop-overs in Guantanamo, Cuba and San Juan, Puerto Rico, before finally arriving in Panama. The Isthmus of Panama is a narrow strip of the Central American landmass with the Pacific Ocean on its southern side and the Atlantic on the north. The forty-eight-mile-long Panama Canal perpendicularly intersects the land and connects the two giant oceans for quick passage between them. Some 15,000 ships pass through the canal each year in an eight to ten hour passage from the Pacific to the Atlantic. It replaced the very stormy, treacherous and lengthy alternative route around Cape Horn, at the southernmost tip of South America; an infamous pathway which has claimed many a ship and their entire crews.

In Panama, Murf grew up swimming early almost every morning at the beach and then fishing off the pier near his house almost every afternoon after school. Once, while horsing around on the beach, he met a shirtless boy with a shocking, shaped series of jagged scars that emanated from his waist and ran in a semi-circular pattern all the way up to his chest. Seems a tiger shark had bitten him as he swam a few years ago and then released him badly bleeding but alive, when it realized the child was not a seal—its intended prey. The boy said that he always stayed on the beach now and no longer swam in the ocean—even where there were metal fencing-type shark nets in place to keep all but small-sized sea creatures away from the swimmers therein.

While it did give Murf a healthy respect for the black tip, mako and hammerhead sharks he frequently saw while fishing from the pier, worries about sharks never even slightly hindered his unbridled delight for frolicking above and below the Pacific waters. That was the case for now anyway. His skin was deeply, deeply bronzed since most of his days were spent running-around in shorts or a swimsuit, without a shirt or wearing any shoes. But the face on this constantly in motion Mother Nature's son was rarely ever without a beaming smile. For outgoing and curious kids of all ages, the waters and jungles of Panama were a Peter Pan-like wonderland of azure blue, sparkling coastal waters and vine-covered trees filled with exotic fruits, squawking parrots and chattering monkeys. The only part of this construct that slowed Murf down, were the countless and ever-present snakes of all kinds. Many, such as the big, thick and dark-skinned pit vipers and tiny multi-hued coral snakes, were highly poisonous and unfortunately prone to nesting inside the darkened corners and closets of homes that dared invade the jungle's edge. There were also giant anacondas about. Murf, his dad and mom, brothers and sister had once lined up and allowed a jungle zoo specialist to drape a fifteen foot-long specimen across their collective shoulders, for a very anxious looking group photo op--"with a FUCKING GIANT, KID-SQUISHING SNAKE!" thought a not often ill-at-ease young Murf.

Once as a bribe to persuade Murf to join the black robe-wearing altar boys, a priest at the base chapel who owned a thirty-foot fishing boat, invited Murf and his dad for a daylong outing of deep-sea fishing. Murf had steadfastly refused to become a real altar boy and to wear the very same type of black billowing robes "the crazy ones," as he called them, did. But the deep-sea fishing boat-owning Army chaplain and his dad cooked up a little scheme to win the boy over. The bait was partially that Murf would not have to commit to being an altar boy. He needed only to wear the altar boy robes to march in the Easter procession wherein he would get to carry a large holy candle. They thought this would give the boy a first taste of the glory of altar-boy-dom that awaited him. The other portion of the reward, to be rendered in advance, was a full day of Pacific deep-sea fishing for giant-size marlins, dolphins, and mackerel. That was more than the young Aquaman could resist.

It took several hours of motoring outward from the military base marina to reach the fifteen-mile offshore areas that the sailfish and game fish preferred. As they trolled farther and farther away from the shoreline, they caught larger and larger fish. Baiting the hooks and managing the heavy-duty fishing poles, heavy-gauge line-covered reels, seat rigs and harnesses, were two dark-skinned, ever-smiling, Panamanian crewmembers. They were also alternately gutting and beheading each fish that was caught so as to render the red snapper, grouper, Spanish mackerel, dolphin (the Hawaiian named mahi-mahi or non-mammalian kind) and such, all filleted and ready to cook prior to returning to the dock. Of course, that meant that the crewmen were slicing up fish and tossing bloody carcasses overboard pretty much the whole trip. And that meant that quite a few fins were now shadowing the fishing party in the wave-emanating wake flowing off the stern. And that meant that, on occasion, when one of them onboard was reeling in a fish and everyone was bent over the side to see the fish gaffed and boated, a huge tiger shark with its mouth wide-open, jaws dislocating and rows of razor sharp teeth slashing, would surprise them by suddenly coming up from the darker waters under the hull. In an instant, the shark would chomp off the fish's entire fleshy body right up to the gills, leaving only a neatly guillotined fish head and steel hook to pull aboard from the now blood-red frothy waters.

That was a sight that would steal your breath away and give you a major case of the willies. The first time Murf saw it, he was scared enough to go inside the cabin of the boat to sit as far away from the water as he could for awhile. It was a sight that none really cared to see a second time, and one that was seared forever into the memories of all who witnessed it.

As the land off the stern of the cabin cruiser became a thin, almost imperceptible line on the horizon behind them, Murf's dad hooked into a large and leaping blue marlin. In the hour and a half spent landing the prize, few, save Murf and the fishing captain priest, paid heed to the tropical squall fast approaching from the west. The next three hours of hell were spent riding six- to eight-foot storm swells and enduring torrential rains and lightening. At one point, with the engines fully gunned and bilge pumps straining, the craft began taking on considerable water as the angry, rolling nightmarish, storm-tossed seas lifted and suddenly dropped the cabin cruiser like a toy.

With worried faces abounding—including those of the two seasoned crewmembers—the Padre then called all but the deckhands to come down below. There he said a prayer for their safety and salvation in a shaken and deeply concerned voice. Murf didn't even mouth the prayer, let alone hear a word the others were saying. All he could think about were the sharks that had followed them and violently savaged their catch all day long. After the praying, Murf was ensconced as far below deck as possible and wedged up inside the pointed portion of the vessel's bow. If drowning at sea were to be his fate, he would still try to put the maximum amount of wood and fiberglass between himself and the must-still-be-lurking-about sharks' jaws.

While all the shaken passengers on the boat did safely reach the marina late that evening and lived to tell the tale, Murf almost didn't get over the frightening ordeal. He was so convinced that the storm was a very clear message from God, that he never joined the altar boys. In fact, he rarely ever set foot in a church again, save for mandatory attendance at weddings and funerals.

Other maritime locales for Murf growing up included three years spent around the Virginia and Maryland coastline and a stint in the Atlantic Ocean-facing northeastern Florida coastal city of St. Augustine—the oldest continually settled city in America dating back to 1565. He also lived in Fort Ord, California—a base built by the U.S. Army as a giant artillery and aerial bombardment practice range amidst the tall sand dunes and green, succulent plants-covered coastline overlooking the dark blue, wind-capped Pacific Ocean; and downtown Chicago on the shores of the immense Lake Michigan, where Murf learned about hundreds of sail, steam-and-coal-oil-powered ships that were prematurely sent to icy graves in howling-wind, giant-wave crashing winter storms. And, of course, he also learned to "root, root, root for the Cubbies," even if it takes forever for them to win another World Series thanks to a stupid fucking curse on the Cubs, allegedly made by a tavern-owning fan whose mascot-intended billy goat was not allowed to accompany him into the stadium!

No wonder the depth of Murf's affinity for pirates, given their predilection for attacking the Spanish ships that traveled on coastal Florida's treasure routes. Not to mention that he'd traveled and lingered throughout the many countless pirate ports of call on assorted rum drinks-blessed Caribbean islands. Further, he had deliberately, one summer as a teenager, hitchhiked to and explored Blackbeard's alleged hideouts on Ocracoke in the Outer Banks island chain off North Carolina. Murf would even attempt to introduce Terri to pirate lore. Together they traveled to Panama on their honeymoon vacation for him to revisit a boyhood haunt, and for both of them to enjoy seeing the Canal and relaxing with a week of R&R at a four-star resort that featured a combination tropical rainforest and coastal-overlook.

While there for a week, he arranged for the two of them to take a day trip to the overgrown-with-jungle-vines ruins of a Spanish castillo on the Caribbean side of Panama called Fort San Lorenzo. It was once invaded and sacked by none other than Sir Henry Morgan, the infamous

English pirate. Captain Morgan, on a mission to plunder the gold of Panama, routed and killed most of the Spanish defenders there during one of his two invasions of the ports and inland territories of Panama. Instead of the romanticized pirate lair visit that Murf envisioned that day, Murf and Terri mostly got lots of heat, humidity, and mosquito bites. And they were constantly worried about encountering deadly snakes as they walked among the pit viper-infested remnants of the castle.

But before leaving the site, their guide arranged for the sale to Murf of a rusted and very heavy lump of metal that had supposedly been retrieved with a metal detector and much digging, at low tide from the temporarily exposed sandbar just about fifty feet out from the built-overlooking-the-bay castle walls. And, indeed, as they spoke, Murf was shown just such an excavation that was then taking place in the flat sand and puddle-covered bay, since the tide happened to be out then. Whether it was an English pirate cannonball fired by an invader, or one fired from Spanish guns back at the pirates, or just a rip-off of $100, Murf was convinced he owned a real piece of history when he brought back home a cannonball that later served as a doorstop in his and Terri's condo. It was also a great conversation piece for anyone visiting his home who expressed—when pressed by him over a cold, rum-tini—even the slightest interest in "Pirates, Matey!"

As for other oceanic exploits, Murf's wanderlust-driven, life-long travels had taken him across the English Channel by high-speed ferry; on cruise ships to the North Sea and Scandinavia where Viking ships once raided; to passages throughout the sunny, turquoise waters and topless beaches of the Greek Isles; to Malta with its many fortresses and Crusader heritage; to the hundreds of miles-long Great Barrier Reef in Australia; to the pristine blue lagoons of Bora Bora in Tahiti; to chasing right whales with a camera in a rubber raft off of South Africa; to many a great deep sea marlin-fishing, tequila-pounding trip out of the coastal resorts of Mexico; to Costa Rica, New Zealand and Hong Kong and too many other ports of call to count. Yeah, you could say that Murf really loved getting lost at sea and, in particular, of late, to sailing out of Sausalito on the sailboat he would purchase and crew with his Pirate buddies.

That Pirates would arise at an advertising agency should surprise no one in that agencies celebrate every single holiday and near-holiday that civil servants and union members take off—plus hastily called celebrations to commemorate big new business wins. And now added to this were the beer and rum-drinking bouts aboard Murf's new love—the *We're in Trouble*, anchored a twenty-minute drive over the San Francisco Bay and just across the Golden Gate Bridge. "Pirates seize any kind of excuse for a pagan celebration," Capt. Murf would tout as their battle cry, but a new account win was the biggest excuse of all for a multi-day bender.

"It's not sailing unless you get wet," shouted Murf at the wheel, as his boat crashed through a cresting, salt-water-spewing wave. PD was busy chumming over the starboard side and the rest of the spray-soaked crew looked like they were waiting their turns to pretty much do the same. Sensing their despair, Murf came about and headed his boat over into the calm waters on the leeward side of Angel Island. Once there, his Pirate mates rebounded quickly. Murf dropped the sails and anchor, and then cranked up some righteous tunes. Fig Newton sprang to life—all waving hair, thrashing arms and leaping legs. Quickly, he was bestowed with the title of Ship's Dancer. The Big Cat then shimmied halfway up the mast and leapt overboard with a 9.9-rating cannonball to claim the moniker, Ship's Diver. The title of Ship's Provisioner went to Mike the Medic for his combination of a special batch of multiple rums-based grog and unbelievably good sourdough roll, salami, Provolone cheese, red onion, lettuce and tomato sandwiches with a major hit of horse-radish-laced, brown mustard.

Murf became a fairly competent blue water helmsman thanks to his incessant reading of anything and everything about sailing—combined with his taking beginner and advanced level instruction one-on-one sailing classes from a marina wharf-rat and part-time instructor.

This was actually not Murf's first experience with sailing. He tried it once on Nantucket on a rare day off from his kitchen work, with an equally sailing-virginal friend. Festooned with, seemingly, gigantic orange life preserver jackets, they set out on a tiny Sunfish sailboat into the relative calm of the harbor. Unfortunately, Murf repeatedly flipped the boat by loosening the boom too much and uncontrollably filling the entire sail with gusting wind. And then he compounded his troubles with his own perverse sense of humor. As he and his buddy clung to the bottom of their overturned sailboat—keel and centerboard pointed skyward—a motorboat approached and hailed them. "Do you need anything?" the concerned boaters shouted.

Murf replied sarcastically, "Yes, we need sun tan lotion." And the potential rescuers turned in puzzlement and quickly sped away.

Murf secretly daydreamed a lot lately about a long sea passage. His cute-as-a-button daughter, Molly, was now eight years old and doing exceptionally well in school. But between his excessive travel and sneaking across the bay for sailing, Murf was missing out on most of her School for the Deaf soccer games and swim classes. And there was even more distance growing between himself and Terri. On weekends, Murf now constantly sailed and twice a week he took night classes to get his seaman's papers as a certified mariner. He wanted to learn everything he could about the sea. He even looked up the words flotsam and jetsam, which sounded to him like what's left floating in a hot tub after sex. And he made one business trip back to New York just for the express purpose of joining a bunch of mostly agency media executives in a visit, sponsored by Forbes Magazine, for lunch aboard Malcolm Forbes' beautiful old wooden yacht.

Murf had read all about Forbes' fabulous boat, but he learned that day about his morbid sense of humor. Below deck, the ship's shiny, lacquered mahogany wooden-plank walls were decorated with numerous gold framed accented paintings of epic disasters at sea—the sinking of the Lusitania and Titanic among them. One even featured a small scene of sharks devouring those in the water who had abandoned ship. It seemed to Murf that he and Forbes had a lot in common including a wicked sense of humor and a love for the sea. But whereas Forbes died on land of a heart attack, Murf believed that he would someday come to his end in the ocean.

Another scheme Murf cooked up in order to get insights into what a life at sea must be like, was booking the family for a vacation cruise to a variety of ports in the Gulf of Mexico and at various Caribbean islands. Stops along the way during this two-week passage included Cancun, Mexico; Roatan, Honduras; George Town, Grand Cayman; Negril, Jamaica; Oranjestad, Aruba; San Juan, Puerto Rico; and Belize City, Belize. Beyond the opportunity for sun and fun, azure blue waters, sugar-sand beaches, and side trips to the haunts of the best-known pirates in history, Murf found other surprising discoveries during that passage. One of the most mind-blowing was the phalanx-like concentration of thousands of oilrigs in the Gulf of Mexico that their cruise ship spent two full days and nights passing through. With the price of oil fairly constantly hovering at very high levels of $80 to $100 a barrel and America's consumption increasing almost exponentially, the saturation of rigs has become far greater than what most Americans realize.

Over 6,600 rigs—some attached to the ocean floor and others actually floating free or tethered by a flexible pipeline—are located in these waters; and yet they produce only about 2 percent of the world's petroleum supply. And some of these rusting hulks, just waiting to deteriorate into major oil-spill disasters, date back to the 1960s.

But what Murf found most amazing was the heavy saturation of bright lights that defined the superstructure of each rig and the way each one created such a Las Vegas casino-type appearance at night, so far out into the open ocean. Murf gazed in awe as their cruise ship sped past rig after rig with their massive four-cornered battleship grey pylons or legs, and multi-leveled platforms and towering superstructures craning up into the night sky. Also amazing to Murf was the speed—some twenty-five knots—at which the cruise ship passed among them as though it were in open water without any chance of collision. More than once Murf said to himself that he could only hope that all of the lights on all of the rigs were fully operable. Surely, he thought, there was some kind of demarked shipping lane in between the rigs that was not apparent to the layman's naked eye. When Murf sat out on the open-air deck of their cabin, he was completely lost in his wonder of the sea, her power and majesty, and constantly shifting nature. When Terri sat out on the deck with or without Murf, she pondered how her marriage could be foundering so badly and so quickly.

One day, back in San Francisco and sailing under the great red-orange rust-colored Golden Gate Bridge, Murf passed one of the many massively vertical container ships that came and went constantly. It was a heavily clouded and gusty day, with the sun only occasionally bursting through like some kind of bright, highly delineated sci-fi tractor beam shining down from the heavens. One such beam now shone directly down from in between two huge cumulonimbus clouds and precisely onto the deck of the ship that so entranced Murf. He was mesmerized by the way the ship was saturated with tall rows of stacked-five-high, red, green, baby blue and yellow rectangular metal containers. Each one of these individual twenty-foot-long and eight-foot-tall steel containers was laden with unseen goods and stacked like so many multi-colored building blocks. The ship looked precariously balanced as though one small wave might trigger a weight-shifting imbalance that would swiftly overturn the vessel like Murf did to that Sunfish so long ago in Nantucket. All of the colorful, stacked boxes were emblazoned with nameplates with mysterious company names like Sinokor, Maersk, Cosco and Hanjin.

Later, from a hilltop perch overlooking the Oakland Shipyard, Murf would further study this unusual industry of worldwide container shipping. Therein, he witnessed a 100-acre highly industrialized waterfront expanse, jammed with row after row of multi-colored stacked containers that had either been off-loaded or were to be loaded onto container ships by giant cranes. At water's edge, rows of these giant giraffe-splaying-their-legs-to-drink-water-shaped cranes were specialized for off loading and stacking the standardized containers quickly and almost automatically. Murf was struck by the general absence of American names on the containers. America had by and large become the world's buyer of goods with far more importing than exporting. When Murf squinted in reaction to the low-on-the-horizon sun in his eyes, it created a wonderful impressionistic visual of lights and structures reflecting off the quivering, ever-moving blue and green palette of swirling ocean water.

CHAPTER 17

Pitch Black

Though now almost an elder statesman in terms of his age relative to his colleagues, Murf still loved getting up for the epic fight that was a multi-agency shoot-out or "New Business" pitch. He enjoyed learning about another industry and leading just-formed teams into battle, with a big, new account to work on as the prize. Murf was no longer the fair-haired kid within the agency, but he was the right choice for this brand called Selectronics Superstores given that he had consumer electronics in his prior accounts experience, that he was almost the lead client's same age, and they both shared middle-class, self-made man backgrounds. In the last few pitches, Murf's traditional role—that of the Big Man on point—had been usurped of late by none other than William Johnston a.k.a. "Danny Boy" of Pirate infamy.

William had risen steadily through the agency ranks with his brilliant command of consumer insights garnered from research, plus a few deft political moves and constant support from Murf that got him out of the background and into the limelight of interacting with clients. He was almost as charming as Murf was, yet he went much further to ingratiate himself with clients by excessively entertaining them and using gifts he purchased and sought no reimbursement for, to gain favor with the more graft-swayed clients. Unbeknownst to his supposedly good buddy Murf, he'd also regularly made wisecracks to the agency's executive committee members about his pal Murf trying to paint him as a bit tired, conventional and past his agency prime. Some friend he turned out to be.

Murf was particularly stoked about the California-based regional chain of electronics stores account. It wasn't just that Danny Boy had led the last two pitches and had landed one of the two accounts. Murf was frustrated with and a bit tired of working on his regular clients' business. And it occurred to him that, as good as he was, the feelings of fatigue might have become mutual. Murf had a theory about this. He called it the Client/Agency Relationship Life Cycle. The gist of it was that just like the Product Lifecycle taught to MBAs—which is charted with a classic bell curve that initially ascends with rising sales, plateaus and then descends with declining sales—so does a client/agency relationship (and possibly even other relationships like marriage). Over the years, he had seen others' and his own relationships with clients wane over time. Cheery and hug-'em-every-time-you-see-'em relationships between a client and the account handlers they initially fell in love with, eventually get predictable and less productive. When compounded by flat or declining sales, even agencies that created fabulous sales successes in the past with tons of glamorous advertising awards bestowed, are quick to get the heave-ho once the thrill is gone.

As he awaited his luncheon appointment or "background on the business informational briefing" with his new prospective client, Murf said silently to himself that even if advertising didn't always, the sea still made him feel young and alive. And there was still so much to learn about it and endless places to explore.

Toward that end, one day the week before, Murf had walked into the U.S. Passport office in downtown San Francisco to get a new passport since his old one was expiring soon. Instead of turning in the old one, he feigned having lost his passport. With just his California driver's license as identification and as an occupation reference, the Mariner's papers he had recently earned studying at night, he applied for a new one. On the replacement passport application he was completing, after twisting his brow with deep thought, Murf wrote-in "Seaman" under the box that said "Occupation." Much to his delight, he would learn some three weeks later when his new passport arrived, that his occupation proclamation had gone unchallenged and was now official.

But today he was meeting the big-shot president of Selectronics Superstores for lunch at a dazzling and critically acclaimed new French bistro. The prospective lead client, named Dan Peterson, whom Murf would get to grill in order to prepare for the big pitch, was mid to late fifties with a bit of slick 'em and a hint of a pompadour in his shiny and unnaturally black hair. From the moment he and Murf shook hands, he was loud, cantankerous and exceedingly full of himself. He looked and acted a bit like a Jimmy Swaggart-type preacher, with spit frequently flying from his lips as he made his immensely important-sounding pronouncements. Murf couldn't help but notice that, although he was dressed in an expensive, dark suit with a monogrammed white shirt and flashy silk tie, he was prone to frequently scratching his crotch and snorting his nose like some vulgar old rummy. He was also a big napkin-sketching man and maybe a bit into pyramid worship. Every grand design he drew out on a napkin for Murf's edification, seemed to have a pyramid at the center of his schematic, separated into multiple layers that formed key stratification of some kind or another. With Murf laying on the charm, the two of them hit it off quickly—especially after Murf shared one of his favorite stories from his past work in the consumer electronics industry.

"We were in Hong Kong meeting with vendors about possible new products," said Murf with a twinkle in his eyes. "The product line in question was radio-controlled toy cars for the Christmas shopping season. And, naturally, we needed the cars to reflect the latest American muscle car designs like that year's hot, new Dodge Viper," continued Murf. "Like this one," I said, showing this Japanese fellow a magazine layout with a half-naked, enormously endowed model leaning on a jet-black Viper."

"Ah-h-h-h," said the speaks-very-little-English Japanese vendor, "WIPE-AAA!! I become you-a WIPAA Wenda!!!" he continued.

"It was all we could do to contain our tittering and bursts of outright laughter," Murf said. "And, not wanting to offend the man, I always carefully said 'Viper Vendor' thereafter to him. But the man just kept excitedly saying 'Wipa Wenda. Wipa Wenda' over and over," Murf said chuckling. "Finally, we just couldn't stop ourselves from falling out of our chairs and laughing uncontrollably until we were wiping away tears in our eyes."

Peterson clearly thought this was a very funny story, because it had the same fits of unstoppable laughter and eyes-tearing effect on him. Two hours, two bottles of wine, and two-dozen bawdy jokes later, they seemed to be the best of friends with innumerable shared experiences and philosophies.

"You'd make a helluva CMO for us," said Peterson to Murf. Though surprised by the suggestion that he jump to the client-side as chief marketing officer, Murf said he was flattered and would love to pursue that conversation at the right time. Then he said silently to himself that said time could be any day now given the mutinous and power-grabbing actions of Danny Boy and the likelihood that his superiors might just one day think of replacing Murf with William Johnston for $150,000 less paid in salary as an incentive. It amazed Murf how often he'd heard of companies that eventually concluded they could get by with someone pretty good but not great, for $150,000 less than they were paying a much better performer.

Of late to Murf, the non-stop pressure and vulnerability of the agency world, seemed a less appropriate place for an older executive with a wife and child to support. Many a great ad man had been swayed to walk on the wild side by becoming a client. Unable or unwilling to rely on their own inexperienced judgment regarding advertising—or unwilling to directly be blamed for it—companies would hire a hot-shot advertising whiz as CMO to manage their ad agency and make those kinds of calls for them. Left to their own devices, most marketing-bereft business people would be satisfied to have an announcer loudly shout the marketing strategy at the consumer. "Let's just tell 'em what we want to tell them," they would rationalize.

But Murf and anyone with any experience with advertising knew that shouting a message with no artifice to engage the consumers' attention is invariably doomed to failure and a wasted expenditure. It's about as effective, thought Murf, as Garrett Morris on the old "Saturday Night Live" show when he'd begin shouting to those who could not hear. "OUR TOP STORY TONIGHT!!!!!..." And on that note, Murf grew sad as his thoughts drifted back to his precious, yet deaf daughter, Molly. He didn't go back to work that afternoon. Instead, he started drinking heavy-pour Irish coffees down at the Buena Vista Café.

It was an afternoon of massive melancholy with all of Murf's misgivings about his life's decisions and his own approaching mortality. "I feel like my life is living me," he said forlornly to the white-apron-adorned and thick-mustachioed bartender.

"I hear-ya brotha," said the commiserating bar man. "I do indeed hear-ya, pal."

Two weeks later, Murf resigned at Lively and took the job as Selectronics CMO that Peterson kept insisting he was perfect for. His first week there was focused on orientation and the pace was far slower than Murf was accustomed to. Later that week at about three in the morning, Murf and Terri were awakened by one of those much-dreaded late night phone calls. "Our sweet brothers are dead," said Murf's crying hysterically sister, Helen. "Killed in a plane crash off in search of god damned bonefish near Christmas Island in the South Pacific."

The next day, Murf flew coast-to-coast to Baltimore to be with his sister and help with the burial arrangements. As he stared out the plane's window thinking of growing up with his wild and lovable brothers and sipping his fifth vodka rocks, a song came on his ipod that further coaxed the tears from his much reddened eyes. It was a Boz Scaggs tune called, "The Ballad of the Sad Young Men." Though now young only at heart, Murf was, indeed, one very sad and confused puppy.

The Ballad of the Sad Young Men

Sing a song of sad young men
Glasses full of rye
All the news is bad again
Kiss your dreams goodbye
All the sad young men
Sitting in the bars
Knowing neon lights
And missing all the stars
All the sad young men
Drifting through the town
Drinking up the night
Trying not to drown
All the sad young men
Singing in the cold
Trying to forget
That they're growing old
All the sad young men
Choking on their youth

Trying to be brave

Running from the truth...

-- *Frances Landesman and Thomas J. Wolf, Jr.*

CHAPTER 18

Maritime Mujahedeen

The warm, salty and moisture-laden Caspian Sea air that filled Abdur's lungs was foreign yet exhilarating after so many years spent in the arid and dust-blown environs of Afghanistan and Iraq. The bright, white-orange Azerbaijani sun warmed his face and he stared at the horizon-wide vista of bobbing fishing boats on the shimmering blue sea with its one-to-two-foot rolling, wind-whipped waves. He coughed a bit as he pulled into his lungs the smoke from the cigarette he held a bit awkwardly in his thumb and forefinger. He was practicing to become a chain-smoking Marlboro man by breathing in just a small bit of smoke and then cautiously exhaling the burning tobacco effluence he—and most reverent Muslims—had religiously avoided all of his life. The cacophony that arose from the hungry and ever-searching sea birds calling out overhead as they soared upwards on the late afternoon thermals and then glided gracefully down, seemed to mock him and the new and as yet ill-fitting image of a grizzled seaman he was trying to project.

In order to pass as ordinary seamen, they were cleanly shaved—shaving sometimes twice a day—and groomed with Western hairstyles to avoid looking even slightly radical. They were clothed appropriately as working seamen, too, wearing rugged, workmen jeans, and white tee-shirts beneath cotton or flannel work shirts. Abdur was still growing accustomed to his much shortened hair length and the removal of his long bushy, black and gray-streaked beard. He occasionally attempted to stroke his phantom beard even now, whenever he was deep in thought, out of a habit of doing so regularly over the last few years.

Abdur knew that it was rare that al-Qaida would mount a sea-based action and assumed it to be of both great import and risk. Keenly aware of Abdur's education and intellect, Zahadid had shared with him the strategic decision that he and the leaders had made to convert loyal and veteran mujahedeen warriors to seamen, rather than trying to recruit, train and command the utmost loyalty and militancy from the available pool of Muslim seamen working in the transoceanic shipping industry. As second in command, Abdur had also been told by Zahadid that the port city of Baku, Azerbaijan was just the site of their maritime training. Their mission would take place elsewhere. Baku was also the capital city of Azerbaijan and was chosen not just for its proximity to the sea, but because it was a site unlikely to be on the radar screens of those looking for a training camp and a cell of terrorists. This was especially true given the failed attack by Islamic militants on the U.S. Embassy there a few years back, which was thwarted by Azeri security forces.

Actually, the failed attack was a feint just to lead Western and Israeli operatives in this theater to believe that militants were no longer active in Azerbaijan. Meanwhile, the sleeper cell still resident there, proceeded with less scrutiny toward their real objective: of training a crew to become transoceanic sailors and to deliver an attack on America by sea. Known as the world's largest land-locked lake, the Caspian Sea is an almost 19,000-mile body of salt water between southeast Europe and western Asia. It's bordered by Kazakhstan to the northeast, Russia to the northwest,Turkmenistan to the east, Azerbaijan to the west and Iran to the south. The Caspian Sea of today is only slightly saline. It was once a part of an ancient ocean connected to other oceans. It was also important as a Mongol-Baltic trade route in the pre-modern times. Now, it is famous for its caviar-producing sturgeon, a large concentration of oil drilling/pumping platforms and massive pollution that flows in from the Volga River basin.

Zahadid had handpicked and molded the obedience of each one of the seven-man group with great care and purpose. Though each carried the nationality of different lands, they were all men of nowhere who fought for Pan Islamist ideology rather than their country. All were in their early to late twenties, save Abdur and Zahadid, the team leaders, who were both in their mid forties. Jamal Ali al-Hakim was from Tangier, Morocco and was a former wrestler whose strength and tenacity had proven vital in hand-to-hand combat. Imdad Saad was once a starving young thief from the slums of Cairo, Egypt who had become a highly trained and experienced bomb designer. Youssef Chababb was a very fast-talking Palestinian from the Gaza Strip. He spoke five languages fluently and could bullshit his way into anyplace or out of almost any sticky situation. Salim al-Mujalami, though from a small town in the mountains of Yemen, had gone on to earn a PhD in Chemistry. Aziz Ahmed Bani was a Saudi like Zahadid, and both, likewise, were from well-to-do families and adherents of strict Wahhabi interpretation of Sunni Islam—just like Osama bin Laden. He served as Zahadid's political officer and chief piety enforcer and nighttime assassin.

Some days the team was based on a very old, forty-foot, multiple-fishing-nets-strewn trawler that chugged slowly in and around the Baku Harbor. On other days, they worked from inside a rusty corrugated metal building in a largely industrial area of the capital city. Their days were spent undertaking an intense and highly unusual regimen of learning to swim, to tie knots, to converse in halting, global-sailor-speak-English, and in studying the comings and goings of the many different types of marine crafts out and about in the very active harbor. They also poured over the schematics of a broad variety of bulk carrier, container and petroleum carrying ships to understand the locations of storage areas, engine and fuel tanks deep below deck, and the large and very vertical accommodations-blocks arising above the engine rooms, most typically at the stern of the ship. They would lay on their bellies for hours on end, at a small, tall-grass-covered hilltop overlooking the harbor. From this concealed position, with the aid of binoculars, they carefully studied the step-by-step procedures of the sailors and dock workers who used the overhead cranes and winches to load and unload the cargos consisting of many different colored and logo-bearing, standardized steel containers.

Two of the men, Imdad and Salim, were also being schooled in the highly automated navigation systems of an open ocean-going ship and on the operation of the ever blinking, modern GPS guidance system. As all of the crew would learn, a global positioning system, or GPS, used in conjunction with an onboard navigational and operational computer, has become the brain or central control for guiding a ship's every movement. In fact, quite a few ships manufactured in recent years could almost steer themselves. With GPS, the ship's watch officer can plot the ship's position pretty much anywhere in the world, under all kinds of operating conditions, and to within just two or three yards of complete accuracy. The ship's computer has become the main instrument used to plot a course, and then while following it, use a series of vectors (just like a plane) for turns made at key junctures, with periodic GPS calibrations for slight course corrections. Salim, who had trained to pilot a small airplane while at college, quickly realized and mastered these modern navigational aids. Of course, what took the most time was learning how not to overreact when they heard the many minor alerts that go off routinely when the ship is driven a little off course by wind, weather or strong currents. This perspective of calm in the face of alarms sounding comes over time and after many transoceanic crossings made in all kinds of weather and with variations in cargo and the fully-loaded weight of the ship.

A hot-tempered and sharp-tongued, mid-forties former Chinese navy officer named Lu-Chi rendered the team's instruction. Many years ago, he had been caught smuggling illicit cargo and had subsequently spent seven years in a brutal prison before bribing his way to freedom. While imprisoned, he studied and solidly mastered, heavily-accented English, Spanish and French. He was a consistently angry man and it was very evident that he resented the very basis of his central charge—to take common terrorists or thugs, as he saw them, and train them in a short period of time to pass as able seamen without really having properly earned that distinction.

"Pay attention you idiots!" he shouted as he read to them from a marine manual. Undermining the seriousness he meant to impart, Lu-Chi was unable to pronounce the letter "L" and, instead, had to substitute "R" whenever a word included the letter "L". "My name is Ru-Chi," he said almost angrily. "Customar-riry, deck officers spend duty hours on da bridge in four-hour shifts, with da turd mate taking the 0800 to 1200 shift. Next, da second mate will cover da 1200 to 1600 hour timeframe, and den da first mate or chief offica will man da 1600 to 2000 shift," he said vacantly in a now disinterested monotone soon to be followed by another angry explosion.

"Write dat DOWN, you FIR-TEE mongrels!! OK. Da captain is on deck as his duties require," he said returning to his rote, monotone presentation style. "Use-urarry his presence is required whenever dere is a harba pi-rot on board, or when da ship is in a prace of row visa-bririty. Dat means ress dan tree mires or in a heav-ary trafficked area. Da captain is being made accountab-re for any and arr probrems dat occur at any hour aboard da ship—whedder he is on deck or not," said Lu-Chi.

What he did not accurately convey to the men was that computer-driven automation and the introduction of highly precise navigating software, have resulted in a great deal of the duty officers' wheelhouse responsibilities becoming checking and double-checking the data, the conditions and then methodically planning for contingencies should any kind of new situation arise. It is speculated that the next generation of ship's gyroscopes may make having a helmsman on the bridge to make minor adjustments expendable. Nevertheless, human beings do have a key role because there are things they can catch sooner than a computer. At least, for now.

The jihadist crew also learned about the much more serious alarms that might go off. The biggest ones were twofold: when the radar triggered a warning of a collision that was imminent, above or below the waterline; and when the alarm for a fire on board was tripped. Fire aboard ships is a major marine industry hazard that results in numerous deaths each year.

Ironically, just about the only learning not imparted in this crash course, was how to do things the old-school way—or how to revert from over relying on modern technology to instead using a magnetic compass, sextant and a chronometer in the event of technological catastrophe. In Lu-Chi's mind, mastery of the manual skills of navigation and time spent at sea are what separated a true seaman from pretenders and landlubbers like this team of Arabs. "And they both are still requirements for earning captain's papers," he said to himself with great satisfaction.

The men of Zahadid's cell were cross-trained in many different jobs. It was almost as though the plan for their deployment would include eliminating some other crewmen—which was dicey, given that the small size of crews aboard most container ships already left little margin for error. First, they were schooled and then repeatedly tested about specifications and governance for any and all-size ships. They were thoroughly drilled on nautical rules of the road and the correct procedures for cargo loading and unloading; and they were given more explanation about TEUs than any of them cared to hear. Technical Equivalent Units or TEUs were the standard capacity measure for how much a ship could carry; 1,600 TEUs was average for a smaller container vessel versus

6,000+ TEUs for one of the modern, high-speed ocean-crossing mega-ships.

"What is a scupper?" screamed Lu-Chi popping an impromptu oral quiz on the men. None had the answer, which is that a scupper is one of many small holes on deck that allows for rain and seawater to drain off. With Lu-Chi's incessant badgering, they absorbed a ton of nautical knowledge in a hurry including how ballast in the form of a water-filled tank lies deep down inside the belly of the ship. This, of course, answered the question that most who see a container ship have asked. "How in the hell does that excessively cargo stacked top-heavy ship keep from rolling over?" The answer is that the mass of its ballast down below helps ensure trim and stability relative to the heavy freight the ship carried. Another esoteric fact that the men learned was that the average 1,600-container ship burns forty tons of fuel a day and that the bunker oil that drives its low speed diesel engines is so viscous and tar-like that it must first be heated and atomized before it can properly fuel the engines.

One day Lu-Chi had organized an ocean swimming drill and it was then that Abdur saw there was a deeply sadistic side to him. Though all had become at least marginally adept in the water during earlier training in Baku, most of the men were far from being really good swimmers. Lu-Chi resented these men for being allowed to pretend to be competent seamen because he had been a real one and a naval officer for a good fifteen years. Prior to the discovery of his smuggling activities, Lu-Chi had attained the rank and papers of a second officer and chief engineer.

"Today, we practice man ova-board dreer," said Lu-Chi tersely. First he commanded Imdad to get into the water without any floatation device. From prior in-water sessions, he knew Imdad to be one of the poorest swimmers and it was apparent that he was also one of the heaviest of the men. Imdad was tentative and bore a worried expression as he rose in the lifeboat that carried the crew, and jumped overboard into a fairly thrashing sea with regular three-to-five-foot swells.

"No swim! Froat!" howled Lu-Chi to his worried subject. Imdad struggled with the waves but remained afloat and reasonably calm as he began quickly drifting away with the current. Next Lu-Chi ordered the smallest man among them, Salim, to go into the water and to retrieve the much bigger man. The rescue method was to get the subject, or Imdad, to lie back while Salim put one arm around his head and neck, using his other arm to side stroke through the water and get them both back to a boat that was now some twenty yards away.

Salim said a quiet and brief prayer and went into the water. Almost immediately after doing so—as he first raised his head above the water-line—a rapidly moving wave engulfed him, forcing seawater down his open and gasping-for-air mouth. Choking, coughing and now taking in even more water, Salim was now in a full panic and thrashed helplessly as though he had completely forgotten everything he had been taught about swimming. "Reeve him," shouted Lu-Chi, as Abdur arose to go overboard to save him. R-E-E-E-E-E-V-E him!" repeated Lu-Chi loudly, glaring bug-eyed and angrily at Abdur. Salim was now slipping under the water, eyes bulging with fear, and Imdad was losing his cool and swimming in panicky small circles as he drifted even further away. With the waves impeding his view, Imdad could only occasionally see the far-away boat.

Abdur was a man of decisive action and could stand by no more. "This serves no purpose, you fool!" he responded to Lu-Chi. "Swim to me now brother," said Abdur in a booming and resolute voice that immediately bolstered Imdad's mindset and guided him directionally. Abdur immediately then plunged head first into the water. When he surfaced some fifteen feet away from the boat, he already had the now unconscious Salim in the classic, lifeguard's clutch. "Here, Imdad, we're here!" he shouted behind him as he swam toward the boat. A very scared-looking Youseff and an outraged Lu-Chi helped pluck Salim from Abdur's arm and hoist him back into the boat. As the others in the boat pressed Salim's back to push the water from his lungs, Abdur had already swum back to reach Imdad and was guiding him to the boat's safety, as well.

Once they were all back in the boat and a reviving Salim was coughing out water and sobbing in gratitude, Abdur grabbed Lu-Chi by the lapels and pulled him up and over to him in one swift movement. With gritting teeth, Abdur said directly into his face as their foreheads butted, "We are here to die for our cause and not for you, you monster! Needlessly risk my men again and I will surely kill you with these very able hands," he said—eyes filled with total conviction. Then he finally released his powerful grip, allowing the now thoroughly frightened Lu-Chi to tumble backwards into the boat.

They almost never spoke again after that nor did Lu-Chi practice his sadism on the men any further. As the launch motored back to the ship with the men, Lu-Chi angrily grumbled to himself yet just barely audible to the others, "Damn A-rabs want me to be turd mate on new ship. I am not damn turd office-a. Ru-chi is sec-rund office-a train by Chinese Navy! Can't make sai-rors outta desert dogs."

After three months of intense preparation in Baku, the crew and their still ill-tempered teacher, Lu-Chi, were then flown to Hong Kong and placed en masse as sailor-interns, on board a "friendly" container ship called the Chandra Express. It was Cameroon-registered and operating out of Hong Kong. The ship—which operated mostly to transport cargos within Chinese waters—was what is commonly referred to as a "coaster" or a vessel that concentrated on plying feeder routes and moving cargo short distances to load or offload other larger, ocean-crossing ships. This meant shorter periods at sea and it gave the crew an inordinate number of days in a variety of Chinese ports. There, in the evenings, with either Abdur or Youssef taking the point position because of their command of English, the crew would begin to practice acting just like sailors in port and all that it implies.

This was to be just another of many steps toward their complete integration into the global maritime world, so the men would be deliberately directed to go to bars in order to observe and record, while consuming some alcohol in moderation to better fit in. Though thought critical enough for the mission for all the men to partake of it (and be forgiven in the name of jihad), Zahadid and Aziz were too absolute in their ways to personally participate in this kind of blasphemy. In preparation, the men had even practiced cussing and they were told typical sailor jokes. They also learned to recount fictitious, yet real-sounding stories of a few thrilling and mostly a lot of completely boring exploits at sea. This kind of fodder, they were instructed, could also be used as a ploy—as in going off on a tangent when answering questions from a prying customs officer. After having lived the intensely pressure-filled and fast-paced lives of constantly-on-the-move guerilla warriors, this kind of socialization was a very extreme challenge of acclimation. It had been an immense shift just adjusting at first arrival in Azerbaijan to the slower and more deliberate pace of life at sea. But once on board the ship in Hong Kong and after settling in a while, they had been instructed to slowly and carefully begin to mix in with the rest of the crew. The objective was to practice, above all, not standing out or coming off as in any way political, given their obvious Middle Eastern features and origins.

To accelerate this process, a few actual shore-leave "nights on the town" were organized and executed. Fortunately for the men, these occurred without the constant and righteous influence of Aziz and Zahadid. For the most part, this consisted of finding the near-the-docks, low-end bars and restaurants that catered to ship crews, and just hanging out and soaking it all up. Their main purpose was to casually eavesdrop whenever possible on the conversations of real seamen. Of course, in order to do so and not be too conspicuous, this also meant they had to have their own sailor-like conversations, speaking as best they could in English and never slipping back into their native Arabic tongue.

Whether on land or aboard the Express, mandatory English lessons taught by Abdur and Youssef, had been a daily two-hour evening drill. It was a top priority, given that most veteran sailors—regardless of country of origin—have developed a decent command of the English language in the course of their travels. And now this was their opportunity to practice English in a real world environment. "Beer please" and the Asian-accented "Sank you" that they so often heard aboard ship, were the usual low-risk utterances made by most of the men.

While slowly nursing beers, they would, for hours on end, try to chat about any topic they could muster that did not involve home, religion or politics. Usually this meant pithy exchanges of philosophy fueled by having read old copies of People Magazine and such that were strewn about the ship. One of them would rant about the latest Britney Spears scandal or another of Kanye West's arrogant and highly public blunders. "But I would still fuck her," Youseff chimed in about Ms. Spears.

This was Youseff's usual capper to most of the men's eloquent Brittany Spears diatribes. Though often oddly inserted and totally out of context, they also worked hard to sprinkle profanity into the mix. "Lu-Chi is horse shit," stammered a sheepishly grinning and slightly inebriated Salim in one such attempt.

"Yes, he is a camel-fucking dog and the son of a filthy whore," a grinning, jumping-on-the-band-wagon Imdad added.

"Here he comes now," said Abdur in a very matter of fact way while pointing at the door behind both of them. The color and smiles immediately vanished from their abruptly lowered faces.

After a very silent moment or two when the ruse was finally realized, Abdur led the team in a hearty laugh spree and Imdad regained enough composure to laughingly say to him, "You ass fuck. You got me!" At that moment they actually could have passed for a bunch of normal off-duty gobs just having a pop and giving each other "the business." And though all were veterans of violent engagements fighting with other insurgent units, since they had not yet served together in combat as a team and were still getting to know one another, these seemingly casual, yet pressure-filled outings, actually were helping bond them together as a unit. They were now a team that cared for each other—with Zahadid and Aziz being the two notable exceptions, or three, if you counted Lu-Chi.

The time the men would spend at sea over the next few months helped accustom them to that which went unnoticed by veteran seamen: everything from the pitch and roll of a ship moving through the waters and a stiff headwind, to the noise and incessant vibration throughout the ship caused by the rumbling engines deep below deck. This also gave them opportunities to learn how to avoid breathing in the nauseating fumes and discharge from the engine room vents that an innocent standing on deck might unknowingly stand next to. Three months at sea—in short, less than a week on-the-water-at-a-time spurts—would have to do as a taste of what the typical thirty to forty day container ship over and back voyages were really like.

Paramount for them was learning not to trip over a line on deck and to always use the safety rails everywhere they went on board. They quickly learned from a bloodied forehead or a deep-thigh bruise from suddenly getting pinched against a metal structure, to be always alert whenever on deck. This was even more of an issue at night and when the deck was wet or smeared with engine exhaust residue. One misstep and a man could fatally slip unnoticed right into the drink. Major and sometimes even mortal injuries could also easily be suffered by those without sea legs who might fall down the many sets of stairs that ran throughout a ship—especially when navigating them in heavy weather.

Of course, all of the men had to learn to deal with seasickness. Unlike cruise ships, container ships do not have stabilizers, so those aboard can really feel the movement of the vessel as it rides up, over and down the waves, or alternately, crashes headlong into them. The team was instructed by Lu-Chi that even if they could not overcome it, they should be confident with the knowledge that even experienced seamen get seasick in stormy weather.

They managed to experience some rough seas in one passage from Hong Kong to Hangzhou, south of Shanghai. During a squall they were engulfed in, waves that were normally in the three to five-foot range, reached ten to fifteen feet in height. The ship and crew were slammed for a good twelve-hour stretch of frequent projectile vomiting and constant clutching of the steel hand railings.

Two days later, in seas that were still far from calm, they participated in a lifeboat lowering drill, which given that it was their ingénue performance, more closely resembled a so-called “Chinese Fire Drill.” Nonetheless, with Lu-Chi’s constant step-by-step haranguing, they managed to lower the boat while inside it. Once they were afloat on the water, Abdur started-up the small engine. As they puttered about, Lu-Chi shouted out where the radio, navigation aid, distress signaler, and small amount of food and water were stored.

In this series of shakedown cruises, the men on the team were thoroughly schooled on the drill when entering a new port, customs procedures and how their bags would be checked upon entry into a new country. Special attention was paid to the tiniest variations if they applied to U.S. procedures. Prior to leaving Azerbaijan, the entire team had been issued impeccable, multi-visa-stamped and well-worn passports. Each one portrayed a merchant Azerbaijani seaman who had already visited most every port in the Far East. The key, they were told, was to not be tripped up by the random and sternly posed questions that might be asked by a customs official. “Feigning poor Engrish is a good first defense,” advised Lu-Chi, “until one has time to correct der taughts for a propa response.”

Lu-Chi even taught them to avoid the pickpockets and thugs who prey on seamen in every port of call. They also came to know about the ship’s rec-room with various table games and stacks of dated CDs and VCR tapes. Then there was the “slop chest” where seamen could buy tax-free and relatively inexpensive sodas, beer, toothpaste and sundries. In the old days, each ship’s policy about whether alcohol could be consumed onboard was left up the captain and tolerated aboard most vessels as long as it didn’t hinder the men in performing their duties. The daily ration of grog is well documented in nautical history as part of the life of a sailor. After the Exxon Valdez debacle—for almost all American ships—alcohol was no longer allowed. Occasional testing had also been started. For other countries—and especially for ships that sported flags of convenience like the Chandra Express—an informal policy of modest off-duty beer or wine consumption was employed. As Zahadid's team became more practiced at the act of kickin' back and poppin'-a-top, the more relaxed they became and more normal they came across.

As they sat laughing and drinking on a night out in a Hong Kong waterfront bar, Abdur scanned the laughing, happy faces of his team. He was struck by the contrast of this unit with the young men he had trained and then served with in Afghanistan. Those not killed in suicide attacks, were subsequently killed fighting against Coalition forces or blown to bits by American missiles. At least on this assignment his men were more focused on learning new maritime skills and Western acculturation versus the constant political and ideological rhetoric Zahadid and Aziz had pounded them with after prayers five times a day back in the Swat Valley. Zahadid's sermons were always about the same thing—justifying the sacred martyrdom of the Islamic warrior, no matter how horrifying the carnage and how many innocents were sacrificed. As Abdur studied the faces of the men before him, he also saw, interspersed in his mind, the faces of the young mujahedeen he had known that had been shot dead or blown to bits. He carried searing memories of each and every one of them and that left him feeling empty and haunted most of the time.

The next day, the men were told they should prepare to leave the Chandra Express in a few weeks in order to move on to their real and still secret final deployment. For the last two weeks aboard, the men were sequestered from regular crew duties to train non-stop. Imdad and Salim exclusively practiced transplanting—with a series of electrical wire splices—a live radio frequency inventory and tracking tag from one container to another identical container. The intent was to make the switch without breaking the circuit, which, if breached, would indicate that a container's RFID tag (miniature sensor, data logging computer, radio transceiver, and GPS tracking system) had been disabled and its rod-hinged door probably opened and contents potentially tampered with.

The rest of the men were concentrated on a single training exercise—using a rarely used auxiliary crane located mid ship. They learned to operate the machine precisely and yet with great speed. The specific task they practiced, was to lift a single shipping container from its position at the top of one row, and then to carefully and precisely lower the nondescript-looking corrugated-steel box into either a truck's cargo bed waiting down below, or onto the deck of a waiting boat down at the water line. The container they repeatedly hoisted up and then lowered down had a blue painted exterior with a Hanjin logo on it. Perhaps this was just a random box. Regardless, this particular logo was the mark of a South Korean shipping company. In this drill there was a step-by-step approach: first, carefully unlash the container from its steel rod bindings and then swiftly raise it up with the crane. Then they were to swing it over the side of the ship, and slowly lower it until they could gently nestle it into either a parked truck's cargo bed or alternately, into an idling-yet-bobbing-in-the-waves boat down below.

Clearly, the boat maneuver was the more difficult of the two. Afterwards, they would latch onto an identical looking Hanjin container sitting either in the bed of another truck or on the deck of the surging up and down boat. The next step was to quickly lift it up and place it precisely back into the slot occupied by the container they had just removed. Abdur was curious as to why the drill was always conducted quickly and with the governance of a stopwatch. The replacement container, though it looked the same, was pronounced to be definitely much heavier and more of a strain on the machine by each of his men as they learned how to make the snatch and exchange. Not one of them would ever have guessed that the cause of the weight variance was not so much due to a heavier cargo load as due to the completely unseen, special lead lining on the inside of the second container's walls.

Zahadid told Abdur that he would be in charge of security and any and all kinds of gunplay that was deemed necessary for the success of this immensely important mission. Though they were alone and not within earshot of anyone, Zahadid now spoke to Abdur in a very hushed tone. His eyes incessantly stared into Abdur's as if searching for hesitance or disobedience from within.

"Our mission is to, once and for all, humble the American Crusaders that are desecrating holy Arab lands with their infidel forces," whispered Zahadid. "We will commit the ultimate propaganda of the deed," he continued with a gleam in his eyes and a lustful grin on his lips. "We have been divinely chosen, my friend, for the great honor of escorting a radioactive "dirty" bomb half-way across the world and into the United States," he spat menacingly as he crushed and twisted his fisted right hand into the palm of his other one. "The plan is, of course, to merely threaten to release the deadly contaminant," he continued reassuringly, "as a means of forcing a massive prisoner release, withdrawal of all Coalition forces from Afghanistan and Iraq, and finally, public American support for creation of an independent Palestine state."

While a single nuclear bomb attack in a major American city could leave millions dead, al-Qaida had yet to obtain such a weapon. What Zahadid told Abdur was that they had gotten their hands on enough spent-but-still-highly radioactive fuel to disperse and poison around a hundred thousand Americans. The materials and bomb had been assembled for $30 million in cash from North Korea, and then transported through China with help from a radically-inclined and virulently anti-American pocket of al-Qaida sympathizers within the Chinese military. A container ship had been chosen to transport the bomb because al-Qaida was convinced that Homeland Security and the CIA were completely fixated on the threat of a small nuke being smuggled in and dropped on an American city via a small, private plane. But an actual deployment of a real nuke, if they were to get one, would not be done according to Zahadid, because of likely nuclear weapons retaliatory attacks by the U.S. on radical hot spots in the Middle East. Such attacks would probably dwarf the bombings of Nagasaki and Hiroshima and decimate multiple al-Qaida supportive regimes and kill millions of Arabs.

The real plan, Zahadid said, was for al-Qaida to use the "dirty bomb" threat alone, including widely broadcast digital footage of the truck-borne bomb, shown parked at a variety of different highly recognizable sites in American cities. Video of the truck, close-ups of the bomb inside, and a complete list of demands, would be fed to the often irresponsible and news-obsessed American media to sow the seeds of abject terror and panic all across the country.

That's what Zahadid told Abdur in confidence; yet the image in the leader's mind was not that of a threatened enemy—but of a mushroom cloud over the burning ruins of a major American city. It was a visual that Zahadid greatly relished and thought of quite often.

Ironically, Abdur now recalled that he had recently read in a dated copy of *USA Today* that a study funded by the Homeland Security Department concluded that "the prospect of a [an enemy's] nuclear device on American soil in the next quarter-century is real and growing. Such a calamitous attack would represent a game-changing event far exceeding the impact of 9/11 on the nation. Today, al-Qaida's nuclear intent remains clear." The article said that every month there are attempts to smuggle either real or purportedly real nuclear materials into the United States. The Energy Department therefore was going to increase its efforts to secure stockpiles of nuclear materials all over the world and to prevent illegal trafficking. In particular, Abdur distinctly recalled the article's last paragraph, "Homeland Security is testing radiation-detection equipment and working at overseas ports to screen cargo containers before they are loaded onto ships headed to the U.S.A."

The article also cited the saber-rattling Israeli Defense Minister, Ehud Barak, as he put it into even more stark and immediately threatening terms: "If it built even a primitive nuclear weapon like the type that destroyed Hiroshima, Iran would not hesitate to load it on a ship, arm it with a detonator operated by GPS and sail it into a vital port on the east coast of North America," he said.

Very acute insight, thought Abdur, only Barak's speculation was incorrectly focused on the wrong and completely opposite coastline.

CHAPTER 19

Slowly Floating Away

Murf had become a shell of his former ebullient self since receiving news of the plane crash and the deaths of his brothers, Kieran and Derrick, just fifty-four and forty-five years old respectively. As kids, Kieran, Derrick and Murf had been very tight. Because they were military brats, the family moved a lot and whether making new friends in each new locale came easily or not, they always had each other to pal around with. They mercilessly and endlessly teased one another and yet always stood together against any kind of adversity. Murf still spoke to both of them by phone at least once a month and they all managed to make their busy travel schedules coincide for a day or two of fishing and carousing at least once a year—until now, that is.

His not-much-fun-to-be-around-anymore drinking bouts with the Pirates had become just a means to a dark, somber end. And that end for Murf was about slipping away from his friends and deep into melancholia. His downward spiral was also making him drift further and further away from meaningful interaction with his wife and daughter. He coffee-ed up every morning and made minimal small talk with them before he went into work. But Murf was mostly just going through the motions.

"You need to snap out of it Murf," said Terri sternly one morning. "Out late every night and, after a gulp or two of coffee, you're right off to work or the airport without even trying to talk with Molly before school. It's unbearable...just completely sucks. We need our old sweet and snappy Murf back," she said, obviously upset and deeply exasperated.

"Working on it," mumbled Murf without looking up from the steaming mug he clutched with both hands.

Terri had also been spending an inordinate amount of time away from their foundering marriage. She had her own busy schedule at work and, whenever possible, she was with Ted, a handsome young teacher at Molly's school. In quiet moments, she had to admit to herself that she was attracted to him both physically and especially because of the passion they shared for working with disabled children. He was making wonderful progress with Molly and had begun meeting Terri for coffee or lunch whenever they could both squeeze in the time. Ostensibly, they got together so Ted could share successful ploys and practices he had uncovered, so that Terri could also employ them with Molly at home. But their conversations had become of a far more personal nature. Ted actually reminded Terri somewhat of a twenty-some-years ago Murf—when he fell all over himself in an effort to charm her. And, she was thoroughly enjoying Ted's company and looked forward to each new liaison.

When Murf first went to work for Selectronics, he tried throwing himself into the company full force. One hundred Dilbert-esque sentences of "Death by Meetings" in the first thirty days nipped this display of new-job enthusiasm right in the bud. While the aforementioned cartoon strip is supposed to present a sarcastic view of the American business world, it seemed to Murf to be a very literal representation of the kind of mindless and endless, waste-of-time meetings and soul-sucking ennui that he'd always feared it might be.

ROAD TRIP! Murf attended every trade show he reasonably could. In order to get himself out of the office even more often, Murf asked to be put in charge of opening up new markets and stores for Selectronics Superstores all over the country. Murf also started further exploring the world as the chain expanded internationally. Work took him to Asia, Russia, South Africa, Greece, London, Paris, Seoul, and repeatedly to Hong Kong. Still, Murf regretted that he was having less and less fun plying his craft.

Instead of being constantly creatively challenged in an upbeat agency environment, he was now working for a sleazy, fat man who wore a pinky ring. Though Peterson was smooth enough that he could sell snake oil to a snake oil salesman, Murf had quickly realized, after he had come over to the dark side, that his boss couldn't tell the difference between a good idea and his own ass. So, as they say, "When the times get tough, the tough get going." And Murf did so. He aggressively used travel to avoid the drudgery and soul-sucking meetings at HQ as much as possible—not to mention ducking his virulently growing personal dilemmas.

As Murf slumped in his seat on the flight later that day to Cleveland and took a deep slurp of his third rum, coke and lime, he stared at the billowing upwards formation of thick and bubbly clouds down below. In spite of the small potbelly and graying hair that were encroaching on his good looks, Murf still possessed dazzling green-eyes and a generally athletic build. But one might not ever notice it given the way he was slumped in his chair and the massively wrinkled conversion his starched blue dress shirt had gone through. Ear buds ran up his chest from the in-his-lap music player. Murf was listening with abandon to a mix of rather ponderous and Anthem-esque rock songs he had made for his travels. As the last chords of "Away from the Sun" by 3 Doors Down faded away, Murf sung along under his breath. "I found myself so far down, away from the sun again…"

The next two tunes that came on were also perfect fuel for Murf's growing case of the blues. The first was the classic "Have You Seen Me Lately" by the Counting Crows. But as opposed to the original rock version, in this version it was performed unplugged. "I don't need anyone these days, feel like I'm fading away…" The second was a more obscure Crows song called "Raining in Baltimore" and it was even more somber than the first song. "I just had no intention of living this way. I need a phone call. I need a plane ride. I need a sunburn. I need a raincoat."

The booze and the blaring, volume-set-to-the-max music seemed to somehow help Murf forget for a moment all of the seemingly profound issues that were constantly banging around inside his head of late.

Did anything at the office remotely interest him anymore? Was there any hope of little Molly ever really knowing her dad? Where had the joy gone that he'd always found in his wonderful, ever-smiling, sweet wife's freckled face? Why didn't they really talk anymore? And how had he so quickly gone from a vital, unstoppable force of nature, to a worthless, hopeless corporate slug? The haunting "Wishful Sinful" by The Doors was next on tap musically and Murf raised his brow and right hand half-way up and signaled the stewardess for another Cuba Libre as he snuggled into the red woolen blanket from his seat back pouch and returned to gazing at the clouds and losing himself in the tunes.

Murf had become quite fond of flying. He deliberately avoided engaging fellow business-class passengers with his glib reparte. Instead, he'd sit in silence and gaze out the window of the jet planes he was being ferried on. He found comfort in the low hum and vibration of the engines as he spent four to five peaceful, blurry and mindless hours per flight, crisscrossing the country while trying not to think about anything and yet inevitably thinking about everything—including the pressures building up back at work and at home.

Some twelve to fifteen times per year, he also flew overseas—usually to Japan, Korea or China—on flights lasting up to fifteen hours. Murf was happily calmed and mesmerized by the 30,000-plus-foot aerial perspective of the earth. He was amazed by the overhead viewpoint looking down upon the geometric shapes of the green or yellow agri-gridded, crop-circled or squared-off-looking fields far down below. Who could not gaze in fascination at the pristine and breath-taking scenes of snow-covered mountain tops, surrounded by blankets of blue-tinged white snow banks spread like icing across wind blown ridges of black, craggy rock. On coast-to-coast flights, he looked forward to flying over the majesty that is Yosemite and looking down at the top of Half Dome from the air. This aerial spectacle was soon to be followed by the brilliantly mottled, rusty orange and cocoa-colored canyons and buttes, typical of the southwestern states. Next came the oceans of brown and dried-out gray scrub-brush that is the barren and scarred topography of West Texas. Of course, his perennial favorite was always the endless and ever-undulating, purple and dark-blue waters of any body of water, with dancing, whipped cream-like wave peaks. Everything was more fascinating when viewed from this enormously expansive, overhead and rum-fueled point-of-view. Something as mundane as a distant grass or brush fire, became a ribbon-candy shaped, long and wispy gray serpent when seen from these heights. Night views were different, yet equally appealing to Murf.

In the darkness, he had watched massive forest fires off in the distance; hills ablaze with destructive fury. Also worth fixating on were the tiny pairs of rounded car headlights—with wide yellow beams that always shined straight ahead even as the road bent and wound. A simple automobile moving mysteriously through the black-of-night engendered wonder in Murf. What kind and color of car was it, and more importantly, what were the people like who were driving inside of it? Where was everyone going and would there be anything worth seeing or doing there when they arrived? Were they happy with their lives or were they tormented by them like he was?

Murf had even, on occasion, seen smoking, flaming red and white-hot lava streams flowing down below in a Pacific Ocean-crossing flight that passed over the "Big Island" of Hawaii. Another time, when Murf was high and passing over Papua, New Guinea, he enjoyed a volcanic fireworks encore. But Murf Morrison's favorite stratospheric vistas were generally of two very specific kinds. First there were those endless, big blue, ocean-crossing ones, which he frequently enjoyed since over three-fourths of our very wet planet is ocean. Murf regularly got completely mentally lost in watching the endless expanses of shimmering blue water with an occasional bobbing-cork-looking ship spotted far below him. And talk about having your head in the clouds, his second favorite airplane visual for alcohol-addled contemplation, was the very clouds which the planes were always flying above and through.

The shapes and formations were infinite in variation, and each cloud seemed to pulse and breathe like a living, thinking entity. There were clouds shaped like bundles of frayed cotton balls, clouds shaped like dragons or rearing-back stallions, and lonely clouds that floated by themselves in otherwise clear blue skies. A particular favorite of Murf's was seeing the enormity and storm-driven power of massively vertical, grey and black anvil-shaped cumulonimbus clouds. Jets would always skirt around them, but in the distance he could see lightning flashes emanating unexpectedly and irregularly from deep inside. Even as Murf pretended to himself that he was temporarily carefree when he took in these spectacles, he would once again slip quickly into rethinking every situation that worried him—from momentous past life decisions, to the biggest question of all, "Where to from here?"

In essence, Murf was alternately wondering about nothing all, and then wondering about the meaning of it all. The questions flowed in an unstoppable and illogically ordered torrent of self-doubt. Crap like, "Should I have married Terri?" to the ethereal, "Is my intended soul-mate still out there?" More second-guessing questions were asked such as, "Should I have played football in college instead of always working at different jobs?" "Should I have dropped out for a while and taken to the road like some latter-day Jack Kerouac, perhaps becoming an author or an artist?" "Should I have gravitated from work in advertising to

Hollywood, to write for sitcoms by day and work on more serious screenplays by night?" And naturally, a few more pithy explorations were also pondered as Murf drifted deeper into a melancholy meltdown—questions like, "How soon and how will I die?" and "What the fuck am I doing with my life anyway?" Inevitably the real doozie always came up. "Will my sweet yet silent little Molly grow up to be happy?"

After his stop in Cleveland, Murf took in a retailing trade show in soul-sucking Las Vegas. Over 120,000 retailers had saturated the town and Murf was extremely unhappy to find his usual reservation at The Mandalay Bay Hotel and Casino had inexplicably vanished. The travel agency was barely able to get him a third-tier, off-the-main-strip, overly priced and under-delivering room at a theme-extreme medieval haunt called The Sherwood Forest Casino. "Lords and ladies, make your way thusly to the registration desk," said a buffoon of a doorman whose costume and pompadour made him look like a collision between the overweight peanut butter, honey and bananas sandwich-stuffing Elvis and a green tights and leather, very effeminate Robin Hood. Once in his room, Murf did a quick inspection. When he pushed on the mattress, it felt like one made of sawed-off Styrofoam. His eye caught sight of the room service table tent on the desk, which touted delicacies that included: Friar Tuck's Bevy of Ye Old Mini-Corny Dogs, Maid Marion of the Bountiful-Bodice's Jumbo Shrimp Cocktail, and The Sheriff of Nottingham's Naughty Deep-fried Twinkies with Au Natural Fresh Strawberries.

Murf grew more depressed by the moment as he trudged through the Camelot Not-looking casino toward the taxi stand and headed to the big trade show. Amidst the bright and flashing colored lights and cacophony of sounds of coins-falling-into-tin-pans, he heard the "Wheel of Fortune!" slot machines all around him with their recordings of the TV show studio audience chanting, "Thousands and thousands of FABULOUS prizes!" They were imploring him to stop, but to no avail. The hardened look of bored and craggy-faced blackjack dealers and overweight and chain-smoking nickel slots freaks, only reinforced his searing discomfort. Given the total artificiality of this place—and really of all of Las Vegas—Murf wondered if the Vegas regulars, who seemed to revel so in the unreal here, loved Las Vegas because their real lives back home in Ohio just sucked so unimaginably. "Hell, why not drink and gamble for three days straight without sleep," thought Murf, "and then get married by Elvis." And by the way, statistically speaking, were marriages conducted in Vegas by Elvis look-alike preachers versus non-Elvis weddings back home, really any less enduring and successful? Serious food for thought there. At the end of the week, Murfs spirits lifted momentarily as he saw Las Vegas looking better now that it was in his cab's rearview mirror. From the airport, it was back to Hong Kong without going home, to scout for new products and meet with key vendors.

The long heavy-drinking "bender" of a flight over exacerbated Murf's pronounced downward spiral. After a post-flight seven hours-long dead-to-the-world slumber at his harbor-side hotel, Murf took a long, slow run along the waterfront for almost six miles until the landscape went from a mix of retail and commercial to decidedly industrial. Murf knew it was time to turn around, but he persisted and crested one last medium-sized hill. Before him lay the breath-taking expanse and bustling behemoth that is the HIT or Hong Kong International Terminal, a man-made and mind-boggling supply-chain and logistics wonder of the world.

Murf sat down, mouth agape, as he surveyed the industrial city of giant offloading cranes and platforms towering over endless thirty foot-tall stacks of containers, taken off the ships in the channel behind them and being stacked and carefully tracked like a maze which comprises tens of thousands of mostly red, blue, orange, and green rectangular building blocks. It was perhaps six or seven times the size of the similar ship loading/off loading site he had studied in amazement for hours back home across the bay in Oakland. The biggest cube-shaped, en masse sections of cumulatively stacked rows of standardized size containers had been stacked twelve containers high and twelve containers wide.

Each stack resembled, in size and shape, a small suburban office building. And there were thousands of these office building-like concentrations.

The biggest of the automated unloading structures or gantry cranes, as they are known, were each the size of an offshore oil drilling platform. They sported topside superstructures that looked like a suspension bridge sprouting from the top-level and forming an inverted L. Smaller cranes, about the size of a single oil derrick, looked like aroused males with one very big arm extended skyward. Down below the dozens and dozens of cranes, was a mid-sized city of rectangular containers stacked into massive, collective cubes. Each individual container—the transport for 80 percent of the world's trade—was painted in a different color and bore a company's name and or logo on each side's facing: HANJIN, MAERSK, COSCO, SINOKOR, QUAYJONG, EVERGREEN, KMTC, LINEA MEXICANA, UNIGLORY, and so on, and so on. Each one also bore a unique RFID tag that, upon arrival in a port, would transmit digital data to a central inventory-tracking computer about the load that it carried.

Murf was again struck by the seemingly non-American posture of most of the names and he intuited that, since the U.S. had become the world's greatest buyer of goods and no longer bothered to make and export as much as it imported, Americans were seemingly blissfully ignorant or completely content with a steadily growing trade imbalance. In fact, as Murf would later read, more than half of the retail goods sold in American stores—with emphasis on toys, apparel, footwear, and consumer electronics—enter through a port. So great is the glut, in fact, that incoming cargo sometimes is trapped for weeks at a time at the two busiest U.S. ports, Los Angeles and Long Beach, into which over one-third of all containerized cargo shipments in the U.S. flows. Alternately, ships originating from Asian ports can go through the Panama Canal and around the tip of Florida to the eastern seaboard U.S. ports like New York/New Jersey, Charleston, and Newport News. So massive is the trade from Asia that a new giant class of container ships—over 1,000 feet long—has recently been coming on line. So large are these ships that they require two harbor pilots to guide them into port. As Murf later on considered just how grossly efficient the worldwide network and the new mega-scale of container shipping had become, he would be struck by how containerized and commoditized his own life now felt. How ironic that he would find a perverse kind of comfort when one Murphy Morrison mentally disappeared into this life's sea of sameness and convention.

After observing the non-stop buzz of this metal-encased and diesel-engine-powered hive for about two hours, Murf walked to a nearby roadway and hailed a taxi back to his hotel in the Harbor City waterfront section of Hong Kong. Later that afternoon, Murf took a ride on the very traditional-looking, wooden, green and white painted Hong Kong ferry. Sitting on an open-air top deck bench and surrounded by mostly Chinese business people and working class types, Murf thirstily gulped from the first of two cans of Heineken beer he had purchased from a vendor or "wenda" in the ferry-building complex, just before boarding. As he took in the view from the Kowloon side across the narrow Victoria Harbor channel to the Hong Kong Island side, he studied the Central District with its staggering skyline of dozens and dozens of 100-plus stories, ultra-modern skyscrapers.

One of the most notable and visible in the center of the approaching Hong Kong Island skyline was the massive, spire-topped Central Plaza building in Wanchai. It was adorned with an enormous, lighted Phillips sign amidst an unbroken wall of other gigantic buildings—each with huge brand name corporate signs: Panasonic, ING, Olympus, Epson, LG, Hitachi, Sanyo, ROLEX, Siemens, Canon, NEC, Sharp, Lippo, SOGO, Nikon. It was an amazing harbor to behold with a motley armada of hundreds upon hundreds of small fishing and transport boats, massive oil tankers, container and cruise ships all intermingling. Most numerous were the ubiquitous Chinese junks and the many green and white Hong Kong ferries crisscrossing simultaneously given that departure times ran about every ten minutes. Right of way was seemingly determined by the size of the cojones and degree of disregard for safety of each vessel's captain. By comparison with the orderly San Francisco Bay waters Murf sailed, here each vessel seemed to be traveling full-throttle at clearly excessive speeds in a supposed nine-knot channel. The jockeying for position and cut-'em-off maneuvers Murf witnessed, looked more vicious than the taxi- and moped-jammed, obscene gesticulation-infested roundabouts of Rome.

The retail environment Murf took in when he disembarked was equally staggering with thousands upon thousands of shops and malls jammed everywhere throughout the city. The designer shop signs were omnipresent—there was Gucci, DKNY, Prada, Burberry, Duty Free DFS Galleria, Louis Vuitton, and Salvatore Ferragamo. Other signs bore oddball names like Sleepcare Museum—the name of a retail bedding store. As an early twenties girl strode by on the street wearing a tee-shirt that said "Snoopy Love Club," Murf wondered what the hell that slogan meant. Was it a club for Peeping Toms, or a Charles Shultz-inspired brothel, or just a bad translation of Snoopy Fan Club? For the next hour, Murf meandered far from the harbor-view Marco Polo Hotel where he was staying. He also walked far from the well-lit main streets and he, therefore, encountered a heavier concentration of raincoat-wearing street hustlers. As he passed by each one they would approach him, smiling, and flash open their coats to reveal hundreds of watches displayed in the lining, as they cried out to Murf and every Westerner walking by, "Copy watch, copy watch!" Murf pressed on and made his way back down to the waterfront.

It was time to leave this neighborhood's garish spectacle and so he took a return trip ferry ride back to the more comfortable and yet also teeming Kowloon waterfront. The primary appeal for Murf of the Kowloon side was the constant ferryboat comings and goings from the dock near his hotel. One after another, each vessel would lurch into or out from the docks—fully laden with passengers and engines loudly and violently churning the murky green and harbor-waste-polluted water into frothy white-water torrents. The humid evening air was thick with the smell of salt water, fresh produce, sweat and tobacco smoke. In particular, he studied the sailors on leave that each day came streaming in from the 400-plus ships that call on Hong Kong each month from all over the world. They laughed loudly and cajoled each other as they clamored for beers, smokes and prepaid cell phone cards to keep in touch with their families so far away. Over the next week, Murf on occasion followed several groups of sailors and further observed them in daylight hours as they toured the town, drinking, eating, making currency exchanges, visiting the Sea Farers Mission for much needed social services and most of all, partying in the countless Hong Kong girlie-bars. Murf even bought a few rounds and chatted up a couple of European sailors one late night in a place called Hot Lips. They loved Murf's innumerable raunchy jokes and generosity. And he loved entertaining the fantasy of a simpler and less pressurized life that he believed they led.

Two days before leaving Hong Kong, on Saturday morning, Murf took the city bus for a forty-minute ride over the densely lush, green and exotic tropical foliage-heavy suburban Hong Kong's hillsides, to the much quieter back-bay town of Repulse Bay. He could easily have afforded to take a cab there, but he preferred to ride the bus with the ordinary folk whom he imagined were consigned to a life of manual labor. As he rode the bus, he saw himself as one of them. Once he arrived in Repulse Bay, he stayed one night in a low-priced room in a small, hillside motel near the center of the waterfront of this bustling market town. Murf killed the better part of a bottle of rum watching the sun go down and staring at the enormous, craggy rocks that arose helter skelter from the water of the quaint and tiny bay. He deliberately slept in the night air in a hammock strung on the deck outside his room.

The next morning, he made an early call back to the home office in San Francisco where it was almost 4 p.m. "Just calling to check in, Dan," Murf said pleasantly.

"A-h-h-h-e-m-m. I hate to break it to you this way, but since you travel so much that you're never here…well, here goes Murf…you're out," stammered Peterson uncomfortably.

Murf hadn't just traveled excessively and missed way too many meetings, his true offense was that he had fallen from favor with his main patron who, in Murf's absence, had found a new drinking buddy and marketing confidant. Peterson told Murf that his termination would not appear to be anything about Murf's personal performance. He was to be part of a planned workforce reduction announced on Friday—a.k.a. another round of corporate beheadings. He further informed Murf that to replace him he was going to be bringing on, at a much lower salary, this "young, bold and brilliant" fellow from the ad agency by the name of William Johnston. The heretofore amazing, fantastic and immensely talented Murphy Morrison was being shown the door. And another masterful, job-hopping strategic move had been made, it seems, by none other than Murf's fellow Pirate in arms, the unctuous and back-stabbing Danny Boy. At a still completely productive and vital age, a very confused and lost former wonder-boy was thoroughly convinced he was done at fifty-one.

CHAPTER 20

The Boredom of Everyday Life

After arriving at the condo, Murf fumbled to find his keys and instead was let in by their doorman who buzzed the unit on the intercom as a courtesy. "Mrs. Morrison is upstairs now, sir," he said to a somewhat surpised but too tired to give it much thought Murf.

"Why are you home at this time of day?" asked the just-back-from-the-Orient Murf of Terri. He had just noisily struggled to simultaneously lift and shove two-at-a-time, his five extremely heavy and over-packed suitcases across the raised threshold of their condo's front door.

An equally surprised Terri, her hair and blouse just a bit disheveled and her face ever so flushed, responded. "Why should you care? You've been gone so damn long, I had no idea when you were coming back!" she stammered.

Murf scanned the room and that's when he saw the man sitting in the living room on their couch. He too looked nervous and fidgeted with his tie as though he had just tied it too quickly and too short.

Terri ended the pregnant pause in the room by saying, "Murphy, this is Ted, Molly's teacher at school." Always the kidder and hoping his imagination had just run amok again, Murf said sheepishly, "You two look like a couple of kids that just got caught with your hands in the cookie jar."

"I've got to get back to the school. Nice to meet you, Murphy. Nice to see you Ter—Mrs. Morrison," Ted said awkwardly as he hurried out.

Terri turned her back to Murf clearly angry and embarrassed. She did not want to look him in the eyes right now.

"We need to talk Terri. It's about my job," Murf said somberly.

"God damn it Murf, to hell with your stupid fuckin' job. Thanks to Selectronics, we never see you around here anymore!" Terri said with her back still turned away.

"That won't be an issue anymore. I got canned," Murf continued.

"Well I'm not one to dog-pile Murf, but I want a god damned divorce," screamed Terri as she fled the living room and slammed the bedroom door behind her.

Murf popped open one of his suitcases and proceeded to strip naked in front of their open-curtained living room window. He quietly put on his shorts, socks and running shoes, and then pulled his head and arms into a well-wrinkled tee-shirt. The ensemble was completed with his favorite Cubs hat snugged tightly onto his head. "Surely I didn't just catch them in the act?!!" Murf mumbled to himself. "It certainly did look that way… but, no, not my sweet Terri. Well, there's nothing like a good long run to settle a troubled mind." And, once again, he was off and gone.

"Maybe the agency will take me back," thought Murf the cockeyed optimist as he plodded stride after stride up a long incline. "And maybe Terri still loves me and would stop seeing that Ted guy." After a short ride across the bridge, he was now running in the fragrant eucalyptus tree-forested Presidio Park, overlooking the stunning Golden Gate Bridge and surging waters at the mouth of the San Francisco Bay. "No way in hell. The agency just lost the Selectronics account and will surely be downsizing," rationalized Murf. "And she sounded like she really meant it when she said divorce." His run that day lasted about two hours and took him through some twelve miles of the vast national park. After he was done, he further avoided going home and sat for another hour and a half staring out at the sea from atop Presidio-based remnants of WWII coastal fortifications where artillery batteries had been stationed to repel Japanese subs. By the time he headed for home, he had come to what he thought was a civilized solution. He'd set Terri free so she could openly be with her young lover without any further pretense or sneaking around. This was the only rational and adult thing to do he said to himself. But, in truth, the very thought of it was eating at his soul. It felt like some stalk-and-slash movie psycho tormentor was slowly dripping pure sulphuric acid onto Murf's exposed yet still living brain.

Murf spent the next three weeks working out of his "home office." As the cliché goes, the tension between Terri and him was so thick you could cut it. And when they tried to have even the simpliest conversation, it quickly deteriorated into an acrimonious one and then a shouting match of accusations and counter-accusations. So Murf and Terri mostly avoided each other and he threw himself completely into working the phone. After a flurry of inquiries calls and emails to all his past contacts, within three weeks that old smoothie Murphy Morrison had, indeed, lined himself up with another client-side job working for "The Mother Ship." That's what he called Samsung, the South Korea headquartered, global manufacturing behemoth. Samsung was the world's largest TV manufacturer and second in terms of mobile-phone production. It was also the lead vendor for Selectronics and many other retail chains. Over the phone, Murf had convinced the Samsung HQ executives he had met with so many times before, that with all his retail marketing industry contacts and superb selling ability, he'd be able to get more of their products into more new channels practically overnight. Truth be known, Murf mostly knew marketing and advertising people who worked for other electronics store chains and most of them would now regard Murf as a competitive threat to take over their jobs. In fact, Murf had very few contacts among the buyers he would now call upon for Samsung—but that was an obstacle he felt sure he could overcome.

The huge strain in his marriage and bare minimum of civil conversation between he and Terri lately was a far more daunting problem. Since his return, Murf had been sleeping on the couch and Terri was supposedly looking into filing for divorce with a lawyer she knew. As he prepared to start up his new job, Murf was somewhat taken aback to learn that the position he had been offered would actually be based in Samsung's Los Angeles office and not San Francisco. Once Murf came to understand the amount of coast-to-coast U.S. and overseas travel involved—and recalling the ease of catching one of the departing-every-half-hour-shuttle flights to and from SFO to LAX—Murf's concern abated somewhat.

His soon-to-be new boss was younger than Murf; a handsome Korean national, maybe thirty-two years old with fashionably longish and impeccably groomed black hair. He was also supposedly the nephew of some very senior executive in the company. This fellow, who went by the name of Kwan, struck Murf as being indifferent to the real work of the company. He seemed only to care about how suave he looked in his expensive suits and with fostering the appearance of being a highly accomplished executive. "Another do-nothing pretty boy," said Murf to himself. There was a distinctively arrogant air about Kwan and he was quick to give people the impression that he was a "made man" or untouchable—due to his serious familial connections.

"For orientation…" said the memo, Murf was to head immediately back to the Orient. There he'd spend a week at company headquarters in Seoul, and then another week touring Samsung manufacturing facilities throughout South Korea. It was going to be a long and stifling trip and Murf was quite upset about the prospect of traveling while losing his almost life-long love Terri and probably along with her, the daughter he wanted so desperately to show that he loved.

As angry and frustrated as Terri was with her husband, she was also quite worried about him—having never before seen him in such an introverted and somewhat pitiful state. He might be surprised to know that she, too, had become bored with work, special-needs childrearing, their relationship and just life in general, at times. But deep down, she still loved her Murf and felt guilty both for her atypical indiscretion and for not asserting herself more to try to stop Murf's spiral downward. Of course, she knew that she and Ted were now outed as lovers and regretted that she had let an infatuation get out of hand to incite their brief affair. "Maybe it will snap Murf out of his funk if he believes that we are over," she reasoned. "Maybe my marriage is not yet too far gone to save."

A day later, she met Ted for coffee and told him that she had decided to not let their relationship proceed any further. He was surprised and grew a bit teary-eyed as she succinctly and leaving no room for equivocation, broke it off with him while also insisting that he continue to give nothing less than his best efforts on Molly's behalf.

CHAPTER 21

I'm a Seoul Man

As Murf relaxed with his usual libation while winging his way to Seoul and his new executive "orientation" at HQ, he dialed up a particular tune from his vast music library. Following the raucous horn-section opening strains, Sam and Dave began bellowing, "I'm a Seoul Man. Ba-dupa-dup Ba-dupa-dup. I'm a Seoul Man," sang Murf. Seoul, South Korea—Murf read in his all-about-Samsung orientation book—is a mere pup of a 600-year-old city. Its modern-architecture-dominated, nothing's-more-than-fifty-years-old look, is because it is, in fact, 99 percent post-Korean War (1950-53) constructed. The old railyard terminal with its distinctive dome is one of a handful of buildings that pre-date the North Koreans and Chinese having reduced Seoul to ashes during the war.

Korea, a 4,000-year-old nation, is known for warm, open people. Though always pleasant, Murf's three prior trips there seemed to blur together in his memory and he fixated on a much-inebriated session he recalled in downtown Seoul, where a cheery middle-aged Korean lady was holding court at a piano bar. Rummy Murf was always partial to delightfully bad piano bar entertainers, but he truly loved taking in those who sang in stilted-English with heavy Asian language accents. This one, he remembered from his last trip to Seoul, sang in oddly pronounced English and probably didn't speak or understand any of this language. Murf distinctly remembered, in spite of the rum haze, that, instead of singing, "Islands in the stream, that is what we are," he heard, "Iran in da steam. Dat az wat we ah. And we can re-ry on deech oda, Ah ha!"

"She was fantastic!" he said to himself with a chuckle.

As he thought about it more and not wanting to appear racist, he asked himself if singing words in a language you don't understand was any more odd than, say, the college student or professional athlete in America, who gets nonsensical Chinese or Japanese alphabet characters tattooed on his body believing that it says something like, "Strong, Brave and Invincible." Of course, when properly translated, the letters actually, instead say, something like, "The chickens are sick."

As Murf spent more and more time in Asia, he noticed more and more strange street signs with goofy, fractured English store-name translations like the Morning Tomato sign that hung over one restaurant door he passed. In China, he once spotted a bathroom-for-the-handicapped sign that proclaimed, "Deformed Person."

Shortly after that odd lingual-translation mental digression, the melancholy started simmering up again. He could not stop thinking about what he had interrupted between with Terri and Ted. He imagined searingly graphic visions that replayed over and over in his head of the two lovers passionately enjoined. "How long had they been lovers?" he wondered. "How many times have they had sex? Was he a better lover than me? And when was Terri planning on dumping me for him anyway?" Murf pulled the red airline blanket up over his head, chewed on a pillow to muffle the sounds and cried at length. Physically and mentally exhausted he finally nodded off two hours later listening to

Billie Holiday singing the my-man-done-left-me blues as only she could.

Upon landing and after transport from the airport, Murf settled into his room and freshened up at the highly upscale Shilla Hotel on the outskirts of downtown Seoul. Later, his hosts for the evening from Samsung headquarters met him in the hotel lobby and introduced themselves. The senior-most Samsung human resources executive was Sun-Yung. He was a portly fellow in his late fifties with an enormous comb-over hairdo that seemed to originate in one extraordinarily lengthy, upwards-combed-swooping-over-from-one-side-to-the-other sideburn that had been forced to try to cover almost the entirety of his largely bald head. Though try as it did, the hyper-aggressive sideburn just could not do enough to cover the shiny, bald chrome-dome that rampantly peeked through his cries-out-to-be-stared at hairdo. The other two, Lee and Yu, were clean cut, mid-thirties, smiling-and-nodding machines, dressed almost identically in dark suits, white shirts and nondescript ties.

"Annyeong haseyo," mustered Murf in the lobby as he shook the three men's hands and used the only phrase—Hello—that he knew in Korean. The evening began in a Korean food restaurant [big surprise] they walked to about three blocks from the hotel, where the initially very formal Samsung executives introduced Murf to a local rice vodka called SuJu. They each had two cups as they noshed on spicy bowls of kimchi.

Many more reciprocal toasts and some grilled-on-the-center-of-the-table meats-veg-and-rice later, his newfound friends took Murf to see some Korean opera. As they drank more SuJu, Murf watched the colorful silk robe-costumed performers keenly. They were mostly men wearing oddly proportioned black top hats. The hats featured large, wide brims and corresponding tiny tops—seemingly way too small to fit firmly atop a man's head. To Murf they looked like Pee Wee's Playhouse-type creations and yet he knew they reflected traditional ceremonial Korean dress of a pre-modern era. Murf was particularly struck by the opera's storyline, as it was shared with the audience by the wise Shaman character.

It was the story of a wayward husband torn between his young mistress and his older wife, whom he still loved and longed for—when she wasn't tearing into him like a banshee for being an old fool. The musical instruments were very unusual. Most were bamboo flutes, roughhewn drums of all sizes and very odd-looking stringed instruments. One of them featured just a single thick string suspended over a curved wooden body that was shaped like an overturned boat. Instead of strumming the string or sawing it with a bow, the musician began striking the string with a stick. It was called a komungo, Murf was told by the still serious Sun-Yung.

Post the one hour-long undertaking of let's-show-the-American-the-great-culture-of-ancient-Korea, the now well-lubricated foursome moved on to another establishment with private sliding door "fun" rooms and walls made of stretched-tight rice paper. The twenty-feet-long, eight-feet-wide room they were ushered into by the hostess, had a sunken seating area in the middle, a karaoke machine by the entrance door, and a small bathroom at the other end. After the men settled in, four barely twenty-something and perpetually smiling women in silk robes brought them drinks. Then one of the girls sat by each man's side, laughing on cue and providing good cuddly company—though they did not join in the drinking. Scotch and beer boilermakers were ordered for all by Sun-Yung for what Murf quickly realized was the beginnings of a friendly drinking competition. "This is what I call a thorough orientation," chuckled Murf.

Numbers were obviously on the Koreans' side and body mass, Irish genetics and a lifetime of training were on Murf's side in the unfolding contest. And yet, the Korean men had little idea how badly overmatched they were. As the drinking game shifted into high gear, Sun-Yung quickly changed his demeanor from senior-most and very serious businessman, to Mr. Big-Daddy-Drinks-A-Lot. The contest was supposed to be about speed drinking and whoever finished his beer and shot last, had to consume an extra shot of Scotch. All four chugged the shot of Scotch down in a blink and then slammed the glass onto the wooden table before depositing it empty into the wide mug of now overflowing beer. As the Koreans each eagerly attacked their first beers, Murf smiled politely and deliberately and steadily drank his beer in one long but unhurried slurp, making sure that he was just a bit slower to drain his glass than them. The Korean men, who had hurriedly choked down their beers, sloppily spilling the liquid onto their suits in the process, roared with laughter and clapped hands in general approval, after winning the first round. Murf just smiled as he glibly knocked back his bonus Scotch shot, asking them innocently and with great sobriety, "You mean I get two drinks to your one, and I'm LOSING the game???!!" he said incredulously with a devilish grin.

After one more identical round, his newfound Korean friends were already getting visibly tipsy from the high-speed drinking and were completely in awe of Murf's unfazed demeanor. To slow the pace of their drunken descent, they now strategically began leaving the table one at a time, ostensibly to use the restrooms, but deliberately missing a round per trip to avoid drinking at the same pace as Murf was. And further, as they filled to bursting with carbonated beer mixed with the masses of air they sucked in as they hurriedly swallowed, they were no longer able to match Murf's seemingly increasing rate of slow and steady-paced beer-drinking. As a result, they began to have to consume the bonus shots instead of him.

As they continued drinking, Murf imagined that he was in the Korean War at the Chosin Reservoir facing wave after wave of Chinese soldiers staging one of their infamous human-wave attacks. But he would hold his ground just as his father did for real there back in 1952, earning a Silver Star in the process. Murf had yet to be born back then, but he grew to love history and to know about and take pride in his dad's military service. For added mischief, Murf now interrupted the Scotch and beer flow to buy the table a halftime round of his favorite-back-in-the-States shots drinking liquor called tequila.

"Teequeewa,???" puzzled the Koreans. Two additional tequila shot rounds later, one white-faced Korean became semi-permanently ensconced in the adjoining bathroom, rooting loudly through the paper-thin walls for that NFL Hall of Fame running back Earl Campbell. "E-E-E-E-A-A-A-A-R-R-R-R-L!" he choked out uncontrollably, followed by coughing and spitting, and then another and another chant of "E-E-E-E-A-A-A-A-R-R-R-R-L!"

Later, Murf learned that two could play at this mixology game. For the final round of the evening, his two remaining drinking buddies retaliated by introducing him to Jinro, a kind of mild-tasting warm, lemony-flavored liquor. This seemingly innocuous drink would make Murf's brain synapses fry and misfire with regularity all of the next day. Murf theorized that it must have been made in North Korea with some antifreeze tossed in to cut it.

The second consecutive night of Murf's continuing orientation/initiation, called for more of the same competitive drinking and then a visit to a karaoke bar. "Rather moist," thought Murf when he met the establishment's two very pretty Korean hostesses. Thanks to the wonders of modern medicine, they sported considerably more "sweater meat" as the Pirates called it, than the average Asian ladies he'd met.

Murf was thereafter subjected to possibly the world's worst rendition of "I Left My Heart in San Francisco" by Sun-Yung, bellowed in Murf's honor. He returned the favor with a howling Bill Murray-esque lounge lizard-version of The Doors' "Touch Me Babe," as the go-go dancing karaoke bar hostesses scrambled to escape Murf's now roaming hands. Afterwards, the Korean men cajoled the two of them into each exposing one bared nipple, which was huge in their minds given that nudity in bars is unlawful and not commonplace in highly modest South Korea—unlike anything goes Hong Kong.

Each woman alternately pulled her blouse aside while looking away dispassionately, and flashed boob for a nanosecond. Then it was over—save for their non-stop nervous giggling, like two dorky teenage girls who had just lost a round of Truth or Dare. Though feeling randy and available, given his wife's seeming indiscretion, Murf was rather turned off by the manner in which this decidedly un-sexy act had unfolded. The girl's tit flash struck Murf as having been no more sexually motivated than a detective who briefly flashes the shiny badge hidden beneath his overcoat.

Later that evening back at his hotel bar, a helpful bartender informed a disinterested Murf that prostitution was illegal in South Korea, but that if a bar girl liked you, there was nothing illegal about you meeting her the next day for sex in your room. "But then you must take her shopping," said the white-apron-wearing barkeep with a knowing grin.

Murf didn't last long at Samsung. He was sent home to San Francisco at the end of his first week, having been summarily rejected by the HR department. In truth, he was whacked largely for the faux pas of drinking better and singing worse than any of them.

CHAPTER 22

Azerbaijani Wannabes

The team for the America mission—code-named "California"—was comprised of the seven mujahedeen warriors who had trained together and grown close aboard a ship in Azerbaijan. Theirs was a brotherhood of righteous discipline and militancy.

Zahadid told the terrorists that they all had something in common. In spite of their origins from countries all over the Middle East, they had all been drawn from different groups of extremist adherents of Salafist Islam, the extreme and strict Wahhabi interpretation of Sunni Islam that Osama bin Laden and his inner circle had long followed. The Wahhabist Saudi sheiks were known for having waged jihad against all of the other forms of Islam, persecuting Shiite Muslims in particular. What the men didn't know was that beyond their shared righteousness, they also had been specifically chosen because they had each suffered terrible personal tragedies that led them to despair and to eventually seek vengeance through extremism. And they had each—like Abdur—been repeatedly tested for unfailing obedience by a highly militant superior who ordered them to commit horrific acts which still haunted most of them. All had, for many months, been drilled on the path to martyrdom. Specifically, they were told that a mission striking the infidels in the United States was the ultimate mujahedeen act and a serious Muslim's obligation; even more important than completing Hajj or pilgrimage somewhere within a lifetime. While most of the men felt privileged to have been selected for such a task, they also felt lucky to have escaped the fate of becoming yet another in a seemingly endless stream of completely expendable suicide bombers.

Most of the extremists had been funneled by jihadist recruitment rings or from online radical-inclined chat rooms to one of the many fundamentalist-bent religious schools, or madrassas, in the tribal areas of Pakistan. It was customary for the clerics of extremist and martyrdom-supportive mosques to send "lost" young men to such a school as a prelude to becoming a mujahedeen. These young men had all but lost hope and desperately needed recognition and any kind of sense of accomplishment. And, as was customary with martyrs for the cause, there was always the promise of seventy-two virgins in heaven and money to be sent to their families or relatives.

"Heaven awaits you," was the standard spiel. "All you need do is serve your people and your god and we will also pay $5,000 or more to buy some land or a house for your loved ones back home. As salaam alaikum (peace be unto you)."

After months and months of lengthy recitations from the Quran and drilling on the specific martyrdom precepts of Wahhabist doctrine including how the jihadi pre-absolves himself of killing innocents and fellow Muslims—each new potential warrior was carefully selected by the school's imam in concert with al-Qaida operatives. The youthful mujahedeen were then sent for further indoctrination, training and toughening in rugged al-Qaida and Taliban-run camps at remote and secret locations. Finally, after about six months of instruction and after repeated tests of commitment and courage in the form of conducting straightforward terrorist tasks, the less promising ones became suicide bombers and the superior ones went on to fight in concert with insurgents operating in Iraq, Yemen, or Afghanistan.

When he was but nine-years old, Salim al-Mujalami's town, Al Hazm, was decimated and his home torched with his family inside, by Yemeni government forces seeking out insurgency supporters. He subsequently grew up stealing fruit. He graduated to bikes, then cars. With deft hands and unbridled daring, he was the team's expert at crime and "resourceful" provisioning. Salim was slender with bushy light-brown hair and green eyes. Though twenty-four years old, he had the face of a fifteen-year-old.

Twenty-six-year-old Imdad Saad was a brilliant and promising young scientist from Minya, Egypt whose wife was accidentally run over and killed by a policeman who was chasing a suspect with his car. Always a voluminous reader, Imdad had gone from being an eloquent, energetic lecturer to becoming a reclusive bookworm. He was of medium build and though wiry, he had a serious and quiet deportment, which his circular-framed eyeglasses only underlined.

While growing up, Youssef Chabab dreamed of and relentlessly practiced singing and dancing to perform on an American Idol-type talent show. That is until his parents were shot to death, allegedly by Israeli Mossad agents, for supposedly being terrorist sect leaders. The twenty-year-old from Khan Yunis in the Gaza Strip of the Palestinian territories was tall at five foot eleven and awkwardly skinny. He could be found during any free time he got, completely wired on coffee inside an internet-wired coffee shop. There he'd be chatting away for hours on Facebook because he was part of the Muslim Diaspora brought together by the social media, Internet phenomenon. Typically Youseff would be ensconced in a Proud 2B Muslim-type discussion group, dissing women who do not dress in accordance with Muslim teachings, while paradoxically also seeking females he could correspond with and fantasize about.

Jamal Ali al-Hakim from Tangier, Morocco was a former heavy-weight wrestler of considerable girth and talent. When fellow students at his university protested state-mandated curriculum changes, troops were called in and subsequently fired on the protestors killing Jamal's inseparable twin brothers. Prematurely balding and short at about five foot four, the twenty-two-year-old had a bushy mustache, huge shoulders and was quick to smile.

The tragedy that had befallen forty-four-year-old Abdur Nidal of Azzun—the loss of his sister and father, as well as his athletic career—were events he rarely ever spoke about.

Twenty-six-year-old Aziz Ahmed Bani from Medina in Saudi Arabia and his mentor Zahadid al-Aboud, a Saudi from Riyadh, were the most militant of the group. Both were generally negative individuals. Similar in height at around five foot six, they were usually almost identically clad—with faces partly obscured behind black cotton shawls and tunics. The unquestioning and instantly obedient Aziz looked as though he could be Zahadid's younger brother. Before shaving it in Azerbaijan, Zahadid had a thick black beard and bushy eyebrows, with deeply sunken and almost frightfully piercing dark eyes. His now beardless face emphasized a jagged scar from a close call in bomb making. The scar ran across his face just under his eyes and over his sharply angled and crooked nose. Joyless was an apt descriptor for both men, that is, if you don't count the kick they both got out of killing. Aziz specialized in extreme piety and in the brutal enforcement of their ultra-orthodox beliefs and policies. He had personally stoned or shot to death more than a half-dozen women in rural villages in Afghanistan and Pakistan. Their crimes? Often, they were accused of adultery. Though, most had actually been raped. Others stood accused of being immodest for not wearing veils, or for riding on the back of a motorcycle driven by a man they were not married to, or worse, for daring to attend school instead of staying home to faithfully serve fathers or husbands.

Zahadid began his terror track record at age fourteen by

firebombing and burning numerous Riyadh stores that sold music after his mullah declared all music to be un-Islamic. That caused relatives to shuttle him off to Pakistan and away from government pursuit. There, he progressed to organizing attacks on fellow students at the religious school he attended, when they did not take the severe Wahhabi doctrine they studied as seriously as he did. At sixteen, he pistol-whipped a teacher at a more liberal neighboring school for loaning books to village girls to study on their own at home. Zahadid then held him upright and shot him right in the eye in front of the entire class. The number of marketplace bombings, assassinations of policemen, explosions of buses filled with commuting workers, and attacks upon Shiite pilgrims that followed from this dynamo of evil, were too many to enumerate. His raison d'etre now was wielding the unadulterated power of a perversely apocalyptic religious mutation, with the intent of emerging as a force in world politics.

After their initial rapid-fire training on the waters of the Caspian and then working on a "coaster" out of Hong Kong for seasoning, Zahadid told his trainees that he had arranged with a bribery-receptive Chinese manning agent for them all to be hired as crewmen on a ship in the harbor. They learned they would go to work on the Panamanian-registered cargo ship called the *Fenix*. It was ironic that the ship chosen for their mission against America was named *Fenix*—which is the Spanish spelling for Phoenix—the bird of legend that arose from the ashes anew after bursting into flames mid flight. Their undertaking was al-Qaida-directed and funded by extremist Iranian and Saudi groups. Orders had come through Mullah Omar's Quetta Shura or Taliban leadership council, but they had originated with the new post-Osama bin Laden supreme leader, Ayman al-Zawahri.

On their final night together in Hong Kong, Zahadid gave the men a minimalist mission briefing. His henchman, Aziz, remained back in the shadows, but Abdur stood by his side given his vast fighting experience and role as the second-in-command line officer for the team. As the men listened attentively, Abdur's was the face of reason and wisdom versus Zahadid's, which emanated absolute authority and instilled abject fear. Zahadid had always thought Abdur to be an arrogant rich kid at heart and, in his mind, he believed that Abdur did not thoroughly enough embrace Salafism. But Zahadid, and all who came to know Abdur, thought him to be a man of great purpose—a brave and cunning warrior and a deeply principled idealist. His valor and commitment had been repeatedly and thoroughly demonstrated. Abdur, on the other hand, thought Zahadid to be unconscionably cruel and manipulating. To him, he seemed all about politics and grabbing power versus being the vigorous defender of Islamic religious beliefs that he pretended to be.

"Tomorrow, when we board the ship, you should separate as much as possible so as not to raise suspicions," instructed Zahadid. "Stay nearby to each other in the sleeping quarters, but do not gather together in groups of more than two and try to mix in with the rest of the crew. You must push yourselves to go out amongst the crew to meet other seamen. You should even try to make friends with them. We must take care never to be seen all together as a group, so meeting will be very infrequent and messages will be passed to each of you through Aziz. When you are seen together in small groups of two or three, remember that you are to act as acquaintances but not close friends," said Zahadid. "And each of you remember your cover story! We know each other only a little, because we worked together on the same ship operating out of Azerbaijan for a few months. A manning agent found us work here in Hong Kong, but it cost each of us a year's wages to relocate here and get these jobs. In about twenty days time we will arrive in San Francisco and from there we will be transported by van down to Southern California to conduct reconnaissance to find the best possible sites for our attack."

Upon hearing this, Youssef stood up and shouted, "I'm going to Disneyland!" like Joe Montana leaving the field after a Super Bowl victory. While Abdur and the team had a brief laugh over his joke, Zahadid was incensed at the frivolity and that Youssef had unknowingly uttered the name of the real target of their mission—which Zahadid intended to keep from the men until very late in the game.

"Enough silliness!" screamed Zahadid slamming his fist onto the table in front of him for emphasis. "You are to be forgiven for not always eating Halal, for not dressing Hijab, for listening to forbidden music, cursing and looking at videos with unclothed women, all in the name of seeming to be ordinary sailors. But if you let yourselves become soft and Westernized like the godless infidels we oppose, you will never see heaven and your families will be punished for your failure!"

Zahadid was extremely irked by his suspicion that the men might be enjoying their immersion in more worldly customs. With the men's attention now completely captured, he continued the briefing, "The California site has yet to be finalized by our high command. We may strike at Hollywood, Beverly Hills, Santa Monica or Pasadena. Perhaps we will hit Seaworld, Knotts Berry Farm, Disneyland or Malibu Beach," said a clearly unfeeling Zahadid most indifferently. "Regardless, careful preparations are being made for precise timings, dependable transportation, and many weapons. Arrangements are even being made for a few females and small children to accompany us in public places," said Zahadid dispassionately as a number of eyebrows were raised and some astonished expressions were borne by the men. "This will be done so that we do not appear to be a large group of Middle Eastern men suspiciously traveling together—but rather we are seen as tourists, with what appear to be girlfriends or wives, out seeing the sights."

Zahadid leaned forward and began progressively glaring—one at a time—right into each man's eyes to gauge their seriousness and commitment. "It is the duty of Muslims to prepare as much force as possible to terrorize the enemies of God. That is what our former supreme commander bin Laden said," laid out Zahadid with the rising fervor of a sermon coming to crescendo. "The bomb we will pick up in Asia and deliver to Southern California will be a large one capable of causing the deaths of more than one hundred thousand Americans. It will be hidden inside a Hanjin container from South Korea, along with a dozen assault rifles, pistols, ammunition, suicide bomb vests and grenades. With the very threat of this massive bomb's destructive power, we will be able to force the swift withdrawal of American forces from every Muslim country they have invaded and free all of the political prisoners they hold," he said with absolute confidence. "And if they force us to detonate the bomb, it will be a glorious death for all of us and a victorious attack on our American enemies that will surpass even 9/11 and bring fear to every corner of the U.S.! We are in God's hands now. That is all," concluded Zahadid who then finished by shouting the Islamist takbir in Arabic. "Allahu Akbar! Allah is the greatest!"

"Allahu Akbar!" replied all of the men loudly and with staunch commitment.

What Zahadid was not telling them was that the bomb was not made just from conventional explosives and it was, in fact, a "dirty" bomb made with both a huge concentration of explosives and about twenty-five pounds of highly toxic depleted plutonium 239. The explosion would both kill and broadly spread radioactive poisoning and death to hundreds of thousands in the short-term and, over a span of just a few years more, would cause radiation poisoning, cancer and death to potentially millions more. This is what accounted for the noticeable extra weight in the replacement container the men had been training to lift and stack. The extra weight was caused by the lead lining of this special-made container. The lead was added not to protect the men from radiation, but to protect the mission from detection via the new radiation detection system that al-Qaida intelligence had reported was being added to the port of Long Beach's security protocols.

The first Pacific Ocean crossing for the men was a tough one with three separate storms torturing them and setting the ship two days behind schedule. Along the way, the work was backbreaking, the shifts very long, and both the food and sleep exceedingly poor. After steaming in under San Francisco's famous Golden Gate Bridge, they reached land again some twenty-one challenging days later. The first real threat to the new marine Muslim terrorist cell was soon surpassed just after docking, when all seven men made it through immigration and customs scrutiny in Oakland, without a single incident. Each then separately made their way walking to a street corner about six blocks away from the dock, where two white vans with drivers were waiting to drive them down to Los Angeles.

"We will soon arrive at our site inspection destination," said Zahadid sternly as he alternated his stare into each one of the men's eyes to ensure rapt attention, while also searching for signs of anything less than total commitment. "Abdur and the main body of men will act like tourists and scout out the park's flow of traffic, spots where the greatest number of people congregate, and for escape alternatives should anything go wrong," he continued.

"Commander Zahadid," interrupted Salim, "what place has been chosen for our attack?"

"It has not been decided yet, but your assignment today is to scout the logistics of an attack on Disneyland," Zahadid said nonchalantly as though he had just cited a local dry cleaners as the target. The others in the van remained silent at the news, but their eyes looked intently from one to another in disbelief. "Aziz and I will concentrate on the Monorail moving overhead all around the park. Now as you know, Abdur and Aziz are inside the other van and they will pick up three local women and their six kids, while we stop for prayers and food. These infidels are being paid to join us in the park so that we will not appear suspicious or get stopped when park security forces apply racial profiling to us as a group," continued Zahadid by way of briefing. "And remember, you are sailors from Azerbaijan. Tell them nothing more. And no pictures! Do not let them photograph any of you. Now Jamal and Imdad can pretend to be husbands to two of the women and the children. The other woman can be positioned as Salim's girlfriend," said Zahadid.

"Excuse me commander," asked a very concerned looking Youssef. "Why has Salim been chosen to have an American girlfriend and not

Abdur, or Aziz or perhaps me?" inquired Youssef tentatively with eyes looking downward from Zahadid's stern gaze.

"SILENCE!! Do not question your orders!" screamed Zahadid. "Just follow them! Do you want a pretend American girlfriend or seventy two virgins in heaven with The Prophet by your side?!!"

"Both would be nice…" said Youssef quietly and all too honestly.

"SILENCE!!! Such lust is haram—forbidden. You filthy dog!!!" Zahadid yelled at Youssef. Now suddenly grasping Youssef by the chin and forcefully jerking on it to raise the young man's eyes up so that he could glare right into them. "You still have living relatives in Gaza and we know just who and where they are. Do as you are instructed or you and what remains of your family will die!" spat a now highly irritated Zahadid, with shocked faces all around him in the van.

In order to re-establish a sense of Islamic decorum as they continued the long drive from Northern California toward Los Angeles and the epitome of Western decadence, Zahadid led the men in a long series of nasheeds or Islamic songs and recitations from the Quran. The enthusiasm in the van for this pious outpouring was weaker than a mixed drink in a strip club.

Meanwhile in the other van, Aziz informed Abdur about the pick-up of the women and the kids, just before they stopped to get them at the prearranged site—a Ralph's Grocery Store on Wilshire near Korea Town. "You have spent time with the infidels in America and speak excellent English," hissed Aziz. "Therefore Zahadid and I have decided that while we focus on the Monorail above, you will lead the men on the ground—with these women and kids amongst you. You are to act just as tourists would act, while also thoroughly scouting the Disneyland Park and its security."

"Where did they come from? Are they Muslim women who are part of our cause, or are they actors?" asked Abdur rapid fire, fearing the vulnerability to his team of outsiders being allowed to join them on a mission.

"They know nothing of our cause or who we are," replied Aziz indignantly. "They each answered a notice our LA sleeper cell leader put in something called Craigslist. I would say they are indeed actors of a kind—for they are all literally whores and some of them have even had children out-of-wedlock who will accompany them. And our men are not to have anything to do with them beyond visiting the park with them and acting like a family on holiday!" commanded Aziz as though he were now in charge of both piety and the entire mission. Abdur rolled his eyes as he could only imagine the context and specifics of this "Single-Mom-Hookers-Wanted" ad on Craigslist.

"Hi there, hon. You're in a white van, just like what was discussed. Are you the sailors from the Craigslist ad?" asked a very loquacious, mid-thirties and heavily made-up woman with tall, beehive shaped bleached blonde hair. She was holding the hand of a pigtailed, brown-haired little girl who was about five years old named Deirdre. She also had a one-year-old boy named Shawon strapped into the stroller she was pushing. Behind them were other painted ladies and kids.

"Yes, please get in," responded Aziz with a feigned smile and a gentle wave of his arm beckoning them inside.

"I'm Shandra, honey," she responded with a smile and a wink. "C'mon everyone, get inside the van. We're going to Disneyland!" The happy and now cheering throng pushed forward. Abdur first helped Shandra with the stroller and then assisted the other children and women up the step and into their seats.

"Ain't chu da gentaman," said a short and buxom-with-enormous-implants Vietnamese lady. "Caw me Littaw Dot. You can be my husban' any day," she said flirting wantonly and speaking in thick, recent-émigré accent. Her eight and six year old daughter and son were both clearly mulatto with the tightly curled hair and handsome African-American features—yet with hair that was reddish blonde and eyes of blue.

"I'm MO-nique, Sugar," said the third female who was a late forties, slightly heavy Hispanic woman with a pleasing smile and ample booty as they say. The only disconcerting aspect to Monique's appearance was that she had spent her ill-gotten gains to get more low quality facelifts than the front row of a Wayne Newton concert. One of her two children was a seven-year-old-boy with red hair, freckles and lighter skin. The other was a very tiny five-year-old boy with Asian eyes and dark, straight hair.

"Now as we agreed," said Shandra with a smile but with an I'm-all-business-right-now tone, "we get paid in advance." she said extending her right hand toward Aziz. "And we were told that we're just going to enjoy a fun day in the park because y'all miss your families back home so much. Right?" she asked batting her eyes with Bo-peep-like innocence. Dutifully Aziz handed her an envelope packed with small bills. As she glanced at and thumbed through the money inside, a very pleased-with-herself Shandra went for broke. "But of course you also have to pay for our tickets to get in," she said solicitously.

"Of course," Abdur replied cutting off Aziz who was about to disagree.

"And then the kids will need lunch…" she continued with her hands raised and palms turned upwards.

"Indeed. And they will have it," assured Abdur as he asserted command. Aziz receded back into the shadows of the van. Once the vans had each parked separately in the as-vast-as-an-ocean Disney parking lots, Aziz called Zahadid by cell phone and the two groups made plans to link up after a three-minute tram ride to the park's main entrance.

"We are in the Captain Hook lot," sneered Zahadid, clearly disgusted as they approached the epitome of Western decadence.

"We are parked in something called Tinkerbell. This tiny woman has wings and a very short, green dress with brazenly bared shoulders and arms bared," said a thoroughly puzzled Aziz. "What do these things mean?" he asked Zahadid.

"It matters not. Just remember the name so we can find our transport when it comes time to leave," he replied tersely.

The crewmen all had dancing eyes as they silently studied the women during the welcome-to-Disneyland-folks-intercom-blasting tram ride. That is until after the group had paid and entered the main gates, and Zahadid and Aziz briefly joined them and then very abruptly bid them goodbye to go ride the Monorail repeatedly. Now the men became jovial and each introduced themselves to the women and kids like competing bachelors on a hokey, dating-game reality show.

"Well, those other two weren't exactly Prince Charming, anyway," said Shandra as they separated. "Let's go have us a good time, people!" she concluded as the kids cheered. A number of the men did likewise—albeit silently to themselves. In moments, the men became wide-eyed, jaws-opened stunned as they began to walk up Main Street U.S.A. accompanied by the sounds of joyfully screaming children and delighted mothers. Clang-clang went the firehouse iron bell as the old-time, horse-drawn fire engine rolled past with its smiling and waving helmet-wearing fire brigade aboard. Heads pivoted constantly, as the bug-eyed entourage passed the Disney character-jammed souvenir shops, ice cream sundae and candy stores, and then reached the circle adorned with the bronze statue of Walt and Mickey holding hands and welcoming all to the park.

And then suddenly, there he was—the man—that is, THE mouse. Mickey Mouse is a character well known even in the Arab world and there he stood before the group with his bulbous black shoes, bright red pants, black jacket with white vest and yellow bow tie. He of the permanently frozen and transcendent face, with his Buddha-type beatific smile, huge, wide-open eyes and raised-in-unbridled-excitement eyebrows, that immediately both welcome and warm all who befall his gaze. The men smartly opted not to actually be captured in any of the photos, but they happily took many pictures of the main Mouse waving at them, hugging the ecstatic moms and their non-stop giggling kids. After Mickey waved goodbye and disappeared back into the crowd, the joyous group began practically skipping together down the cobbled street and they were soon in sight of the distant view majesty of Sleeping Beauty's castle, which anchors the Fantasyland section of the park. Off to their right and far away, yet looming large, arose the picturesque Matterhorn with individual red, yellow and dark blue bobsleds descending in downward circumnavigations. Also on the side of the mountain was an oversized-white-furball of a Yeti, periodically popping up mid-mountain with arms raised threateningly. Abdur was amazed at what he saw, but was still managing to take mental notes on the layout of the expanse and the mostly behind-the-scenes security he spotted. The rest of the men were wearing massive smiles and were now completely swept up in the wonder that is a first-ever-trip to Disneyland.

As the men curried favor with the three professionally accommodating ladies, there was an endless stream of questions from them. "Why does the beauty have to sleep so much?" "What job has this Peter Pan to dress like this?" "And how does this a Jim-a-nay the Cricket animal come to talk like a professor?"

The women patiently answered what seemed to them to be the dumbest questions from the biggest dopes on earth. Their answers varied between the truth and just a good story, made up in absence of knowing the real answer. But there was no stopping the kids from wanting to ride the rides. Abdur instructed the men to partake because they were, after all, tourists. And they did so with obvious relish. With Shandra and the Disney attendants help, they were quickly separated into ride-sized groups and soon soared with Peter Pan and his band of brave lads, over Captain Hook's ship and a giant, jaw-snapping crocodile.

As they pushed deeper into the park, they encountered the absolute-must-ride for all. Even Abdur was chided into joining in with the group and spinning himself senseless alongside Shandra in a white on the outside and bright teal inside, over-sized teacup and saucer. This was quickly followed by the equally classic ride, which the Middle Eastern men called Dumbo-the-giant-eared-flying-elephant ride.

Afterwards, the now thirsty group stopped for a fresh-squeezed lemonade. As they were sipping the cool, sweet-and-sour home-made delight, Cinderella waltzed through the area waving like a beauty queen with her million-dollar smile, baby-blue gown with puffed sleeves and matching blue ribbon holding back her blonde hair. Even without the costume, the young lady playing the role was a stunning beauty and the men were transfixed by her every move and utterance. "Hello everyone, I'm late for the ball," she cooed.

As had been agreed with Shandra in advance, Abdur paid for everything. He kept track of the mounting expenses as best he could and he carefully peeled off bills to pay for lemonade, caramel corn and even one red helium balloon for each child. The kids' smiles and squeals were priceless. While they sat, Abdur eavesdropped on a conversation going on between two fathers seated at the table next to him. Realizing that they were in the middle of telling a joke, he zeroed in on it. "You know why Mickey is pissed at his girlfriend Minnie Mouse don't you?" asked the one man to the other.

"No, I don't," he replied playing along dutifully.

"Because he thinks she's fuckin' Goofy," came the response.

Later, as they stopped for lunch and more thoroughly studied the park map, a common theme emerged from the men and was shared with Abdur as a master plan for approval. The theory advanced was that since they were all seamen, all rides that featured marine vessels must be experienced. This led to an afternoon of non-stop fun, first with a taste of nautical history on the three-masted sailing ship Columbia, then floating through the subterranean Pirates of the Caribbean lair, followed by canoeing in tandem on Davey Crockett's Explorer Canoes, then receiving the Captain's permission to toot the heard-throughout-the-park steam whistle aboard Mark Twain's Riverboat. Next, they experienced the exotic sounds and sights on the Jungle Cruise, then they went plunging beneath the sea inside the formerly Captain Nemo's now Finding Nemo's submarine in Tomorrowland. After that, came a thorough soaking and the automatic stationary-camera photographed remembrance of a five-story plunge in a huge log boat on Splash Mountain. Finally, they capped off the day with the quintessential Disneyland ride—that-damned-repetitious-tune-is-permanently-lodged-inside-my-skull-slow-boat-through "It's a Small World After All" hell. But of course to the collective group of ultra-happy campers, it was heaven on earth.

After the Small World coup de grace, warm farewells to the kids and ladies were exchanged by all with several of the men receiving whispered-in-the-ear invitations for no-charge-extracurricular-activities at a later date by the three ladies, who were genuinely thrilled with the good time they and their children had been shown. A look of post-pleasure melancholy befell the faces of the men as they waved at the departing families they had just helped into two cabs. Youssef, in particular, seemed very down and a concerned Abdur approached him as he leaned against a fence staring off into space. "Youssef, what troubles you?" asked Abdur in a consoling tone.

"I don't want to kill all those sweet, happy babies wearing the Mickey-Mouse ears and Goofy hats," said a visibly upset Youssef with head bowed.

"One-thousand Disneylands will be yours in heaven, Youssef," said Abdur dutifully and convincingly—though he now had his own doubts. "Remember that those nice children will go instantly to heaven, too. They will never feel any pain and will become martyrs for jihad. And when we are someday martyred, we will all be together again, enjoying Disneyland rides forever," said Abdur with affection for a young man who in spite of his life's hardships, had still not completely forgotten the not too distant joys of his own childhood. It was a memorable and extremely revealing day. Especially amazing was the revelation of a considerable spark of humanity that still burned within the hearts of most of these hardened killers.

Meanwhile up riding in the Monorail and often whispering their disgust for such unimaginable American decadence, were Zahadid and Aziz. "Prevailing evening winds blow west to northwest," said Aziz perfunctorily.

"Yes, this is good, replied Zahadid with the wolfish grin of a man with an insatiable appetite for terror. "From the Tomorrowland Monorail stop, the poison would create a kill zone running from Anaheim up toward Fullerton, Placentia, Yorba Linda and Chino Hills."

CHAPTER 23

A Flag of Convenience

Back now from Korea and packing for his planned bender on the coast up at Salt Point, Murf had given up on looking for work. Lively & Partners and the other ad agencies he called never quite got around to getting back to him with an answer. Murf was now resigned to his failure as a working professional, a husband and a father. Given his life-long love for all things aquatic, he had imagined once or twice before what it might feel like to someday meet his demise at sea. When he could resist it no more, arms too dead-tired to paddle farther, he would cock his head back and then slip beneath the salty water, which would then fill his lungs and end his life. He imagined that with the life-in-ruins resignation now pouring in on him, this might just be the way it feels to drown. Murphy Morrison was now drowning in his own life.

Hangdogged with his going-down-for-the-last-time blues, Murf told Terri in a note that he was going camping by himself up on the north coast to do research for the great American novel he was now planning to write. He decided that, just like his Hermann Melville favorite, Moby Dick, it was going to be all about the sea.

After Murf attempted to clear his head with a bit of campfire coffee, following his bizarre Good Morning Webelos-encounter, he began thinking back to that container ship on the horizon. Murf was reminded that he'd really gone camping to test-drive the idea of dropping out of his current life and essentially abandoning his family and the career he once loved so. Maybe the solution to escaping all of his problems was aboard one of the ships he'd been fascinated with all of his life. He then started to brainstorm ideas.

He reached into his duffle bag and retrieved a file he had kept hidden among his most personal things for many years. Labeled, "The Sea," it contained scraps and clips related to the ocean-going life. There was a clipping from an old newspaper re-telling how a bunch of scouts from the local summer camp had been badly stung by jellyfish after their canoes overturned. Only now could he laugh about that debacle. There was a program from a Jack London play he once talked Terri into seeing with him. It had been staged by an acting troupe that actually performed inside the tall-masted and historic sailing ship Balclutha, docked along the San Francisco waterfront. There was a fading color snapshot of a young and very-much-in-love couple, Murf and Terri, taking a boat ride on the Seine in Paris on vacation. His eyes puddled up at the sight of it and the tender memories it conjured.

They pretty much managed to work a boat-ride or ship cruise into all of their vacations. There was another very unusual Polaroid of a buck-naked group of men and women smiling and waving happily to the camera from atop a houseboat deck. It captured a too-weird-not-to-be-true story of how Murf and Terri had come unanchored from an overnight sail during a fast-moving storm. The wind gusts and waves pushed Murf's untethered boat across the channel. When he failed to get the engine started, the now adrift *We're in Trouble* truly was. Spying a nearby and well-anchored houseboat, Murf used the tiller for propulsion and nearly killed himself by pushing it back and forth again and again to move his boat enough to eventually drift alongside of the houseboat. When he shouted for permission to come aboard, he was quickly greeted by the naked people in the photo, who came up from down below deck. They'd been in the midst of a swappers' party when Murf interrupted to ask for an assist. Though Murf and Terri accepted the invitation to tie-up until the storm had passed, Murf declined the invitation the swappers also extended to join in on the immediately resuming sex party.

There was also a National Geographic story all about the difficult life of manual toil experienced by Louisiana oilrig workers and shrimp fishermen. There was a twice-read copy of Annie Proulx's *The Shipping News* which had led Murf to begin seeing himself—much like the protagonist—as a bit of a doofus and a misfit in life, in spite of outward appearances to the contrary. There was a coaster he'd saved from Red's Java House, an old rummy bar and café at water's edge over by the working docks. Murf had begun to frequent Red's just to hang out a bit with real seamen and to hear their stories and tall tales of life on the water. There were also reams and reams of paper that he'd printed out from web sites he'd been using to research ocean-going ships. At the bottom of the pile, was a copy of a book he'd bought and forgotten to read called, *The Outlaw Sea* by William Langewiesche.

"A world of freedom, chaos, and crime," promised the book cover provocatively. "Forty-three thousand gargantuan ships ply the open ocean carrying nearly all the raw materials and products on which our lives are built. Many are owned or managed by one-ship companies so ghostly that they exist only on paper. They are the embodiment of modern global capital, and the most independent objects on earth—many of them without allegiances of any kind, changing identities and nationalities at will. Here is free enterprise at its freest, opportunity taken to extremes. But its efficiencies are accompanied by global problems—shipwrecks and pollution, the hard lives and deaths of the crews, and the growth of two perfectly adapted pathogens: a modern and sophisticated strain of piracy and its close cousin, the maritime form of the new stateless terrorism."

Murf was completely hooked and began hungrily pouring through the book.

Langewiesche's central tenet was that the system known as "flags of convenience" had created enormous fleets of dangerously operated ships and that the oceans have become beyond governmental control. Ironically, the U.S. initiated this "flags of convenience" maritime construct on the eve of WWII as an end around its own neutrality laws to allow shipping of restricted cargo to countries that would later become formal allies after declarations of war. In essence, the open-registry convenience construct allows any country—both those with coastal access and those that are land locked—to recognize ships for a fee. Thus they become registered as being from that country's homeport and said country can apply or not to them whatever laws it chooses. The reality is that the more lax the regulation and enforcement, the bigger the fee-based revenue enjoyed by this country. As a result, Panama is the largest maritime country in the world, followed by Liberia. Therefore according to the author, tens of thousands of ships bearing "flags of convenience" sail the seas with little, if any, oversight and no legal accountability for criminal actions unless they are captured inside a country's twelve-miles-from-shore sovereign territory zone.

"In some of the worst case scenarios, aged and unfit ships are loaded with volatile cargo like petroleum, and manned by impoverished multinational crews with dubious training, hired by sometimes unscrupulous Third World manning agents, at the behest of offshore management companies with elusive ownership," wrote Langewiesche.

"Of the world's commercial-sized ships," continued Langewiesche, "43,000 fly flags of convenience—many from countries with lax safety standards and with low-paid crews held in what, in some cases, amounts almost to slavery. Crews are paid as little as $1.50 an hour and do not really undergo thorough background checks. The oldest (25 plus years) and most decrepit of these ships can sometimes slip unchallenged through what little port inspection exists, and worst case scenario, are later lost with their crews at sea in massive storms, and then ultimately cause massive levels of lethal pollution when the oil washes ashore."

According to Langewiesche, dozens of large ships are lost every year. But horrific pollution from shipwrecks and the loss of crew lives are only the tip of the iceberg, to use a horrible maritime pun. There is an even worse case scenario. "The United States has ninety-five thousand miles of coastline," wrote Langewiesche, "and more than a hundred seaports capable of handling large ships... more than sixty thousand port calls by ocean going ships, the great majority of which are foreign flagged, owned by offshore companies, and crewed by anonymous sailors—almost all of whom come from troubled parts of the world where America is resented, corruption is rife, and authentic documentation can easily be bought."

The resulting influx of six million containers a year cannot all be checked and, according to the writer, the U.S. manages to intercept and search only 16,000 ships per year.

"Of course, what is on everyone's mind," wrote Langewiesche, "is that a nuclear device or some other weapon of mass destruction will pass through a port without being discovered, and will subsequently be carried by truck or train to whatever target is deemed most desirable."

Despite an ability to run intercepts that has expanded greatly in recent years, there is not much the allied navies and U.S. Coast Guard can do to stop every such threat. "Osama bin Laden is said to own or control up to twenty aging freighters..." said Langewiesche. "In 1998, one of them delivered the explosives to Africa that were used to bomb the U.S. embassies in Kenya and Tanzania."

In a post 9/11 world, the Langewiesche's contention is that "...in the United States, many officials have come to regard the ocean with grave concern, believing that a full blown maritime attack would make those of September 11 seem puny by comparison," and that "such an attack currently poses the most serious threat to national security, and that when the attack comes it will involve the use of merchant ships."

As Murf read this expertly crafted narrative about the calamitous world of ocean shipping, there were other key passages that burned into his brain, like they "are crewed from pools of the poor...largely who are mixed without reference to such petty conventions as language and nationality." Murf read into this particular passage the word, OPPORTUNITY.

From other articles on the shipping industry, which he later downloaded and devoured, Murf learned that heavily advertised airborne freight giant FedEx notwithstanding, ninety-five percent of the world's total cargo volume is transported by ship. Hong Kong, Singapore, Shanghai, Shenzhen (China), Busan (South Korea), and Kaohsiung (Taiwan) are the biggest shipping centers in the Far East and the top ten U.S. ports for container ships were from east to west: NY/New Jersey, Charleston, Norfolk, Hampton Roads, Savannah, Houston, Los Angeles, Long Beach, Oakland, Seattle, and Tacoma. Each had its own specialization with the West Coast ports focused on consumer goods, apparel, machinery and vehicles, and the eastern and southern ones centered around agriculture, furniture, pharmaceuticals, and petroleum. And the growth therein has been exponential due to Americans' love of imported goods and a doubling of U.S./International trade during the 1990-2000 period. The explosion of the container shipping business or using standardized, corrugated metal containers—moved from ships to rail and trucks—had taken off as a worldwide industry in the 1950s. A former North Carolina trucker named Malcolm McLean drove it initially. He was the first to load trucking freight trailers on a conventional ocean-going tanker in New Jersey. Sea-Land was the name of McLean's company and the network that unfolded thereafter. Eventually, R.J. Reynolds acquired it. But over time, U.S. companies had difficulty remaining competitive in the container shipping arena, because of the growing dominance of low-cost Asian crews used by those who operated exclusively under flags of convenience. As a result, AP Moller-Maersk of Copenhagen—the world's largest container-based network—now owns Sea-Land.

In one magazine article about the industry, Murf read, "In terms of the ships—or 'box boats' as they are known in the business—economies of scale are driving a trend toward enormity. Demand for the new 1,000+ feet-long super-sized container ships being regularly launched during the ongoing worldwide trade boom, have driven a shipbuilding spree. As a result, the new mega-ships must squeeze carefully into U.S. ports that were designed for smaller ships. The ports were also built to handle less volume than they are now handling and most are upgrading and expanding as quickly as they can.

"For comparison purposes, the Titanic was some 883 feet in length and the massive new generation of container ships that are now hitting the seas range from 1,100 feet or nearly a quarter mile long, to as big as 1,300 feet long. Such a behemoth is more than three football fields in length and far too wide to fit inside the Panama Canal; which, incidentally, is also being widened. The above and below deck payload or container capacity of the big ships can run as high as 15,000 of the standardized twenty foot long cargo containers stacked both below deck and above, and sometimes as tall as six or seven stories high. Speed is another modern ship construction differentiator. Versus the almost thirty-five knots or forty mph maximum speed of a nuclear-powered aircraft carrier, one of these industrial sea giants can run twenty-six knots or thirty mph all-out. Older, smaller container ships and bulk carriers crawl along by comparison at fifteen to seventeen knots, which adds considerable time to an oceanic crossing. This translates into a passage of twenty-some days at a rate of about 400 miles a day, from Los Angeles to Australia (known to seamen as the Boomerang Run). Since the advent of modern day trade levels and bigger payload ships, ocean-transport now runs year 'round. The peak-season is August through October, which coincides with the ramp up to fill American stores with goods for the fourth quarter. And that means ports are open nights and weekends then to help fill shops and stores throughout the land with toys, electronics and clothes prior to the big holiday shopping season."

A little known fact about the industry is that foreign companies—and in some cases companies controlled by foreign governments—already partly or wholly manage over 60 percent of the terminals at America's largest port. When information like this surfaces in the post 9/11 U.S., a political firestorm can ensue. As one newspaper story put it, "such was the case recently when it became well spot-lit in the news, that Dubai Ports World was in line to be named to operate large U.S. port facilities. While that move was derailed by a burst of opposition by the U.S. Congress, the foreign operation of U.S. ports is a fait accompli and really is a result and reflection of the global nature of the maritime industry and the dominant position the global shipping lines based in China, Taiwan, Japan, Singapore, and Denmark have built. And the logic is hard to argue with from an efficiency perspective, because integration strategies rationalize that they should run the facilities that are handling the cargo they ship. Since each terminal is technically leased to an individual operator that is responsible for moving the containers off the ships and to the storage areas for pickup, volume of trade is the decisive factor as to who ends up running most of the port's terminals. Long Beach is a good example of this with COSCO (China Ocean Shipping Company) in the catbird's seat due to the enormous volume of goods brought into Long Beach from China."

Another reporter really honed in on shipping industry security. "Today, only 5% of cargo containers entering U.S. ports get inspected. And relative to issues of national security, container ship inspection remains in the hands of our federal enforcement agencies, which include the U.S. Coast Guard, U.S. Customs, and Border Protection, the TSA or Transportation Security Administration and the FBI. As a direct byproduct of 9/11, the Coast Guard, our first line of defense, is now reporting in to the Department of Homeland Security. It also now receives incremental funding to combat terrorism. The result of these changes is that the number and frequency of ship searches are up significantly. Nevertheless, they still represent searching only a minority of the incoming traffic, as well as the proverbial finding a needle in a haystack type of search. Given that there are a total of more than thirty million boats on the waters and container ships' cargos are stacked to towering heights and nearly impossible to thoroughly search, the task is a nearly impossible one. Opening most arriving containers would take too much time and would slow an industry that puts a premium on speed and efficiency unacceptably. Some container ports do have radiation detectors, but unexploded nuclear devices—while radioactive—when hidden beneath lead coatings, emit almost undetectably low levels of radio-activity. And using radiography technology to look for abnormally high concentrations of lead inside of containers, is almost unheard of largely due to the enormous size of such an apparatus. Handheld scanners are the appropriate solution but unfortunately are a long way from coming to market. Seemingly, the strategy of our authorities, at present, is to frighten away terrorists by convincing them through our public conferences and rhetoric, that the security of the U.S. maritime industry is now a paramount priority and that therefore, any attempt to attack the country through ships arriving in our ports would be doomed to fail."

Evildoers beware, thought Murf. We are on it, big time!!! The article concluded, "The other port security facet of shipping via the oceans, is in the area of the dockside unloading and loading. The onset of another recession, has exacerbated an already tenuous situation in that there have been significant reductions in both jobs and hours to be worked. This creates the kind of economic pressure that invites corruption. Throw some corner-cutting hiring practices into the mix—can you say felons working at the docks?—and then add in sloppy screening for security risks. For good measure, then mix in some graft, bribery, dancing around federal rules, cargo 'gone missing' and you potentially have the formula for chronic chaos and crime, and potentially, far more dire consequences."

What Murf selectively garnered from all this information that other folks would largely find frightening, was that his hair-brained plan had a fair chance of succeeding. With all of the shipping industry information now well digested, he set about bolstering his confidence by making more frequent visits to the docks for further observation. Murf was beginning to feel thoroughly prepared and comfortable enough to potentially go ahead and let his wild fantasy scheme actually unfold.

Back in the city, he visited a bookstore for reference material so that he could learn the rudiments of the crews' many different native languages. Murf purchased a copy of Mandarin for Dummies, Thai for Dummies, Filipino for Dummies, Albanian for Dummies, and a bunch of other linguistic short-cut books, with the later-on regrettable exception of Arabic for Dummies. His intent was to be able to understand enough of the basic languages he'd be overhearing, to where he'd be forewarned if he were, in fact, suspected of being an imposter in the new role he planned for himself as a ship's cook. He also wanted to be able to converse a bit, in order to get input from the crew to keep them well-fed and happy. A web site named edgylingo.com that he discovered later, had more of the really useful foreign language slang phrases that he desired. He thought they'd come in handy so he could casually toss in a few raunchy lines and authentic profanities to spice things up and help him come off like a worldly seafarer. "Slow down this cab right now or I'll vomit on your neck," was one such phrase (translated into English from Albanian), that Murf had read and found amusing. But that one seemed more applicable for a crazed taxi driver in Rome than for where he wanted to go. In preparation, Murf was also bolstering his repertoire of recipes at web sites that featured prize-winning Asian, Indonesian and Eastern European dishes.

The next week, Murf was down and hanging out at Red's Java House again. This time he was dressed even more so like a working seaman with unfashionable and well-worn jeans, boots with non-slip boating soles, and a beige work shirt. Since he had not shaved from the time he had left for his Salt Point camping escape, he now sported a close-cropped reddish-brown beard with gray streaks. At Red's he sat right next to two squabbling, seagoing types—a Filipino manning agent whose name he never discerned and a so-called galley boy who was actually a fifty-one-year-old Thai named Prachai Loong. Murf couldn't help but overhear their-louder-than-normal and somewhat strained conversation. The agent was trying to persuade the galley boy to take over for the cook who had just had an emergency appendectomy that morning and wouldn't be able make the ship's departure two days hence. The galley boy felt the job was too big and complicated for him alone and he was only comfortable doing just prep work and clean up. The ship that they would depart on was of Panamanian registry. It was named *Fenix*. The vessel was well past retirement age and had been used primarily to haul dry freight throughout the Pacific between Far East and U.S. ports. One other tidbit Murf learned that day was that their ship's captain was a very big and somewhat fussy eater. And he also had a sweet tooth.

CHAPTER 24

Steel and Saltwater 101

That night, Murf looked up the specs on the *Fenix* online at the International Shipping Registry. He learned that the twenty-two-year old steam-powered, Panamanian-registered vessel was 514 feet long and eighty-two feet wide. It had a displacement of 17,000 tons, which translated to a maximum haul of a little more than 1,100 standard-sized containers, depending upon the actual mix of different length containers. And finally, he learned that it was manned by a crew of twenty and featured a lumbering top speed of sixteen knots. It was the proverbial "Slow Boat to China" that Murf had been looking for.

Next, Murf began to pore over all of the container ship information he had amassed with enormous urgency, like a college student cramming for finals. He was now intensely boning up on what several industrial publications he'd gathered described as Intermodal Freight Transport, a.k.a., container shipping by ship, truck and rail. According to the industry background articles, standardization was the driving influence. In other words, by universally and interchangeably using truck-sized eight foot wide, 8.6 foot tall, and either twenty or forty foot long containers to ship goods in, either a truck, train or ship could be loaded in seconds by a harbor-side crane operator so that a steel box carrying up to twenty tons could then immediately be on its way. That it was all about standardization and commoditization was patently clear. And Murf perversely found comfort in the prospect of losing himself in a world of commoditization. Like the commodity contents of the ubiquitous and standardized steel shipping containers, Murf felt that his career and even his life had become just another commodity, with actuary-calculated tables dictating standardized life stage junctures such as being too old at fifty-one to remain on top of a youth-dominated industry like advertising.

Murf also spent a couple of hours visiting several different container shipping websites like containership-info.com and The Internet Guide to Freighter Travel. These kind of sites feature orientation materials for those non-working passengers who seek passage on the some 300-plus, out of the thousands of container ships at sea, that actually regularly take ten to twenty passengers on board per trip. From these varied sources, Murf was able to glean some very useful information. For instance, he learned that nine months at sea is the average term for a seaman to sign on for and that such a span would entail about thirteen transoceanic Pacific crossings for a ship like the *Fenix*. "About one-third of the crew will turn over every few months. This happens, of course, in port and usually at the major maritime hubs like Hong Kong or Singapore. During this transition, the 'old' crew starts teaching the 'new' crew the variances relative to each particular ship and the preferences and personalities of the officers who run them. As for training, the unique maintenance each individual ship needs is a top priority. The emergency and safety procedures are equally important and holding a lifeboat drill very soon after new crewmembers come on board is of fundamental importance but unfortunately is not always implemented."

"When a vessel makes port," said one site, "…the sailors who have just finished their contracted terms and have been paid by the Purser, try to quickly recapture some semblance of a "normal" life for a couple of months at least. The normative likelihood of such a career is that most seamen will neither marry nor raise a family. As for the ones who do wed, the stereotype of disproportionately high divorce and alcoholism rates is unfortunately one rooted in fact. Many of them are simply ill equipped to deal with routine social conventions. While totally at ease around their own kind at sea, the men seem nonconversant and uncomfortable around land-based folks. Since this is less of an issue among family, sailors in port will often visit parents, if living, and siblings. Their stays are usually kept short given that they are conscious that they are interrupting the rhythm of their relatives' busy lives."

Another source said, "the legend of sailors with a girl in every port is just that. The highly atypical life of seamen is very far from advantageous relative to meeting women and long separations do not have a positive effect on the marital bliss of the few who might encounter a willing lady." Brothels, on the other hand…

"The size of a crew manning today's container ships is significantly smaller because navigation, speed control and GPS guidance are relatively recent developments. Crews range from twenty to forty now, whereas in days of yore, it took more men to keep things on an even keel. Back then, most ships at sea were powered by steam engines. They also had to carry most of their own fresh water. Today, desalinization provides more than adequate drinking and bathing water. Some of the vessels also did their own loading and unloading in port via onboard cranes. Ports then were often a far cry from the highly automated facilities we see today."

Since Murf has always imagined he would be accepted more readily by an older, less desirable and therefore less discriminating ship, he was keenly interested in reading about twenty-plus year old ships. "Ships now being built have a life expectancy of only twenty years. This is because their diesel powered engines have greater efficiency and output, but as a result, they wear out faster than the 'steamers' of old." But according to the site, many older, should-have-been-long-retired-by-now ships were registered to Third World countries and continue to ply the seas and somehow miraculously pass annual inspections.

Versus bulk carriers that fill their holds with oil or grain, box boats are focused on the manufactured goods or dry cargo sector. This includes finished consumer items of all kinds: household goods, clothes—even Murf's favorite—consumer electronics. Also a big focus, were food products and even refrigerated or perishable goods. These were carried in specialized and insulated refrigerated containers called "reefers." These containers were plugged into the ship's electrical system to maintain their preservative state of a constant and cooler temperature. The reefers were usually stacked below deck and away from the elements in cargo holds as opposed to the above deck containers. The exposed outside boxes were lashed into stacking frames with wire ropes, steel rods and chains all pulled tight with a tension-based system of levers and locking mechanisms. In one article Murf read in WIRED® Magazine, the author reported that there were now enough shipping containers in existence on earth, that they could be used to construct an eight-foot-high wall that would circle two times around the equator. "Equa-tor!!!??? Hell, I hardly knew her," Murf chuckled to himself as he read on.

With so many of these generic and nondescript containers in play worldwide, it's a wonder that they can be kept track of. Murf read that as many as 10,000 containers per year are estimated to get lost overboard at sea during storms—which, in turn, generates offbeat news stories and amusing beachcombing when thousands of single and mate-less sneakers wash up mysteriously on a shoreline somewhere. One of the most famous of these incidents involved the mid-Pacific loss in '92 of 29,000 toys made by a company called First Years. As a result, many thousands of yellow rubber ducks showed up in great numbers on the shores of first Alaska and then Japan. At this point, they have now circumnavigated the globe and appear in small numbers in oceans and on beaches everywhere.

Cargo losses in ports happen far less, due to the use of modern technology. Most containers nowadays are tracked by attached radio frequency emitting chips. While they are loaded and unloaded and at sea, they can be regularly and instantly inventoried. In addition, this allows a vast maze of precisely organized containers, each transporting different kinds of goods, to be quickly unloaded in port in a highly orchestrated plan wherein each container goes on a specific railcar or truck, headed to the right location of intended delivery.

"The most challenging aspect of loading and unloading is the delicate dance that is maintaining constant balance. Since each container has a completely different gross weight, a loading plan that takes this into account and creates an appropriate orchestration is essential. Vessels that are poorly loaded and whose center of mass is off-kilter because the cargo weight is not properly distributed, can unexpectedly capsize. If cargo is not well secured and shifts violently in a storm, the result can be one where the ship suddenly is cracked in two and all cargo and hands aboard are forever lost," said one quite sobering article.

"Jesus, they all look like they are so over-stacked that a small wave is all it'd take to tip 'em over," said Murf nervously. And then he plunged right back into his speed-reading mode.

"Steel crossing lashing rods are used to secure the first few rows of containers which are stacked on the deck to prevent any movement. Stacks of containers eight-deep are lowered down into slots found in the below deck hatches."

As he read on about the logistical marvel of loading and unloading, Murf remembered how much he enjoyed watching the ships unload—which he had witnessed from both sides of the Pacific—in both Oakland and Hong Kong. "In the back bays of the port of Hong Kong, one could pull his car off the highway and onto the shoulder of the road, and peer down into massive fields of boxes stacked in rows five to seven high. In between are transport lanes for the broad variety of machines that lift and set in place the multi-colored sealed boxes. In some spots, the twenty- or forty-foot-long, truck-sized container stacks actually rose from sea level to heights well above the freeway.

"Right after after a container ship docks and is tied securely to its moorings, streams of digital data begin pouring into the control center. Then an extremely automated and complicated process unfolds. Operators sitting inside glass booths that are located high on the gantry cranes, begin lifting the heavy boxes in precise accordance with the computerized master plan. An embedded metal track running parallel to the dock allows the cranes to move to service the stacks aboard the ship as is necessary. And to move a container takes a crane less than sixty seconds. Harvesting or picking up the containers three at a time, are numerous tall, four-legged traveling lifts. Men wearing hard hats and glow-in-the-dark orange safety vests operate these machines. They scurry to and fro stacking steel boxes in the appropriate slots plotted out on a concourse that has been heavily gridded by lines and cross stripes painted in bright reflective colors. Working non-stop, in just hours the cargo is relocated from the ship to the terminal. Now the process renews but in reverse as the ship is rapidly reloaded so that it can sail with the outgoing tide, often on the very same day of its arrival."

"No doubt," thought Murf, "the creators of the movie WALL-E drew inspiration from watching such a container ship offloading exercise, before folding an interplanetary version of it into their robotics dominated, stack-'em-as-high-as-a-skyscraper construct."

Harbor entry was another area Murf thought he would need to be familiar with. "Entrances to harbors vary greatly," advised one source. Some, like the San Francisco one Murf regularly sailed on, was as wide as the Golden Gate Bridge is long. By contrast, down south at Long Beach, the entrance is narrow and requires extremely precise manueuvering. Of course, little is left to chance or a helmsman unfamiliar with a given harbor. That's because the standard procedure for port entry is for harbor pilots to come aboard, even as the ship is still cruising, and for tugboats to shortly thereafter take charge of the propulsion and steering.

Murf was up and jamming until about 3:30 a.m. that night. And then the next morning, he rose at about 8:00 a.m. and headed to his neighborhood Whole Foods all-natural-grocery story. There he shopped with the wild-eyed look of Dr. Frankenstein assembling critical ingredients. Murf bought key items as though setting up his own restaurant: three large bottles of barrel-aged balsamic vinegar; blends of dry spice seasoning rubs for meats; tins and tins of beef and veal demi-glace and chicken stock for sauces; key lime juice extract; large bags of dry, jasmine infused rice; coconut milk for Filipino and Thai-style soups; red and yellow curry sauce mixes; bottles of dark and tangy stir-fry sauces; two wheels of parmesan cheese; a case of Italian espresso coffee; four cases of number ten cans of fire-roasted crushed tomatoes; organic honey; dried, golden raisins; fresh and canned berries; the ripest bananas he could find; four big bottles of the best Mexican vanilla; ultra-rich Belgian bakers chocolate; black strap molasses; cinnamon; brown sugar; flour; a ton of salted-butter; and a hand-held fruit zester to later scrape strips of orange peel into a sweet, golden batter. Murf also got $400 in emergency cash from a next-door Bank of America ATM. As he turned away from the machine while tucking the money into his wallet, Murf looked up and couldn't help but see the large window poster in the liquor store across the street. It was advertising a special promotion to "Win a Caribbean Cruise Courtesy of Captain Morgan's Rum."

"No thanks, matey. The *Fenix* only needs one captain and besides, it's about time this sailor got himself clean and sober," Murf said out loud.

About 5:00 p.m. after a half-day of intense work in the kitchen using many of Terri's favorite recipes, Murf showed up at Red's again hoping to encounter the fellows from the *Fenix* he'd met the day before. Only one was there, but it was the important one. Murf explained to ship's galley boy Prachai Loong, that he was doing research for a book about the container shipping industry and wanted to treat him to dinner at the best and most expensive Thai Restaurant in San Francisco, in exchange for information on feeding a ship's crew at sea. Such a feast was an offer too good to be refused and Murf struck him as a trustworthy sort.

The evening began with two rounds of potent, three-kinds-of-rum Mai Tais and Murf made sure Prachai's favorite Singha beer was ever-present during dinner. Murf had a four-fold advantage in a drinking contest with this particular opponent. Beyond the combination of usual body mass, extreme-rum training regimen, and Irish constitution, there was the olive oil Murf had chugged before meeting Prachai at the restaurant. This was a little drinking contest trick Murf's army sergeant dad had told him about from back in his WWII days. Seems that, right after the war in Berlin, our Russian allies regularly challenged American dogfaces to vodka drinking contests, which the Yanks mostly survived by coating their stomachs with olive oil, allowing most of the alcohol to pass through the system without entering into the bloodstream.

During a sumptuous feast, Murf learned more from Prachai about the crew's composition and what to cook for the Filipino members that made up almost 40 percent of the total crew. This was not unusual, given that about one-third of the world's merchant sailors are from the Philippines. Besides the Filipinos, other crew nationalities were Albanian, Uzbeks, Romanian, Croatian, Spanish, Turkish, Azerbaijani, Liberian, Nigerian, Tanzanian, Indonesian, Malaysian, Thai, and Chinese.

After dinner, they returned to the restaurant's bar for Mai Tai after Mai Tai, until the galley boy was completely incoherent and extremely unlikely to make the scheduled departure of the *Fenix* at 8:00 a.m. the next morning. To make sure of this, after helping him to fall into bed at the motel he'd been staying at, Murf unplugged the clock radio and drew tight the double curtains on his windows. For good measure, Murf posted the Do Not Disturb sign on his outside doorknob.

And then Murf returned home, just before midnight to finish his baking (and packing). He told an irritated and disbelieving Terri that he had volunteered to make baked goods for a benefit fund-raiser for unemployed San Francisco business executives. When Terri awoke the next morning at 6:00 a.m., Murf was already gone, but he had left her an enormous sink full of dirty dishes

When Murf showed up about 6:45 a.m. that morning at the Oakland dock, where Prachai had told him *Fenix* was tied up, he spied a white with red-trim container ship much larger and more modern than how the *Fenix* had been represented at the online shipping registry.

"That's not the *Fenix* is it?" he asked an older sailor on the dock who was headed in the opposite direction.

"Not hardly, mate. The *Fenix* is that ol' scrapper just off this un's stern," said the seaman, chuckling a bit. As the *Fenix* came into view, Murf immediately encountered a very unhappy ship captain and the Filipino manning agent he had observed with Prachai at Red's two days before. From what Murf quickly grasped of their conversation as he approached, no replacement had been found for the appendicitis-afflicted cook. And the backup plan, Galley Boy Prachai, was nowhere to be seen.

"I hear down at Red's you need a cook," said a sheepishly smiling Murf, dressed in very nondescript working clothes as he approached the two men. His arms were fully laden with four baskets of gingham cloth-covered, sweet and just-warmed muffins, killer cookies and brownies with coconut and honey-glazed walnuts. As Murf uncovered one of the baskets, the captain's blue eyes sparkled with interest. He was a portly, balding man in his late fifties with a heavy salt and pepper beard of medium length, thick, hairy arms and a redwood-tree-circumference neck with a thin, gold chain encircling it.

"Murf Morrison's the name," said Murf as he offered samples of his work to the two highly engaged men. "Made these just a little while ago," Murf said with a twinkle in his oh-so-skilled-at-selling eyes.

"M-m-m-m-m," said the captain, as his thick-fingered, stubby hand relocated a sugar-frosted orange and cranberry muffin from the basket to his lips in a blur.

"I've only just recently taken to the sea," Murf explained to the still stunned manning agent and wide-eyed captain. "Messy divorce after our only child died," said Murf convincingly as the seemingly ravenous captain started in on a second fresh muffin—this one bursting with whole blueberries and laced with extra Mexican vanilla. "So I left my job at the restaurant. Now I'm used to cooking for a crew of twenty to thirty," Murf rattled on without pause. "Been on the circuit from the U.S. West Coast ports to Asia and back. You know, Hong Kong, Shanghai, Seoul and such," said Murf now sounding less than completely authentic.

The captain eyed him carefully as he ate, with a look that said he suspected such a last-minute rescue was too good to be true.

"I'll sign on for nine months for $900 a-month," Murf continued, knowing that his price was attractively set below market.

"Eight hundred is what the job pays," replied the unctuous-acting manning agent, sensing that Murf cared little about the wages he'd receive, and eager to regain favor with the captain by landing the prize at an extra low price. The captain gave the weasel-resembling agent a look that said, "You'd better not blow this," while he turned his attention to investigating the brownies.

"That'll do just fine," said Murf almost too eagerly. "I'm just ready to get out to sea again." This sounded exceptionally suspect to both, in that days-off on shore leave were never enough for most seamen, and most were more likely to bitch about the long hours and hard work aboard a ship, than to express upbeat anticipation for putting back out to sea.

"I'll need a passport for the register," said the captain studying Murf's eyes carefully as he swallowed and licked his fingertips for clinging crumbs. As he scanned the document Murf readily handed him, he noted the stated occupation and the unshaven appearance and working clothes Murf had deliberately conjured up for his new passport photo. "How old are you?" asked the captain to see if Murf's answer would match the birth date.

"I'm OK if you want to call me 'The Ancient Mariner,' Murf replied with a chuckle. "I'm a very strong and able fifty-one," Murf said with a now determined tone, as he secretly worried that he was once again going to be the victim of age discrimination. After a very uncomfortable pause in the conversation, Murf interjected, "Would you prefer a dinner of steaming Italian sausage and three-cheese lasagna or oven roasted fennel and lemon chicken, with garlic and cheddar cheese-studded potatoes?" asked Murf craftily of the big man.

The captain kept looking down at the passport and noted that Murf's answer to the "gotcha" age question was indeed correct. He also noted, as he paged though the book further, that the ink stamps on Murf's passport were more typical of those made by an airport official's than the kind he was accustomed to seeing on a seafarer's passport. "I like the sound of both of those meals," said the caving-in leader. "My name is Benjamin. Get your things on board in the next hour." He then added matter-of-factly. "And I'll take these," as he picked up the other three baskets of goodies Murf had set on the dock. He immediately turned and began to go up the ramp with his prizes in tow.

"There are papers to sign," said the now smiling agent to a surprised looking Murf. "Come over here with me."

Afterwards, Murf jumped into a cab, which would take him across the bridge to Belvedere and to his condo building. There he planned to keep the meter running, get his two completely-packed-with-supplies footlockers from the doorman, and then give him a big tip along with an envelope to hand to Terri at the end of the day when she returned home with Molly. As the taxi sped toward his condo building, Murf penned his brief Dear Terri goodbye note.

"Let's face it Terri, as a husband and as a father, I just completely suck. You and Molly deserve so much more. And I know that you two will be much better off without this drunken slug in your lives anymore. Murf."

Note delivered and cargo loaded, Murf instructed the cabbie to return to the dock as quickly as possible.

CHAPTER 25

Solitary Sea

In spite of his gruff countenance at first meeting, the captain was an altogether jovial chap named Benjamin Harold at birth—but everyone on board just called him Skipper. Though his accent was largely British, he sounded like he had, indeed, been raised in a combination of Liverpool, Istanbul and Shanghai and that he might break out in any one of several languages at any moment. Captain Benny was actually Hong Kong-born to a working class family of English expats. He was imbued as a youngster with an amalgam of the many cultures to be found in Hong Kong and was solidly educated in public schools there. Afterwards, he struggled to get into and pay his own way through the city's Merchant Marine academy. After graduating in the lower third of his class, he had slowly worked his way up over the course of twenty-five years, as a senior officer aboard many different vessels ranging from oil tankers to grain haulers, and now box boats. He'd been a captain now for three years and yet, surprisingly, he was able to discern little about the aging *Fenix's* true ownership. But although it was not much of a ship, it was his to command and he did so with a sense of pride and confidence that Murf found reassuring. While he generally ran things with an even temperament, Captain Benny rarely fell behind schedule for anything other than legitimate act-of-God reasons such as large-scale storms. Nonetheless, he was fair and considerate of the generally hard-working crews and he stayed on time without driving the men into the ground, as some other ship commanders did.

Murf was more than a bit taken aback by the ship's aged appearance and, though a layman, his perception of her dubious safety. The ship had a smell about it that made Murf think of death, though, in fact, it was a combination of fuel oil, soured water that had dripped from refrigerated containers, tobacco, salty air, and still-pending sewage disposal that was well overdue. As Murf was being shown to his quarters by the curt and largely non-conversant manning agent, at times the overbearing and acrid smell of smoke stack gasses prompted thoughts of nausea. So Murf stepped lively and avoided breathing deeply.

The *Fenix* was a little longer than half of a football field. It was painted stem to stern with a badly faded sky blue color, with red trim lines on the superstructure and a faded gray hull below the top deck. Its exterior was badly mottled in many places with massive orange-brown rust spots and downward dripping yet long-dried, rusty stains. With a 4,000 TEU cargo capacity, the *Fenix* was considered just slightly larger than the "feeder" ships that worked intra-coastal waters quickly moving cargo from port to port. Small by comparison to large and modern container ships, the *Fenix* was fairly versatile in that it was equipped with its own installed gantry crane. In the old days when backwater ports didn't always have shore-side cranes, this feature made the *Fenix* more self-reliant—though the ship no longer used its own crane much, given that it operated much slower than the modern shore-side ones. The ship's seven-ton bow anchor was black and tinged with rust, but was massively impressive at eleven feet tall and about eight feet across.

Walking the *Fenix* deck was like walking the aisles in a seamy warehouse that stored leaky containers stacked precariously high and poised to fall. The drab, faded colors and preponderance of gray and variable rust colors almost everywhere, reminded Murf of the times he had sailed past the huge collection of abandoned, horribly rusted WWII and Korean War-era merchant marine and warships that were lashed together and anchored en masse in the East Bay backwaters of Suisun Bay, near a large oil refinery outside of the metro San Francisco/Oakland area. They were known as the Suisun Bay Reserve Fleet and, judging by its appearance, Murf figured the *Fenix* might well be just as seaworthy as the oldest of these so-called ghost ships—the WWII "Victory Ships"—that were built in 100 days or less in the early 1940s for the war effort. That they were still afloat long after their ultra-short, planned obsolescence—and that an eyesore like the *Fenix* was, as well—was nothing short of incredible. As darker thoughts about the ship's possible purposes beyond shipping crept into Murf's mind, he reasoned that she did not look competently enough managed to be a drug or arms smuggling ship. The old gal was just cut-rate, risky transport for those with no other option.

Given his station as one of the key specialized talents aboard, Murf had his own small cabin with a porthole. His room was on the seventh level of the aft superstructure or bridge castle that rose vertically above the rows of thirteen-across-and-four-high-stacked containers that ran the length of the ship toward the bow. The officers' quarters were on the top deck, with the multi-window encircled bridge or wheelhouse just below them. Most of the working crew shared cabins on the fourth, fifth and sixth levels and even those with front-facing port holes, had the view blocked by stacked containers. Directly below the aft deck from whence the bridge castle arose was the ship's massive engine room and the surrounding storage tanks for the heavy fuel oil that powered it. Throughout the ship, and even subliminally ever present in each individual room, were the constants of the almost hypnotic hum and vibration of the huge engines turning the shaft that spins the propellers to power the ship through the sea. Omnipresent was the smell of bunker oil, engine exhaust and salt water. The cawing sounds of the white-bodied, gray-winged seagulls were ever-present, along with the whistling wind rushing over the faded gray deck and stacked containers and the beastly roar of breaking seas on a steel hull.

Though Spartan even compared to the average Motel 6 room, Murf's new home had an adequate built-in bed, desk and a small reading light with a bendable neck that Murf could crane either straight down or toward the bed for reading. To the 220 volts outlet on the back wall in between one of his two small shelves, Murf plugged in his power cord adapter-festooned laptop loaded with his music collection. His well-compiled music library allowed him to mindlessly enjoy a shuffle between the likes of a brilliantly written and played Steely Dan or Van Morrison tune, to a soulful Boz Scaggs covering a great vocalist's standard, to the sublimely mellow alto sax play of jazz master Grover Washington, to the irresistibly dance-inducing back beat of Stevie Wonder, and then to the gnash-your-teeth, rock 'n roll grit of The Boss, The Stones or Chrissie Hynde wailing with The Pretenders. And of course, he also had a ton of the more contemporary artists he enjoyed like U2, the Black Eyed Peas, Red Hot Chili Peppers, John Legend, Green Day and the alternative rock band, The Shins.

Music does more than just sooth the savage beast; it can set a badly troubled mind and soul right, at least for a time, thought Murf. Since he associated reading with work and his advertising career (he read *The San Francisco Chronicle*, *The New York Times* and *The Wall Street Journal* religiously every morning over coffee before work), mistakenly Murf didn't bring a single book with him. He had little space for them anyway, given that he'd crammed two footlockers to the brim with the culinary supplies that he bought to insure success in his new role.

Later, Murf would find himself with considerable free time between meals and prep work. Fortunately, and in spite of stereotypes about sailors, the ship had tons of old paperbacks in the rec-room and a fervent core of eager-to-swap book junkies. However, Murf just loved to spend as much free time as possible standing and walking on deck and in awe of the sea. The intra-ship passageways located just below deck were functional for transit, but too narrow to facilitate walking for pleasure. So Murf's favorite place for free-form exercise—there actually was an antiquated fitness room below deck with a few older-model cardio machines—was on the sunken deck located just below the last towering stack of containers aft and right above the ship's stern. The semi-circular deck was about forty yards long and twenty yards deep. Its outer perimeter was encircled by a chest-high, metal frame railing that was open at the bottom and beneath, through which a man's body could easily slide. That railing was the final separation barrier between man and water and it overlooked the ship's bubbling white water wake. While there were smaller decks elsewhere aboard—including a tiny smokers deck outside of the galley and the usually very windy and wet deck near the bow and around the foremast—Murf preferred the sunken deck. There, the wind was greatly mitigated by the containers looming above it and he enjoyed sharing it with the seabirds that loomed in the air all around it, diving occasionally into the water to feast on the aquatic tidbits the propellers flushed to the surface from waters deep below. The deck was large enough to accommodate the entire crew and spacious enough for walking for exercise—though most of the men just hung out here to smoke and to chat.

The *Fenix* had two different and sizeable galleys—a holdover from the old days when the ship had a crew of over sixty. More than twenty years after she was commissioned much had changed. Container ships now operated with far less fixed cost. New technology advances and the retrofitting of a considerable amount of automation equipment had led to the *Fenix* operating now with a crew one-third that size. The smaller galley on deck eight was originally just for the officers, but it had now been converted into a rec-room that was open to all. Murf would keep it stocked with coffee and snacks, 24/7. It was, in times of inclement weather, a wet room for those seeking quick recharge while on watch. Often harbor officials would spend a considerable amount of their time on board loading up here in lieu of inspections and safety checks. The much larger galley on the third deck is where Murf served scheduled meals. It was self-segregated into two areas—one for the officers and skilled sailors and engineers, the other for the poorly paid common crewmen.

When he began settling in and unpacking his supplies, Murf noticed that both galley areas were in need of a good cleaning. Dead roach carcasses and rat droppings were noticeably evident. The first thing he did was put on the new pair of comfortable, thick rubber-soled cooking shoes he'd recently bought. While not ideal for the deck of a ship, they'd allow him to spend eighteen-hours a day on his feet. Then he made a pot of French roast coffee.

The aroma drew an appreciative fan in the late-thirties Filipino second officer named Daniel Aquino. After two delicious cups and hearing Murf rail a bit about "the filthy bugs and vermin," Daniel procured traps and bug spray from the ship's supplies to help Murf rectify the situation. The food supplies arrayed in the canned food storage area and walk-in refrigerators were about what Murf had anticipated—pedestrian but adequate in a middle-class family regimen sort of way. It was just like the kind of food that Murf had grown up with. The dry-goods shelves were heavily stocked with staples such as rice, flour, beans, sugar, and soft drinks. Since the now appendicitis-sidelined former cook had completed and turned in the supplies list as the ship made port, the 'fridges had just been stocked with fresh vegetables and fruits of all kinds, whole chickens, ducklings, hams and modest pot-roast-and-skirt-steak-type cuts of beef, plus giant, waxed-cardboard tubs of vanilla, chocolate and strawberry ice cream. With this base to work with—supplemented by the secret-weapon-seasonings and sauces Murf had brought with him—Murf was confident he had the ingredients he needed for success in his new life.

The first night's dinner was a tour de force and more than a bit overdone. Murf attacked his nerves over this new challenge by serving up a repast that so far exceeded expectations as to make the crew wonder if they had mistakenly boarded a four-star cruise ship instead of the *Fenix*. Murf deluded himself into thinking he wasn't getting carried away by telling himself he was just using simple ingredients that should be enjoyed before fresh produce was no longer an option. The starters included perfectly ripe and sweet red, orange and yellow tomato slices with buffalo mozzarella and avocado slices interspersed and drizzled with aged balsamic and olive oil; made-from-scratch, piquant Caesar salad with garlic and butter-brushed sourdough croutons and large shreds of thin-sliced parmesan cheese; and crisp chopped and spicy red pepper and vinegar kimchi. While whole chickens were an almost generic ingredient, Murf slow-roasted them with an herb rice dressing inside and red wine reduction cassoulet-style sauce of wild mushrooms and peppers atop the birds. The fish served was just catfish, but coated in ground pecans, flour and spices and then simmered in soy sauce and olive oil with a few hits of wasabi added for zip and jasmine-infused white rice and sautéed bok choi as accompaniments. The desserts included fresh blueberry-and-peach cobbler, decadent German-chocolate saturated mousse, and white cake with toasted-coconut frosting and a Grand Marnier cream sauce on the side.

As everyone finished up their meals, Murf nervously paced the galley dining room asking its bloated occupants if they needed more dessert or tea. Most of the big-eyed, belly-bulging belch machines callously waved him off. Afterwards one disbelieving Filipino sailor approached him cautiously and asked if he had been a cook on container ships for long. As Murf unconvincingly said, "Uh, no, well ah, just one small ship actually," all those within earshot of his reply broke out into hearty laughter. They knew a rookie when they saw one. But as they stood and began clearing the galley, they were considerably cheered by their great fortune of having a cook of this caliber for the voyage.

Several said as much to a very pleased-with-himself Captain Benny. Murf was quickly seen as a real asset, especially since the specialty of the last cook seemed to be re-heating canned foods and boiling chicken, beef and fish into flavorless gray masses, surrounded by equally flavorless potatoes and rice.

Murf settled quickly into the galley life. However, instead of keeping to himself and living a somewhat solitary life of a quasi-hermit that he had imagined, he was more like the Murf of old—buoyant and affable. Likewise the sailors who had seemed to be generally quiet and introverted in port, were downright raucous and talkative when at sea and at ease among their own kind. Murf quickly won newfound friends among the crew for his inspired fare, and his cheerful personality and great jokes. He also got along well with the officers for the most part. To give himself regular breaks from his galleys' windowless environs, Murf took fresh coffee, tea and snacks up to the bridge where he usually lingered for small talk and because he liked learning about the ship's control center.

Food aboard a ship is typically served formally three times a day at 0700, 1200, and 1800 hours, with about an hour and a half allowed for each meal. In addition to after midnight sandwiches and hot soups for the night shift, there were also thirty-minute caffeine breaks at 1000 and 1500 hours, with light, mostly sweet snacks. Murf served more sweet baked goods than the ship's large population of Asians was accustomed to. But they were very fast learners and, given the extreme succulence of Murf's, by way of Terri's, muffins and pastries, he won over a ton of converts as was evidenced by many of the crew's newly bulging waistlines at the end of the multi-month term. The skipper, in fact, put on a solid ten pounds more.

As for beverages, fresh coffee was served at breakfast and at the 10 a.m. break. After that it was available in thermoses or fresh, in small periodic gourmet coffee batches, when Murf personally wanted some. The universally popular tea was available around the clock. In his preparations-cramming, Murf had read that, "After hours, the crew is usually allowed to scavenge for snacks with the proviso that they put away all food taken from storage and clean up any dish they might soil." Murf learned quickly that all aboard indeed did so—save one individual, the rather arrogant and short-tempered Chinese Third Officer Lu-Chi.

"In light of the menu planning autocracy granted to most shipboard cooks and the lack of an alternative in the form of making one's own meals," Murf remembered reading on one web site, "few crewmen risk the cook's displeasure by disparaging the fare within earshot. Aboard some ships, an exception is made when it involves food preparation of traditional foods from sailors' native lands and cultures." Knowing this led Murf to very overtly invite his diners to make favorite meal suggestions and to collaborate with him in the preparation of special dishes more attuned to native palates.

Murf's basic menu was dominated by high-calorie comfort foods, along with delicious, fresh-baked breads, pies, cakes, cookies and liquor-laced flans. Salads were served for the first week at sea, after which carrots, beets, onions and frozen and canned fruits and vegetables predominated. With the luxury of two galleys, Murf focused one on real meals and the other—the rec room—on snacks. It was run just like the craft services table at TV shoots with regular replenishment. To fuel the harsh-manual-labor-driven crew, Murf maintained ever-present quick energy snacks like his now famous fresh killer muffins, assorted candy from American, European and Asian groceries, and always lots of coffee and hot tea. As for the meals, for the Asian crew's palates, there would usually be a hot congee, which is a porridge-like dish Murf made with small grained rice, mushrooms, scallions, tiny shrimp or roasted pork shreds, pickled radish or carrots, a bit of cilantro, and decorative and zesty dashes of sesame oil and soy sauce in the center of the steaming, tan colored mush. The captain was partial to pastas and Murf's deep and cheesy, stacked lasagna Bolognese with a hearty veal and Italian sausage ground-meat sauce imbued throughout. The dish was a broadly hailed favorite among all and soon came to be expected on at least a weekly basis. Pizza was a daily staple and also universally revered, but Murf made pizzas a daily surprise with varying sauces and ingredients like salami slices, bacon, sausages, pineapples, stewed tomato chunks, spicy Thai ingredients, and Tandoori-style chicken chunks. These largely improvised pizzas were variations of those he remembered eating at California Pizza Kitchen restaurants.

As was the maritime custom, Murf generally served the seated officers plates that he had prepared for each of them, and the crew, dressed mostly in blue overalls and hardhats, helped themselves to the steam-dishes and containers that he set up buffet-style. But since Murf took pleasure in seeing their reactions to his work, he often stood behind the food and served up portions for the crewmen as they passed through the line. He would join in the meal once everyone was served, though he ate only a little, preferring to move among the men replenishing favorites and chatting them up.

Most of the crew possessed surprising intellect, given that the seaman's life was one of bursts of strenuous physical labor followed by lengthy periods of down time. As a result, most sailors were extremely well read—not just via pulp fiction, but many were better versed in the classics than most of the college graduates Murf knew. Most of the men had wonderful senses of humor and a general joie de vivre. Two of Murf's favorites to bend an ear with were Willie Espinosa and Miguel "Danny" Diaz, two Filipino sailors in their early thirties. They were both short, olive-skinned men, yet sinewy and with ant-like disproportionate-to-their-size strength. Both of them were almost professional-caliber side-men with booming and ready laughs. They played Ed McMahon for Murf's Johnny Carson-type post dinner comedic monologue. Not surprising—given that the majority of their days were spent at sea—most of the men were either divorced, long-time singles or downright marriage-phobic. So they particularly liked Murf's universally appealing and easily adaptable "I hate my wife" jokes. Early on, he enthralled a couple of Serbian hands over strong hot coffee, with the joke about Franz who is dying and says, as he lay in bed to his unconcerned wife, "'Please, can you grant me one wish?' She said to him, 'Very well, I will.' Her husband then says, 'When I die will you please promise me that you will marry my boss, Slobodan?' 'Yes I will,' says the wife, 'but I thought you hated Slobodan?' she responded. As he breathed his last gasp," said Murf, whispering for the dramatic effect, "Franz smiled and said, 'Yes, I do.'"

The laughter erupted and Willie and Danny provided a bit of applause.

"Speaking of wishes," Murf smoothly segued like a Vaudeville comic, "A man named Samir is walking down a beach and finds an old brass bottle with a hard cork jammed into the top. He wrenches it open and out comes clouds of billowing smoke," Murf continued, gesticulating upwards with his arms dramatically. "As the smoked cleared, there stood a magical Genie in ancient costume," said Murf knowing well that the two Serbs might not understand every word he said, but they clearly were mesmerized by his histrionic storytelling style and would probably get the punch line.

"The Genie tells Samir he has been granted three wishes for freeing him. He had been imprisoned for hundreds of years as the brass bottle floated across oceans all over the world and back," Murf said playfully. "'But there is a catch,' said the Genie; 'whatever I grant you, I must give your ex-wife twice as much,'" said Murf in a deepened Genie-like voice. "Not yet really believing in the Genie's supposed powers, Samir made his first wish. 'I want you to give me $5 million dollars,' he said and POOF! He was instantly surrounded by stacks and stacks of money," said Murf waving his outstretched arms all about again. "'But remember the catch,' the Genie said. 'Your ex-wife just got $10 million dollars.' Samir was not pleased with that twist, but he now believed in the Genie's magic, so he made his second wish," said Murf holding up two fingers. "'I want seven beautiful lovers, a different one for every day of the week. They will get along sweetly, never get jealous, and will always want to make sweet love whenever I so much as wink at them,'" Murf said with a twinkle in his eye. "POOF and suddenly Samir was surrounded and sweetly hugged by the most beautiful women he had ever imagined with luscious lips, beautiful eyes and hair, and the most amazing curves," Murf said seductively as he moved his hands simultaneously downward sweeping in and then outwards, drawing imaginary curvy women's figures in midair. "'Presto!'" said Murf loudly in the Genie voice, "'and your ex-wife just got fourteen handsome lovers.' Samir winced at the thought and gripped his chin as he thought long and hard about his third and final wish. Finally," said Murf moving into crescendo mode, "Samir spoke his third wish out loud. 'Please, oh great and powerful Genie, I want you to beat me half to death.'"

After a bit of a pause, the two Serbs faces lit up in understanding and they bellowed heartily with appreciative laughter. "Got dat BITCH," said the twice-divorced taller one as they ambled out of the galley still laughing and high-fiving each other awkwardly. As they left, Murf noticed an olive-skinned, late forties man, who had close cropped black hair with wisps of gray, sitting close by and smirking as though he had overheard and appreciated the joke too.

"Nothing like a good ex-wife joke, huh?" said Murf. The man nodded affirmatively as he sipped his hot tea. "You married?" Murf inquired.

"No, no…but there was this one girl at University, many years ago," said the man in English that sounded as though it carried an Arab accent, "But I went away and we lost touch…" his voice trailed off with a sigh of regret.

"So this man and his wife come upon a wishing well," said Murf sliding back into his shtick. "The man leans over the bottomless well and tosses in a penny as he silently makes his wish. Then his wife steps up and leans over the well to make her wish. But she leans over too far and falls head over heels into the darkness down below. 'Shit, this thing really works,' says the man," Murf finished as he studied the crewman's serious face for a response.

He smiled and nodded again, enjoying the humor, but with pronounced reserve. After a few moments of awkward silence he spoke. "That joke IS funny and I've heard it told in many different languages. I haven't heard it in years. My name is Abdur," he said extending his hand up and toward Murf. The scars on Abdur's hand were grisly and Murf wondered as to their cause but did not ask. They were, in fact, caused by a faulty timer, which had prematurely exploded. On his deeply tanned and handsome Arab face, Murf noticed a small one-inch jagged scar (shrapnel) to the left of his narrow nose. Abdur bid Murf a "Good evening" and Murf noticed that he walked with a slight limp as he left.

Murf was on a voyage scheduled for two months without significant or multi-day shore leave. The *Fenix* would roam across the Pacific and back three times, with infrequent stops at ports for just-in-time-re-supply of fuel and provisions. Usually this meant the crew would get that day off in port, but would sleep on the ship that night and depart early the next day. This meant that almost all of the overworked crew would spend the day and night drinking at nearby bars and restaurants, before returning to the ship after the bars closed, to sleep it off. For some, a life on the sea and long twenty-day crossings without setting foot on land was an utterly lonely and enervating experience—isolating, disorienting and alienating. For Murf, it had a different effect, exuding calm and considerable mollification for a troubled soul. With him, it wasn't about escaping debt or legal proceedings by fleeing to foreign shores—as with some of the men. Nor was it about making a living or seeing the world, because Murf could otherwise earn a living and had already traveled the world over. The escape was one from overwhelming career and home pressures, and into a life of mindless, manual labor, which came with an intoxicating sense of freedom. However, Murf's real deep-seated fear concerned raising a deaf and mute child to find happiness in a harsh and unforgiving world.

Murf was completely excited at the prospect of his first trans-Pacific crossing by ship. It would take the twenty-five-year-old bucket of rust around twenty days, weather permitting, to cross the Pacific with its American industries' cargo of mostly machinery, pharmaceutical and medical products, and agricultural exports. On the return trip from Far Eastern ports, the ship would carry a broad variety of consumer goods that had been manufactured in Asian factories. Food product imports and exports, of course, always filled the reefers.

Murf was most unusual in that he didn't mind when capricious Mother Nature kicked up her heels and inclement weather set in. The sight of the ship rolling and crashing through the twelve to fifteen foot-high frothing waves, as stacks of grooved vertical channel, metal containers rose and fell—as though being set down by a card-dealing Neptune, would bring great fear and foreboding to a more objective, less detached mind. For the most part, the Pacific Ocean voyages of the *Fenix* were done in calm to moderately turbulent seas with maybe two or three bad storm days per crossing. Tropical typhoons were not that difficult to circumvent, and Pacific storms were routinely tracked and course adjustments made by the ship's computer in order to mitigate them. The really treacherous ones that crewmen and officers alike really feared—and that were nearly inescapable—were the winter storms in the North Pacific, pouring down from Alaska and stirring up bad weather fronts and treacherous seas for almost a thousand miles, hammering West Coast cities from Vancouver to Seattle to San Francisco and down to Los Angeles.

Murf's nearest outside perch to take in all of the ever-changing majesty that is a ship plowing through the sea, was the small aft smoking deck outside the main galley. About three weeks into his new life adventure, on a windy and twelve-foot-seas, wave-riding night, Murf was on this deck and steadily gazing upwards. In spite of an increasingly building cloud cover, he was still able to see large sections of sparkling black night overhead. The *Fenix* was at a point in our rotating earth's celestial presentation when the Milky Way is obscured from the majority of Americans and about a fifth of the world. And yet Murf saw it clearly in the dark night sky. Murf was taking a well-deserved cigar break from his post dinner clean-up, and he noticed the Arab gent who had introduced himself the other day, was also out on the aft deck for a smoke. He, likewise, seemingly drew personal calm from the turbulence and spray. Murf said hello and waved him over. They briefly made small talk, at first, and warmed further to each other's company as the sky quickly clouded-over and all around them became gray up above and dark, swirling blue down below the ship. When the blackening and stormy clouds began to spit wind-driven rain, both men said goodnight and went inside. When you live together with a crew 24/7 for forty to fifty days without much of a break, you do inevitably talk and tend to get to know at least a few people fairly well. It seemed to Murf as though this fellow—who was articulate, though a tad somber—might be one he would enjoy conversing with regularly.

While he perversely enjoyed being on deck in large swells or when they muddled through a storm, he did have dark thoughts about being below deck in his berth in the middle of the night, when the ship might be struck by a 100-foot-high rogue wave. Rogue waves are believed to grow up to 200 feet in height, measuring from from trough to crest. They are thought by some to be fairly spontaneous, and without any argument, on occasion have been known to suddenly sink some very sizeable ships sans any real warning save the startling visual approach of the huge freak wave just prior to striking a vessel. Murf's sailing training had taught him that common waves are formed by the wind blowing across open water. The force of the wind and its duration drives the mass of the swells, with large blowing storms as the key determinant of the waves' height. At sea, waves six-feet-high are commonplace and waves that run twenty- to forty-feet-tall are not considered unusual—though they do scare the hell out of people. According to the scientists who study them, as many as ten rogue waves happen per day across all of the oceans. A constant characteristic is that just before striking, they are preceded by a deep trough. The resultant roller coaster experience is one that even the most modern, massive and seaworthy of ships sometimes cannot survive.

Rogues are thought to be caused by waves and wind that head directly into powerful ocean currents moving in the opposite direction. These contrarian-pressures cause a huge surge of water to rise up from the depths. Rogues generally do not happen near land, but largely in areas with extremely powerful currents like the Gulf Stream in the Atlantic (can you say BERMUDA TRIANGLE?!!). In the Pacific, the Kuroshio off of Japan, which the *Fenix* frequently passed, is another such locale. Rogue hot spots exist all around Norway and South Africa where wind and current collide and monster waves are spawned. For sailors who frequently ply these waters, it is well known that therein, two or three ships a year were massively damaged and almost did not survive monster wave incidents.

According to industry statistics, in the past few decades, rogue waves are believed to have sunk several dozen large ships—taking hundreds of sailors to their deaths. Should one of these seven-story tall freaks strike the *Fenix*, it would undoubtedly capsize and sink in a scant few minutes. The thought of being flipped upside down mid-sleep and then struggling to make your way through darkened, quickly-flooding passageways, with few if any viable escapes, was a sobering one and it promised the kind of suffocating, horrific death that would fuel abject terror in most already borderline claustrophobic sailors. And though Murf was strangely and serenely fearless when outside in a storm washing over the deck of the *Fenix*, whenever this particular trapped-inside-the-sinking-ship nightmare came to him, it gave him serious pause. Even if he miraculously did escape the sinking ship, he calculated that the odds of finding a buoyantly big Shelley Winters-in-Poseidon Adventure-type floatation device to save himself within in the open seas, were even less likely. So in his nightmarish dreams, even when he somehow did emerge from inside the bowels of the sinking ship's corpse, he was left to tread water for hours until in complete exhaustion, he was finally forced to relent, let himself slip beneath the dark water's surface and surrender to drowning. It was more than a little ironic that a man, who dropped out when he felt like he was slowly drowning in his own life, would, in this scenario, give in to the sea and actually drown.

Awakened from this recurring nightmare, Murf was resilient and would chug several large swigs from his bedside water bottle, wishing it were rum, and then slowly settle down and find comfort in the white-noise drone of the slow-moving ship; the hypnotic engine and propeller-spinning hum, the howling of the wind whipping across the metal ship and the deep swishing sound that the bulbous bow parting the waters made.

Two weeks after the *Fenix* left port in San Francisco, Murf took part in an anti-pirate drill on deck, which was quite poignant given his former membership in a band of same-named goofballs back in San Francisco. Beyond fire, collision, grounding, and consistently running so far behind schedule that the shipping company would fire the officers and raise a new crew, pirates were a more distant, but nevertheless legitimate, threat. The drill largely involved pulling up the accommodation ladder and pilot ladder from the sides of the ship. There was also the manning and aiming of powerful water-spewing fire hoses at imaginary pirates coming alongside and attempting to come aboard using rope launchers to latch onto cargo containers or railings to then ascend from their boats. The officers and a few of the men would be given small arms from the ship's lock-up to further aid in repelling boarders.

The *Fenix* made runs almost exclusively between Asia and the U.S. West Coast ports, and did not ply the waters in eastern Africa's Gulf of Aden where pirate attacks and highjackings were common, weekly occurrences. Nonetheless, pirates were still an active threat in Asian waters, too. In the '90s, a South China Seas pirate named Sister Ping became quite notorious for almost a decade of piracy, before her capture and trial in America. She and her men specialized in hijacking ships, converting them into unidentifiable phantoms and smuggling illegal immigrant human cargo into Europe and the U.S.

As Murf pretended to aim the unloaded shotgun he had been given, he spied and aimed at a bucket aboard the ship with a printed label on it that said in large block letters, "Lacquer." Naturally, Murf said to himself, "Lacquer? Hell, I hardly knew her!!!" as he fired imaginary pellets into the offending pirate/bucket. And then, as the second officer shouted out the check-offs for the captain's checklist, Murf's mind drifted to the huge white clouds up above—cumulus cloud masses of thick cotton-ball clusters set against a brilliant blue sky. Murf thought about the clouds and the ever-changing sky, wind and sea around them, but he did so without a whit of the depression that had accompanied his previous cloud-contemplations on airplanes, back when he was a white-collar corporate captive.

Less than a week later, as the *Fenix* neared Singapore—its first stop after crossing the open ocean—Murf was, again, on the aft deck relaxing and enjoying the only constant of the sea: change. The play of light and shadow on the water resembled an impressionistic painting with sparkling, cloud-filtered light colliding with blue-green, undulating water. The ocean's color had begun changing a few days back from that deep-ocean dark, almost purplish-blue, to the more sublime azure color typically found in the tropics. It also indicated a sandy bottom beneath the water. Overhead soared three brown pelicans whose rhythmic and graceful wing flaps and elongated, sword-like beaks contrasted sharply with the goofy-looking, drooping pouches under their mouths—mouths that they loved to and lived to fill with silvery, wriggling fish.

A nearly inaudible and far away sound of men in conversation emanating from the foremast deck down below pulled Murf's attention away from his daydreaming. Almost hidden from sight from his perch, he saw Third Officer Lu-Chi meeting with a six-pack of sailors in the shadows of a six-story tall container stack. He recognized Lu-Chi from his white officer's cap and Asian face, but the sailors' faces were hard to recognize at that distance. Murf also couldn't make out any of what must have been an intense conversation, given the broad arm-waving gesticulations of Lu-Chi. Murf did finally spot one familiar face among the group. It was Abdur, the older, Middle Eastern sailor whom he'd chatted with a few times. In a few moments, when a sailor using the railings walked near them on the deck, the group quickly broke up and dispersed in different directions like someone had just kicked an anthill.

CHAPTER 26

Always Avoid Politics and Religion

With so much to be done and no galley boy to help him, Murf was of necessity and predisposition, a bundle of tireless energy aboard the *Fenix*. He, in fact, enjoyed being lost in the beehive of a ship's daily activities and was completely enthralled about his first crossing—save the evenings in his cabin alone when he was constantly overwhelmed by despairing thoughts about the cowardly way he had dropped out on his life, his wife and his daughter. To escape those thoughts, he either drowned them out with iPod music blaring directly from his ear buds into his brain, or he'd go back out on deck to stare at the ocean again.

One evening, just one week out of port, Murf was plating up dinner for the officers and grooving to the rhythms of his workflow when The Rolling Stones mainstay "Get Off Of My Cloud" came on. Murf had taken the two small, portable speakers he packed into his gear, and attached them to the galley wall so he could listen to tunes hands-free while preparing and serving meals. The music wasn't played particularly loud, but the song selections were impeccable and the men sometimes rocked to them as they passed through the line. Just five minutes after serving the officers, the skipper returned to the line where Murf was now serving the men, for seconds. Respectfully the crewmen parted their line to let the captain through. As they stood back, the grinning-like-a-Cheshire-cat skipper wiped the still-clinging spaghetti sauce off of his beard with the back of his hand and then unexpectedly spun completely around, bustin' a little dance move as if he had now become Captain Boogaloo. The men and Murf had a very hearty laugh at this sight.

The next song on the tape was "Walken" by Wilco and the entire mess seemed to be alive with toe tappin' and finger snappin'. Steve Earle's "City of Immigrants" came on afterwards. Besides having an exceptionally infectious tune that had the men ducking and popping their heads appreciatively, the lyrics and happy melting-pot message of this ditty were completely apropos for the *Fenix*, given that the composition of the crew resembled the diversity of a United Nations assembly.

Livin' in a city of immigrants
I don't need to go travelin'
Open my door and the world walks in
Livin' in a city of immigrants

Livin' in a city that never sleeps
My heart keepin' time to a thousand beats
Singin' in languages I don't speak
Livin' in a city of immigrants

City of black, city of white, city of light, city of innocents
City of sweat, city of tears, city of prayers, city of immigrants

About thirty minutes later, Murf had a run-in that could have escalated into real trouble. It was with the always-belligerent Third Mate Lu-Chi, who had come to the galley near the end of the mealtime. The Chinese officer and ship's chief engineer became even more quarrelsome than usual after clumsily spilling his hot tea into his lap just as Youssef, a slender, smallish young seaman was passing by. Frustrated by his own clumsiness, Lu-Chi blamed the young sailor, who apologized even though he didn't really come close to Lu-Chi. "You ba-ba-ba-bump me, you ba-ba-bump Ru-Chi!" accused Lu-Chi belligerently. The third officer also had an unbeknownst-until-now problem with stuttering when angered, which then usually embarrassed him and made him even angrier and more stutter-prone. "You s-s-s-s-s-tupid A-ru-ru-ru-ru, A-rab!" screamed the now literally spitting-mad fellow. As it happened, Murf was nearby pouring coffee. Disinclined to allow any loud friction in his galley, he interceded.

"See here Mr. Lu-Chi. As a well-trained and experienced officer like you knows all too well, accidents happen aboard a moving ship. No one's fault, they just happen," Murf posited in a calming voice while he handed him a dishtowel to sop-up the spill.

"He is stu-stu-stu-stu-pid du-du-du-dog!" screamed the still furious engineer as chuckling could be heard from the other seamen in the dining room.

Murf deftly slid himself in between the Chinaman and the rattled young Arab sailor and asked, "Did you know, my good officer, that you two have much in common. Why his ancestor Arabs invented Algebra, and had hugely advanced medicine, natural sciences, astrology, and even engineering, while most of Europe was still in the Dark Ages. Your Chinese forefathers were also far more advanced in all the sciences and arts than their Western counterparts. The men of the West were the stupid ones," said Murf self-deprecatingly with a smile. "The fault is mine," Murf continued. "There must have been a spot of kitchen grease. Terribly sorry, I'll clean the floor twice tonight."

Duly distracted, the third mate now turned his rage on Murf and denounced his decadent American menu describing his food as "pu-pu-pu-p-p-poison." Then he threw the wadded wet rag toward Murf's face. Murf snatched it out of the air without missing a beat and turned away from the red-faced anger management flunkee before his Irish got the better of him and he gave-in to his searing urge to drop him with one swift fist to the chops.

"That must be why you had seconds," replied Murf quietly with his back now to Lu-Chi so he could not quite make out what Murf said. As he moved further away and back toward his kitchen, Murf then piled on more sarcasm with his best Ricky Ricardo-style Cuban accent, "You got some 'splainin' to do, Lu-Chi." Clearly Murf's final remark was overheard by a couple of sitting-nearby seaman, who laughed vigorously as Lu-Chi fled the galley in a huff. One of those was Abdur Nidal. And unbeknown to Murf, he also just had to stifle, like Murf, both his anger and a predisposition toward swift retribution.

"That was funny and very well played," said a now smiling Abdur. "My thanks for helping the young man," he said to Murf as he, too, exited the galley.

Later, Murf ran into Abdur again out on the sunken deck where he was smoking and staring at the roiling sea. It was a faintly moonlit night with a troubled sky overhead and storm clouds out in the distance. A gusty wind was flowing over the ship's nine-story superstructure at about fifteen miles per hour. A fingernail or thin crescent moon provided intermittent illumination between passing thick gray clouds. "Mind if I join you," asked Murf as he torched his cigar after chewing the tip off the other end and spitting it overboard.

"Please do," said Abdur with a welcoming tone as he turned around to face Murf.

"That Lu-Chi is a piece of work," said Murf as he puffed away.

"He is too quick to anger," replied Abdur as he lit a cigarette and continued, "but he's a very competent engineer." Abdur's comment reflected his own equivocation over whether it was wise or not to publicly disparage an easy-to-dislike ship's officer who was secretly on his team.

The ship and containers down below the two men were hidden in dark shadows. The main deck lights were not used at sea—just the running lights that alerted other ships to their presence. This, plus the peril from stacked containers, machinery, slippery surfaces and combustible materials on deck, made it a place where night visits were discouraged and smoking was prohibited. The waves were in the ten to fifteen-foot range, causing the *Fenix* to dip and bob vigorously as it rode the waves down and then back up. Murf heard the sounds of distant thunder and could smell and feel the threat of rain in the thickening air. Seagulls overhead drafted on the thermals or updrafts of warm air, seeming to float up and down effortlessly and endlessly, as though powered by some invisible source of thrust, with little need for flapping of wings.

As Murf and Abdur continued smoking and conversing, dusk turned to darkness and moonlight soon began reflecting on the shimmering water. "I have a very apropos joke given tonight's incident," opened Murf. "I don't usually make fun of anyone with a disability, but that third mate is a major dickhead. So…two men go into a bar and the first one says to the other, who happens to be our third officer, 'Hey Jackass. What do you want to drink?'" said Murf. "Lu-Chi then says 'A-a-a-a-p-p-p-p-int of bu-bu-bu-bu-beer please,'" Murf said spraying saliva like an errant water fountain as he spat out each syllable.

A sparkling-eyed Abdur giggled uncontrollably at Murf's over-the-top delivery. "The first man goes over to the bartender and says, 'A pint of beer for my friend, Jackass, and a rum and coke for me,'" Murf continued. "The man takes the two drinks from the bartender and hands one to the third officer saying, 'Here you go, Jackass,'" Murf intoned smugly. "After the guys both finished their drinks, the first man says to the third mate, 'It's your round, Jackass,'" said Murf. "Lu-Chi goes to the bartender and says, 'A-a-a-a-p-p-p-p-int of bu-bu-bu-bu-beer, and a ruh-ruh-ruh-ruh-rum and ca-ca-ca-ca-coke, p-p-p-p-please,'" Murf said, spraying even more profusely. "The bartender, unable to control his curiosity, says, 'Why the FUCK do you let him call you Jackass anyway?'" Murf asked indignantly. "The stuttering Lu-Chi responds, 'He-aw, he-aw, he-aw'" brayed Murf, "'he-always c-c-c-c-calls ma-ma-ma-ma-me that,'" concluded Murf. Both he and Abdur now had to hold the rail tightly as they swayed back and forth laughing hysterically to the point of crying.

"Now let me tell you mine," said Abdur upon recovering his composure.

"Yours?" a surprised Murf asked.

"Yes," said Abdur gathering himself into storyteller mode. "A handsome young Arab man sits down at a café and orders from the waiter. 'I-I-I-I-I'd like a p-p-p-p-pot of t-t-t-t-tea p-p-p-p-please,'" stuttered Abdur in the role of the young man. "Sitting next to him at the café is none other than our third officer Lu-Chi," said Abdur grinning broadly as Murf bellowed his approval of the performance. "'Sounds like you have a stuttering problem,'" said Abdur playing the part of a surprisingly non-stuttering Lu-Chi. "The now-perturbed young man then says. 'N-n-n-n-no, sh-sh-sh-shi, kidding,'" said Abdur. "'I used to have a stuttering problem, too,'" Abdur continued as he made the voice of Lu-Chi again, "'but then my wife cured me. She put her mouth down below on my root. She did this once, then again a second time after I recovered, and then one more time before I left,'" said Abdur with a wry smile. "'Fa-fa-fa-fa-fantastic. Thank you and g-g-g-g-g-good-bye' said the young man who then left. The next day, the SAME young Arab sits down at the SAME café and says to the waiter, 'I-I-I-I-I'd like a p-p-p-p-pot of t-t-t-t-tea, p-p-p-p-please,'" stuttered Abdur once more. "The third mate, again sitting at the very SAME table next to his, says in disbelief, 'So you didn't try the cure I told you about,'" said Abdur as Lu-Chi. "'Y-y-y-y-yes, I d-d-d-d-did. Bu-bu-bu-bu-but it d-d-d-d-didn't wa-wa-wa-wa-work. Bu-bu-bu-bu-but your apartment is very na-na-na-na-nice,'" said Abdur, as he and Murf buckled over again and commenced another imitation of a pack of staccato-howling hyenas.

Afterwards, Murf offered Abdur a cigar. Abdur's acceptance of his offer surprised Murf a bit and emboldened him to again risk unintended offense. "You are Arab I believe, Abdur?"

"Yes, I come from Azerbaijan … but I am really Palestinian," said an initially hesitant Abdur, stumbling ever so slightly between cover story and the truth. "With no work or even any hope alive in Palestine, I left my country many years ago. But I am not a terrorist as most Westerners automatically assume about anyone from my country," Abdur said earnestly without any hint of deception.

"Of course not," interjected Murf.

"It's not that I don't care…I'm just not really political," said the Arab seaman. "And the sea is my home now. After fleeing Palestine, I was raised by my uncle who was a fisherman on the coast of Lebanon," continued Abdur. "Then I got work on a ship that worked the Caspian Sea out of Azerbaijan. Baku is the capital of this oil-rich, largely Muslim nation on the Caspian Sea," said Abdur attempting again to weave-in the cover story narrative. "There are a few other Arab men on board who also sailed with me on the Caspian. But then shipping industry levels subsided drastically and we could find no other work. Then we used the last of our money and came to Hong Kong, where we signed on with the *Fenix*." Abdur studied Murf's eyes and expression for any sign of doubt as he relayed his story. He could find none, so he allowed Murf to reciprocate.

"I used to work in restaurants in San Francisco," responded Murf. "But then my marriage broke up after our young child died, so I went to work at sea to get away from things," said Murf in the most matter of fact way.

"I am sorry about your child," said Abdur commiserating.

Wanting to change the subject in order to move away from his own cover story, Murf said, "If you don't mind Abdur, let's talk openly about the problems of the Middle East. I studied the subject a bit in college and

I see a lot of wrong on both sides of the issues. And while the two of us may not be able to save the world by talking, I'll bet we can learn a lot just by understanding each other's perspectives."

"If you wish," Abdur said wincing slightly at the risk-riddled prospect. Thus began the first of a continuing series of historical, geopolitical, religious and philosophical after-hours exchanges between Murf and Abdur.

With Murf's governance, the consistently substantive discussions were usually rooted in terms of his recollections about the history of the Middle East, contrasted with Abdur's point of view having been born and raised in Palestine. Intertwined with the historical expositions, were Murf's central philosophical constructs such as the need to stand up for good versus evil and for constructive versus destructive actions, and the importance of moving toward flexibility, growth and evolution of thought versus militancy and intolerance for different points of view. Of course, in Murf's mind, these were tenets that he assumed were almost universally held, regardless of where someone grew up and what challenges they had faced. Abdur attempted to skirt discussions of terrorism, extremist politics and the Muslim religion, but inevitably the meandering conversations would circle back to precisely the topics Abdur most wanted to avoid. As the trust between them grew a little deeper in each discussion, Abdur found himself opening up more and more in spite of the risk.

"As I recall from ancient times, it is known that both Arab and Jew sprang from the same basic gene pool—the descendants of Abraham and Noah," said Murf a bit pedantically. "I believe Abraham is, in fact, known as the father of both Judaism and Islam. And furthermore, both Hebrew and Arabic are very similar Semitic languages and, racist as it may sound, both Palestinians like you and Israelis are characterized as being very intelligent and intellectual but also prone to argument," Murf said as quietly and as non-provocatively as possible.

"How dare you say that!!!!" Abdur screamed, shocking Murf with his explosive reaction. Only after a wry smile began to replace the feigned outrage shown on Abdur's face, did Murf understand that Abdur had just played a joke on him.

"Good one," Murf said hesitantly after catching on.

"OK, so back to Murphy Morrison's recall of Middle Eastern history. The non-stop Middle Eastern and European invasions and counter invasions of Persians, Greco-Romans, Christian Crusaders, Ottoman emperors and such, left the biblical lands of the Middle East a muddle of credible claims and counter claims," said Murf with his best attempt at Swiss-like neutrality. "My friends who are Jewish maintain that Israel was part of ancient Judea and Samaria, and say it was stolen from them in ancient times." Abdur nodded his head once and raised his hands slightly with palms toward the skies as if say either, "Shit happens" or more probably, just to confirm that he understood what was being said without necessarily agreeing. Then Murf continued his playback of college history classes and his incessant *New York Times* readership. Abdur nodded some more, puffed steadily on his cigar and listened in earnest. "The post-WWII 1948 creation of Israel, which was imperially decreed by Western powers, was certainly motivated by regret for not doing enough about the Holocaust persecution of the Jews by the Nazis."

"That is correct, Murf," interjected a now more energized Abdur. "But how can one terrible injustice sanction another, just to assuage the guilt Europe and America felt for the initial indifference they showed to the plight of the European Jews?"

"I agree," said Murf, pleased at the even-tempered nature of their discourse so far.

"So Jews get murdered in Europe and then they steal land from Arabs who did them no harm," said Abdur in an angry tone. "And later when Arabs defend themselves from Jewish aggression, they are declared murderers and terrorists and further justification is granted for the Israeli theft of even more land from Arabs. Look again at your history books, Murf," Abdur continued as Murf looked on with slight concern for the growing intensity of their discussion. "Next time you are at the library, take a look at the Israeli-owned or sanctioned land in Palestine on a map from 1947. They show up like a few small spots on a large dog—mostly concentrated around Tel Aviv and Netanya on the coast. Now take a look at any of the maps published by the West today and you will see that the Israelis have taken over everything. There are now over 100 Israeli settlements with 300,000 Israelis living on occupied Arab lands. Over one million Arabs must submit to the occupiers' governance. The Jews will never really leave lands they have occupied and they will consume the last remnants of Palestine in Gaza and the West Bank if they get their way," said Abdur with extreme conviction. Then he caught himself and deliberately feigned a small smile to let Murf know that it was OK to proceed with the discussion.

"So let's back up. Help me recall, Abdur, the historical progression," said Murf in a tone that promised objective investigation. "If memory serves me, Abdur, after the Western-sanctioned formation of Israel in '48, the first Arab-Israeli War quickly thereafter broke out with Egypt, Syria, Lebanon, Jordan and Iraq, all fighting in Palestine against Israeli forces," said Murf.

"Well, it was far from the first time Arabs and Jews had fought, but this was the beginning of the Israeli border expansions," said a now somewhat dispassionate Abdur. "And if I may, Murf, then much later in 1967, when Egyptian President Nasser closed the straits to Israeli shipping, as was Egypt's right..." laid out Abdur, "Israel responded with a surprise attack much like your Pearl Harbor. And as they destroyed all of the defenseless Arab air forces still on the ground, they were also attacking everyone by land forces as well. Do you remember the Israeli attack on the American spy ship Liberty?" asked Abdur provocatively but with an even mannered, measured tone.

"Yes, I vaguely remember that Israel mistakenly strafed an American ship in international waters off the Sinai Peninsula and that quite a few American sailors were killed," said Murf, recollecting.

“Thirty-four Americans died at the hands of your so-called allies, who repeatedly strafed and bombed the ship, in spite of the huge American flag it was flying in perfect visibility weather. And then they sent torpedo boats and machine-gunned the lifeboats that were lowered into the water,” said a very wide-eyed Abdur.

“Yes, Abdur, I have seen recent articles to that effect, although this account of the incident did not come out until twenty-five or thirty years later,” said Murf nodding his head as he puffed his cigar. “Apparently what is just now being declassified and coming to light, is that the Israelis deliberately attacked the ship and President Johnson refused to send help, supposedly preferring that the ship be sunk so Egypt could be blamed and the U.S. could enter the war on the side of Israel,” Murf said as they both nodded agreeably. Whereas initially, Abdur seemed rather guarded and a bit conflicted to Murf, he now seemed to be genuinely enjoying the conversation.

“You are a very different sort, Murf Morrison,” said Abdur with a look of surprise on his face. “Most Americans I have met just knee-jerk agree with Israel and all of its actions.”

“Israel is our ally and we generally want to stand by them,” responded Murf. But I think there’s been plenty of wrong done on all sides. And keep in mind, Abdur, that terrorist attacks tend to make people react based more on emotions instead of rational thought.” Abdur remained silent and cast his eyes downward pensively. Murf then filled the silence with a resumption of the historical narrative. “Without any question, the facts show that the Israelis did strike first in the 1967 War,” Murf said. “And after the Six Day War, Israel’s overwhelming defeat of the Arab countries gave rise to the occupation of East Jerusalem and the onset of Israeli settlements in the West Bank, Gaza and tremendous expansion of the borders of Israel,” Murf recounted. “And then again if memory serves me, in the 1973 Yom Kippur War, Egypt, Syria and the Arab states attempted, without success, to regain those captured territories.”

“This is accurate,” said Abdur without emotion. “And now Israel has more than tripled its occupied land mass. But let's shift to more recent times. In the early '80s Lebanon War, the Israelis invaded Lebanon and attacked the PLO." Murf raised a hand as though taking exception to this opening salvo.

"The PLO had repeatedly committed horrible terrorist acts against Israel," Murf stated as Abdur rolled his eyes.

Up until now, they had been chatting fairly amicably like a Siskel and Ebert review where both men liked the movie under scrutiny. Now the two men were beginning to clash, albeit in a civilized, verbal jousting only manner, akin to the give and take of two retiree Central Park chess players.

Abdur continued undeterred with his version of modern Middle Eastern history. "In 1987, still trapped by Israeli occupiers, the first intifada began. The flash point occurred when a careless Israeli driver killed several Palestinians in a traffic accident. As word spread, Palestinians poured into the street and began rioting. This led to violent clashes with troops that culminated in heavier Israeli occupation. And the uprising spread throughout Palestine and in the West Bank and Jerusalem," stated Abdur. "A second intifada against the occupiers began in 2000 and has yet to officially end," Abdur noted.

"As I recall, Palestinian mobs lynched two Israeli soldiers that day," added Murf solemnly. Abdur ignored this remark.

"And by now, you have the formation of the PLO, then later on Hamas and Fatah. With Fatah's loss of legislative elections for Parliament to Hamas in recent years, the radicalization of Palestine deepens. And then Hamas' call for a third intifada and resumption of missile attacks on Israel."

"Whoa. That's a lot of detail to swallow, Abdur. So what is the difference between Hamas and Fatah anyway, and haven't they been fighting with each other lately?" asked Murf with genuine interest.

"Yes, that's true about these rivals' in-fighting. Fatah, a mainstream faction of the PLO and a more secular group, runs the West Bank. Hamas is more militant and wants Palestine to be an Islamic state. They run Gaza and they also maintain a military wing," replied Abdur.

"Terrorists, as the Israelis and the Westerners call them…right?" qualified Murf.

"Well, that is a matter of one's perspective," replied Abdur. "And most Palestinians are willing to accept an independent Palestinian state limited to the West Bank, Gaza and East Jerusalem, versus demanding all of the land taken in the '67 War back."

Not to be outdone and as a contrarian counter to Abdur's ongoing contention that Israel always maneuvered to gain more and more Arab land, Murf mentioned that he thought he recalled that the Israelis removed their civilian and military presence in Gaza five years or so ago.

Anger rose in Abdur's flushed face though his voice remained in control. "They blockade and choke the life from Gaza and its people. They routinely commit assassinations of the leaders there. Demolition of civilian homes is a weekly occurrence. Some Israeli departure," huffed Abdur who then thought better of it and quickly regained his composure.

"Murf," said Abdur now in a tone much less confrontational, "The United States is committed to preserving Israel's military superiority over the so-called Arab states. And as for Iran, which is not Arab at all but is ethnically Persian, the U.S. is not so much really concerned about nuclear proliferation. Your country will do just about anything it can to deny Iran or any other Muslim country, save Pakistan, from possessing even one single nuclear weapon to defend itself against Israel's hundreds or thousands of them."

"Yow, I can't believe what we forgot. It's the classic elephant in the room that goes overlooked," said Murf as one of those infamous blinding glimpses of the obvious flashed into his head. "Abdur, what is your perspective on 9/11 and al-Qaida moving the attack to America?" Murf asked in a hushed and serious tone.

Abdur sat quietly with his head bowed for almost a full minute to convey the appropriate reverence. "Sad," he said. "Terribly, terribly sad.

And yet many Arabs feel this event was caused by the West because of the one-sided role it has played." Even as he segued into putting a fervent Islamist's spin on 9/11, he was also thinking fleetingly and with a bit of melancholy, about his own brief, yet happy college times in America at MSU. And that, in truth, he was a bit uncomfortable because of this prior America-based happiness, with attacking Coalition troops.

Murf now piqued, suddenly interrupted Abdur by placing a hand on his wrist for emphasis, "You couldn't possibly side with the 9/11 attackers could you!!??" he said with a voice simmering with potential anger.

"No, no, but Murf," said Abdur, "you must admit that the intense and prolonged media attention it commanded alone was the biggest influence on the Western World in all of modern times. And don't forget that the resultant invasions of Afghanistan and Iraq by what many Arabs refer to as 'The Crusaders,' has helped to fuel hatred and radicalize the Muslim world like no Middle Eastern war ever has."

The conversation had come to an awkward impasse here. And not surprisingly, since it is very difficult for most Americans to relate even slightly to the sense of victimization and alienation that motivates an Islamic extremist faced with the overwhelming might of Israel and the West, to blow themselves and innocent bystanders literally to pieces. On the other hand, there is the moral quandary for a terrorist of viewing themselves as former innocents—men of religion and moderation who were forced by oppressors to in turn kill other innocents and often themselves with their extremist tactics—in order to prevail against their powerful enemies. Yet the Quran explicitly forbids suicide. Though jihad and martyrdom have been applied here to turn self-destruction into self-sacrifice, have the extremists not, in the end, destroyed the very righteousness and way of life they sought to defend? Murf had once even asked in a bar room philosophic discussion, "Are terrorists who murder innocents in the name of God any better than pedophile priests who also prey on innocents and hide behind the robes of a man of supposed faith?"

Murf was clearly disappointed with Abdur's response. "Wait just a god damned minute, Abdur," said Murf angrily as he raised his right hand with a finger pointed toward Abdur's face. Abdur realized the very bad turn the discussion had taken and stood up.

"Look at the time," he said evasively. "It's well after midnight, Murf and we've got a busy day tomorrow," Abdur said, abruptly ending their stirring conversation.

"Right, right. To be continued, Abdur," a now cooling down Murf said as he patted Abdur's shoulder. "I very much enjoyed our spirited discussion and look forward to our next one."

With that said, both men now craned their necks in the direction of a pulsating, thumping sound coming from the distance. Off to the ship's starboard side they could clearly see another ship—an extremely well lit one. Passing another ship at sea was by no means an extraordinary occurrence. It happened every day or so. But this one looked and sounded like a Las Vegas casino with its flashing strobe lights and blaring music, which grew louder as the two ships grew nearer. Both men now had walked to the railing and were looking at what appeared to be a bevy of arms-akimbo dancers on a portion of the ship's deck, which seemed to have been turned into an outside disco. The song was growing clearer as the Japanese cruise ship neared.

"Good gracious, ass bodacious. It's getting hot in here, so take off all your clothes. I am getting so hot, I'm gonna take my clothes off," chanted the dancers to the song's chorus. Several of the other ship's dancing passengers who had seen the *Fenix's* lights, were now close enough that the too-bright-lights from their ship illuminated Murf and Abdur standing on deck and watching them. They began to wave at the two men as though encouraging them to give up a reciprocal dance. Murf was only too happy to comply and that induced a big cheer and more excited waving from the Japanese tourists dancing across the waves from them. Abdur was unable to stop himself from laughing loudly at the sight and he even managed a little hands-clapping-over-his-head action to join in.

The ships began to move further and further apart. Still laughing, the men had turned toward the hatch and began readying themselves to retire for the night.

"Candy?" Murf said as he took a paper bag out of his pocket that said "Liquorice" on it and offered some to Abdur.

"No thanks, but thank you," said Abdur, still slightly rattled by the intense discourse, followed by, of all things, dancing. As Murf noticed the spelling of "Liquorice" on the bag, his still stimulated and buzzing brain made the automatic joke in silence, "Liquor –ish???!!! Hell, I hardly knew her-ish!" The two men shook hands and slowly began working their way off the sunken deck. Murf stumbled when his kitchen shoes failed to stick to the deck. Abdur, with his lightning fast reflexes, grabbed Murf by the arm and steadied him.

"You need to get some proper shoes to wear out on this slippery deck," said a concerned Abdur.

"I know. I know Abbie. And thanks pal," Murf said with sincerity. Together they carefully navigated the early morning precipitation-slicked surface, with deliberate hand-over-hand use of the ships continuous system of handrails.

CHAPTER 27

"So Jesus, Muhammad, and Buddha are in a Lifeboat..."

"That talk last night went too far," Abdur thought as he headed for the galley for some tea and breakfast. Zahadid would slit my throat as I slept if he knew we were discussing the conflicts between Arabs and infidel Crusaders."

"I heard you were up on deck for several hours last night talking with the American cook," said Zahadid as he suddenly appeared behind Abdur on the stairwell. "What were you discussing with him?" Zahadid asked with an undercurrent of menace to his tone.

"He likes to tell jokes. You must have noticed him doing so as the men eat their meals," said Abdur without hesitance or nervousness. "He does most of the talking and I learn many things about America listening to him," Abdur continued. "I talked about life at sea and growing up working on my uncle's fishing boat in Lebanon. I also told him about working in Azerbaijan on the Caspian with the other men. Let's hope he repeats that story to others in the crew who may ask him about us," Abdur said coolly.

"Excellent," said Zahadid with a sinister smile on his face. "You set a good example for our team by infiltrating the *Fenix* crew and building trust." Zahadid grasped Abdur by the arm and stopped their stair climbing for a moment. "We will soon be in Singapore and then three days later we reach Korea and we make port in Busan. By next week, we will be in Shanghai for the exchange. Do you think the men are ready for the mission?"

"Yes, indeed. They are young, but every one of them is completely dedicated and they took to their training with great seriousness," said Abdur as he resumed his path up the stairs.

"Good. I will speak with you later," Zahadid said as they climbed the last stairs leading to the galley deck. "Meet with him some more…" he whispered to Abdur, "and tell me what you learn." The two men then separated as they entered the galley.

There had been much change introduced into Abdur Nidal's life, lately. Abdur had been, for many years, unquestionably an Islamic fundamentalist by way of philosophy, but of late, more and more reluctantly so. He saw himself as a devout Muslim, but not as truly a Salafist who justifies the killing of innocents. Since coming aboard the *Fenix*, he prayed only at irregular intervals and no longer stopped five times a day to recite his ritual prayers of Salah as he had done relentlessly since leaving Palestine so many years ago to become a holy warrior. He hated Zahadid, and not just because of the cruel and murderous acts he had ordered Abdur to commit. He hated him because Zahadid was the most dangerous kind of sociopath imaginable: a complete anarchist who loves creating violence and mayhem, and one who kills without remorse or discrimination between man, woman, young, old, soldier, civilian, colleague or countryman. Abdur had become a prolific killer in the name of jihad and seeking to exact vengeance on Western invaders, but he did so without joy. In fact, he was shaken inside each time a fellow

Muslim or innocent was sacrificed for the cause.

Zahadid on the other hand, seemed to actually enjoy terrorizing people and the very act of killing, as well. Abdur has been disgusted when he noticed the beaming smile and almost glowing light on Zahadid's face, whenever the light was fleeing one of his dying victim's eyes. And the more spectacular, inappropriate and unspeakable the act, the more delight Zahadid extracted. An attack on a marketplace or a group of police conscripts was mundane for him. His favorite ploys included attacking soccer matches, schoolyards or, even better, a funeral procession caused by another murder he had deliberately committed a few days prior, just so that he could torment and kill the mourners. Abdur was now becoming more and more disenchanted with extremism, hatred, and mindless killing and destruction that was not truly in the name of God, but in the name of one monster's perversion and his incessant struggle to attain more and more power. And with forces converging to his benefit—like terrorism becoming global, the costs of weaponry shrinking, and the demand to seize power and commit larger-scale atrocities mushrooming—Abdur viewed Zahadid as the epicenter of evil and a one-man weapon of mass destruction.

Abdur was becoming increasingly disillusioned with militant politics in general and, in particular, with his commander's excesses during the period when Zahadid repeatedly tested his commitment. Of late he had found it difficult to rationalize to the young men on his team in late night private quarters discussions, many of the more extreme Islamic jihadist actions and al-Qaida's legitimacy as a political and religious touchstone. And now Abdur was also worrying about where his next discussion with Murf might lead. Broaching the subject of 9/11 late last night did not go well. He knew he needed to come off as a relatively non-political type, and yet, as a man with an Arab view of the world dissimilar to the average American's. Abdur worried that if too much of his own real voice slipped out, he might accidentally convey to Murf both a too radical, borderline terrorist posture or worse—his own growing dilemma over the mission he was on and the potential it held for killing innocents on an unprecedented and massive scale.

"You know that there is always hope when people can still come together to talk," said a soothing and familiar voice behind Abdur.

"This is true," replied Abdur turning around. "Murf, how are you this evening?"

"I am FAN-tastic," said Murf ebulliently. "'And how did you find your dinner?' asked the cook of the always hungry fat man," Murf mugged. "'"Well, I just moved the parsley and there it was,'" said Murf in his best Catskills comic manner.

"Dinner was excellent, as usual. Shall we continue our discourse on solving all of the world's problems?" suggested Abdur.

"Indeed, good sir. I'll meet you out on the sunken deck with cigars directly," responded Murf.

"So when we left off, we were recounting history and had gone from the Western-forced partition of Palestine to the growth of Israel post several Arab-Israeli wars. And we had ended our session discussing the use of weapons of mass destruction in 2001—highjacked airplanes—against innocents on American soil," Murf said as he handed Abdur a stogie pre-wrapped in a plastic sleeve.

"Well actually, we were discussing the 9/11 tragedy—not to be mistaken for the other terrorist deployment of a WMD on American soil. An American, in fact, did that later that same year. Have you forgotten the attention-seeking germ warfare scientist Bruce Ivins' 2001 Anthrax attack in Frederick, Maryland that killed five people?" asked Abdur.

"Shit, that's right," nodded Murf in agreement as he lit his cigar. "You brought your A-game to the debates tonight, my friend. Well played."

Guessing that it might be wise to move the focus away from the geographic areas where Abdur and his family had suffered their tragedies, Murf shifted gears. "What about the other players besides Palestine, Israel and the immediately adjoining countries? The Egyptians accepted a truce after hostilities with Israel didn't they? They got the Sinai back from Israeli occupation, too. And the Saudis seemed to have aligned their interests with those of the West?" asked Murf rapid fire.

"The Saudi and Egyptian aristocrats of the Arab league countries care only about the maintenance of their kingdoms, inbred royal families and personal wealth," responded Abdur with a slight smile and a shoulder shrug.

"What say we get Iran, Iraq and Afghanistan into the mix?" asked Murf. "Let's see, after the Russians invaded Afghanistan…" said Murf wrinkling his brow and scratching his head. "Then anti-Soviet and Arab forces became allied with Afghan guerillas. Ironically, the U.S backed them. After years of heavy losses, the Ruskies eventually withdrew and, again, ironically, those very same Afghan guerilla fighters the U.S. helped, ultimately permutated into al-Qaida, bent on global jihad with the aim of Islamic religious law becoming supreme in all Muslim countries."

"Essentially correct," confirmed Abdur. "As for Iran, the U.S. and Iran have been mortal enemies since the overthrow of the Shah and the embassy hostage crisis. And in Iraq, Little Bush or, how do you say… Bush Junior, invades Iraq claiming to have been threatened by Saddam's infamous Weapons of Mass Destruction."

"And," Murf interjected, "that was after years of warring between Iran and Iraq, with hundreds of thousands of casualties on both sides and the use of deadly poison gases not seen in warfare since World War I."

"And now in Iran," Abdur continued, "you have the very real and growing threat to Jews and the West, of a fundamentalist-Islamic-ruled Iran, with its Hezbollah militia in Lebanon and Syria and its budding nuclear arsenal. Plus the Iranians give overt financial and military support to violently anti-Israel and U.S. movements of all kinds throughout the Middle East."

"WOW! That's one helluva tinderbox waiting to go up in flames," said a very chagrined Murf.

"And it's essentially been that way going back to the days of infidel Crusaders battling the Arabs defending their motherlands," concluded Abdur.

"So explain to me just exactly what the difference is between a Sunni and a Shiite Muslim anyway? It can't be minor because Lutherans and Methodists in our country don't go around attacking each other just because they are not identical in their protestant faith," said Murf with mock exasperation.

"That's an excellent question. Though I'm not really very religious, I was raised a Muslim and can tell you about the differences," Abdur said. Abdur's own mixed religious upbringing actually gave him a firm grasp of both faiths and had also allowed him to mix as needed, with both orthodox Sunni and Shiite militants.

"It is not easy to explain, but I will keep it very basic and I will start at the beginning, as you say, with the similarities between all Muslims," said Abdur slightly pedantically as Murf listened intently. "There are five basic pillars of Islam or duties for a Muslim. The first is Shahada, the profession of faith and a belief in one god, Allah, and in the finality of his messenger, the Prophet Muhammad. These days, some say Shahada is also just as much about declaring commitment to the struggle against the enemies of Islam," said Abdur, who then consciously faded away from this direction as one that might be too revealing about his militant point of view and recent past activities. "The second is Salah or the prayers Muslims say five times a day on our knees in the direction of the holy city of Mecca. Next is the regular giving of alms to the poor or Zakat. Charity is central to being a Muslim. In caring for the poor and the community, one is also purifying one's self and achieving personal growth," continued Abdur. "Then there is Sawm or fasting to burn away one's sins; fasting from dawn to dusk during the holy month of Ramadan during which Allah sent down to earth his holy word, the Quran, to guide us."

"What month of the year is Ramadan in?" asked Murf.

"Ours is not a solar calendar like yours, but a lunar one. So our months begin when the first crescent of a new moon is sighted. And because the Islamic calendar year is eleven to twelve days shorter than the solar year, Ramadan migrates throughout the seasons over the years." He could see that Murf was getting a bit glassy-eyed about the calendar, so he moved on. "During Sawm there is no food, drink or sex with your spouse allowed between dawn and dusk. At the end of Ramadan, we celebrate breaking the fast with a festival called Eid-ul Fitr, one of two major holy days in the year. People celebrate by gathering with relatives and friends, even by visiting and honoring the dead in cemeteries," said Abdur his face aglow and smiling as he, no doubt, remembered a few such happy holiday occasions of his own. "Small gifts are sometimes exchanged and the children go door-to-door receiving chocolates, dates and treats," continued Abdur.

"Sounds like our Halloween," Murf responded.

"I have never really understood the religious significance of this Halloween. And what is this business with werewolves and vampires all about???" said Abdur.

"We'll save that for another time; go on," said Murf.

"Eid-al Adha is the other holy day and it is a four-day celebration of sacrifice. It occurs at the end of the day, after the pilgrims descend from Mount Arafat, during their Hajj, which is the fifth and final pillar of Islam. Hajj is the annual pilgrimage of millions each year to Mecca in Saudi Arabia, made by Muslims worldwide. Now this greater Eid holiday of sacrifice is rooted in the obedient Ibrahim's willingness to sacrifice his son Ishmael, as it was Allah's will. But God spared Ishmael and a ram was slaughtered instead," said Abdur.

"Right, right, Abraham from the Old Testament!" injected Murf.

"Yes, Abraham or as we say, Ibrahim," resumed Abdur patiently. "He was a prophet or messenger from God and Muslims believe that so were Moses, Jesus, David, Soloman, and Noah. But Muhammad was THE messenger and law bearer who brought us Allah's divine revelations that form the Quran. And even more so, with his own life, Muhammad was 'the example' of how to follow that word and to live the true life of Islam. Before he died, Muhammad galvanized Muslims into the belief in one god versus many; he gave us God's revelations—revelations that transcend the ability of human reason, and he began the Islamic conversions that unified all of the Arabian peninsula under one faith—a faith that has now spread all across the world."

"Not to be disagreeable, Abdur, but wasn't Muhammad also a general who used the sword to force conversions—meaning convert or you die—just like the Catholics and Crusaders and countless other religions have done?" asked ever-the-catalyst Murphy Morrison. "That's what I like least about all of the 'organized' religions, except maybe for the Buddhists who don't want to harm any type of creature; animal or human. I think it's just fundamentally wrong to be out there killing your fellow man in the name of 'my God is better than your God.' What a crock of hypocrisy!"

"Well, this is a very complicated thing and, as you say, the historical context for the schism is rooted in the dispute over succession after Mohammad's death almost fourteen centuries ago. A Shiite believes the succession of power followed the Prophet's lineage. They regard Ali as the true successor to Muhammad and believe that the Caliph or head of the church is appointed by divine will. A Sunni sees this as heresy; they believe that the whole community should choose the Caliph and that the first four Caliphs after Muhammad were, indeed, the rightful successors. They also believe that a Muslim must literally walk in the Prophet's path or live by his example. Over the many, many years since the split, the two faiths have also developed many differences in the traditions and customs they follow, even in how clothing is worn. About 80 percent of the Muslim world is Sunni with this denomination predominating in Afghanistan, Egypt, Turkey, India, Saudi Arabia, Southern Russia, the Balkans, Southeast Asia, China and Africa. Shiia Islam is predominant in Iran, Iraq, Azerbaijan, Lebanon, and Syria. But let's move on for now and come back to that," Abdur said with hope that Murf would acquiesce, which he did.

"As I was saying," resumed Abdur, struggling slightly to regain his train of thought, "the fifth pillar, again, is Hajj or the pilgrimage during the last or twelfth month of the Islamic calendar. Hajj is an obligation to visit Mecca where Muhammad was born, and several other holy sites on a pilgrimage. This must be done at least once during your lifetime if you are able. It is a process that involves cleansing your body, mind and soul. It includes wearing simple pilgrim's clothing, shaving your head, and taking part in a series of vigils, prayers, and sacrifice. It brings Muslims together as one people from all over the world."

"Please, Abdur," Murf interjected, "with all due respect to your faith—which sounds altogether wonderful, so far—please explain to me why Sunni Muslims attack and kill Shiite Muslims every year, it seems, precisely during their once in a lifetime Hajj pilgrimage to Mecca to join in love and cleansing with all of the Muslim brothers of the world???!!!"

Abdur with the color now gone from his face and clearly exasperated, began slowly and deliberately with disappointment apparent in his voice, "The concept is called takfir, whereby the jihadi pre-absolves himself of the killing of a fellow Muslim. And the innocents that are sacrificed feel no pain and are martyred, so they go directly to heaven when they die."

"Excuse my French," said Murf removing the cigar from his lips for emphasis, "but that's a lot of horse shit."

"How different is Muslim-on-Muslim violence from Irish Protestants killing Irish Catholics in the name of God?" demanded Abdur. "I'll tell YOU what's horse shit," exploded Abdur as he seethed in response to Murf's sarcasm. "For more than forty years of occupation, the Israelis steal our land, murder our innocent women and children and repress all Arabs systematically! They come to our towns and, as they say, they CLEANSE them, as they are really preparing them for Israeli settlement. And when we defend ourselves, the Western world has the temerity to call us terrorists!!!?? We have no jets and tanks, just small arms and a few RPGs. The only way we can make the Israelis pay a price is if we fire at them from within civilian areas. So that when they attack us, they also kill many civilians in trying to kill us. That way the world sees horrifying images of dead and maimed women and children and can see the Israelis for the ruthless infidels they are!"

Murf sat in stunned silence at Abdur's intensely vehement outburst. Realizing that he had blown up, Abdur checked his tone and took it down several big notches. "Murf, there is no end to the Israelis' hunger for our lands. In addition to swallowing up Palestine, subsequently the Golan Heights was stolen from Syria, the Gaza Strip from Egypt, and the West Bank and East Jerusalem from Jordan in the 1967 Six Day War! And they immediately sent in their settlers to build and occupy the lands that they captured! And this is all justified by centuries of lust for a sacred land of Israel which they think is their birthright dating back to biblical times!"

"So let's go back to the beginning; back to ancient times," said Murf seeking to calm Abdur with a friendly pat on the shoulder. "As I understand it, most people of the Fertile Crescent share one common gene pool of Semitic ancestors, and that includes the ancient Hebrews, Christians and Muslims."

"The ancient Arab peoples, from which we descended, were rulers and the Jews were constantly creating uprisings," said Abdur dissenting.

"Look, Abdur, from what I recall from the history books, before Muslim rule, Ancient Israelites did rule for around one thousand years until falling to Muslim conquest. Then came, I think, the Assyrians rule; and in the Middle Ages, I think it was the Babylonians who were on top; followed by the Persians, then the Greeks led by Alexander, and next by Romans who persecuted, enslaved and scattered the Jews. And then you've got Byzantines, and then the Crusaders bent on taking back the quote/unquote "Holy Land" for Christian Europe; then Muslims again kicked them out. I loved studying that period of history in college," said Murf excitedly. "I remember that the Arabs were led by the great General Saladin, who stopped Richard the Lionheart from re-taking Jerusalem. And finally, after that, you've got the Ottoman Empire in charge leading up to World War I and siding with the Germans," said Murf ticking off the regime changes with impressive recall. "My God," said Murf quite pleased with himself, "the Middle East has seen more invasions and assholes than a Turkish border guard."

Abdur looked at Murf somewhat unsure of what he meant by his attempt at humor and whether or not to be offended. Nonetheless, Abdur was quite impressed with his sparring partner's encyclopedic litany of facts. Murf's favorite non-major courses in college were always in the area of history and he also had barroom-honed his recall like the Cliff Claven character on the TV series Cheers. "As I was saying," Murf continued, "the Ottomans were on the wrong side of WWI, so the British took over after the war and began to support formation of a Jewish state. The U.K. also made a lot of conflicting promises in those days, given that they were faced with both the rise of Zionism and Arab nationalism. After the next 'war to end all wars,'" Murf said sarcastically, "World War II, the Brits supported dividing Palestine into two states—one Arab and one Jewish. But under violent attack by elements from both sides, they dumped the dilemma into the lap of the United Nations who DID mandate just such a partition. Israel bought into that immediately and declared its independence, but the Arab states refused to accept the plan and the first of many Israeli-Arab wars ensued."

"Bravo Murf. But don't just recite history. What do you think of all of this," Abdur, his brow deeply furrowed, demanded in a moderately loud but firm tone.

"Well, no matter how much one group has been persecuted and chased all over the world, it doesn't suddenly make it right to just take away the land and homes of families who lived in Palestine for so many generations and who had nothing to do with mistreating the Jews in Europe," Murf said with sincerity.

"Fuckin' A!" said Abdur pounding one fist into his other hand's palm, "as you say in America," he added to create quick distance from his comment.

"Unfortunately, as you pointed out last night, the '67 Arab-Israeli War nearly tripled the land Israel occupied at the expense of Egypt, Jordan, Lebanon, Syria and, most of all, Palestine. And a Palestinian state never really came into being thereafter, with both Israel and Jordan taking land from the Arab state grant of the British.

"It was never their land to parcel out in the first place," stated Abdur, defiantly.

"Well now that you mention it," said Murf with brief pause, "if you go back into U.S. history, America actually made conquest of the entire southwestern United States from Mexico—including the great state of California where I'm from." Abdur was astonished that Murf was so forthcoming about his own country's occasional bouts of outright imperialism.

Murf, wanting to lighten the mood to end the night on an up note, then said that this reminded him of an old joke. "So there's an elderly Jewish man who was walking on the street in the formerly very seedy, Times Square area of New York City, with all its flashing lights advertising strip clubs and peep shows," said Murf as he turned on the charm. "There, he encountered a tall and bushy-haired hooker. And she keeps lifting up her dress and shouting, 'Super Pussy! Super Pussy! Super Pussy!'" Murf said in his most tawdry-lady-like voice. As he shouted, "Super Pussy!" Murf stood on his toes and raised a pretend skirt over his head repeatedly. "So the old man looks at her and says, 'I think I'll have the soup,'" said Murf suddenly sounding both old and Jewish.

Abdur laughed long and well. "I will reciprocate. Let me tell you a couple of jokes about your American presidents," a once-again thoroughly jovial Abdur said. "One day when President Clinton was getting off of Air Force One, a secret service agent sees that he is carrying a pair of pigs; one under each arm," Abdur said seriously. "'Very nice pigs and welcome home, Mr. President,' said the secret service agent," he continued. "'Those aren't pigs,' President Clinton drawls. 'Those are genuine Arkansas razorbacks. This one I got for Hillary and the other one I got for Chelsea,'" said Clinton nee Abdur. "The still-at-attention agent, sunglasses covering his eyes, replied crisply. 'Excellent trade, sir.'" finished Abdur with gusto.

Murf let loose a hearty and genuine laugh and then Abdur closed the evening. "A just elected George W. Bush is spending his first night at the White House and the ghost of the first American President, George Washington appears to him," said a winking Abdur. "'Tell me how I can best serve my co-u-u-n-try?' says Bush. Washington responded, 'You cannot tell a lie,'" said Abdur. "Later that night the ghost of Thomas Jefferson appears to Bush, who once again, asks, 'Tell me how I can best serve my co-u-u-n-try?' Jefferson replies, 'You must listen carefully to the people,'" Abdur continued. "Still later that night, the ghost of the great Abraham Lincoln appears to Little Bush, who repeats his question, 'Tell me how I can best serve my co-u-u-n-try?' Lincoln thought a moment and then said to Bush, 'I think you should go to the theater.'"

CHAPTER 28

Provisioning

"Operated continually since 1819, the Brani Port terminal in Singapore, is an enormous hub for Asian trade and the largest container port in the world," read Murf, as he checked the reference materials he kept in his cabin, on the night before the *Fenix* was to dock in Singapore. "In modern times, Singapore was the world's busiest port, in terms of total tonnage until surpassed by Shanghai in 2005. It remains the world's busiest in terms of container goods with over 400 million freight tons per year passing through its three giant container terminals each year. Brani is also a shipping hub for over 600 other ports in dozens and dozens of countries around the world."

The only break he took from reading and working on his galley supplies provisioning list for the next crossing, was a brief one on the sunken deck for a quick smoke around 10 p.m. As Murf looked out at a sky filled with a scattering of low-lying clouds beneath a star-sprinkled black canopy above them, he could now make out extremely distant lights on the approaching shoreline.

The next morning, about an hour after serving breakfast, Murf was "invited" by Captain Benny to come up on the bridge and take-in the ship's entry into port. Reading between the lines, Murf showed up with fresh coffee, tea and still-warm muffins for the Buddha-shaped skipper and the harbor pilot who had just come aboard.

The harbor pilot was a short, wiry Malaysian man in his mid-thirties. He had come aboard by making the arduous climb from the pilot boat's deck, up the long ladder lowered down the side of the *Fenix's* steel hull. It was an amazing sight to behold when a pilot came on board the moving ship. Murf had watched in fascination from the aft deck, as the pilot boat pulled alongside the *Fenix*. The boat had enormous black hard-rubber bumpers all the way around it. After pulling parallel to the still moving *Fenix*, the wave action began to thrash the tiny, by comparison, pilot boat repeatedly into the side of the massive ship. Once the distance between the vessels had been sufficiently closed, the pilot lunged and grabbed hold of a ladder leading up to the pilot's hatch. He then climbed about two-thirds of the way up the ship's side to the entrance.

While the view of the horizon from the ship's bridge was often somewhat obscured by huge billowing white clouds at sea, today was a mostly sunny day with a few intermittent clouds, but largely vast and clear visibility. Gusting winds created dancing whitecaps atop the blue-green water. Off the port side, Murf noticed two much larger bulk-type carriers, both with the name EUKOR painted boldly on their sides, which were headed back out into deep waters. In between the ships, two brown pelicans sat floating upon the water, completely unimpressed with the comings and goings of the behemoths. An assortment of small, wooden dhows with sails brimming and tiny inboard motor-powered fishing boats were moving away from them on the starboard side.

Murf loved being on the bridge with its commanding view and he took a seat next to the captain's to enjoy himself. As he did so, he saw the first mate seated behind him with head down and his eyes completely transfixed on the ship's computer—just as he almost always was when on the bridge. As conversations between the captains of other nearby ships crackled over the speaker for the bridge-to-bridge VHF radio, the skipper and the pilot enjoyed multiple sweet treats. The skipper engaged in friendly banter with Murf in between repeated finger licks. A mostly silent Murf was simply taking it all in and delighting in watching slices of land slide past the window as the ship came in through the Strait of Singapore. Next, it swung around a mid-sized land mass called Sentosa Island, which provides beaches and recreation areas for the million-population city. As the *Fenix* began entering the busy harbor, the tugboats that had come alongside took over. Murf could see that the harbor was teeming with hundreds of huge, anchored ships with dozens and dozens more under way and heading either into port or back out to sea. As he began watching more intently through the wiper-blade-equipped main bridge window, he noticed that the *Fenix* was gently rolling and plowing through five-foot, wind-whipped waves.

"These muffins are fantastic," cooed the pilot enthusiastically, putting two extra roadies inside his jacket pocket. Murf smiled and acknowledged the compliment and then looked away and tuned-out the conversation as he got lost in the magnificent sights of their harbor entry. Today, as they came into port, he saw from a distance three giant container stack-congested terminals with dozens of berthed ships and gantry cranes fixed atop them. The cranes looked like gigantic yellow-metal giraffes looming at water's edge and waiting to poke their heads aboard each new ship in search of something good to snatch away. The blue-green waters of the Keppel Harbor behind them were quickly giving way to the massive concentration ahead, of countless stacks of metal, multi-colored containers. Vast warehouses were immediately behind them, and still further in the distance Murf could see the side view of an elevated superhighway leading toward the immensely tall, sleek and elegant towers of the downtown financial district. The city skyline was modern and the harbor waters at its edge commingled there with the Singapore River, which ran through the city and into the harbor. The river was buzzing with water taxis, tour boats and passenger crafts of all kinds. Nearer to the container terminal area, the ship was now approaching a tall building with a revolving restaurant and a lounge atop it—with a no-doubt inspiring view of the entire harbor and the sprawling city.

Singapore was a metropolis that prided itself on cleanliness and booming industry. This was evident because of the contrasting juxtaposition of the downtown skyline and entertainment and nightlife complexes within sight of the intensely industrial containerized concentration. As he scanned the endless rows of stacked metal boxes, Murf remembered flying over such areas in both Hong Kong and Oakland. Whether on final approach or just having taken off from the airport, from 10,000-feet, the myriad of colorful containers, cranes, and machines down below appeared to be a colossal high-tech circuit board, composed of thousands of different colored component parts, lightning quick microprocessors and brilliant bits of shiny copper and silver connections.

"I know of many captains who would pay handsomely for a cook with his talent," the pilot said knowingly to Captain Benny. The longtime captain of the *Fenix* was savvy in this regard and, in fact, he believed that the most important person on board a well-operated and highly productive ship was actually the cook and not the captain. On cue, he asked Murf to go below to the galley and make a list of the necessary provisions the purser would acquire once dockside. As Murf stood to leave, he continued to watch the massive ocean-going tugboat that had cruised alongside the *Fenix* from open seas almost to dockside make its departure. He turned to leave. Out of the corner of his eye, he noticed six or seven crewmen, including Abdur, gathered mid-ship between the container stacks and conversing on the deck of the *Fenix*.

Whereas port calls in days of old lasted for weeks, the stop in Singapore was scheduled for only six hours—that's just how automated and efficient the terminal operation was. Murf helped Adam Santez, the purser and the officer he reported to, finalize the list for provisioning. Murf knew that once the list was completed, he had four hours of free time to put to good use. He walked down the railed accommodations ladder gangplank to ground level at the dock. He was immediately almost overwhelmed by the buzzing hive of activity as a small army of gantry cranes, bulked–up forklifts, side loaders and wheeled mini-cranes and their operators, the longshoremen, stevedores and truckers, all converged on the forest of steel boxes and rapidly and very noisily began tearing down and building back up perfect stacks of inbound and outbound cargo.

Murf started to walk away, and then he stopped and turned to take a moment to fully appreciate the spectacle. The *Fenix* was now tied to the dock. Perpendicular to it, were ten or more gigantic gantry crane spans that now loomed overhead and above the containers on the ship. They were set at precise intervals that made them look, from above the ship, like fat, steel ten-yard line markers superimposed over a football field. Murf marveled at the sight for a few more minutes and then hurried off to catch a waiting shuttle from the Tanjong Pagar Terminal, where the *Fenix* was one of forty-five ships berthed that day. It would take him to a marketplace three miles away.

To his surprise, he was able to reload on quite a few of his exotic secret ingredients in a gourmet grocery store. He also replenished his cigar supply, treated himself to some sizzling garlic prawns served at an outdoor café, and then visited several Asian groceries for goodies he had learned about in his future menu-planning foodie discussions with the Asian-dominated crew. Afterwards, he had a good smoke and a large pot of strong green tea with honey and mint leaves before he began his return to the ship. A cab took him most of the way, but dropped him short of his destination at the terminal gates past which the public was not allowed. Now he had a good quarter-mile to traverse carrying six plastic bags of groceries that soon were doing a thorough job of squeezing every last drop of blood from his pinched, circulation-starved fingertips. As he made his way through the sea of containers, in spite of the irritation to his hands, he veered a bit off the main pathway to get a little peek at what lay in between the endless rows and rows of stacked steel boxes. Just a couple thousand yards away from the deck, he was forced to put down the sacks and give his hands a brief respite.

As he stooped over and nestled the bags to the ground, he thought he heard muffled voices. In the center of a small clearing, he could see that there was a group of men standing about four rows ahead of him. They were the same fellow crewmen he had seen gathered on the deck of the *Fenix* earlier from the bridge. He noticed that, in addition to Abdur and several of his Middle Eastern Azerbaijani acquaintances, the bitter and eternally irritable Third Officer Lu-Chi was also among them. Lu-Chi was speaking at the moment and with anger written all over his face. He was waving his arms and gesticulating forcefully with his hands toward a man that Murf had never seen before. Murf thought that he appeared to be Korean.

The scene had the look of some kind of transaction that was going bad. As Lu-Chi argued with this gaunt, mid-forties suitcase-carrying Korean character, who looked like a recently escaped refugee from a jungle prison with Papillion, Murf saw the third mate aggressively grab the other man. Lu-Chi yelled at ballistic levels into his shocked and frightened face. They both began to shove each other and then wrestled themselves to the ground as the other men drew closer around them. Suddenly, after they both struggled back to their feet, still clutching each other, Murf saw the quick flash of a silvery knife blade, which Lu-Chi had pulled from his coat. His opponent saw it, too, and he reeled back in shock.

At that point, Abdur quickly stepped in between the two of them, his arms perpendicular to his chest and the palms of his hands bent up at right angles. Lu-Chi then lowered the knife and resumed his shouting at the clearly frightened man. He then removed an over-stuffed letter-size envelope from his coat and angrily tossed it at the Korean. It bounced off his chest before he could react to it. The Korean then lowered the suitcase he'd been holding to the ground and scooted it with his foot toward Lu-Chi. The frightened man picked up the envelope, turned and quickly hurried away. Murf, who was watching in disbelief, had seen enough. He picked up the grocery-heavy bags and began walking in the ship's direction. He couldn't help but think he had just witnessed a drug smuggling transaction and pricing re-negotiation going down. He also wondered whether or not and how he might bring up what he had seen in his next conversation with his friend, Abdur.

In an hour, the last of the bulk-loaded strawberries, tea, motorcycles and fertilizer that were added as cargo, were stacked aboard. The lines were then cast off and reeled in by the *Fenix* crewmen. Slowly, with Benny at the helm and another harbor pilot beside him, she backed away from the dock and turned in the direction of the channel that led back to the open sea. They were off once again and heading to the port of Ulsan, South Korea, some three days away. There they were to take on a cargo of automotive parts to transport over to Shanghai. Once there, they would load up with electronics to take back across the Pacific to the port of Long Beach, California.

CHAPTER 29

Bombs Away

Murf spent the next few days in a fairly constant state of wonderment and deep worry—hardly the state of mind he sought when taking refuge in a mindless, yet pleasurable, job on a clunky old ship at sea. Given the repeated gatherings he had witnessed and the Arab nationalities of Abdur's "acquaintances," Murf's mind was racing between possibilities. Was there a plan afoot involving an act of piracy and taking over and re-naming and re-flagging the *Fenix*? Could it be a drug deal or smuggling operation that might result in a bloodbath of murders if revealed? One afternoon, Murf, in need of a break from his paranoia, grabbed a magazine from the rec room en route to the head. Turns out it was published in the U.K. two years earlier. "The Growing Threat of Nuclear Terrorism" crowed the large-type-headline on the cover. "That's just great," sighed Murf, as he dropped trou and sat down on the toilet seat. He then opened up the periodical to the cover story and started feverishly reading it.

"Dr. Mohamed ElBaradei, the head of the U.N.'s International Atomic Energy Agency, reported recently in his annual address to the U.N. General Assembly that there are around 250 cases a year of illicit trafficking of nuclear material," read Murf who was now transfixed. "According to The New York Times, some material that is reported stolen is never recovered, and conversely, a lot of the material recovered has never been reported stolen. The possibility of terrorists obtaining nuclear or other radioactive material remains a grave threat. Dr. ElBaradei also expressed hope that North Korea would rejoin the Nuclear Nonproliferation Treaty that it left in 2003, and he criticized Iran for impeding the agency's attempts to verify whether it was developing nuclear weapons."

The article went on to recount how the leading scientist in nuclear weapon-equipped Pakistan, had confessed to secretly exporting expertise and components to terrorism-disseminating Iran. "These brainiac nuclear watchdogs think terrorists can't really pull off actually making and deploying 'the big one?!!!'"

Murf skeptically thought to himself. "Have they not seen the countless movies and TV shows where the super-cool secret agents of the free world always just barely intercede in time, to foil nuclear terrorists who inevitably always got their bombs from a former iron curtain Eastern European country still holding remnants of Russia's stockpile of decommissioned warheads?????!!!!!!"

Perhaps that was the popular action movie portrayal because the experts' focus had always been on nuclear terrorism emanating from black-market devices obtained from Russia. Unbeknownst to Murf, an alternative scenario that his new friend Abdur knew about, was a nuclear device that was obtained from North Korea in secret dealings with rogue military officers desperate for money to escape their own country; and that a worn-out, nondescript container ship would play the key role as the delivery mechanism.

Murf now read even faster, given that he was ready to conclude his restroom business. "blah-blah-blah...fissile material," he mumbled as he read. "In Graham Allison's Nuclear Terrorism: the Ultimate Preventable Catastrophe, he concludes that, 'On the current course, nuclear terrorism is inevitable.' The task is, indeed, a highly daunting one, yet not impossible. Nuclear warheads must be scrupulously maintained, overcome arming codes that safeguard them. The quantity of nearly impossible to find and almost entirely cost prohibitive bomb fuel is great—100 pounds of it would have to be secured from rogue individuals within a nuclear or former nuclear nation. Then it would have to be transported over thousands of miles of terrain to a safe site. Building the actual bomb would require the terrorists to get nuclear expertise and extraordinarily complex equipment together. In the end, there would be no way to pre-test it. Delivery of such a device is yet another huge challenge. Potency is not arguable—a ten-kiloton nuclear explosion (10,000 tons of TNT equivalent) would completely destroy buildings up to a mile away, create 900-mile-per-hour winds and a deadly radioactive cloud that would drift and coat the land for hundreds of miles."

"They must be smuggling drugs or I'll bet it's actually counterfeit products like copy watches, fake Gucci handbags and such," Murf said to himself as he broke into a having-reassured-himself smile. Surely Abdur could be involved in nothing worse than shipping and selling fake Chinese-made designer scarves and bags at flea markets and low-end retail shops. "Your secret is safe with me my friend," said Murf with a smile and a flush.

Wanting a proper conclusion to his reading, Murf skimmed quickly and saw that the story, thereafter, went on to talk about the unconfirmed rumors, that, at the height of the cold war, more than 200 suitcase-nukes supposedly had been covertly manufactured by both sides, allegedly for use against each other in urban warfare and domestic terrorism efforts. "Great, another new doomsday scenario to worry about," said Murf as he closed the magazine.

CHAPTER 30

Extra Special Cargo

The evening before the arrival of the *Fenix* in Ulsan, South Korea, Murf asked Abdur while they chatted on the aft deck, whether he cared to join him for a quick trip to Seoul during their two days off after a month at sea. "I thought I'd pop up to Seoul. There's an Asiana flight that's just $120 round trip and from there I plan to visit the infamous Demilitarized Zone at the 38th Parallel," said Murf with his sales savvy, persuasive tone. Noting the puzzled look on Abdur's face, Murf explained further. "Over three million lives were lost in the Korean War back in the early 1950s and the DMZ is the buffer zone and a demarcation line created after the war to keep the two countries from resuming open hostilities," Murf continued. "The DMZ is some 160-miles-long and cuts the Korean peninsula roughly in half, into North and South Korea. And ironically, though it's called the Demilitarized Zone, it's the MOST militarized border in the world with both sides having huge divisions of infantry, tanks and such poised and waiting to attack."

"Thank you, Murf, but I must stay with the ship in Ulsan to earn extra wages," replied Abdur. He was part of a skeleton crew that would watch over the *Fenix* while most of the crew and officers were on shore leave. The lone officer in charge for these two days was Third Mate Lu-Chi.

Both Murf and Abdur turned in early that night anticipating a big day tomorrow, but for decidedly different reasons. Murf was up by 4:00 a.m. and breakfast was served early beginning at 5:45 a.m. because the *Fenix* was scheduled for an early morning arrival.

Murf poured over his web sourced reference materials in preparation for this new destination. "The port of Ulsan, is South Korea's seventh largest city and is situated on the southeastern coast facing the East Sea also known as the Sea of Japan. It is dissected by the mouth of the Taehwa River, which runs through the city center and far inland. Ulsan is an enormously industrialized city of just over one million, and it's where a vast sea of about-to-be-exported Hyundai cars undergo their final assembly, and then are driven onto ships and stowed below the decks in massive car carriers. In addition, the port is home to the largest ship building facility in the world and a huge petrochemical complex with multiple refineries." Not in the information, Murf had gathered, was a revelation that rattles many Westerners to learn. And Murf would discover it later, as he walked past a large sign next to an odd looking bright red ship, with a harpoon gun mounted atop its bow deck. Ulsan is also home to the South Korean whaling industry.

After turning in his provisions request and getting some Korean currency from the purser, Murf took a shuttle to the main gate, where he caught a bus into the city and then another directly to the airport. Murf had cash to take taxis and the cost was generally less than 10,000 won, or ten bucks, to go just about anywhere by cab. But Murf wanted to be true to his new rudimentary role in life. Plus he liked watching the regular working-class people who took the bus versus the self-absorbed executives—like he once was—that largely traveled by high-speed train, limo and taxi. The flight was a mere fifty minutes long. By 10:30 a.m., he'd be in Seoul.

"It sure is strange to be back up in the clouds again," thought Murf as he sipped a bad cup of lukewarm coffee on the plane ten minutes later. "And even stranger," he thought, "to not be drinking a rum, Coke and lime." It now occurred to Murf that he'd, in fact, been without booze for thirty days and he had never really given its absence a second thought until now. Murf gazed out the window to begin contemplating the billowing masses. Shaped like elongated lines, the clouds he saw looked like delicate, hazy white streamers with a contrasting rich-blue sky as a backdrop. "Mare's Tails" is what Murf had heard these type of cirrus clouds referred to. He had admired them countless times while sailing on his boat or cruising on the *Fenix* at sea.

Once in Seoul, Murf caught a bus into the city center where he got a modest room at the Novotel in the Insadong area—which he remembered was popular for shopping for traditional Korean crafts. Insadong was a bustling district in a neighborhood not as tony as the one he stayed in while at the posh Shilla Hotel during his last trip to the capital city as a soon-to-be-summarily-rejected, prospective employee of Samsung. In the lobby business center he went online to the Lonely Planet website to download information on both Seoul and the DMZ. He did a quick scan of the first paragraph of the pages he printed out, and then smiled and scratched his head as it struck him. "Seoul has been revived, phoenix-like from the rubble of the Korean War and locals like to call their 600-year-old capital 'the miracle on the Han [river].'" The irony of the phrase "phoenix-like" and the name of the ship that he'd arrived on, escaping what he saw as a life in ashes, was sublime.

After gathering up the printout, Murf took a short walk to meet up with a tour bus for the hour-and-a-half-long ride north to the DMZ. The bus would take him to Mount Dora or, as the Koreans called it, Dorasan. Atop its heights was the Dora Observatory, notably painted in a splotchy, olive-brown-green military camouflage scheme, with bold pro-Republic of Korea slogans painted on its fascia. Murf's fascination with the DMZ, of course, stemmed from his dad having fought in the Korean War before Murf was born. There he rose from private to corporal, and finally to master sergeant—winning three battlefield promotions in a three-year tour of duty with the U.S. Army infantry. Murf's dad was, indeed, a brave and skilled soldier. He had even survived the frozen retreat from the Chosin Reservoir when tens of thousands of Chinese troops poured over the border in a surprise human-wave, dead-of-winter attack on a nearly victorious U.N. force that had all but driven the North Korean invaders back and into oblivion. There he won two Bronze Stars for valor and two Purple Hearts for wounds suffered. In this battle, so many of his fellow troops were killed or wounded, that whoever was left standing and survived, probably stood a good chance of advancement just due to scarcity.

The Dora Observatory structure totaled about 300 square feet and could hold approximately fifty people. There were dozens of extraordinarily long-distance telescopes mounted out on the open-air deck and also inside for visitors to use in scanning the thin strip of territory between North and South. Therein lay the North Korean "propaganda village" called Kijong-dong, which had been built across the wooden and marshy area in between. It was so-called, not just because of the recorded propaganda that blared across the distance from the loudspeakers mounted atop huge wooden poles. It also had been thusly named because the atypically modern town built in a highly rural setting, had a bevy of colorful poured concrete, blue-roofed, multi-level apartment buildings, that were in fact empty shells. They had been constructed to show the health and modernity of the North Korea nation to South Koreans and other visitors who had come to this vantage point to see for themselves.

"Der are no people living inside these buildings or in the village," said the tour guide for Murf's group. He spoke excellent English—as did most Koreans—versus the lack of command of the English language

Murf had encountered elsewhere in his travels. English was rarely spoken by common folks in Japan, and throughout most of China—save Hong Kong—where English is commonplace. "At night, many believe that tanks rumble out from within these buildings. The North Koreans are famous for their underground complexes as is evidenced by the four massive tunnels we have discovered over the years, that they dug for use in future invasion scenarios," explained the guide.

Murf could visualize a sea of tanks parked in a hidden subterranean depot beneath the buildings, and how, when given the signal, they would come roaring out of the seemingly tranquil, residential complex, like so many angered red army ants once their anthill has been kicked. And just such a scenario was especially easy to imagine, since the fearless leader of the North was crazier than any dictator since Idi "the Cannibal" Amin. And he was sitting on nukes that could be launched by missile from the North to strike Seoul with the Big One less than a half hour later. In fact, significant fighting has periodically broken out in the DMZ with over 500 South Korean, fifty American and over 3,000 North Korean soldiers killed in action in the sixty-some years since the armistice supposedly stopped the deadly conflict in 1953.

After the two-hour visit to the observatory, the bus stopped on the way back at a quaint, nearby restaurant that was set up just to take advantage of visiting tourists from the city. There Murf enjoyed a highly flavorful meal that began with spicy, fermented kimchi cabbage, and then moved on to grilled-over-hot-coals, marinated beef strips skewers with rice. The meal concluded with a spicy noodle soup with giant dumplings floating in the broth. But what he enjoyed most that afternoon was having somebody else doing the cooking for a change. And as he read over the menu before the delicious food was brought out, he said quietly to the confusion of those seated around the table, "Skewer??!! Hell, I hardly knew her."

Back in his Novotel room a few hours later, after having napped on the long bus ride back, Murf lay fully clothed on his back in his bed, just staring at the ceiling. That's when the realization hit him; he really was all alone now. Without the constant camaraderie he manufactured each day in his well-run galley on the *Fenix* with the always-happy-when-well-fed crew, he began to feel lonely. His bizarre dropping-out-on-life actions of the past month and the weight of his loneliness suddenly bore down on Murf. He picked up his wallet off the nightstand where it lay along with his early-morning return flight ticket to Ulsan, and opened it. He pried out with his fingers from a small, hard-to-spot crease where he had stashed it, a single, wallet-size photo of himself, Molly and Terri. In it they were hugging and smiling broadly together in an instant-photo booth down at Pier 39 in the Fisherman's Wharf area within the highly touristy, waterfront part of San Francisco. Murf glanced at the photo, smiled briefly, and then almost immediately began shaking and sobbing. For the next ten minutes, he sobbed uncontrollably, until he finally passed out from anxiety and the complete exhaustion of having both driven himself and so completely denied himself for over a month. Little did Murf know what he was missing back aboard the *Fenix*.

While Murf was in Seoul, Lu-Chi and the Arab crewmen, who had also deliberately "volunteered" to remain behind, had overseen the first-day-in-port unloading and loading of the ship by dockside workers who used their nimble machinery to stack standardized containers five-high, looming over forty feet high from the deck. The *Fenix* also topped-off with bunker oil to fuel the container ship's engines for when they headed out after tomorrow on a four-day cruise to Shanghai. And tomorrow, while the vast majority of the officers and crew were still away, the men would do a little loading of their own. A single Hanjin container, filled with stacks of giant burlap sacks of rice, as well as a hidden-between-them cache of assault rifles, Glock 9mm pistols, about a dozen grenades and one long and very fragile 250 pound wooden crate filled with molded foam to form-fit over and protect some kind of device inside. Once they had used the auxiliary crane to remove one blue Hanjin container from the ship and had replaced it with an identical-looking one from the engine-still-running truck down at dockside, Aziz and Zahadid would personally carry something that they removed from the crate below deck with great care—as though nitroglycerin or the like was contained within. Meanwhile, the team's best bomb-making members, Imdad and Salim, were transplanting, with a series of electrical wire splices, the RFID tracking tag from the original container on to the new container, without breaking the circuit.

They had chosen a Hanjin-branded container because they didn't think anyone would expect illicit cargo within a Hanjin Shipping Company container of South Korean origin. The container in question would eventually be supplanted by another identical container at the next port and then buried beneath a row stacked above it, after the final cargo stop to load was made at the Yangshan Deep Water Port in Shanghai.

When his morning flight landed, Murf was still quite unsettled from his evening alone in the motel room in Seoul. He took a cab instead of waiting for the bus to take him from the Ulsan airport back to the docks. He returned much earlier than he had originally planned and was seeking refuge in his kitchen and the solace of cooking—even if it was just for the small, skeleton crew left to secure the ship during shore leave. As he slung his overnight bag over his shoulder, he noticed something quite odd. The *Fenix* was scheduled to have been fully loaded the day before, and, at first glance, it had been and was now stacked high with new containers. And yet, aboard his ship this morning, he could see a small group of crewmembers operating the almost never-used fixed crane mid-ship, to lift a single blue container into place atop one of the stacks. Normally, the crew would be involved in loading or unloading only in an emergency situation. So it was highly unusual to see them doing so and on a day when no activity was scheduled for the *Fenix*. As Murf took in this scene, one of the Arab individuals turned in his direction and seemed to be staring at him in mutual recognition.

As it turned out, that individual was Zahadid. He had, indeed, spotted Murf and noted that he had witnessed their actions. "The cook must be eliminated, or he could be our undoing if he talks," he later said to Abdur with emphasis underlining that it was an order.

"Murf will not say anything. I will reassure him straight away and everything will be fine," said Abdur hoping to dissuade Zahadid from this course.

"Do as I command you! You are to kill him and dump him overboard. And you will do it after we make our quick stop in Shanghai and we are back out at sea and heading back to California!" Zahadid said angrily.

After stowing his bag, Murf went back off the ship and purchased some nice steaks, fresh seafood and fruit to make something a bit more gourmet for the small crew. The capper to the meal was a dark chocolate fondue pot with wooden sticks for dipping plump berries and slices of fresh pineapple into a rich, sweet cocoa and orange-brandy Grand Marnier-based sauce. Afterwards, Murf was virtually alone and enjoying a cigar out on the deck, when Abdur popped his head out the door, saw Murf and then walked out to join him.

"You are back early," said Abdur quizzically. "Is everything all right?"

"Oh sure, I went to the DMZ and it was fascinating," Murf replied. "But then the city and its noise made it hard to sleep, so I came back on an earlier flight than I had planned to."

After a bit more small talk, Murf just had to sneak in the question still eating at him. "I've just got to ask you, my friend," said Murf hesitantly, as he used his lighter to light Abdur's cigarette and then his own cigar. "What in the world was going on this morning with that crane and the single container?"

Abdur's face initially showed alarm as he issued a quick denial. "I don't know what you're talking about," said Abdur sounding completely defensive and angered. "Everyone knows that the shore workers are all unionized, Murf, and they do all of the loading and unloading," Abdur continued with a nervous, almost apologetic smile.

"I know what I saw," said Murf firmly. "And I saw some of the guys from your last crew in Azerbaijan, loading that single crate."

Given that he'd now had a moment to recover and think, Abdur's tone calmed and a confident smile returned to his face. "Oh, that's right. I forgot that Lu-Chi received a special order to add one more crate after the dock crews had done all their work yesterday," said Abdur speaking very evenly and looking Murf right in the eyes. "Something about an outbreak in China and the need to transport extra backup vaccine serum and some specialized equipment."

Murf quickly decided to accept the explanation because he wanted to believe Abdur, even though flying vaccines in mere hours made more sense to him than taking four days to transport them by ship.

"Well let's hope they nip it in the bud," said Murf agreeably. "We don't need another swine flu or another new disease sending the whole world into a frenzied panic."

Abdur now grew silent as he smoked his cigarette and wondered to himself if Murf really believed him. He also wondered if, perhaps, Zahadid was right and that Murf must be eliminated to protect the secrecy of their mission.

The final Asia side stop for the *Fenix* was Shanghai, a little less than two days directly southwest from South Korea. The Yangshan Deep Water Port, where the ship would make its last stop in Asia before heading back to the U.S., is amazingly located twenty miles out to sea from the city center of Shanghai, amidst a cluster of islands in the East China Sea. The port was built in waters almost fifty feet deep and is connected to the mainland via a six-lane bridge that took two and half years to build. There, during the partial unloading of the Ulsan cargo and loading of supplemental cargo from China, Murf went ashore for half a day to stretch his legs and think.

After walking around the terminal and seeing the sights for about an hour, he ate lunch at a small family-run restaurant on the top level of a two-story concrete building. The place had an outdoor observation deck with a few tables overlooking the docks, so Murf ate there to take in the view. When it was time to order, he deftly avoided the civet cat kebabs special on the highly-exotic-for-a-Westerner menu, and had a simple meal of boiled eel mixed with scrambled eggs, scallions, rice and a splash of sesame oil. Leery of the complimentary glass of water he was brought with his food, and having been dry for more than a month, Murf decided to demonstrate to himself that he could consume small amounts of alcohol without slipping back into his Pirate excessive-drinking-haze. So he chased the fairly tasty lunch with a Yanjing beer, which he drank directly from the large, green bottle it came in.

As he nursed the beer and relaxed on the deck, he thought he could make out the *Fenix* off in the distance. Next to the red-chili paste, soy sauce and other condiments on each tabletop, was a small pair of inexpensive binoculars that allowed patrons to do a bit of ship-spotting. He put them up to his eyes and quickly confirmed that it was the *Fenix* and that the dock crews were leaving, having completed their work. Murf put down the field glasses and resumed sipping his beer for the next ten minutes. As he readied himself to depart the restaurant and start his walk back to the ship, Murf thought he saw two pickup trucks pull alongside the ship. Again, using the binoculars, he noticed that there were, indeed, two trucks alongside. And, once again, the mid-ship auxiliary crane was being used to lift and lower a single container from on top of one of the stacks. After placing it in the bed of the empty truck, it was then used to lift a container from the other truck up and then putting it back on the stacks exactly where the original container had come from. "Vaccines my ass, Abdur," said Murf as he continued to watch the action. "That's another major payload of copy watches, my friend," he said with an all-knowing smile.

The blue Hanjin container the men had substituted, again, as in the last transfer in Ulsan, looked identical to the one it replaced. After the old one had been been lifted and lowered overboard to a position on the dock side-by-side with the new one, great care was again taken to splice the RFID tracker from one container to the next without breaking the circuit and signaling to inventory tracking sensors that there was an issue with this particular box. After lifting the new one back aboard and lowering it into place, the men laughed aloud at one tiny visual discrepancy between the boxes that only they would ever see or know about. While the two containers looked completely identical, upon extremely close inspection, there was a difference. Versus the number 1466 that had been stenciled in white paint in one-inch tall letters on the original, their terrorist collaborators who supplied the new container had displayed a perversely evil sense of humor by painting a new number, 0911, in tiny white type on the substitute container.

CHAPTER 31

S.O.S.

Happy to be at sea and headed across the Pacific again, Murf settled back into the ship's routine quickly and he found comfort in the regular repetitions and rhythm of each day. After dinner had been served and the galley cleaned, it was Murf's favorite time of day. Even in the darkness of night, the ocean left Murf spellbound. By moonlight he would contemplate the infinite panorama of wave-breaking highlights on an endless liquid body of churning, dancing black velveteen-colored water.

Though Abdur seemed a bit distant at first, Murf's evening discussions with him resumed and became as engaging as ever. With each night's exchange they knew more and more about each other's philosophies and beliefs and their friendship continued to flourish. Tonight the *Fenix* was struggling mightily against strong headwinds and eight-to twelve-foot swells. The ship was about two and a half weeks out of Shanghai and just days away from the California coast.

One night, when Murf and Abdur were on deck and chatting, Murf suddenly got the bright idea that he could get Abdur to open up and talk about his smuggling ring by interjecting a series of chess-like feints in the conversation. So he nonchalantly brought up things like, "the skill and practice it would take to operate the auxiliary crane," and "the copy watch he had recently bought in Hong Kong," and "I wonder if that Chinese epidemic is in check yet, Abdur?" While his intent was only to see if he could get Abdur to admit that he and his buddies were involved with smuggling counterfeit goods, Murf's delicate dance backfired on him when Abdur suddenly took umbrage and accused Murf of "meddling in his personal affairs." The two men then argued briefly and, in a mutual huff, they separated from each other to lean on opposite sides of the deck's railings. Abdur knew that now was the time to follow his order to do away with Murf, but could he bring himself to act against his friend?

After a few strained minutes, Murf turned around quickly to apologize to Abdur who was now walking carefully—given the ship's rolling pitch—away from the railing and toward the hatch and stairwell.

"Abdur, wait please," Murf said in earnest. As he turned, one of his comfortable, yet inappropriate-for-a-ship shoes that he wore to cook in, first stuck on a bit of tar and then twisted sideways. Suddenly, Murf slipped and fell when kitchen grease that had accumulated on the side of that shoe came in contact with the metal deck. "Oh, shit N-O-O-O-O," Murf said in that instant as he realized he was tumbling backward and heading under the rail. He had probably just made a fatal maritime-operating error. "AB-D-U-U-R-R!!" Murf yelled as he plummeted sideways overboard. In an instant, he was gone.

Abdur turned just in time to see Murf falling overboard with arms reaching out and clawing at the air, disappearing from sight with only the offending shoe that caused his plunge left behind. Shocked by the sight and reaching his own arms out, wanting to help Murf, Abdur then thought for an instant that, per Zahadid's directive, the prying American would no longer be a threat to their mission.

Then suddenly, with the stark realization that a friend now

desperately needed his help, with both arms, Abdur grabbed an empty red and white heavy-duty plastic Coleman ice chest, and spinning around, he hurled it toward Murf like a torso-twisting shot-putter throwing a heavy ball and chain. He then, without hesitation, jumped over the rail right after it into the dangerous propeller backwash of the ship's wake. It took only a few minutes of modest swimming effort for Abdur to reach and clutch the cooler and then to join the dog-paddling Murf with the improvised floatation device he had brought along. "You crazy son-of a-bitch!" said Murf exasperated that his friend had joined him in the serious plight his damn cooking shoes had created. "Why in the world did you jump in? Now no one knows we're both 'Man Overboard.'"

"I just acted out of instinct, thinking you might have been hurt in the fall or knocked unconscious," responded Abdur. "Clearly it would have been smarter to have alerted the crew," said a now much more sobered Abdur. "I should have known better. Only a fool acts on impulse without thinking first."

"Well I, for one, am glad you did," replied Murf. "They will realize we are missing sooner or later and hopefully this ice chest will keep us afloat until they can find us," Murf said attempting to reassure the both of them.

Shocked at the sight of the *Fenix* growing smaller on the horizon and the all-enveloping ocean all around them growing more and more immense and threatening by the second, Murf and Abdur very deliberately chatted even more so than usual, while they floated and rode up and down the waves. The two men took turns letting go of the chest and swimming a little in hopes of generating body heat to stave off the hypothermia that would probably eventually claim them both.

"So what do the letters S.O.S. in the international distress signal stand for anyway," asked Murf, rhetorically.

"In my maritime training this question came up," answered Abdur in between his heavy breathing from a just completed swim. "I thought it might stand for Save Our Ship or Save Our Souls," he continued. "But it turns out that the letters stand for nothing. They stem from the ease of sending a Morse code signal comprised of a continuous sequence of three-dits/three-dahs/three-dits. And because, in Morse code, three dits form the letter S, and three dahs make the letter O, adding words after the fact just made it easier to remember that the distress signal order of the dits and dahs spelled out SOS," recalled Abdur from his lessons in Azerbaijan.

Murf decided to finally go for broke and ask Abdur about the struggle with the Korean man and Lu-Chi, which he had witnessed. Abdur laughed it off and then coolly explained that it was just a meeting to pay for the return of Lu-Chi's sister's possessions. Seems she had fled the Malaysian household where she had been deployed as a domestic and her brother was just sticking up for her. Before doing so, she took from her employers some critical business papers to ensure that the exchange for her left-behind possessions would, indeed, finally take place. Murf accepted the story, though it didn't seem to quite match the scene that he had witnessed and did not explain the subsequent container transfers that he later observed.

As thirty minutes in the water turned into three hours, Murf and Abdur had exhausted all their small talk. In order to keep panic and delirium at bay and possibly as a perverse type of confessional as they realized they might not get out of this alive, they began to share more and more truths.

Murf started it when he suddenly blurted out that he had abandoned his wife and child when he sailed with the *Fenix*. And further, that his career had been in marketing and advertising and not cooking, for some twenty-five years before he got canned because a backstabbing colleague was younger and less expensive to pay.

Abdur was now ashamed at his reserve in the face of a now highly likely death alongside a true and honest friend. He then told Murf that he must apologize to him because the story of Lu-Chi's sister he told just a little while ago was a lie.

"You cooked that up on the fly like that?" said a much-impressed Murf.

"Yes, I have been trained to quickly fabricate such cover stories," said Abdur, his eyes downcast.

"Trained by whom?" said a now very confused Murf. Abdur then admitted that he was a Western-educated terrorist schooled both at Michigan State and in training camps in Afghanistan and Azerbaijan.

"I became radicalized when my family was destroyed by Israeli occupiers back home in Palestine, in a small town called Azzun where I was born," Abdur continued as Murf listened in amazement bordering on disbelief. "In Palestine it was more about fighting against other Palestinians in a political struggle between Gaza-based Hamas and Fatah in the West Bank. So I joined al-Qaida seeking jihad against not just Israel, but also against all of the Western or Israeli allies in Iraq and Afghanistan. I have fought extensively against coalition troops in both of those places."

For five minutes thereafter, the only sounds heard by the men were the splashing of the ocean water against the ice chest and their own deep breathing.

"You know, Murf," said Abdur with a tone of regret to his words, "when I was growing up, my father taught me that jihad actually had another meaning beyond 'holy war.' It's rooted in a broader Islamic concept of the struggle to manage to do well with one's life and to live the true ideals of the Muslim faith. Versus the extremism I have come to represent, jihad can be just as much about achieving moderation in all things. My jihad, I think, has been only about revenge and probably is an affront to the true spirit of Islam," said Abdur now choking on both seawater and emotion.

"So what's a nice guy mujahedeen like you doing floating here in a place like this?" asked Murf trying to inject some levity.

"I cannot tell you about our mission, Murf," said Abdur with a smile. "If I did, then when we are rescued, I'd have to kill you," he said with a chuckle and the wink of an eye. "No more talk for a while, my friend, we both should rest."

By morning, the chill of the cool water had taken effect and hypothermia was robbing Abdur and Murf of what little energy they had left. The two shivering men's desperation had become palpable, and they both clung to the ice chest side-by-side with their heads held up by it just above the water line. Suddenly, a white tern landed with a splash in the water nearby—thoroughly startling them both. "For a minute there when I heard that splash, I thought something much larger had joined us here in the water," said Abdur not wanting to actually say the word shark for fear of precipitating such a scenario.

"Abbie, sometimes we think too much alike," said Murf with audible relief. The two watched the bird preening and smoothing its feathers as it floated oblivious to them just twelve yards away and highly visible with its white coat contrasted against the dark, one- to two-foot pummeling swells-infested ocean. "Thank God my friend, um…Allah be praised that is, that buzzards only live in the desert and not at sea," said Murf making light even though he knew he was beginning to lose his will to fight. The seabird made for a welcome, yet temporary, distraction from their deepening-by-the-minute dilemma. After it settled, it began to crane its long neck and then to rhythmically sway back and forth like a cobra listening intently to a tune emanating from a crude and nasally sounding reed instrument. Murf was immediately reminded of his daughter Molly and he told Abdur how she would sway back and forth rhythmically like that bird, with a huge, beatific smile on her face whenever "Copperline," a James Taylor song, came on.

He said, "Though she could not hear the music, she clearly felt the song's vibration and beat and loved to dance to it." Murf's eyes quickly filled with tears, and he lowered his head onto the top of the chest. Overflowing with fatigue-charged emotion, he was unable to stop the steady stream of tears and began quietly sobbing and whispering her name. "I love you Molly," he said quietly to himself but audibly enough for Abdur to hear. Abdur, now thinking of his sweet sister Amal, told Murf all about the special things she used to do and he began crying steadily, as well.

"My heart has suffered a wound that can never heal," sobbed Abdur. "There is only hatred and cold inside me now."

"I don't buy it, Abbie. You just threw away your life to help a friend," countered Murf. The two emotionally-wracked men, with their chests resting on the cooler, now draped arms over one another's backs as they both cried long and hard.

Ten minutes of tears later, suddenly out of nowhere, Abdur spoke, "I was planting Iranian-made IEDs in the Swat Valley at the direction of Zahadid, our commander," said Abdur with a gasp, the truth now flowing as freely as their tears. "I was sure we were targeting Coalition convoy vehicles, but there was so much dust being kicked up that I couldn't make them out." Abdur said with clear regret as he further unburdened himself. "I could hear an engine," he continued, "'The lead Humvee is approaching the bomb,' screamed Zahadid into my ear. 'You must trigger the blast NOW!' And I pushed the button down. When the dust from the blast finally cleared, I saw that I had become the monster," sobbed Abdur as he spoke. "There was no convoy, just the twisted, burning wreckage of a bus carrying twenty-some school children. They were all about the age of my younger brother Khalil when I left home and, because of me, their bodies were torn apart into bloody pieces," confessed Abdur in an outpouring of pent-up shame.

"Before Osama's death, he gathered his mullahs in secret and issued a fatwa decreeing that his martyrdom was inevitable, and after his death, the time would be right for another major attack on the U.S. to demonstrate the continuing strength of al-Qaida. We are on that very mission Osama pre-planned. We have a radioactive dirty bomb on board the *Fenix* that will kill more Americans, by far, than perished on 9/11. The target of our crusade against the West for Islam…is Disneyland." Abdur said without emotion as the two men were now completely spent, with their heads down against the chest, silently fighting even to continue to cling to it.

"No, you can't, Abdur..." Murf said as he raised his head with great effort. He was almost too tired to respond further to what he was hearing. But his eyes had widened with enormous alarm at the prospect of such massive carnage and he managed only to spit out, "God damn it, Abdur!"

"I believe that Zaha...Zahadid wants our suppliers in North Korea and Ch-Ch-Ch-China to be implicated," Abdur continued shivering almost uncontrollably, "so that the U.S. will be forced out of the Ma-Ma-Middle East to fight a massive Asian war against them. Regardless, if they succeed, America will never be the same and the f-f-f-i-fighting will broaden and go on and on and on."

"Terrorism cannot ever be religious, Abbie," said a totally exhausted but now fighting-mad Murphy Morrison. "It's just plain murder and lawlessness and it leads to hell and not paradise. Invoking the name of God while killing innocents is a complete and hate-filled perversion, whether it happens in Iraq, Northern Ireland or..."

"Or in Iraq and Afghani-st-st-stan," added Abbie nodding his head in agreement.

"I have been thinking a lot lately about terrorism. In the end, I think it is a-a-a crime against the true spirit of Islam. And I will never see heaven because of that," said Abdur who then paused to reflect further. "Did you know, Murf, that strange as it m-m-m-ay sound, none of the t-t-t-terrorists who bombed the two towers in New York were from Afghanistan or Ir-Ir-Iraq where America now fights? They were mostly from Saudi Arabia and Egypt, the so-called f-f-f-friends of the West."

"Nine eleven was planned and executed by al-Qaida from Afghanistan," interrupted Murf. "Stop philosophizing and rationalizing, Abbie. You need to stop wallowing in self-pity and fatalism," he added with unbelievable irony, given his own personal decisions and actions. "I know the West has failed to rectify the tragedy of Palestinians that we, in fact, created," Murf continued. "And I realize that we stereotype and demonize Arabs and overlook countless legitimate grievances. But it is men of principle and substance on both sides, just like you, who must overlook human failings and renounce violence. We must both make a stand to personally do something that makes a helpful difference to stop this endless cycle of violence, that only engenders more violence." said Murf with a lot more pleading than his highly refined skills of persuasion in his appeal.

"I pray we will get that chance, my friend," concluded Abdur, audible only to himself. He looked utterly sad and ashamed as he lowered his head to the ice chest again.

Four hours later, the two desperate and completely enervated men were now becoming feeble in their resistance to the pull of the sea. Murf suddenly opened his salt-encrusted and burning eyes and let loose his grip on the ice chest. He then began to gently float away from it on his back. In this final moment, Murf could think only of the family he foolishly abandoned and of his friend that he hoped might survive if he could have the floatation device all to himself. "I'm all done, Abbie," Murf said, now far enough away that it was audible only to himself. "Take good care, my good friend. And save me some of your stockpile of virgins," he said in between coughing out saltwater.

Abdur, though fading in and out of consciousness, sensed a change with the absence of Murf's bodyweight and finally looked up. "Murf, you can't give up. Swim back here," screamed Abdur hoarsely. And then he, too, let loose of the ice chest, but in order to swim to Murf whose head was now slipping beneath the water.

Since a crewman found Murf's black shoe on the aft deck and reported it to him, Captain Benny had been on his feet now for the better part of sixteen hours, firing lingering red flares overhead during the night and scanning the horizon. He personally operated the searchlight that had been shone for hours, in vain, onto the infinite expanse of darkened water. Daylight helped expand their line of sight, but this was a veritable needle-in-a-haystack search. Nonetheless, the skipper stubbornly refused to quit. Container ships on long passages routinely run a few hours to a few days off schedule. But his search would put them three and a half days behind and that could cost Benny his job. He thought about this as he searched and about how much he loved Murf's fresh-baked muffins and steaming deep-dish lasagna. And then as he was about to give it up in spite of his deep-seated desire to protect his much-prized galley asset, he thought he spotted something amiss in the sea of sameness. As he brought his field glasses into focus, he saw a red ice chest but no sign of Murf. And then he saw a man in the water with his arm around another. They were both struggling to stay afloat. Captain Benny began repeatedly sounding the immensely loud ship's foghorn to alert them of the approach of the *Fenix*.

Adbur and Murf were both fairly delirious at his point, but Abdur swore to Murf that he had heard a ship's horn. "Allahu Akbar!" whispered Abdur to Murf as his tears began flowing in joy. "God is great!

Even with the *Fenix* approaching the men at full steam the skipper could see through his binoculars that they might not be able to hold on for much longer. As they drew near, with incredible nimbleness for a man of his considerable heft, Benny kicked of his shoes, grabbed three life vests and jumped in after them. Looking a bit like a large whisker-faced walrus in the water, Benny swiftly made his way to them and slipped a vest around Murf.

"Thank you my captain," said Abdur with heartfelt appreciation as the skipper held Murf with one arm and slipped a jacket onto Abdur with the other. Suddenly Abdur's eyes widened and his face bore a highly startled expression at the sight of something he had never seen so close up before. It was a golden Star of David at the end of the chain around the captain's wet and hairy neck. Though all who might look could easily see that the ship's captain wore a thin gold chain around his neck, Benny had always kept the symbol at the end of it tucked out of sight under the white tee-shirt beneath his work shirt.

CHAPTER 32

Attacking the Magic Kingdom

After the lifeboat from the *Fenix* had retrieved the three men, Murf and Abdur were given dry clothes, saline for their dehydration, and warmth and rest to counter the debilitating effects of exhaustion and hypothermia. Though now only fourteen hours from making port in Long Beach, Murf was still intermittently delirious as he slept. Once upon briefly awakening, the captain gave him a shot from his personal bottle of five-year-old reserve rum. It was ironic, given the many times Murf had in the past joked about his drinking being for medicinal purposes, that the first hard liquor to touch his lips since they set sail out of San Francisco some fifty-eight days earlier, actually was. During the brief stretch of lucidity and consciousness it facilitated, Murf was able to tell the captain about the terrorist plot and the Hanjin container carrying a dirty bomb.

Unfortunately, the mission of the mujahedeen was already well underway. It began when Third Officer Lu-Chi manned the watch two nights earlier. Almost all of the crew and officers slept very deeply that night, with a little extra help from some sedatives the extremists had added into the evening's coffee and tea thermoses. At about 3:00 a.m., the container in question had been lowered by the auxiliary crane onto a fishing boat. The vessel had, by prearrangement, pulled mid-ship alongside the *Fenix*, which had slowed to a near stop. Lu-Chi, Zahadid and the supposedly-from-Azerbaijan boys, had then fled along with the lethal cargo. It was then that Zahadid told Abdur he was to stay behind to take care of unfinished business by dispatching the cook who had witnessed their prior container swap in Shanghai. Afterward, he would go overboard when the *Fenix* was close enough to shore for him to swim. Then Abdur was to quickly make his way to the warehouse to help lead the attack.

Once Murf made the captain aware of the plot, the skipper called for an immediate crew muster wherein the men were confirmed missing and identified. Normally, a muster was done by work shift every day during a passage. But in all of the recent excitement it had been overlooked when it was needed most. The skipper immediately notified the authorities, which quickly amassed a large-scale search for the fishing boat and terrorists. Plus, they were sending FBI agents on a harbor pilot's boat to meet the *Fenix* to arrest and begin questioning Abdur, Murf and Captain Benny. Soon, a Navy P-3 reconnaissance plane would arrive on the scene and begin circling to keep constant watch over the *Fenix* for the day and a half it would take for her to reach port. There were sure to be many challenging questions for the captain to deal with. He was worried about the kind of outcry that would ensue even if the terrorists were caught. It could cost him not only his job but his freedom if he were held responsible.

As night fell on this momentous day and with the coast of California now visible on the horizon, Murf and Abdur were both soundly asleep and recovering from their ordeal, unaware that a team of Navy Seals and a CIA operative were also en route via chopper to be lowered onto the *Fenix* to take charge. Almost as though some instinctual, internal alarm had gone off, Abdur awakened suddenly and willed his dead-tired body up and out of the bed. Then he crept silently to his secretly stashed contingency supplies and recovered and then donned a wetsuit. He swiftly filled, via a small compressed air tank, a semi-circular inflatable that would support his chest and yet allow him to propel himself through the water with his black rubber swim fins. Abdur moved with speed and precision as he strapped a pair of Glock pistols to his chest and washed down a handful of amphetamines with a bottle of water, to help him regain the drive to lower himself back into an ocean that had so recently tortured him to the breaking point.

"Allahu Akbar" said Abdur as he dropped the final twelve feet from the ladder on the side of the ship to the water down below. As he recovered and mounted his inflatable and began to kick, the coastline was now looming large on the horizon and he could hear the faint sound of a helicopter approaching far in the distance. It would probably take a near impossible performance by a world-class swimmer to reach landfall successfully. And once the authorities discovered his disappearance, there would also likely be a helicopter or a dozen, searching the water for him.

Meanwhile, on shore, the terrorist team had removed their cargo from the steel container on the fishing boat deck and trucked it to the warehouse they had maintained in the City of Industry since their trip the month before to scout the theme park they targeted. Zahadid suddenly began to argue furiously with Lu-Chi. Moments before, while Zahadid was busy preparing the men, Lu-Chi had examined the contents of the container carefully and demanded more money now that the true end game of attacking Disneyland with a dirty bomb had come together for him. "Filthy dog," spat Zahadid, as he turned his back on Lu-Chi. The other Arabs gathered together in readiness to help if there was a fight. Zahadid then swiftly turned back around toward Lu-Chi with the pistol he had drawn from its hiding place now aimed right at him. Without hesitation, he fired two rounds into the sneering Chinese seaman's forehead, saying, "Here is your reward, infidel!"

Afraid that his plan might be starting to unravel, an uncharacterisitically rattled Zahadid blurted out, "All of you hurry up now and load the dirty bomb into the van." For the now staring-in-surprise men, it was the first time they were learning about a dirty bomb. They had thought up to this point that the weapon they were transporting just used a massive amount of conventional explosives. Now they clustered around Zahadid with contemplative expressions that reflected their comprehesion of the magnitude and implications of their true mission.

"But commander," protested Youssef in the most diplomatic and gentle way he could muster, "we should not waste our efforts targeting a few thousand children and mothers at Disneyland. If we attack downtown LA or a government center with this nuclear bomb, we can surely kill many, many more of the infidels," he pleaded persuasively with a cloying smile.

Zahadid's reaction was swift and shocking. He raised the still-smoking pistol to just beneath Youssef's chin and fired a single shot deep into his brain. "We are obedient martyrs and there will be no wavering from our foresworn duty to Allah!" shouted the thoroughly evil Zahadid. And then he shouted, "First Lu-Chi and now Youssef dared to question my orders. Both have now paid the ultimate price and they both died for nothing. Are YOU completely committed to jihad and martyrdom?!!" he asked as he turned to look at the remaining crew. The men nodded affirmatively in fear, as they alternated their gaze between Youssef's body with dark red blood now pooling beneath the head, and the seething Zahadid, pistol still in his raised hand. Even Zahadid's faithful henchman, Aziz, was momentarily taken aback by the sudden dispatch by the militant, of the youngest and most affable member of their now grown-very-close team.

"Great Commander Zahadid," said Imdad with his eyes downcast. "When is Abdur to rejoin us?"

"As you know, Abdur was ordered to stay behind and push that nosy cook overboard or to die trying to," said Zahadid with great disdain. "He is to swim ashore when the ship is close and then make his way here. If we do not hear from him soon, we will assume he has drowned," said the vile leader without the slightest concern for the missing team member. "And then we WILL go on without him."

Back on board the ship, Captain Benny awakened Murf. The talented cook was now recounting every word he could recall that Abdur had shared with him about the plot. The CIA operative and an agent of Mossad sent by chopper to the *Fenix* to "facilitate" Abdur's interrogation, listened intently. In the meantime, onshore and via helicopters in the air, a small army of police and government agents were scouring every shipyard and marina in Southern California to locate the fishing boat, the terrorists and "the device," as they called it.

Shipping industry statisticians report that between the Los Angeles and Long Beach Harbors, about fifteen million containers are handled each year or about half of the container cargo that the U.S. imports. Zahadid had chosen this entry point both for its proximity to their target and in hopes that the overwhelming usage and crowding at the port would help them go little noticed.

CHAPTER 33

Jihad Realized

After entering the harbor escorted by aerial reconnaissance, the harbor pilot boat and a Coast Guard cutter that joined them about two miles out, the *Fenix* tied up at the port's very cramped Middle Harbor docks. Murf, the captain and all of the crewmen were detained onboard the *Fenix* and thoroughly interrogated in hopes of finding the slightest clue as to the whereabouts of the maritime terror cell. Murf was smart enough to know that a simple background check on him would raise suspicions, so he was absolutely truthful about dropping out on his white-collar, yet frustrating, life by becoming a cook on a container ship. That Murf willingly did so, and that he worked such long hours at such a minute fraction of his former salary, was immediately perceived as highly suspect by all of the Feds. One much older FBI agent ventured that maybe Murf and Abdur were in "cahoots" on the whole thing.

"No, I had no idea. I thought they were smuggling copy watches," Murf said eyes cast downward. "I'm no terrorist or criminal, just a simple coward for abandoning my family."

Just then, one of the agents burst into the room. "Found it!" he said excited and enthused. "It's a van rental confirmation. We're lookin' for a white GMC van and the plate number is HY2729," he stated rapid fire.

"I want an immediate APB on that van," ordered the CIA agent-in-charge loudly. "And alert all the choppers and video surveillance units. We've got to find that god damn van and now!"

The dirty bomb was now loaded into the van and the five remaining men had all changed into their theme park-appropriate civvies or casual clothes, under which they had hidden small arms and suicide vests. Zahadid split the team into two. Aziz would be in charge of the van group that included Jamal, Imdad, and Salim. Zahadid would travel separately to the park via a taxicab that had been called. He would arrive at Disneyland before the van. Meeting him there at the front gate by prearrangement with the team's LA sleeper cell, would be the blonde prostitute named Shandra, her five-year-old daughter Deirdre and one-year-old, stroller-bound son Shawon. Since Zahadid would be wearing a pair of black Mickey Mouse ears saved from their prior visit, and he'd be accompanied by what would ostensibly be his wife and children, he should arouse no suspicions.

After entering the park and walking through the main entrance, Zahadid planned to eliminate the main gate Disney security guards so that the van team that followed him could penetrate the park with the dirty bomb unopposed. He would then proceed to the park's nearby administrative building where he would ambush the park headquarters station security forces as they attempted to respond to the alarms that would be sounded. The plan was for the team to shoot and suicide-bomb-detonate their way through the crowd, if necessary, until reaching the Matterhorn. Zahadid told the men that the plan had changed and no longer would the bomb be detonated from the Monorail. Instead, they would overpower the Matterhorn ride's attendants and enter the back lot and then climb the ride's hidden-from-sight evacuation ladders to a spot even greater than the Monorail's height appropriate for detonating the bomb and releasing its radioactive contents into the consistently blowing breeze.

"What exactly is a 'dirty bomb' anyway?" asked Imdad of Zahadid at the close of the briefing.

"It is when radioactive material is packed into a very powerful explosive device for wide dispersal of its deadly contents by means of a conventional explosion versus one that features a nuclear chain reaction. But it does not matter that you, Islam's holy warriors, do not technically have a nuclear warhead like the Western powers," Zahadid concluded. "All you need to know is that millions of our enemy will die at your hands and America will be brought to its knees," snarled Zahadid impatiently. Zahadid closed the briefing by adding that the team would, of course, die glorious, instantaneous and painless deaths in the bomb's explosion, and then awaken in heaven with all the virgins and Disneylands their hearts could desire as rewards for their historic martyrdom.

"My taxi is here now and the van will follow it after another ten minutes." said Zahadid. "Allahu Akbar!" shouted Zahadid with his handgun raised high above his head. The men, in turn, raised their weapons and shouted in response, "Allahu Akbar!"

Zahadid then went to a back room and very gingerly removed from its wooden crate, a long, hard-plastic piece of gray-colored luggage with a black handle. It had initially been concealed inside the first Hanjin container they picked up in South Korea. Zahadid and Abdur had removed it and they hid it below deck. Inside this protective encasement was a bazooka-like weapon. Zahadid's face now beamed with a completely malevolent smile because he knew that the dirty bomb was just a feint or distraction to draw the park's security away from him and toward the others. Truth be known, his supreme leaders had told him that they were unsure if the dirty bomb they loaded in Shanghai had ample radioactive material or would even work at all. Zahadid was now fondling the real weapon, which could instantly disperse the 1,500 kg of Anthrax spore-laden gas contained in the brushed metal cylinder embedded at the center of the launcher. With a steady breeze blowing inland from the park, this was enough to infect and kill well over one million people in Southern California if properly sprayed at a significant altitude. And the Monorail, which Zahadid still planned to go to immediately after entering the gates, was at just the right height and its Tomorrowland stop was at just the perfect angle to maximize the wind-spread dispersion of the hyper-lethal gas.

Zahadid then closed the suitcase with the weapon safely inside it, snapped down the safety latch and carried it outside where he gently nestled it into the back of the cab. Once inside, he rested it on his lap. “Disneyland,” he said without emotion to the driver.

The van departed the warehouse as scheduled precisely ten minutes after the commander had left. It was less than a five-minute ride to get to the freeway entrance. But just two minutes after reaching the highway, a helicopter pilot spotted a white van and moved in to survey, via advanced optics, the vehicle’s license plate. “We’ve got them!!! Repeat, we have them just outside of the City of Industry on the Orange Freeway, Highway 57, heading south to Anaheim! We have them at mile marker 22, just past the exit with the elevated In-N-Out-Burger billboard!” said the pilot with evident excitement.

“Roger that. Well done,” replied the central command transmission. “All vehicles and choppers converge immediately to intercept. I repeat, “CONVERGE IMMEDIATELY and surround that van. Assume occupants are heavily armed and use multiple stun grenades to disable the vehicle and render occupants unconscious. Immediately after stopping the van, SWARM the vehicle to prevent demolition of the device or any suicide vests. I repeat. IMMEDIATELY SWARM and shoot anyone that moves. Let’s send them a message—big time!”

The battle of the Orange Freeway was brief and yet quite bloody. Without being noticed by Imdad—who was driving with Aziz in the van’s front passenger seat—unmarked government vehicles quietly moved into position in front, to the side and behind the van. Then, after slowly segregating it from the rest of the freeway traffic, the order was given, and they struck the vehicle with stun grenades fired from all four sides simultaneously. The van immediately swerved and then flipped over and skidded to a grinding, screeching halt as scraping metal caused sparks to fly all about. Most of the occupants were just momentarily shaken and Salim and Jamal in the back of the van, threw the doors open as soon as they could stagger to their feet. A hail of mutual assault rifle fire ensued with two agents wounded and both of the terrorists shot more than a dozen times. At the exact same time, other agents were assaulting Aziz and Imdad by firing repeatedly through the front windshield. Though Aziz was immediately hit and killed, a mortally wounded Imdad managed to detonate his suicide vest and three government agents died with him.

Neither the devastating gunfire nor the detonation of the vest had much impact on the footlocker-sized and ruggedly packaged dirty bomb in the back.

Though the scene was a horrifying one of blood, smoke, extreme gore and barely identifiable body parts, only minute radiation levels were subsequently detected via the Geiger counters that the federal agents and scientists who were flown to the scene, wielded. After complete analysis, the still-intact dirty bomb was revealed to have been nowhere near as potent as a modern-day one made from weapons-grade Plutonium 239, the radioactive fuel common to most nuclear weapons and reactors. It was actually a crude and inefficient one by today's nuclear weapons standards because it consisted of only about a twenty percent concentration in about 100 grams of Uranium 235. Though not state-of-the art, Uranium 235 is what was used in the "Little Boy" nuke that laid waste to Hiroshima.

Because of the suicide vest explosion's damage, the disintegrated bodies and subsequent fire, and the threat of radioactive poisoning, it took several hours to stabilize the scene and ascertain the exact number of terrorists killed. And that bought Zahadid the time he needed. Unbeknownst to him, as he neared the park, word was spreading quickly throughout the all-on-high-alert police and security forces throughout Los Angeles, that the terrorist threat had been eliminated and the half-assed radioactive weapon they planned to deploy had been captured and disarmed.

Back at the *Fenix*, the agent who was stationed outside of Murf's cabin, soon also got the good news over his cell phone and briefly left the once-again sleeping ship's cook, Murphy Morrison, to go celebrate with a cup of coffee. Within seconds after he departed, Murf was out the door and had slipped away. He only hoped that he might still be in time to stop the man who had saved his life, from potentially and senselessly becoming another misguided martyr.

"Hello, lady. Hello, little kiddies," said Zahadid to Shawon and Deirdre when he came upon them just outside the front gates of Disneyland about forty-minutes after leaving the warehouse. They were puzzled to see him, the dour man they remembered, now wearing silly Mickey Mouse ears and a bright aquamarine colored short-sleeved sport shirt. His appearance created a mind-blowing contrast given the frivolity of the headgear set against his black eyes, long, angular nose, hairy forearms and almost blue-colored cheeks due to the fact that the excessively hairy man had just recently shaved. "I have tickets. So let's go have good fun," he continued, doing his best to act as though he might be able to foster a good time in spite of his naturally nasty demeanor that they all too well remembered.

"They said you'd pay double this time," said the all-business-to-be-transacted-up-front-minded Shandra. "Of course," replied Zahadid. "Here is money and I brought picnic umbrella inside this case for later. Allow me to attach to little boy's stroller, please," Zahadid stated. Without waiting for a response from Shandra, he tied his gray case between the stroller's long arms.

"Whatever," said Shandra nonchalantly as she finished counting the money. "Let's go to Disneyland again, kids!" she said with genuine excitement.

"Just one moment more, I make call first," said Zahadid as he stalled for time until he could spot the other team members assembling behind them. First he dialed the number for Jamal's cell phone and, after it rang and rang, he called Aziz's, Imdad's and then Salim's. "OK, we go now" said a now agitated Zahadid. Despite the fact that something had clearly gone wrong, the party of four headed for the entrance line.

In spite of Zahadid's best attempt to make nice and present his group as the epitome of domestic American bliss, the attendant at the entrance immediately balked at letting them in without examining the contents of the strange-looking carrier Zahadid had strapped to the stroller. "It's just an umbrella, honey," said Shandra with a genuine smile.

"The park has many shady areas ma'am, I need to see inside the case, please," said the attendant with polite persistence. Zahadid could see that a security guard had noticed their discussion and was now walking their way.

"Child gets sick from too much sun," pleaded Zahadid with feigned fatherly concern. "Doctor says we must always carry with us."

The guard had arrived and overheard this. "Sorry Sir, park rules. Please open up the case," the guard said more sternly. A second guard who was nearby had now spied the budding confrontation and was moving briskly toward the group. Suddenly Zahadid unsheathed his Glock and instantly pumped two bullets in the first security guard's chest and then spun in the direction of the approaching second guard and shot him in the forehead. Screams and cowering people became ubiquitous.

"What the hell are ya doing!" screamed Shandra as she attempted to wrestle her son's stroller away from Zahadid. He immediately and without hesitation, wheeled and shot her once in the chest. Both children started screaming and crying in extreme terror as Zahadid desperately tore the case from the stroller and began to run toward the Monorail station ahead, waving his gun threateningly at all he passed along the way. As he did so, a swiftly moving figure running at full speed tackled him from behind. The force of the impact sent both men rolling quite some distance over the concrete walkway, but Zahadid managed to keep hold of his gun. Sprawled face down on the ground, he swiftly rolled over on his back, sat up and then screamed "YOU! You meddling fool!"

He had instantly recognized his now rising pursuer as none other than the ship's cook. Clearly, Abdur must have betrayed their secret to him. WHAM! The force of a bullet ripping into Murf's body forcefully knocked the cook and former advertising wizard down to the ground and sadly ended his attempted heroics. As the light in Murf's eyes faded, his face bore a look of stunned surprise. He realized too late that security, police and military actions are best left to professionals.

Upon reaching the inclined Monorail entrance line, Zahadid vaulted past ten or so people waiting for the approaching train. In moments, he was on board where he shot another attendant who approached him. The other passengers in the car began screaming and dropped to the floor, save one man who turned and began walking toward Zahadid. As he raised his pistol to fire yet another bullet, he recognized the man's face and was extremely startled to see it. "Abdur???!!! So you and your cook friend both survived?" Zahadid said with extreme disbelief and disgust.

"Is the dirty bomb in the case?" asked Abdur firmly as he drew nearer.

"That is not for you to know. Your job is to obey me." Zahadid snapped arrogantly.

"Answer me now you filthy mongrel!" said Abdur in a booming and absolutely determined tone of voice that left Zahadid's arm shaking as he pointed the gun.

"It is deadly Anthrax gas, something infinitely more powerful than a dirty bomb. And you stop right there, Abdur," spat Zahadid as he steadied with both hands the pistol he had aimed toward Abdur's chest. "The gas was always the real plan of attack," continued the terrorist commander. "The dirty bomb is a ruse to draw them in and let them think the crisis has passed. Then the second and truly meaningful attack can commence. The release of poison gas from the Monorail over the Magic Kingdom will create an image of lasting horror to be forever seared into the memory of all Americans. And I, Zahadid al-Aboud, will be forever remembered for a victory even greater than Osama's!"

In an instant, Abdur was upon him and, at the same time, Zahadid had discharged the Glock. With pain searing from the shoulder wound he received when the bullet went right through him, Abdur was relentless. He grabbed Zahadid by the throat and lifted him off the ground. He used his powerful arms, weathered hands and overflowing anger as he ever-tightened his grasp around the commander's throat. The consummately evil one gasped for air and wrenched his face into an even uglier than usual appearance. As his eyes bugged out and his face contorted, every horrible deed Zahadid had forced Abdur to inflict on innocents rushed through Abdur's brain and fueled his unstoppable frenzy of choking the life out of this supreme mullah of murder. After one minute of throat choking and unbridled struggling, Abdur saw the color drain from his tormentor's face and the light leave his eyes. He now felt the pain in his shoulder anew and he dropped Zahadid's lifeless body to the floor of the Monorail car.

Abdur had been shot on several occasions before and he had always been fortunate enough to have the bullets pass through his body without damaging organs or causing massive bleeding. And so it was again this time—though, once again, pushing through the considerable discomfort of a gunshot wound required great discipline and pain tolerance. Unnoticed in the struggle, Disneyland had begun implementing emergency procedures and the Monorail controls had stopped the car's movement.

Abdur removed Zahadid's suicide vest from him, picked up the case, slung it over his bleeding shoulder, and then used his other, stronger arm to pry open the rubber sealed doors of the car. As they gave way to his strength, he leapt from the car and grabbed the gray, steel support structure's railing. He descended downwards until he could leap carefully just a few feet to the ground. In a flash, he moved with speed and stealth as he escaped through the tree line on the park's periphery. From there, he made his way to a side area of the parking lot where, as luck would have it, a family was exiting a cab and paying the driver. Swiftly, he slid around the opposite side door and slipped into the back seat of the cab where he rested the case on his lap and shoved the suicide vest out of sight on the floor. Almost before the driver even realized he had a new passenger, a smiling Abdur was handing him four hundred dollar bills and saying, "I'm having a family emergency and need to get to San Diego in a hurry."

"You got it pal," replied the pleased-at-his-good-fortune cabbie, who then sped the sedan away from the park with professional expedition.

Unbeknown to the driver, Abdur's true intent was to get the device away from heavily populated areas and perhaps to head for the Mexican border. One very standard procedure taught in terrorist training camps is to always have a preordained alternative detonation means set up for each bomb in case of detonation failure. Given Zahadid's extreme paranoia, Abdur knew that a timer-based secondary detonator—to release the gas in case of Zahadid's death—was likely. Abdur asked the driver to keep the windows rolled up and the AC on as he sped away from the park and up onto the freeway. Abdur deftly located and disengaged the timer.

Two hours later, on the southern side of San Diego and off of both the 5 Freeway and all main roads, Abdur relieved the driver of his vehicle but left him unharmed on the side of the dirt road he had stopped on. It would be a good five mile walk for the driver back to civilization, and the dirt road seemed to be heading into rolling foothills covered in cactus, scrub brush and tumbleweeds. The GPS-based driving directions app on his cell phone told Abdur that this backcountry road that veered southeast from the San Diego metro area toward El Cajon, was still headed in the general direction of Mexico. He was thinking now mostly about how to dispose of the Anthrax-spewing bomb permanently, just in case Zahadid or Aziz had, in fact, programmed some other kind of redundant booby-trap to trigger the device should they be incapacitated. Just then, he spied some ramshackle tin-roofed wooden buildings ahead on the hillside in a state of great disrepair. The sign on the chain-locked gate guarding the side road that led to them said "Danger! Abandoned Mine. No Trespassing."

Two bullets later, the lock was blasted open and the gate swung open wide. Abdur drove the cab down the quarter mile of dusty road to the old tungsten mine's entrance. The mine had been abandoned since just after World War II when tungsten was a mineral critical to the war effort and for manufacturing penetrating projectiles, in particular. With his mind set on sealing the Anthrax in this deep hole in the earth forever and then heading for the border, Abdur took the case and Zahadid's suicide vest from the cab. He then popped open the vehicle's trunk where he found a black magic marker and an old Eveready flashlight that worked only intermittently, with a frustrating flicker that would have dim light going on and then off every few minutes. He put both of them inside his jacket pocket. To lighten his load, he then unlatched and removed the weapon, with its attached aluminum gas cylinder, from its protective, hard-plastic industrial-grade case.

The mine entrance was sealed with a locked, chain-link fence door with a danger sign posted on it. Abdur very gently set the weapon on the ground and then he stood. Using the marker, he added the word "Anthrax" to the sign. Another blasted lock later, and he was ready to move inside the mine. But first, while still in the bright sunlight, he bent down again to rewire the suicide vest to allow for detonation from a safe distance.

With his preparations completed, Abdur again lifted the weapon and walked carefully into the mineshaft, which quickly descended about seventy-five yards down a steep incline. In spite of the ever-cooler temperatures in the progressively further-below-ground chambers, he had begun to sweat profusely. Determined not to drop it, he tightly gripped the Anthrax bomb with one hand as he made his way further into the darkness guided by the flickering light he held up high in the other. Though he turned his head and took note of the old rusted self-propelled rail cart sitting off to the side for just a moment, it was long enough to keep him from noticing the obstacle on the ground directly in front of him. When his right foot hit a protruding wooden strut, he stumbled but was still nimble enough to quickly begin to recover his balance, as he clutched the bomb with an unbreakable grip to his still-throbbing shoulder and chest.

In the relative darkness, Abdur had no way of knowing this piece of wood was the beginning of a railroad-type track that ran thousands of feet more down into the mine. And when his left foot struck the next of the equally-spaced-apart wooden struts, his bad knee buckled on him and he fell, still holding the bomb tightly.

In that instant, as he fell, he knew that his luck as a warrior who always managed to somehow survive the most harrowing situations, had finally run out. As he tumbled out of control to the hard ground, the weapon of mass destruction that he carried hit solid rock on the side of the shaft and immediately began emitting a hissing sound as a thin plume of gas started leaking from the cylinder's coupling to the firing mechanism. From what he recalled of his initial training at the camp in Afghanistan many years ago, Anthrax was always fatal at high concentrations, but he did not recall how fast-acting it was. While he was most certainly a dead man now, he was determined to accomplish one last mission—to insure that no other innocents would die as a result of his actions.

"Allahu Akbar," he shouted one last time as he pulled the detonator cord, which blew up the suicide vest and sealed the poison gas under tons of hard rock, deep in the earth's core.

CHAPTER 34

And This Too Shall Pass

Though traced to a phantom middleman company who had chartered the *Fenix* for the passage to Long Beach, and then further, to an obscure and supposedly Swiss-owned façade of a company, the real ownership of the *Fenix* was believed to be al-Qaida. So the ship would remain docked at Long Beach for some weeks until it was finally relocated by the FBI's West Coast operation to, of all places, semi-permanent anchorage in Suisun Bay in the back-bay waters of San Francisco.

After more than a week of questioning by the authorities and incessant media interviews that led to stories that implied incompetence on the part of the ship's captain for allowing the whole escapade to unfold, Captain Benny Harold was finally allowed to slip back into obscurity. Eventually, he was even given another ship assignment, but as first officer and not captain of a Pacific-based container ship that was just as, or more, decrepit than the *Fenix*.

Incredibly, on the day of departure, alcohol incapacitation had rendered the ship's incumbent first officer unfit for duty at the last minute and while Benny was down at the docks pretty much every day pestering anyone who would listen about hiring him. The skipper needed badly to get back out to sea, so Benny grabbed at the chance to do so even if it meant a demotion and pay cut. Since the food was absolutely awful on his new ship, and because the first officer normally makes as many or more decisions than the captain does, Benny was able to hire, as the new ship's cook, another notorious *Fenix*-ex named Murf Morrison.

Murf was to start work immediately once the vessel finished its initial crossing and reached Seoul, South Korea—that is, if he was now fully recuperated from his bullet wound and could tolerate flying in an airline jet across the ocean to meet the ship. Murf jumped at the chance and left the next day from Los Angeles for Seoul. Even though he had received the telex from Captain Benny mid-crossing and ten days before the ship would make port in Seoul, Murf decided he would continue doing his prescribed rehab exercises in South Korea, shop for supplies and visit museums to kill the time until his ship came in.

When the stewardess offered to bring Murf a drink after take-off, without thinking he replied, "Rum and Coke with lime, please." Though she dutifully brought it to him, the drink sat untouched for the entire flight as Murf dared not risk slipping back into his rum-loving Pirate-on-an-airplane ways. And all he could think about as he was running away from home and family again, was the wonderful, beautiful wife he did not deserve and the face of an ever-smiling angel that his daughter, Molly, possessed.

Once again, Murf stayed at the Novotel in Insadong and, after sleeping-off his long and sleepless flight over, he woke up to a frosty and clear mid-winter morning in Seoul, and decided to go for a jog. With a temperature of about eighteen degrees Fahrenheit, Murf had to wear a knitted hat and gloves to help brave the cold. But still, it savaged the parts of his face exposed to the bitter wind. After a short walk, Murf found himself standing alongside the wide and serene Han River, with over twenty bridges spanning it, connecting the south of the city with the downtown area. The usually un-picturesque and muddy river that flows west through the city and eventually into the Yellow Sea had become an interlocking mass of frozen mini-icebergs. He wasn't alone there, for a half dozen mostly elderly Korean men and women were out shuffling up and down the paved river embankment or stretching and doing Tai Chi exercises.

Murf tried to think of nothing and just listen to his own heart pounding and lungs heaving. But the thought that recurred anyway was that he would no longer find it satisfying to escape into sailing the seas. For sure, the pithy conversations with Abdur on deck would be sorely missed. But Murf was also beginning to realize that his affection for the sea had been irreparably altered. Throughout his life, Murf held that whether swimming in it or sailing upon it, there was some kind of energy transference from the waters to his very soul that always left him feeling stoked and happy afterwards. Since his near-death in the ocean with Abdur, something had changed. It wasn't resentment that the waters he so loved had almost killed him. It was the creeping realization that it was time to stop always thinking first and foremost about himself and to start thinking about something that mattered much more.

Later, Murf took a walk and visited the War Museum of Korea. It featured historical exhibits depicting all of the many wars in Korea—almost all against invaders dating back to ancient wars with the conquest-centered Chinese, Japanese and Manchurians. As he studied the more modern-day Korean War, in which his father had fought, he pondered whether his dad and that generation had any clearer understanding of the true meaning of life, given their cataclysmic experiences. Afterwards, he walked by an Anglican Church situated near the waterfront. On the marquee sign with its posted service times, it also had a long-standing message that said, "Christian Seamen Welcome." The changeable-weekly-message beside it said, "Self-pity is the worst emotion of all."

Murf thought long and hard about that statement. It started him thinking about his own failings, his vanity, the shame that consumed him, and his inability to accept the loss of status after being fired from the world of advertising.

Later that afternoon, as the day began to warm up, shoppers filled the streets picking out purchases from the fresh fruits and vegetables to the woven handbags and baskets being sold in the tented stalls. Murf found himself occupying a centrally located park bench and watching passers-by as he slowly sipped a weak cup of coffee. Then he spied a grandmother and grandfather out with a teenaged child. Though almost as tall as most Korean men and stockier than many, it was clear that he was very much a child, still. This was most evident in his face, which bore as beatific and unchecked a smile as any of the Renaissance masters ever painted. Yet in his eyes, Murf noticed a glassy expression—one that strongly suggested a tragically lessened intellect or possibly mental retardation of some kind. Murf wondered why his mom and dad were not with their beaming and joyous boy on a Sunday in the park outing. He theorized that the grandparents, by default, had become the child's caretakers. Perhaps they were the only ones in the family who honored the special value and respect that each and every person merits, no matter his or her IQ or physical state.

The temporary center of attention for all three of these happy and constantly hugging kin was a single orange helium-filled balloon aloft overhead yet restrained by the string at its end which ran down into the boy's plump hand. Given that the boy was respectably clad in clothes not more than a few months old and that his loving, very gray grandparents' clothes were well worn, patched and thinning to the point of collapse, Murf imagined that these two eighty-something caretakers, were sacrificing perhaps meals as well as new clothes, to afford their sunshine-faced man-child, the best care they could. Their great love and sacrifice seemed immensely discernible even beyond the obvious affection they showered upon him. It was a warm and wonderful scene Murf was taking in of a grandpa and grandma repeatedly bouncing the balloon tirelessly up and down for the child's amusement, blowing his hair with gentle, highly tactile puffs from their mouths, and rubbing his belly in a near sensory overload outpouring of love.

Just as Murf's fascination had settled in for a long ride, a sharp and sudden gust of wind caught all of them by surprise and wrenched the balloon high into the air and completely out of their reach. The crushed looks on the boy's and his panicked grandparents' faces were enough to break anyone's heart. And with thoughts of his daughter suddenly flooding his mind, Murf rushed to the nearby balloon vendor, bought the entire bunch of balloons and brought them to the thankful trio in a flash. Minutes later, he was in a cab and headed back to his hotel room to gather his belongings while the cab waited outside. Within the hour, he was at the airport, booking a one-way flight home to San Francisco.

CHAPTER 35

"What in the Hell Were You Thinking!!??"

Terri's and Murf's conversation from the airport in Seoul was brief and very strained. Murf could hear both anger and tears in her voice, but she soldiered on and agreed to meet with him at the condo when he arrived back in San Francisco. Terri had broken down and cried in torrents when she first learned from the FBI of the events in Los Angeles and that Murf had been wounded. Though his mug was all over the news as a brave citizen who had stood up against terror, since Murf had not called her that day or in the week afterwards as he recovered in the hospital, she did not run to be at his side even though she wanted to.

On the fourteen-hour flight home, Murf deliberately didn't touch a drop of alcohol. He thought long and hard about what he would say to Terri and Molly and composed and re-wrote his plea for forgiveness many times over. Though Terri had cheated on Murf and he was still heartbroken about that, he figured that he'd probably contributed to that situation with his negligence and excessive behavior. And he knew now, absolutely, that regardless of what had transpired, Terri was his one true love and soul mate. He wanted and desperately needed her in his life forever and would do anything to accomplish that. Before landing, he shaved in the lavatory and put on the clean, light blue dress shirt and navy blue blazer he'd purchased at the Seoul airport to go with his jeans and black, thick-soled cooking shoes. He was about to attempt one of the toughest pitches of his life and he badly wanted every chance to make the sale.

Upon landing in San Francisco, Murf gathered his things to ready himself for deplaning. He moved, seemingly with patience through the crowd of passengers ahead of him, though he was truly terribly anxious to rush to the cabstand and head into the city. As he fumbled with his gear momentarily, he was roused by a highly familiar female voice that had called out his name. "Murf!" He looked up to see his beautifully coiffed and made-up wife, dressed in her best tailored black silk suit for a big board meeting that she was actually now missing. Alongside Terri was his surprisingly taller and enormously beaming daughter, Molly. She was holding up over her head, a colorful, orange balloon-festooned sign with the words "Welcome Back Daddy" written on the paper in crayon.

The two of them rushed up to Murf and smothered him in the most wonderful and prolonged hug of his life. When the embrace ended and each of them stepped back from the other, Terri slapped Murf in the face with all the might a good woman taken for granted could muster. It sent him reeling backwards, and greatly shocked both Murf and the onlookers who just moments ago had been taking in the just moments ago tender and highly sentimental airport homecoming scene.

"What in the hell were you thinking, you big idiot!??" said Terri in a serious-as-a-heart-attack tone with both fists now clenched and shaking in front of Murf's face for emphasis. "How dare you just drop out on your family and life to run off to sea like some adolescent, circus stowaway—and without an ounce of discussion whatsoever," spat Terri as she thumped Murf forcefully in the chest once and then twice more. "Don't you think I'd like to run away, too, sometimes?!! I know it's hard dealing with life's problems, Murf, and the terrible mistakes we all sometimes make. But God DAMN it, we love you and we will fight like hell to help you beat back any kind of problem you ever have!"

Murf was flabbergasted by Terri's passionate and majorly pissed-off outburst, and he was rubbing his cheek, which bore the hot red imprint of Terri's five fingers and hand across it. As good as Molly had become at reading lips, she had wisely chosen to avert her eyes downward until the Vesuvian eruption had run its course.

"I am an incredible idiot, Terri," said Murf as he abandoned his carefully written and rewritten script. "I don't deserve to have a wife as loving and brilliant and beautiful as you. Nor a sweet and wonderful girl as magical and special as Molly is. But, at least, I have learned a lot from all of this. I've gained a clear perspective on what's really important in life." Murf continued with fat tears now flowing freely down his cheeks, "I've learned from running away, living alone at sea, and all of this madness I got involved in, that it's…it's not supposed to be all about me. Or about my selfish ambitions and schoolboy fantasies. That's the kind of graven-idol crap that lures a lot of folks into making profoundly stupid choices. Like I did. I know now that the important thing in life is to not waste the precious opportunity we are all given to do some good in this world, instead of just chasing after the latest trendy cheese. And if you'll give me just one more chance, I'd like to spend the rest of my life loving and cherishing you and Molly. And also helping out a few people who are really in need, especially little kids. I want to help make a difference now," concluded Murf with a completely committed countenance. "And I can't do it or live without both of you beside me."

After a second group hug and a bucket full of much happier sobs, tears and tender kisses, the Murphy, Terri and Molly Morrison family finally set a course for home.

CHAPTER 36

A-Camping We Will Go

That Terri had taken Murf back and forgiven him for his mid-life meltdown and his bizarre and completely irresponsible disappearance, still utterly astounded him. Though he'd never stopped loving her in spite of the heartbreaking choices each had made, their romance had been passionately rekindled after his sudden absence and equally sudden return. And he had come to appreciate that there was nothing more important than actively fostering the love and nurturing of family and friendships. In fact, he now had a new role in life as "Camp Cookie" or the cook at the almost year-round camp he and Terri now ran—a camp that integrated both typical and special needs kids and taught children to appreciate the differences in each special individual. Children had become the second-stage rocket of Murf Morrison's now re-ascending life.

Murf often pondered his thoughts during that now-long-ago instance of nearly drowning. He realized then, that he was afraid of dying alone, lonely and without having contributed anything worthwhile to anyone else. He now clearly saw how relatively unimportant career, job status, conquest and mindless bad-boy adventure were in the overall scheme of things. Murphy Morrison had come to the realization that he needed to personally commit to making an unshakable commitment to loving and appreciating his family and his own life. And with that foundation, he could create something a lot more meaningful than a memorable meal, or another clever advertising campaign, or a snappy slogan to spur mindless consumption of another new product or brand. Murf's only brand focus now was FAMILY & CHILDREN IN NEED. And given this painfully-earned perspective he was more alive than ever.

Upon Murf's return from his misadventures at sea and before he'd had the brainstorm of starting a camp for kids and investing all of his and Terri's considerable retirement funds into it, one day he'd run into Cat Man crossing a street downtown and he learned that the Danny Boy was no longer the chief marketing officer at Selectronics. In fact, he was dead. It seems that after he became the big shot head of marketing, he'd fired his old agency Hal Lively & Partners. After a too-many-glasses-of-Pinot-Noir celebration lunch, hosted for him by the brand new advertising agency he had hired, William "Danny Boy" Johnston was driving back to the office in the new red Porsche convertible he'd bought the day before. He was momentarily distracted by an unfamiliar instrument in the dashboard panel. When he looked back up from it, he did so just in time to see that the eighteen-wheeler that had been far in front of him was now at a dead stop only inches away. The impact of the collision sheared the windshield and Danny Boy's head clean off. The next driver coming up from behind and approaching the accident might well have asked himself, "What's that in the road, a head?" as opposed to the more usual "What's that in the road ahead?"

Murf also found out that his old job at Lively had been taken over again, after William Johnston's departure to become a "client." Seems she was a crackerjack executive with a Harvard MBA and a rising star whom all the clients just loved. The Big Cat raised an eyebrow as he whispered to Murf, "She's a real looker, this one. Very moist. And given to wearing tight-fitting black skirts along with those hyper-expensive high heeled Manolo Blahnik shoes," he said to Murf as though revealing classified government secrets.

The world of his seemingly long-past career mattered little to Murf, now. Together with his lovely and ever-supportive wife, they would soon thereafter develop a simpler, yet extremely more profound purpose for their future lives. His wit and charm and ability to persuade people to try something new were actually still invaluable assets, but now he would be using those and his talents as a cook, to help provide a more substantive kind of nourishment and positive life-course-altering experience for kids. He and Terri would provide opportunities for kids who needed to understand that, in spite of their challenges, happiness and productivity could be found for them in this world if they worked hard and always treated other people well, no matter how different they seemed at first. In fact, Camp Abbie, as their new business would be known, advocated universal humanism, and the differences in people were specifically celebrated.

The camp's charter deliberately focused on each term bringing an extremely diverse set of kids together in order to show them how fascinating and wonderful the differences in people are. The real activities and experiences at Camp Abbie focused on the importance of resisting conformity and making decisions individually on each one's merits without succumbing to "Group Think" and antiquated social norms. The point of it all was to show the kids that the differences in people made life more interesting for everyone. In fact, the camp's flag was a pirate flag but one that portrayed a truly Jolly Roger and had hundreds of smiling kids' faces behind the larger pirate skull and cross bones. The intended message was that all who went to Camp Abbie should become helpful, caring pirates in the sea of life—the kind of people who would actively defy convention and regularly seek to meet interesting kinds of people who are different from themselves, and to always try to help anyone they encountered who was in need.

Murf and Terri worked to teach kids to be fiercely individual, conscientious, ever-curious, and flourishing human beings, and they were encouraged to spread the word and try to get other kids to respect and celebrate the wonderful differences in people of all kinds. Toward this end, Murf, in fact, had gone back to school as the camp was in its planning stage and began to work toward a Master's degree in child psychology and theology. Informally, Cookie was known for looking after and doting on the most challenging of the children who came to them with each new session of campers. More formally, in addition to his culinary duties, he also taught a course called "Believe" that exposed campers to the foundations of many different religions and centered on the common cause of humanism, which was at the heart of each doctrine. And right alongside Christianity, Judaism, Hinduism, Native American tribal spirituality, and Buddhism, the precepts of the Muslim faith were shared—and not the Islamic extremist version kidnapped by militants. The Muslim faith was touted for its commitment to kindness, tolerance, hospitality, family and the service of both God and man.

Terri, by special arrangement with the Homeland Security and State Department, also saw to it that every group of new campers included seven kids from Israel and seven kids from Palestine to be mixed into the camp's general population and then returned home after camp with a perspective markedly different and more progressive than their peers back home. Funding for this came each term from an anonymous company headquartered in Southern California—one that had been sold on implementing the "Small World" philosophy after an impassioned ad man presentation that a very persuasive marketing wizard named Murphy Morrison made to them in his final appearance in his expensive Madison Avenue selling suit. In this session, one of the teenagers from Israel was a fifteen-year-old with a speech impediment. He had been brutally teased by other kids back home. His name was Isaac and he was both a deserving "scholarship" camper but had also received very "connected" help through a phone call made to Murf by Isaac's Uncle Benny, who was once again a "box boat" ship captain sailing the Pacific. Benny, had of course, long-since forgiven Murf for the slight of calling and canceling out on him at the last minute as the cook for his ship out of Seoul.

In the mess hall, the walls were adorned with the usual painted arrowhead and pine tree shaped varnished wooden platters, made by each different cabin's crew to commemorate their team's camaraderie and accomplishments.

Murf had also stenciled these words boldly on one otherwise clear wall of the dining room:

We shall not cease from exploration
And the end of all our exploring
Will be to arrive where we started
And know the place for the very first time
Little Gidding
T.S. Elliot's Four Quartets

The camp was situated on about twenty-five heavily wooded and pristine acres that hugged the Maryland coastline and overlooked the Chesapeake Bay. At the camp's main gate there stood, on two giant vertical logs, an overhead-spanning, rectangular sign that denoted the name "Camp Abbie" in red block letters engraved into the flat wooden sign's facing board. It also had three symbols on each opposite side of this lettering. The first three on the left were a cross standing for Christianity, the Hindu symbol Om, and a silhouette of Buddha. On the opposite side, there was a Jewish star, a thunderbird eagle for native American beliefs, and a Muslim crescent moon.

Murf had chosen the name Camp Abbie, not because he believed that Abbie's final act of sealing himself inside the mine with the deadly gas equated to redemption for all of the prior acts of terrorism he had committed. Murf chose the name because Abbie's final act was a conscious choice of siding with good versus evil. The federal agents and Homeland Security specialists who conducted the post mortem on the terrorists' attack could not fathom why he did this instead of exploding the bomb around people, and why he had even written the word "Anthrax" on the sign outside the mine to forewarn them of its deadly contents. Abdur had chosen to protect the lives of hundreds of thousands or even millions of innocents, instead of committing a heinous act of murder and terror on an unprecedented and enormous scale, to create headlines, fear and propaganda for a political cause, no matter how much he believed in it. So Camp Abbie was so named to underline—if only in Murf's mind—that it was a place dedicated to instilling in kids the will to make the right choices, regardless of their religion or politics or whatever kind of inevitable tragedies that life had in store for each of them. And since its launch, eight months after Murf's adventure aboard the *Fenix*, Camp Abbie had been doing so for over a dozen highly successful years.

Then again, what's in a name? According to a twelve-year-old darling blonde, freckle-faced camper named Abby with coke-bottle thick glasses and Down's syndrome, Camp Abbie was named after her. "I'm Abby. And Mr. Cookie, this is my camp. So may I have more dessert please?" she implored of Murf.

"What's that young lady? Camp Abbie is yours??!!" responded one very puzzled Murf Morrison, a.k.a. Cookie.

"Yup. My name is Abby Sprechter from Sacramento. And since the camp's named after me, can I have more please?"

Murf mentally started to respond with "Sprechter!!??? Hell I hardly…" but he stopped himself. He immediately dished her up a big scoop of the still warm peach cobbler. "Well, Miss Camp Abby. May I put some extra vanilla ice cream on top in your honor?"

"Yes please," said the girl with a killer smile and a joyful giggle.

The camp had been master planned by a world-class talented designer that Terri secured. And Terri had also personally managed every detail of its construction. Whole pine logs of an immense girth and varnished, roughhewn planks abounded. Each structure was surrounded by numerous towering evergreens on three sides. No clear-cutting had been allowed, which posed considerable challenges for vehicles and men during the building phase. But the harmonious end result of buildings integrated into dense forestland was amazing. The two dozen large cabins, one massive dining hall and administrative offices all uniformly featured the same Kelly green shutters and doors, and cedar shake shingles adorning the rooftops. Terri had really outdone herself on this undertaking. And in addition to her genius, she was still a dazzling beauty with a very lovely figure and those ever-sparkling eyes. Other than the streaks of gray that now accented her hair, she could easily have passed for a very attractive forty-five-year-old woman—some fifteen years younger than her true age. Terri was the subject of many a crush among the adolescent campers and counselors and was also deeply admired by all the young women who emulated her example of a strong yet sublime woman with many accomplishments throughout her career, marriage and motherhood. Murf was immensely lucky to still be married to her and he knew it.

For the past week, Murf had an assistant—though not necessarily a terribly willing one—helping him in the kitchen for two hours each day before dinnertime while the other campers were enjoying two hours of "free time." Seems that a young man named Isaac from Israel had punched two campers who had been teasing him about his speech impediment. And they always took great delight in doing so whenever a group of girls from the cabin next door were walking by. Isaac had divulged to another cabin-mate that he had a crush on a pretty young lady from a small town in Palestine whom he had met on the long plane ride which they and the other "scholarship" campers all made over to the

U.S. together. And when the troublemakers, who always taunted him, found this out, they made a point of embarrassing him every time she passed by. When Isaac had finally suffered enough, he floored one of them with a gut punch and the other with a solid uppercut to the jaw.

"You know, Isaac," Cookie said as they peeled potatoes together, "I've done a lot of stupid things in my life trying to impress the ladies or trying to show off and be one of the guys. It took me a long time and a lot of trouble to finally learn that showing off to buddies or fantasizing about females is not what life's really about. And violence, though it feels justified in some cases, only leads to more violence and more misunderstanding and hatred. In the end, what I learned is that life is not supposed to be all about ME. It's about something far more important than anyone, really. It's about how we go through life the right way, and that means just trying to be a good person and especially helping others who are struggling and need a hand. You learn to do that, and that young lady or some other one you are meant to be with, is going to fall head over heels for you because she will know you're really special and much smarter and better than the idiots who teased you. And then someday you can teach the same thing to your son or others who lose their way. You get what I'm saying, dude?" asked Murf gently.

"Yeah, my dad told me that too," he replied remorsefully. "I know it's good advice, but sometimes, if I can be honest here, life can be…well, you know, life can be a real bitch, Cookie." Isaac said hesitantly.

"I hear ya brutha, I sure do hear ya," said Cookie with a chortle. "Here, knock off with the peeling and take this platter of cookies with you back to your cabin. And you get right in those guys' faces with a big Isaac smile and offer the very buttheads that teased you the first taste," he said with a wink.

That Sunday was a big day at Camp Abbie. As was customary there, the morning wake-up consisted of musical selections from a mix tape Murf had made. "Better Days" by the Goo Goo Dolls was playing now with its lyrics highly resonating to Camp Abbie's mission. "I wish everyone was loved tonight. And somehow stop this endless fight. Just a chance that maybe we'll find better days. So take these words. And sing out loud. Cuz everyone is forgiven now. Cuz tonight's the night the world begins again."

Murf was in a total dither today, frantically packing gear for his flight to Fort Lauderdale on the very day that the third and final session of summer camp was ending and campers are scurrying all about as the buses came to pick them and their luggage up for a return trip home to their families. Murf had told Terri precious little about his "special getaway"—just that he's traveling solo to Florida for some beach time away to recharge his batteries.

"Have a wonderful trip, Murf," said the camp's guidance counselor Shandra. She and her two children all worked full time at Camp Abbey and she was a rock of dependability. "Don't worry about anything here. We can handle whatever comes up."

Murf came to know Shandra when the FBI was interrogating them both about the events that had unfolded from the sequestered room they shared at the hospital while recovering from their gunshot wounds. After returning from Korea and reuniting with Terri, he looked her up when she had fully healed and was badly in need of both money, and, like Murf, a new start. He and Terri had practically adopted her and her brood. They moved them to an apartment in San Francisco and paid for Shandra to go to community college, while Camp Abbie was still in the planning stages.

After the drive to the Baltimore Airport and a two-hour flight down the coast to Lauderdale, Murf met up with his liaison at the prearranged spot: the Wayfarer Hotel. They had previously agreed to meet there for dinner at 8:00 p.m. before driving together early the next morning down the Florida Keys to Key West. Upon meeting her, Murf realized that she was taller, and far more vibrant and gorgeous than he had expected. She embraced him with a warm, long hug and a quick kiss. Thereafter, they had a delightful and rambling three-hour dinner conversation that later, in his hotel room, left Murf wringing his stiff and slightly sore from gesticulation hands.

The next morning, after driving down to Key West, they caught a boat out to the dive site. It took almost three hours of full-throttle cruising to reach it. Once everyone was briefed by the dive master and had geared up and had done their buddy system pre-dive safety checks, they descended into the Atlantic Ocean. The dive took place some twenty miles off the Florida coast in waters that were about forty-five to sixty feet deep, with moderate currents.

Amidst dozens of strands of upwardly cascading air bubbles, their conversation of last night began anew—and was not in any way restricted to the classic sign language of scuba divers. Murf and his now twenty-three year-old daughter, Molly, were chatting away with the deaf signing language he was so very glad to have finally mastered. She also was now an expert lip reader and could eavesdrop on other conversations going on around her at a busy restaurant or even pick up on a sarcastic waiter, who she'd tear right into if they had it coming. Molly had also worked extremely hard after her cochlear implant in her teen years to master solid speaking skills based on the inner ear vibrations and sounds she could now roughly discern. In fact, her first words to Murf, after, perhaps weeks of practice, were, "I love you, Dad." Murf was stunned as though hit by a two-by-four and then he collapsed sobbing with joy as he hugged his girl.

Molly was now in her junior year and studying marine biology at Princeton. She was a strong, independent and exceptionally bright young woman who had not allowed her handicap and later than usual grasp of language, to lead her into social isolation. And though she loved her deaf school, her classmates and the deaf culture that allowed her to flourish in her early years, she worked hard to purposely integrate herself back into a regular high school by her junior year. And she now had many, many good friends. Plus, because she was killer good lookin' like her mom, a hugely smitten and doting boyfriend. Murf and Molly both had their own unusually deep connections to the sea, and their passion for diving had been cultivated and shared from its inception every step of the way.

Initially, based moreso on hearsay than fact, those with cochlear implants were thought not be able to play contact sports or scuba dive. But both of these misconceptions had been righted over time and Molly was able to dive with only the limitation of an eighty-five foot depth versus the recreational diving limit of about 115 feet. But this was no ordinary dive today—even though they already had dove more than a dozen shipwrecks together on assorted vacations since they had studied and become certified PADI divers in Molly's senior year of high school.

Today's dive was very special and the result of some elaborate and long-in-advance arrangements made by Murf. To facilitate the dive, he had bought a modest twenty shares of the treasure hunting legend Mel Fisher's corporation stock for both himself and Molly. And as stockholders, the Morrisons had become entitled to dive an unlimited number of days each year, at any of the Fisher Corporation treasure-recovery sites. Today, they were diving another unexplored quadrant on the map in an area that had come to be known as Hurricane Alley. A cabin cruiser took the two of them out to the semi-permanently anchored Fisher ship that was the hub of the treasure recovery effort. It also housed the propeller blast-powered excavation device they used to blow away the years and years of accumulated sand in hopes of revealing something worthwhile buried below it. The specific site they would dive was one of thousands of such sites mapped for exploration. It was part of an almost endless, but disciplined process of systematically searching mathematically charted underwater excavation areas indicated on a Mel Fisher Corp. master map. They and the ship's six professional treasure hunters that staffed it were in search of lost silver, gold and emeralds from the Spanish treasure ship Atocha that sunk in 1622. While the first (Mel and his wife) and now second generation of the Fisher group had already recovered over $100 million from the Atocha wreck over the course of twenty some odd years, the ship and its treasure was strewn in a hurricane-driven sinking over a fifteen mile-long area and the main cargo of hundreds of silver bars had yet to be located.

Maybe today was the day. Regardless, it would be a day that Murf and Molly would treasure forever.

Acknowledgements

Amis, Martin. "Terrorism's New Structure." *The Wall Street Journal:* August 16, 2008. Web. http://online.wsj.com/article/SB121883817312745575.html>

Campbell Law Review. Web. 24 July 2011.

containership-info.com. Web. 24 July 2011.

Elliott, Andrea. "The Jihadist Next Door." *New York Times Magazine:* January 31, 2010. Web. 24 July 2011. <http://www.nytimes.com/2010/01/31/magazine/31Jihadist-t.html?pagewanted=all>

freighter-cruises.com. Web. 24 July 2011.

Hall, Mimi. "Experts to Testify of 'Real and Growing' Nuclear Threat to U.S." *USA Today:* April 2, 2008. Web. 24 July 2011. <http://www.usatoday.com/printedition/news/20080402/a_nukes02.art.htm>

"Internet Guide to Freighter Travel." seaplus.com. Web. 24 July 2011.

"Israel Warns U.S. of Iranian Nuke Attack." *USA Today:* December 18, 2008: Web. 24 July 2011. <http://www.usatoday.com/printedition/news/20081218/wobs18_st.art.htm>

jms.janes.com. Web. 24 July 2011.

Keefer, Wendy J. "Container Port Security: A Layered Defense Strategy to Protect the Homeland and the International Supply Chain." Campbell Law Review. Web. 24 July 2011. <http://law.campbell.edu/lawreview/articles/30-1-139.pdf>

Kershaw, Sarah. "The Terrorist Mind: An Update." *The New York Times:* January 10, 2010. Web. 24 July 2011. <http://www.nytimes.com/2010/01/10/weekinreview/10kershaw.html>

Langewiesche, William. Excerpt from *The Outlaw Sea: A World of Freedom, Chaos, and Crime* by William Langewieshe. Copyright © 2004 by William Langewiesche. Reprinted by permission of North Point Press, a division of Farrar, Straus and Giroux, LLC. Print.

Levinson, Marc. The Box: How the Shipping Container Made the World Smaller and the World Economy Bigger. Princeton, NJ: Princeton University Press, 2006. Print.

MacFarquhar, Neil. "Rate of Nuclear Thefts 'Disturbingly High,' Monitoring Chief Says." *The New York Times*: October 28, 2008. Web. 24 July 2011. <http://www.nytimes.com/2008/10/28/news/28iht-28nuke.17299463.html>

Mayo, Anthony J. and Nitin Nohria. "The Truck Driver who Reinvented Shipping."

Harvard Business School Working Knowledge: October 3, 2005. Web. 24 July 2011. <http://hbswk.hbs.edu/item/5026.html>

Mike Vaughn's Ship Information Center. Web. 24 July 2011. <http://www.best-maritime.net/index.php/l/en/mod/vc_general/company_id/49767>

Navy Fact File: Container Ships

providence.edu/polisci/students/megaport/ContainerShips.htm. Web. 24 July 2011.

providence.edu/polisci/students/megaport/ContainerSource.htm Web. 24 July 2011.

Shipbuilding Dictionary Picture. Web. 24 July 2011. <http://forshipbuilding.com/shipping-worldwide.com> Web. 24 July 2011.

Taggart, Stewart. "The 20-Ton Packet." WIRED® 7.10: October 1999. Web. 24 July 2011.

Yachting and Boating World. Web. 24 July 2011. <ybw.com>

Reference materials and invaluable background information for many of the characters and situations fabricated herein have included the many fine stories from war correspondents and other reporters for *The New York Times*, the *Associated Press*, *The Wall Street Journal* and other newspapers. I have also sponged liberally from Wikipedia, and a broad variety of online web sites about the shipping industry. In addition, my thanks to the many talented advertising agency co-workers I have known, whose stories and ideas helped me.

www.ingramcontent.com/pod-product-compliance
Lightning Source LLC
Chambersburg PA
CBHW030812310726
48980CB00006B/469/J

* 9 7 8 0 9 8 3 7 8 6 8 0 1 *